An Investees' Anthology

Selected Contributions to

The MX Book of New Sherlock Holmes Stories

by Members of
The Baker Street Irregulars

AN INVESTEES' ANTHOLOGY

SELECTED CONTRIBUTIONS TO
THE MX BOOK OF NEW
SHERLOCK HOLMES STORIES
BY MEMBERS OF
THE BAKER STREET IRREGULARS

SOUTHAMPTON
STREET

359

EDITED
by
David
Marcum

OFFICES

TRADITIONAL HOLMES
ADVENTURES
COMPILED FOR THE
BENEFIT OF THE
RESTORATION OF
UNDERSHAW

ISBN Hardback 978-1-80424-137-0
ISBN Paperback 978-1-80424-138-7
AUK ePub ISBN 978-1-80424-139-4
AUK PDF ISBN 978-1-80424-140-0

Published in the UK by
MX Publishing
335 Princess Park Manor, Royal Drive,
London, N11 3GX
www.mxpublishing.co.uk

David Marcum can be reached at:
thepapersofsherlockholmes@gmail.com

Cover design by Brian Belanger
www.belangerbooks.com and *www.redbubble.com/people/zhahadun*

Internal Illustrations by Sidney Paget

CONTENTS

Forewords from Previous Volumes

(Continued on the next page . . . .)

·Poems

Adventures

(Continued on the next page . . . .)

(Continued on the next page . . . .)

**These additional Sherlock Holmes adventures
can be found in the previous volumes of**
The MX Book of New Sherlock Holmes Stories

(Continued on the next page . . . .)

PART III: 1896-1929

PART IV – 2016 Annual

(Continued on the next page . . . .)

PART V – Christmas Adventures

(Continued on the next page . . . .)

PART VI – 2017 Annual

(Continued on the next page . . . .)

PART VII – Eliminate the Impossible: 1880-1891

PART VIII – Eliminate the Impossible: 1892-1905

(Continued on the next page . . . .)

Part IX – 2018 Annual (1879-1895)

(Continued on the next page . . . .)

The Lambeth Poisoner Case – Stephen Gaspar
The Confession of Anna Jarrow – S. F. Bennett
The Adventure of the Disappearing Dictionary – Sonia Fetherston
The Fairy Hills Horror – Geri Schear
A Loathsome and Remarkable Adventure – Marcia Wilson
The Adventure of the Multiple Moriartys – David Friend
The Influence Machine – Mark Mower

Part X – 2018 Annual (1896-1916)

Foreword – Nicholas Meyer
Foreword – Roger Johnson
Foreword – Melissa Farnham
Foreword – Steve Emecz
Foreword – David Marcum
A Man of Twice Exceptions (A Poem) – Derrick Belanger
The Horned God – Kelvin Jones
The Coughing Man – Jim French
The Adventure of Canal Reach – Arthur Hall
A Simple Case of Abduction – Mike Hogan
A Case of Embezzlement – Steven Ehrman
The Adventure of the Vanishing Diplomat – Greg Hatcher
The Adventure of the Perfidious Partner – Jayantika Ganguly
A Brush With Death – Dick Gillman
A Revenge Served Cold – Maurice Barkley
The Case of the Anonymous Client – Paul A. Freeman
Capitol Murder – Daniel D. Victor
The Case of the Dead Detective – Martin Rosenstock
The Musician Who Spoke From the Grave – Peter Coe Verbica
The Adventure of the Future Funeral – Hugh Ashton
The Problem of the Bruised Tongues – Will Murray
The Mystery of the Change of Art – Robert Perret
The Parsimonious Peacekeeper – Thaddeus Tuffentsamer
The Case of the Dirty Hand – G.L. Schulze
The Mystery of the Missing Artefacts – Tim Symonds

Part XI: Some Untold Cases (1880-1891)

Foreword – Lyndsay Faye
Foreword – Roger Johnson
Foreword – Melissa Grigsby
Foreword – Steve Emecz
Foreword – David Marcum
Unrecorded Holmes Cases (A Sonnet) – Arlene Mantin Levy and Mark Levy
The Most Repellant Man – Jayantika Ganguly
The Singular Adventure of the Extinguished Wicks – Will Murray
Mrs. Forrester's Complication – Roger Riccard
The Adventure of Vittoria, the Circus Belle – Tracy Revels

(Continued on the next page . . . .)

Part XII: Some Untold Cases (1894-1902)

PART XIII: 2019 Annual (1881-1890)

(Continued on the next page . . . .)

PART XIV: 2019 Annual (1891 -1897)

(Continued on the next page . . . .)

(Continued on the next page . . . .)

Part XVII – Whatever Remains . . . Must Be the Truth (1891-1898)

Part XVIII – Whatever Remains . . . Must Be the Truth (1899-1925)

(Continued on the next page . . . .)

Part XIX: 2020 Annual (1882-1890)

(Continued on the next page . . . .)

(Continued on the next page . . . .)

Part XXII: Some More Untold Cases (1877-1887)

(Continued on the next page . . . .)

(Continued on the next page . . . .)

Part XXV: 2021 Annual (1881-1888)

(Continued on the next page . . . .)

(Continued on the next page . . . .)

Part XXVIII: More Christmas Adventures (1869-1888)

(Continued on the next page . . . .)

(Continued on the next page . . . .)

The Adventure of the Chained Phantom – J.S. Rowlinson
Santa's Little Elves – Kevin Thornton
The Case of the Holly-Sprig Pudding – Naching T. Kassa
The Canterbury Manifesto – David Marcum
The Case of the Disappearing Beaune – J. Lawrence Matthews
A Price Above Rubies – Jane Rubino
The Intrigue of the Red Christmas – Shane Simmons
The Bitter Gravestones – Chris Chan
The Midnight Mass Murder – Paul Hiscock

Part XXXI 2022 Annual (1875-1887)
Foreword – Jeffrey Hatcher
Foreword – Roger Johnson
Foreword – Steve Emecz
Foreword – Emma West
Foreword – David Marcum
The Nemesis of Sherlock Holmes (A Poem) – Kelvin I. Jones
The Unsettling Incident of the History Professor's Wife – Sean M. Wright
The Princess Alice Tragedy – John Lawrence
The Adventure of the Amorous Balloonist – I.A. Watson
The Pilkington Case – Kevin Patrick McCann
The Adventure of the Disappointed Lover – Arthur Hall
The Case of the Impressionist Painting – Tim Symonds
The Adventure of the Old Explorer – Tracy J. Revels
Dr. Watson's Dilemma – Susan Knight
The Colonial Exhibition – Hal Glatzer
The Adventure of the Drunken Teetotaler – Thomas A. Burns, Jr.
The Curse of Hollyhock House – Geri Schear
The Sethian Messiah – David Marcum
Dead Man's Hand – Robert Stapleton
The Case of the Wary Maid – Gordon Linzner
The Adventure of the Alexandrian Scroll – David MacGregor
The Case of the Woman at Margate – Terry Golledge
A Question of Innocence – DJ Tyrer
The Grosvenor Square Furniture Van – Terry Golledge
The Adventure of the Veiled Man – Tracy J. Revels
The Disappearance of Dr. Markey – Stephen Herczeg
The Case of the Irish Demonstration – Dan Rowley

Part XXXII 2022 Annual (1888-1895)
Foreword – Jeffrey Hatcher
Foreword – Roger Johnson
Foreword – Steve Emecz

(Continued on the next page . . . .)

Part XXXIII 2022 Annual (1896-1919)

(Continued on the next page . . . .)

(Continued on the next page . . . .)

Part XXXVI "However Improbable . . . ." (1897-1919)

Editor's Foreword:
From All Quarters Received
by David Marcum

Pastiches. There can't be enough of the good ones, and their importance in The World of Sherlock Holmes cannot be over-emphasized. As I've mentioned elsewhere, they are the third leg in the Sherlockian stool – along with The Canon and Scholarship. They are all the threads that provide nuance and depth within *The Great Sherlockian Tapestry*, winding through and enhancing the strong main fibers of the Canonical sixty adventures. Generation after generation, new Sherlockians find their way to The Canon by way of pastiches, and sixty Canonical stories are never enough to tell the entire lives of Our Heroes.

Even as The Canon was originally being published, extra-canonical stories were appearing – although sadly these were parodies, where Holmes and Watson were given shabby new names and behaviors that the authors presumably felt were funny. The first true influential pastiche was William Gillette's 1899 play *Sherlock Holmes*, and it opened a door that has never since shut.

In the 1930's, Edith Meiser, BSI, recognized that the Holmes stories would make perfect half-hour plays for the new medium of *radio*. But after a few years, and repeating the Canonical Sixty over and over and over, she obtained permission from the litigious Doyle Heirs – whom she would ironically sue at a later date, correctly pointing out that her bringing Watson forward from simply a narrator in the shadows to a co-starring role fundamentally changed The Game – to write new cases, including an account of The Giant Rat of Sumatra, and another intriguingly called "The Hindoo in the Wicker Basket" (broadcast January 7th, 1932). These narratives from beyond The Canon, both by Meiser, and later by Leslie Charteris, Denis Green, and Anthony Boucher, BSI, helped pave the way for easier acceptance of cases that didn't have to be routed across the First Literary Agent's desk. But there were still far too few of them.

Other pastiches followed in bits and pieces. Adrian Conan Doyle and John Dickson Carr's *The Exploits of Sherlock Holmes* (1954) are actually twelve really good stories, but the well-earned ire that Adrian had accumulated in the Sherlockian community meant that the actual Holmes book was often the baby thrown out with the bathwater.

1954-1955 brought us over three-dozen early television pastiches starring Ronald Howard, and in 1959, Hammer produced the first color

1

Holmes film, *The Hound of the Baskervilles* – mentioned here because it's full of pastiche elements – a *tarantula!* – before going full pastiche at the end, with a conclusion completely altered from the book.

Occasional Holmes pastiches popped up in subsequent years, including the 1965 Holmes-versus-The Ripper film *A Study in Terror*, and there is no doubt that each of these pastiches led new fans to The Canon. That's how it worked for me: In 1975, I owned an unexamined Holmes book, and it might have stayed that way, but one rainy Saturday afternoon I saw *A Study in Terror* being re-run on television and decided to read the book. And there was no going back.

That was a perfect time to enter The World of Sherlock Holmes, because just the year before, Nicholas Meyer, BSI, had published *The Seven-Per-Cent Solution*, (subsequently made into a 1975 film), and a worldwide Sherlockian fire was ignited that has never since gone out – *all because of a pastiche.*

New Holmes adventures began to appear more often as publishers recognized the increasing interest in Mr. Holmes. Pinnacle reprinted all of the Solar Pons stories by August Derleth, BSI, known to exist at that time, and commissioned some new ones. More of Holmes's investigations appeared here and there – Nick Meyer wrote another, *The West End Horror*, in 1976 – still one of my all-time favorites. That same year, Nick Utechin, BSI, and Austin Mitchelson wrote a couple of Holmes novels, *Hellbirds* and *The Earthquake Machine*, and in 1979 Sean Wright, BSI, and Michael Hodel, BSI, wrote *Enter the Lion*.

This was the way it continued for the next few decades – some Holmes stories were published in very obscure editions or magazines or journals known only to small select groups or collectors, and a couple of times a year, a "real" Holmes novel or anthology from a "real" publisher might show up unexpectedly in a bookstore.

And then came the internet.

And then came the new publishing paradigm.

And then came MX Publishing.

Thank Heavens.

MX didn't start out to be the world's leading Sherlockian publisher. Steve Emecz founded the company to produce books for children with learning disabilities. But in 2008, he published Alistair Duncan's *Eliminate the Impossible*, a book of Holmes scholarship dealing with both page and screen. Cannily recognizing that there was a massive Sherlockian void in the publishing world, and that the new print-on-demand paradigm was far better than the old dinosaur publishing approach, Steve and MX began providing other Sherlockian works, both scholarship and pastiche, for those like me who very much wanted to read them, and an outlet for Sherlockian writers who had no other path.

My association with Steve began in late 2012 when I asked him to pass on a message to another MX author. Then, not long after that in January 2013, I took the plunge and emailed him again – truly a life-changing experience – about republishing my first – and at that time *only* – book, a collection of Holmes short stories. He did, and soon after that I sent him my first Holmes novel, which was also subsequently published. In Autumn 2013, I made my first Holmes Pilgrimage to England and Scotland and met Steve in person in the lobby of the Sherlock Holmes Hotel in Baker Street, where I was staying. On that same trip, he arranged for me to have a book signing at the Hotel.

MX published another collection of my stories in 2015, and that was the same year I had the idea for *The MX Book of New Sherlock Holmes Stories*. It literally came to me in a dream, in which I had edited a Holmes anthology. I woke up early and, instead of rolling over and going back to sleep, I got up and looked around at my shelves to see who I might ask to participate. I ran the idea by Steve, who was encouraging (as always), and I asked the opinion of a couple of Sherlockian friends. They approved, so I started sending invitations.

At first, I feared that no one would be interested, and at best I'd have enough new stories for maybe one small paperback volume – which was okay with me, because there would be more Holmes stories than before, and I would have been able to contribute an anthology to stand beside all those others that I'd admired over the years. Due to my insecurity about the success of the project, I sent invitations to every pastiche author that I could think of or locate – and I knew of a lot. Then – to my amazement – people started to say yes. Other people that I hadn't initially invited – mainly because up to that point they hadn't written traditional pastiches – also wanted to join the party, (and it turned out that they wrote *great* traditional pastiches). And then, after all those invitations were sent, the most incredible thing of all: New Holmes stories started showing up in my email inbox, and sometimes paper stories were mailed to my physical mailbox – all raw and fresh from The Tin Dispatch Box.

As 2015 progressed, the idea for a small book had to be revised to accommodate the immense participation. In the end, we had over sixty Holmes adventures, to be published in three massive simultaneous volumes – the largest collection of its kind ever. (We would go on to surpass that.)

From the beginning, Steve and I had planned for the author royalties to go to Undershaw, one of Sir Arthur Conan Doyle's former homes. For several years, MX had been very involved in trying to save Undershaw, then in terrible shape, from developers. By mid-2015, when the books were starting to take shape, Undershaw *was* saved. It had been purchased by the DFN Foundation as the new location for the Stepping Stones School for special needs children, then located in a small and crowded facility in nearby Hindhead. Therefore, the royalties would be re-directed from saving the building to helping support the school.

After the initial and very-successful publication of the first three books, I thought that was the end of it – until I immediately began hearing from authors asking about the *next* books – both those authors who had previously contributed, and new participants who wanted to join us. As Steve and I had already made all the tough formatting decisions, it was easy to re-start the engine for new stories – and it hasn't stopped since.

We are currently up to 36 massive volumes, with more currently in preparation – *New stories are always welcome!* The books have over *750* new Holmes adventures. We've raised over *$100,000* – that's *One-hundred-thousand dollars!* – for the school – which has since changed its name from *Stepping Stones* to *Undershaw.* And the school tells me that even more important than the money is the worldwide awareness of the school that the books have generated.

In addition to providing support to Undershaw, MX also financially supports the *Happy Life Mission*, a baby rescue center in Nairobi that has saved the lives of over 800 abandoned babies, the *United Nations World Food Programme* – Steve Emecz is an advisor and technology mentor, and the team won the 2020 *Nobel Peace Prize* – and *iHeart*, which works to support and improve teenage mental health.

Another great aspect of *The MX Book of New Sherlock Holmes Stories* is that a number of authors – both old and new – found their way to the prolific world of pastichery, and they have gone on to write so many that they now have books of their own collected stories. Some had never written before. Along the way, other Holmes anthologies have followed from other publishers – *We can't have enough traditional Holmes pastiches!* – and in particular, the MX anthologies directly led to the formation of the other powerhouse Sherlockian publisher, *Belanger Books.* Founded by the equally brilliant Derrick and Brian Belanger, Belanger Books has also done an incredible job of producing amazing and high-quality Holmes collections, while also feeding the Holmes adventure addiction for me and many other people around the world.

Another really wonderful thing is that the MX anthologies have had contributions from over 200 incredible people worldwide – including a number of members of *The Baker Street Irregulars* (BSI) . . . .

4

The BSI was originally "The Three Hours for Lunch Club", created by Christopher Morley, BSI, as an informal New York literary society that discussed arts and literature over drinks – lots of them, apparently. The first meeting under the name *The Baker Street Irregulars* occurred in 1934. Initial gatherings were indeed *irregular*, but when leadership passed to Edgar W. Smith, BSI, in 1940, the proceedings became more formalized.

I have a particular fondness for Mr. Smith, who wrote:

> *There is no Sherlockian worthy of his salt who has not, at least once in his life, taken Dr. Watson's pen in hand and given himself to the production of a veritable Adventure.*

Strong words from the man who shaped The Baker Street Irregulars. And words that should not be forgotten or swept aside with a jibe and a sneer in the pursuit of the scholarly side of things.

From the very beginning, members of The Baker Street Irregulars have supported the MX anthologies with their contributed stories, forewords, and poems – some on multiple occasions. (Below I mention some ways in which they have contributed.)

From the beginning to the most recent volumes, BSI members have remained involved in these books, and I'm particularly grateful to Sean Wright, BSI and noted pasticheur, for suggesting this special volume collecting representative contributions from nearly every participating BSI member.

My goal when first coming up with the idea for these books was to have more (and more and more) stories about the Canonical Sherlock Holmes, with adventures that could have appeared alongside the originals in *The Strand.* It would not have been possible without the incredible contributions of the 200+ authors – including over two-dozen BSI members – *from all quarters received,* and also the countless supporters who have bought and collected the books. I can never adequately express my gratitude to all of you for making this happen, and for allowing me to have this chance to play in the Sherlockian sandbox.

* * * * *

"Of course, I could only stammer out my thanks."
– The unhappy John Hector McFarlane, "The Norwood Builder"

As always when I finish a book of my own or an edited anthology, I most want to thank with all my heart my incredible, patient, brilliant, kind, and beautiful wife of thirty-four years, Rebecca – every day I'm more stunned at how lucky I am than the day before! – and our amazing, funny, creative, and wonderful son, and my friend, Dan. I love you both, and you are everything to me!

I'm thrilled to have gotten to know so many Sherlockians – both in person and electronically – by way of these books. It's an undeniable fact that Sherlock Holmes authors are the *best* people!

I wish especially thank the following:

- *Steve Emecz* – Even before my first association with MX in 2013, I saw that MX (under Steve Emecz's leadership) was *the* fast-rising superstar of the Sherlockian publishing world. Connecting with MX and Steve Emecz was personally an amazing life-changing event for me, as it has been for countless other Sherlockian authors. It has led me to write many more stories, and then to edit many books, along with unexpected additional Holmes Pilgrimages to England – none of which might have happened otherwise. By way of my first email with Steve, I've had the chance to make some incredible Sherlockian friends and play in the Holmesian Sandbox in ways that I would have never dreamed possible.

  Through it all, Steve has been one of the most positive and supportive people that I've ever known.

  From the beginning, Steve has let me explore various Sherlockian projects and open up my own personal possibilities in ways that otherwise would have never happened. Thank you, Steve, for every opportunity!
- *Brian Belanger* –I initially became acquainted with Brian when he took over the duties of creating the covers for MX Books, and I found him to be a great collaborator, and wonderfully creative too. I've worked with him on many projects with MX and Belanger Books, which he co-founded with his brother Derrick Belanger, also a good friend. Along with MX Publishing, Derrick and Brian have absolutely locked up the Sherlockian publishing field with a vast amount of amazing material. Luckily MX and Belanger Books work closely with one another, and I'm thrilled to be associated with both of them. Many thanks to Brian for all he does for both publishers, and for all he's done for me personally.
- *Michael Keen, BSI ("Wiggins")* – I haven't had the chance to meet Mr. Keen in person, but we've emailed several times, and it was

6

he who suggested the title of this volume, *An Investee's Anthology.*

- *Roger Johnson, BSI* – I first became acquainted with Roger when I sent him a copy of my first Holmes book. He was incredibly supportive, and I was able to meet him on Holmes Pilgrimage No. 1 in 2013. He and his wife, Jean Upton, BSI, met me at The Sherlock Holmes Pub, whereupon he allowed me to enter the amazing museum and examine the Sherlockian artifacts therein. (On a return trip, I was able to hang out in there for several *hours!*) When I was assembling the first MX anthologies, I knew that I wanted Roger to write a foreword – and he's been part of the books ever since. So many thanks for so many things!
- *Nicholas Meyer, BSI* – With *The Seven-Per-Cent Solution* (a pastiche!), the current Sherlockian Golden Age began, and it's never ended. All that, and saving *Star Trek* too, is reason for great gratefulness from all of us, but I'm also personally grateful that Nick contributed to these books, and later wrote a foreword to a collection of my own stories.
- *Steve Rothman, BSI* – I'm very grateful to Steve for taking time to correspond with me over the years, for kindly reviewing some of my books, and for publishing four of my essays in *The Baker Street Journal*, the BSI's official publication which he masterfully edits. Also, I very much appreciate him writing a new foreword for this collection. And in another way, Steve deserves some background thanks and credit leading up to the MX anthologies. In early 2015, I suggested to him my idea of me pulling all the previously published pastiches from all the old *Baker Street Journals* – back when they used to include pastiches – and then editing them into a separate book. Steve declined, and with that out of the way, I then went on to have the idea of the MX anthologies. Thanks, Steve, for saying no, and allowing all of what followed to occur.
- *Lyndsay Faye, BSI* – When I first sent out invitations to the initial MX books, the very first "Yes" reply was from Lyndsay. And then she returned a few years later to contribute a foreword. Her initial affirmative was my first sense that this whole project might work.
- *Sean Wright, BSI* – I was first aware of Mr. Wright when, as a boy, I found his brilliant and definitive Mycroft Holmes novel,

Enter the Lion. We later began to correspond after I published a book of Solar Pons stories, and I was able to recruit him to write more Mycroft tales. (His most recent, co-written with his son, DeForeest B. Wright, III, appears in this volume). It was Sean who had the idea for this special BSI edition of MX anthology contributions, so when you see him, be sure to thank him!

- *Otto Penzler, BSI* – Otto's incredible and brilliant work in the mystery field needs no description, but I personally want to thank him for all that his work has meant to me over the years, and for the support he's given in selling my books, especially for the first one in the early days, and for asking me to sign my books one day at The Mysterious Bookshop – truly a bucket-list item!

- *Nick Utechin, BSI* – I'd heard of Nick for years as a famed Sherlockian, and occasionally communicated with him. I was finally able to meet him in 2015 on Holmes Pilgrimage No. 2, when he took a day of his time and gave me an incredibly in-depth behind-the-scenes tour of Oxford, where he lived. After that we stayed in touch, and he contributed several stories and forewords to books that I've edited. (His mother and my mother were both Rathbones, so we had that family connection in common as well.) His passing in 2022 was and is an incredible loss to the Sherlockian world.

- *Tracy Revels, BSI* – I first met Tracy in 2012 when we were sharing a table selling our books at *A Gathering of Southern Sherlockians.* She is a great person, and has contributed *twenty-eight* new Holmes adventures (so far) to the MX anthologies. I'd like to include all of them in this volume, but you'll have to wait for Tracy's own book to find them in one place. A sincere tip of the deerstalker to Tracy for the incredible support!

- *Marino C. Alvarez, BSI* – I first met Marino at meetings of the Nashville Scholars of the Three Pipe Problem, my home Scion – although it's a four-hour drive from my home, and my attendance is limited because of the time and distance involved. He is truly a gentleman and a scholar, and I was thrilled when, one day, he sent a story to be considered for the MX anthologies. I'm very glad that – although Marino has since retired and moved – another Nashville Scholar is represented here.

- *Chris Redmond, BSI* – Within days of discovering the internet, I discovered Chris Redmond's invaluable *Sherlockian.net.* Back then, it was an incredibly useful jumping-off place, particularly with its links to on-line pastiches. Later, it was a thrill to communicate with him. Having him contribute to the MX anthologies was an extra added treat.

- *Catherine Cooke, BSI* – I met Catherine on Holmes Pilgrimage No. 1 in September 2013, when she graciously gave me a tour of the Holmes collection at the Westminster Library, and also accepted copies of my books (up to that point) into the collection. I met her again in person in 2015 at the London launch party of the MX anthologies. I very much appreciate her contribution and support.
- *Jayantika Ganguly, BSI* – Although I've never met Jay in person, we've corresponded a lot over the years, ever since she first expressed interest in contributing to the initial MX anthologies. Since then she's written a lot of stories, both for the MX books, and other anthologies that I've edited, and I look forward to reading many more. (She also edits the brilliant journal for *The Sherlock Holmes Society of India*.)
- *Bonnie MacBird, BSI* – I met Bonnie in September 2013 at the same lunch at The Sherlock Holmes Pub where I met Roger Johnson and Jean Upton. At that time, she indicated that she was working on a Holmes pastiche, but no amount of hinting convinced her to let me see it early. I next met her in person at 2014's *From Gillette to Brett*, and then again in 2015 at the MX anthology launch party in London. She's gone on to write five Holmes novels since then, and her MX contributions are very much appreciated.
- *Mark Levy, BSI* – Mark was always a great supporter of these books and me personally, and I'm very glad that I had the chance to meet him in person when he once went out of his way to pass through East Tennessee once to have lunch, and again on several occasions in New York in 2020 during the Sherlock Holmes Birthday Weekend. I'm also glad that he and his wife, Arlene Mantin Levy, were able to be part of these books. Mark's passing is a great loss, and he is much missed.
- *Carla Coupe, BSI* – I first "met" Carla by way of her editorship of the *Sherlock Holmes Mystery Magazine*, when she accepted and published two of my Holmes scripts. (I was thrilled that payment for one of them, based on the word count, worked out to a very Sherlockian *$221*.) She contributed a story to the MX anthologies, and I was able to finally meet her in New York in January 2020. Thanks very much!

- *David Stuart Davies, BSI* – David is a Sherlockian who has been on my radar for decades. Soon after discovering Holmes in the mid-1970's, I received several related volumes as Christmas presents, including his *Holmes of the Movies* (1976). After years of correspondence, I was thrilled to meet him in person at the 2014 and 2018 *From Gillette to Brett* conferences – and to get many of his Holmes books in my collection autographed. Having him contribute to these books – with both a foreword and a story – was very personally gratifying.
- *Sonia Fetherston, BSI* – I initially "met" Sonia when she submitted a story to a Belanger Books anthology that I was editing, and then she contributed two pastiches to the MX books. After that, we co-edited a book (with Derrick Belanger), and I got the meet her in New York in January 2020. She's an incredibly nice and supportive person, and I look forward to seeing what she writes next.
- *Leslie S. Klinger, BSI* – I've met Mr. Klinger a couple of times at *From Gillette to Brett* conferences, but because of his work in "freeing" Sherlock Holmes in a lawsuit that went all the way to the Supreme Court, I knew that I wanted him to write the first foreword to the first volume of these books – and he graciously said yes. He stays busy with all kinds of projects, but I – and many others – thank him for the work he's done in the Sherlockian field.
- *Mark Alberstat, BSI* – I was first directed toward Mark by the late Peter Calamai, who suggested that I invite him to contribute a pastiche to the initial MX anthologies. Mark wrote a fine story – and I'm not sure, but it may be his only pastiche. He definitely needs to write more of them. Several years later, he asked me to contribute an essay to the very fine journal that he edits, *Canadian Holmes*. He is very supportive, and I'm glad that he's a part of these book.
- *Peter Calamai, BSI* – When the initial MX anthologies were being assembled, we tried to spread the word as far as we could to generate submissions – and it clearly worked, because I was emailed by Mr. Calamai, asking if he could submit a story. He had one that had been published several years before in an obscure volume, and even though it wasn't "New", it was new to me, and probably almost all of the anthology's readers. I glad said yes, and I'm very glad that he was included in the books. He passed away several years ago, before I had a chance to meet him in person, but I enjoyed the time that I was able to correspond with him.

10

- *Stephen Mason, BSI* – I'd seen Steve on Sherlockian social media for quite a while before I was able to meet him in January 2020 at the New York Holmes Birthday Celebration. He is a great and enthusiastic fellow, and having him be part of these books is a wonderful thing – and I hope he writes some more stories sooner rather than later!
- *Julie McKuras, BSI* – I have a lot of on-line Sherlockian contacts, but – living where I do – getting to the in-person events is rather difficult. While attending my second *From Gilllette to Brett* in 2014, and knowing very few people, I had the good fortune to sit next to Julie at dinner. She amazed me when she said that my book – there was just one then – was at the University of Minnesota Holmes Collection, and then we proceeded to spend quite a bit of time talking about the conference and discussing some of the speakers. When it turned out that she wrote pastiches too, I knew she had to be part of these books – and I'm glad that she agreed!
- *Jacquelynn Morris, BSI* – I first heard of Jacquelynn when I was in England on one of my Holmes Pilgrimages, and it was mentioned by a Sherlockian friend-in-common that she was over there then too – but I didn't get to meet her. She did a lot of work to save Undershaw before it shifted to become a school. I finally met her in person at 2018's *From Gillette to Brett*, and again in New York in January 2020. She contributed a pastiche to an anthology I edited for Belanger Books and four poems to the MX anthologies. I'm very grateful that she's part of these books, which is very fitting considering all the work she did for Undershaw.
- *Ann Margaret Lewis, BSI* – 2011's *From Gillette to Brett* was the first Sherlockian event I'd ever attended, and it was mind-blowing. (Being around beuing awed in the Dealer's Room, I met Ann, who was working one of the many tables. I'd read and enjoyed her Holmes pastiche, *Murder in the Vatican*, the previous year, and now I was meeting the author. That night, as I introvertedly joined a table for dinner at the banquet, she was there and was most gracious at working me into the conversations. When it was time a few years later to recruit for the MX anthologies, she was on my A-list of invitees, and she didn't let us down. Many thanks for being part of these from the beginning.
- *Nancy Holder, BSI* – Nancy is an award winning author and Sherlockian, and I've been trying to recruit her to write a pastiche for quite a while. I haven't succeeded yet, but I'm very grateful that she contributed a foreword – and the invitation for the story

hasn't gone away! (I was glad to finally meet Nancy in person in January 2020, and she's just as nice in person as she is in emails.)

- *Jeffrey Hatcher, BSI* – I'd been aware of Mr. Hatcher's work for several years before he spoke and presented his play, *Holmes and Watson*, at 2018's *From Gillette to Brett.* I was very glad when he agreed to contribute a foreword to these books and to have have him as part of the MX anthology "family".
- *John Farrell, BSI* – Mr. Farrell passed away in 2015, and I was never able to communicate with him. However, his friend, Sean Wright, had an umpublished pastiche that Mr. Farrell had written and sent it to me. I received permission from Mr. Farrell's family to use it, and was thrilled that it could finally be shared with the world.
- Although they chose not to participate in this volume, I also want to thank the remaining two MX BSI contributors, Bert Coules and Ashley Polasek, for their past contributions – Bert with three of his BBC scripts, and a poem from Ashley.

And finally, last but certainly *not* least, thanks to **Sir Arthur Conan Doyle**: Author, doctor, adventurer, and the Founder of the Sherlockian Feast. Honored, and present in spirit.

As I always note when putting together an anthology of Holmes stories, the effort has been a labor of love. These adventures are just more tiny threads woven into the ongoing Great Holmes Tapestry, continuing to grow and grow, for there can *never* be enough stories about the man whom Watson described as *"the best and wisest . . . whom I have ever known."*

David Marcum
October 25th,, 2022
132rd Anniversary of
"The Red-Headed League"

Questions, comments, or story submissions
may be addressed to David Marcum at

thepapersofsherlockholmes@gmail.com

Foreword
by Steven Rothman

David Marcum has edited an astounding 36 volumes in this series. He has urged, cajoled, demanded, hounded, and bargained a wide-ranging list of authors out of far more stories about Sherlock Holmes than Arthur Conan Doyle ever produced. So many, indeed, as to warrant this "best of" volume with a theme: All the contributors (including me) in *An Investee's Anthology* are members of The Baker Street Irregulars, that slightly mysterious group of Sherlockian scholars and enthusiasts.

But we are really not all *that* mysterious. Looking over the Table of Contents, I see librarians, lawyers, schoolmasters, playwrights, radio producers, film directors, bookshop owners, anthologists, cataloguers, novelists, short story writers, teachers, professors, university administrators, film writers, journalists, publicists, and editors. They come from three continents and make up about ten per cent of the contributors to this series. Irregulars are just everyday folk who love Sherlock Holmes a little bit *too* much, though in a thoroughly sociably acceptable way. We like to gather to talk about Sherlock, write about him, read about him, toast him, sing about him (some of us on key), and generally think about him.

Ask any Irregular the best part of being a Sherlockian and the answer will be the same: The people. Just as the Canon is really the story of the friendship between Holmes and Watson, so the Irregulars is a gathering of friends, a sort of family, that meet officially but once a year.

So dive in and enjoy. Re-read a favorite story or enjoy one new to you. And think about joining your local Sherlockian society so you too can make new friends and celebrate those two old ones who make Baker Street resonate within all of us.

Steven Rothman
Philadelphia
18 October, 2022

An Ongoing Legacy
for Sherlock Holmes
by Steve Emecz

Undershaw
Circa 1900

*T*he *MX Book of New Sherlock Holmes Stories* has grown beyond any expectations we could have imagined. We've now raised over $100,000 for Undershaw, a school for children with learning disabilities. The collection has become not only the largest Sherlock Holmes collection in the world, but one of the most respected.

We have received over twenty very positive reviews from *Publishers Weekly*, and in a recent review for someone else's book, *Publishers Weekly* referred to the MX Book in that review which demonstrates how far the collection's influence has grown.

In 2022, we launched The MX Audio Collection, an app which includes some of these stories, alongside exclusive interviews with leading writers and Sherlockians including Lee Child, Jeffrey Hatcher, Nicholas

Meyer, Nancy Springer, Bonnie MacBird, and Otto Penzler. A share of the proceeds also goes to Undershaw. You can find out all about the app here:

https://mxpublishing.com/pages/mx-app

In addition to Undershaw, we also support Happy Life Mission (a baby rescue project in Kenya), The World Food Programme (which won the Nobel Peace Prize in 2020), and *iHeart* (who support mental health in young people).

Our support for our projects is possible through the publishing of Sherlock Holmes books, which we have now been doing for over a decade.

You can find links to all our projects on our website:

https://mxpublishing.com/pages/about-us

I'm sure you will enjoy the fantastic stories in the latest volumes and look forward to many more in the future.

Steve Emecz
September 2022
Twitter: *@mxpublishing*

The Doyle Room at Undershaw
Partially funded through royalties from
The MX Book of New Sherlock Holmes Stories

A Word from Undershaw
by Emma West

Undershaw
September 9, 2016
Grand Opening of the Stepping Stones School
(Now *Undershaw*)
(Photograph courtesy of Roger Johnson)

It seems not so long ago I was writing with news from Undershaw, and here we are again with even more achievements to report. The school is now well into our new academic year with an unprecedented number of students on our roll, and we are busy firming up our place as a Centre of Excellence for SEND education, not only in our locality but further afield.

As an example of the positive culture we have at Undershaw, we received the most wonderful feedback from a work experience placement student we hosted recently. Here's what she had to say about our school from the time she spent with us:

> *Coming to Undershaw was a fantastic experience. I really appreciated the opportunity to spend time with your students, and even to take part in some drama improvisation! Your students were articulate, confident, and thoughtful. Sports Day was a real highlight for me – I felt it was inclusion at its best. The range of activities on offer, and the careful thought*

16

that had gone into the design of the day to ensure that every child could enjoy and achieve was inspirational.

Earlier in the summer we took our accolades to new heights when Undershaw was awarded a Gold Award by the Skills Builder Programme. This is a framework which identifies eight vital life skills, such as problem solving, leadership, and listening. When mastered, these skills ensure our students are fully equipped to take their places as economically and socially independent young adults. At Undershaw, we work tirelessly to ensure our students are immersed in every feasible aspect of their academic and character education, both of which furnish them for their rich and dynamic futures, wherever they may lie.

Undershaw is making a mark as a great seat of learning, proven this year with a fantastic set of GCSE, BTEC and Functional Skills results. We are so very proud of the results which are testament to the students' hard work, resilience, and perseverance. The way that they approached the examinations, having had their previous learning and opportunities to practise with mocks disrupted by the pandemic, is remarkable. Our students move on with a great set of qualifications and achieved the school's first ever Distinction grades, but just as important, they have developed their social and communication skills, built their confidence, and have become the most delightful group of young people. We look forward to hearing all about their next steps and their future successes.

I often say we have the best "job" in the world, as we are privileged enough to witness these remarkable students, who may not have had the best experiences in education before they came to us, find and fuel their passion under our tenure and ready themselves to spread their wings. My inbox is awash with emails from alumni telling me of their latest triumphs as they carve out their niche in the world. I will leave you with the sign-off from one alumnus who wrote to me recently and signed off with the words, *"Thanks for the confidence in me"*. That just says it all.

On behalf of all the wonderful students, committed and talented staff, and the families we support, I extend my heartfelt thanks to you all for being by our side. Undershaw would not be the school it is today without the selfless dedication of all at MX Publishing. We are honoured to have such friends in our midst.

Until next time…

Emma West
Headteacher
October 2022

"Undershaw," Hindhead, Conan Doyle's House.

Editor's *Caveats*

When these anthologies first began back in 2015, I noted that the authors were from all over the world – and thus, there would be British spelling and American spelling. As I explained then, I didn't want to take the responsibility of changing American spelling to British and vice-versa. I would undoubtedly miss something, leading to inconsistencies, or I'd change something incorrectly.

Some readers are bothered by this, made nervous and irate when encountering American spelling as written by Watson, and in stories set in England. However, here in America, the versions of The Canon that we read have long-ago has their spelling Americanized, so it isn't quite as shocking for us.

Additionally, I offer my apologies up front for any typographical errors that have slipped through. As a print-on-demand publisher, MX does not have squadrons of editors as some readers believe. The business consists of three part-time people who also have busy lives elsewhere – Steve Emecz, Sharon Emecz, and Timi Emecz – so the editing effort largely falls on the contributors. Some readers and consumers out there in the world are unhappy with this – apparently forgetting about all of those self-produced Holmes stories and volumes from decades ago (typed and Xeroxed) with awkward self-published formatting and loads of errors that are now prized as very expensive collector's items.

I'm personally mortified when errors slip through – ironically, there will probably be errors in these *caveats* – and I apologize now, but without a regiment of professional full-time editors looking over my shoulder, this is as good as it gets. Real life is more important than writing and editing – even in such a good cause as promoting the True and Traditional Canonical Holmes – and only so much time can be spent preparing these books before they're released into the wild. I hope that you can look past any errors, small or huge, and simply enjoy these stories, and appreciate the efforts of everyone involved, and the sincere desire to add to The Great Holmes Tapestry.

And in spite of any errors here, there are more Sherlock Holmes stories in the world than there were before, and that's a good thing.

David Marcum
Editor

Sherlock Holmes (1854-1957) was born in Yorkshire, England, on 6 January, 1854. In the mid-1870's, he moved to 24 Montague Street, London, where he established himself as the world's first Consulting Detective. After meeting Dr. John H. Watson in early 1881, he and Watson moved to rooms at 221b Baker Street, where his reputation as the world's greatest detective grew for several decades. He was presumed to have died battling noted criminal Professor James Moriarty on 4 May, 1891, but he returned to London on 5 April, 1894, resuming his consulting practice in Baker Street. Retiring to the Sussex coast near Beachy Head in October 1903, he continued to be associated in various private and government investigations while giving the impression of being a reclusive apiarist. He was very involved in the events encompassing World War I, and to a lesser degree those of World War II. He passed away peacefully upon the cliffs above his Sussex home on his 103rd birthday, 6 January, 1957.

Dr. John Hamish Watson (1852-1929) was born in Stranraer, Scotland on 7 August, 1852. In 1878, he took his Doctor of Medicine Degree from the University of London, and later joined the army as a surgeon. Wounded at the Battle of Maiwand in Afghanistan (27 July, 1880), he returned to London late that same year. On New Year's Day, 1881, he was introduced to Sherlock Holmes in the chemical laboratory at Barts. Agreeing to share rooms with Holmes in Baker Street, Watson became invaluable to Holmes's consulting detective practice. Watson was married and widowed three times, and from the late 1880's onward, in addition to his participation in Holmes's investigations and his medical practice, he chronicled Holmes's adventures, with the assistance of his literary agent, Sir Arthur Conan Doyle, in a series of popular narratives, most of which were first published in *The Strand* magazine. Watson's later years were spent preparing a vast number of his notes of Holmes's cases for future publication. Following a final important investigation with Holmes, Watson contracted pneumonia and passed away on 24 July, 1929.

Photos of Sherlock Holmes and Dr. John H. Watson courtesy of Roger Johnson

An Investees' Anthology

Selected Contributions to

The MX Book of New Sherlock Holmes Stories

by Members of
The Baker Street Irregulars

Forewords from Previous Volumes

Study and Natural Talent
by Roger Johnson
From *Part I: 1881-1889* (2015)

Greenhough Smith, editor of *The Strand Magazine*, hailed Arthur Conan Doyle as "the greatest natural storyteller of his age". Over a century on, Conan Doyle's genius keeps us reading, and, because many of us feel that sixty adventures of Sherlock Holmes just aren't enough, we write as well. The original tales are exciting and often ingenious; they're intelligent without being patronising, and they're never pretentious. The characters of Holmes and Watson – the apparently contrary forces that actually complement each other like Yin and Yang – stimulate our imaginations. Surely every devotee believes that the world needs more stories of Sherlock Holmes, and as, barring a true miracle, there'll be no more from his creator's fondly wielded Parker Duofold pen, we should provide at least one or two ourselves. We know the originals inside-out, or we think we do; we have a grand idea for a plot, and the style seems to be – well – elementary. How hard can it be?

In fact it's a sight harder than most of us think. Believe me: I know! To set a story convincingly in late Victorian or Edwardian London can require a fair deal of research just to avoid simple anachronisms and similar errors of fact. There are aspects of personality that may need careful attention – not just Holmes and Watson, but other established characters such as Messrs Lestrade and Gregson, and Mrs. Hudson (who really *was* the landlady at 221B, and *not* the housekeeper). Vocabulary and speech-patterns are important . . . .

Some will say, of course, that it's impossible to replicate the Doyle-Watson style. Nevertheless, there are writers who have come acceptably close to the real thing. Edgar W. Smith declared that *The Exploits of Sherlock Holmes* by Adrian Conan Doyle and John Dickson Carr should be re-titled *Sherlock Holmes Exploited*, but it is actually a remarkably good collection. Nicholas Meyer, L. B. Greenwood, Barrie Roberts, and Michael Hardwick are other names that come to mind, of authors who have, as Holmes himself said in a different context, applied both study and natural talent to the writing of new Sherlock Holmes adventures. For the current monumental collection, conceived and published for the benefit of the house that saw the rebirth of the great detective, David Marcum has coaxed stories from the best of today's generation of Holmesian chroniclers. Some of the contributors are famous, and some perhaps are destined for fame, but all of them bring intelligence, knowledge, understanding and deep affection to the task – and we are the gainers.

Roger Johnson, BSI, ASH
Editor: *The Sherlock Holmes Journal*
August 2015

Foreword
by Leslie S. Klinger
From *Part I: 1881-1889* (2015)

The urge to write new stories about Sherlock Holmes is not new. The first parody appeared in November 1891, after only a handful of Watson's tales had been published in the *Strand Magazine*. The public was fascinated by Holmes and wanted *more*. Parodies, an exaggerated version of a writer's style, written with humorous intent are exempt from the copyright laws, and so the author of the genuine Sherlock Holmes stories said nothing when these appeared. Pastiche, however, a reproduction of a writer's style without humorous intent, has long been restricted, as it should be, by the copyright laws granting the original author the right to control the use of his or her own characters.

Klinger v. Conan Doyle Estate Limited did not make new law. It merely recognized what the Estate had tried so hard to deny, that many of the elements of the characters of Sherlock Holmes, Doctor Watson, and their milieu, including not least the character names, had passed into the "public domain" throughout the world. This book celebrates the possibilities of that freedom, as creators tell their own stories about the beloved characters. Some may find it ironic that the celebration is dedicated to preserving the memory of Arthur Conan Doyle, whose heirs so bitterly fought the loss of their control of the characters. But, in the words of John Le Carre, "No one writes of Holmes and Watson without love."

Leslie S. Klinger, BSI
August 2015

Foreword
by Catherine Cooke
From *Part II: 1890-1895* (2015)

It all depends on your point of view. Fifty-six short stories and four long stories. Sixty cases of Sherlock Holmes spanning forty years. Sir Arthur Conan Doyle thought that was quite enough – probably too many even. While some commentators have opined that not all reach the same high standards, it cannot be denied that for the legions of Holmes's students, 60 is not nearly enough. They beg, *desire*, *DEMAND* more.

Sir Arthur was a man of action. His wife Touie was diagnosed with tuberculosis. He took her abroad to climes more suited – to Switzerland and Egypt. Hearing from a friend about "Little Switzerland", an area of Hampshire considered to have a climate as beneficial, he rushed down to Hindhead, bought a plot of land, and had a house built, specially designed for himself and for his ailing wife: shallow stairs, easy to open doors, and a couple of splendid heraldic windows. It is a tragedy of recent years that this house, Undershaw, and its beautiful grounds have been allow to fall into rack and ruin while legal disputes rumbled on.

But now there is cause for rejoicing on both fronts. A collection in three volumes (count 'em, *three*) of new Sherlock Holmes stories from well-practiced, well-known pens, as well as from newer writers – surely here there is something for all tastes. Furthermore, all royalties are to go to projects in the redevelopment of Undershaw by Stepping Stones. Conan Doyle's house will rise again offering specialist educational facilities to enable its students to achieve their full potential.

Congratulations are due to the editor, David Marcum, to MX Publishing, and to all those writers and supporters who have given their time, talents, and money to make these volumes possible. Now settle back and enjoy new accounts from the classic years of Holmes and Watson's partnership, which may shed new light on the mysterious years of the Great Hiatus.

Catherine Cooke, BSI, ASH
August 2015

The Sherlock Holmes Mystery
By David Stuart Davies
From *Part III: 1896-1929* (2015)

The real mystery about Sherlock Holmes is his universal appeal. What is it about this character created by a young Scottish doctor over a hundred years ago that has caught the imagination of readers worldwide? His stories have been translated into many languages; there are Holmes fan clubs all over the globe, in countries as diverse as Japan and India; and statues have been raised to this man who never lived in England, Scotland, Switzerland and Japan. His fans range from teenagers to pensioners, from labourers to aristocrats, from postmen to politicians. Why?

Well, the appeal of Sherlock is not new. Conan Doyle's tales about Holmes fascinated the Victorian reader and they became the mainstay of the *Strand* magazine – the sole reason why people purchased the publication. When the author tried to do away with his detective creation by casting him into the swirling waters of the Reichenbach Falls, the public mourned his loss, wearing black arm bands as a mark of respect. One outraged lady wrote to Doyle in protest, beginning her letter, "You brute!"

However, by this time the Sherlock bandwagon had begun rolling. After his supposed death at Reichenbach, Sherlock Holmes gradually grew into a media star. The first actor to portray the Great Detective in public was Charles Brookfield in a bit of comic nonsense called *Under the Clock* at the Royal Court Theatre in London in 1893. The piece made great fun of Holmes and his fawning companion, Watson. In 1894, Richard Morton and H. C. Barry penned a popular song, *The Ghost of Sherlock Holmes*, which did the rounds of the music halls. Both these ventures reveal how famous Holmes had already become so early in his career.

Holmes's fame received a boost when William Gillette appeared in the successful production of a play he had penned himself from an early draft written by Conan Doyle. *Sherlock Holmes*, a melodrama, with a plot largely drawn from "A Scandal in Bohemia" and "The Final Problem", opened in New York in 1899. While the critics sneered; the public cheered. It came to London in 1901 and ran for six months, playing to capacity houses at the Lyceum Theatre.

Then came the movies. As early as 1903, Holmes was up there on the silver screen. The first known film to feature the sleuth was *Sherlock Holmes Baffled*, made by the American Mutoscope and Bioscope Company in 1903. This humorous movie, which lasts less than one minute, is little more than an exercise in primitive trick photography but it appealed because the detective's name was in the title.

And so Sherlock Holmes began to have a parallel career: on the page and in the media. And it has remained so ever since. For over a hundred years Sherlock Holmes, along with his friend and biographer Dr John H. Watson, has appeared in numerous stories, films, plays, radio shows, television dramas, cartoons, musicals, etc., delighting a growing legion of fans. Doyle only wrote fifty-six short stories and four novels featuring his detective hero – but this Canon has been added to greatly by other hands. The desire for more Holmes continues to grow.

And yet, this still does not quite explain the appeal of the deer-stalkered one. Of course there are some rational explanations. There is the playing of the light-hearted academic game started by Ronald Knox, which involves investigating the anomalies and omissions in the Doyle Canon caused by Watson's slip of the pen: establishing the true date of certain cases, providing solutions and theories with respect to some obscure point – exactly how many times was Watson married, which university did Holmes attend, who was Mrs. Turner, and why were the Moriarty brothers both called James? The friendship between Holmes and Watson, one of the great literary bondings, is another vital and appealing aspect of the stories. We know that despite his cold aesthetic nature, Holmes is lost without his Boswell, and to Watson his friend is "the best and wisest man" he has ever known. Then there is the enjoyment of the period and the wonderful atmosphere evoked by the stories: it is a world where no matter what nefarious deeds were being planned, the world's more foremost champion of law and order was on hand to set things right – an England of thick, rolling fogs, where "gas lamps fail at twenty feet." In the company of Conan Doyle's mythical occupants of Baker Street, we return to a magic childhood. Sir Arthur himself indicated that the stories appealed to the boy who was half a man and the man who was half a boy. As we immerse ourselves in these wonderful tales, we shed the shackles of the present day and are free to thrill to the hansom cab ride through the darkened streets, knowing once more that the game is afoot.

All these reasons and more may be proffered in response to the question – why Sherlock Holmes? And in some way they are all applicable to solving the mystery. But there is something else. Something that lies in the heart and beggars description. We experience what it is. We feel it. We all share it. But it is too intangible, too precious to verbalise. That is why there is no truly clear and appropriate answer to why Sherlock Holmes? Only a feeling – one that brings intense and enriching pleasure.

David Stuart Davies, BSI
August 2015

Foreword
by Steven Rothman
From *Part IV: 2016 Annual* (2016)

Not everyone loves Sherlockian pastiche. Many readers find the sixty canonical stories sufficient. Good for them.

Others need as much Sherlock Holmes as they can possibly read – plus more Holmes to watch, Holmes to listen to on those long drives, and perhaps a videogame Holmes to fill the dozy hours. Sherlockian parody followed almost as closely on the heels of the birth of the Canon as Jacob did Esau with the earliest parody, "My Evening with Sherlock Holmes", appearing in 1891, the same year as "A Scandal in Bohemia". Pastiche is parody's only slightly younger sibling: the earliest known example, "The Late Sherlock Holmes", was published in 1893.

It is almost as if the world realized that however much Conan Doyle produced, there would never be enough Holmes to satisfy. Is this the greatest compliment ever paid to a writer? Quite possibly. Many popular writers have imitators, but only a very few can claim to have given birth to an industry. (Yes, there is Tarzan and Conan – and perhaps, other than Sherlock, characters' names should end in *–an* to earn worldwide affection. But do either the Lord of the Jungle or the Lord of Cimmeria hold the same place in as many hearts as the Lord of Baker Street?)

One of those who can never get enough Sherlock Holmes, certainly in written form, is the father of this continuing series of volumes, David Marcum. Marcum knows in his soul that Holmes is where the heart lies. This is the fourth volume of *pasticherie* that Marcum has conjured into being – cajoling stories from a wide range of authors, both old hands and those new to the Sherlockian game. And all offered to the world by MX to help preserve Undershaw, the house that Sherlock built, as it is being prepared for its bright new life as a school. "Lighthouses, my boy!" as Holmes said to Watson in "The Naval Treaty". So here is to the bright future of Sherlockian pastiche. Start reading!

Steven Rothman
Philadelphia
12 February 2016

Foreword
by Nicholas Utechin
From *Part VI: 2017 Annual* (2017)

Forty-two years ago, Nicholas Meyer published *The Seven-Per-Cent Solution* – an immense success out of left field. Forty-one-and-one-half years ago, a colleague and I at a radio station thought we would try and write a Holmes pastiche. Austin Mitchelson edited news bulletins which I read to some thousands of people in London. Every half hour, we would scribble notes of plot and dialogue. We wrote separate chapters and stitched them together.

The end result was something called *The Earthquake Machine*. For some reason, we were pleased with it, so we thought of another and called it *Hellbirds*. They were published in the U.S. in 1976 and neither was particularly good.

We thought we had been so clever to use Rasputin, Winston Churchill, Baron von Richtofen, and (very briefly) a young Adolph Hitler spread around the two books. (After all, our guide, Meyer, built his whole novel around Sigmund Freud.) We thought that a death atop the Eiffel Tower or a robbery at the Tower of London would add so much pizazz. Did Doyle ever insert Mr. Gladstone or Sir Arthur Sullivan into his works? Was there good reason that he only wrote four long stories?

Mind you, I was only twenty-four. (Mitchelson was older and should have been wiser).

Paramountly, we thought that we had the Watson/Doyle style nailed. Vitally, we eschewed Americanisms ("gotten to Baker Street", etc.). Crucially, it didn't work: An erudite Scottish minister who doubled as a literature/computer expert looked at how Doyle used words, how Mitchelson-as-Doyle used words, and how I used words as both myself and as Doyle. I was easily differentiated from Doyle, as I was from Mitchelson. All very disheartening.

This is a precursor to saying that writing Sherlock Holmes pastiches – good ones – is very difficult indeed. With good reason, as a veritable tsunami of often merely average and sometimes downright bad attempts at being Watson rolled out over the decades, I stepped back until a couple of years ago, when I was enthused by Editor David Marcum – on a visit to Oxford – to return to the fray and contribute to the preceding two volumes in this MX series. Others may comment on their quality (or not), but I think that is probably *that* from me. Just as I have always avoided

38

contributing to the chronology of Sherlock Holmes's cases – because it is too damn hard – so I believe that the art of a goodish pasticheur is to write little and rarely. How many did Starrett pen, or S. C. Roberts? Steer clear of the bandwagon unless you are very sure of your abilities.

All that said, there are some crackers in this latest collection and I am grateful to David for having afforded me some space to surmise.

Nicholas Utechin, BSI
Oxford, U.K.
January 2017

Foreword
by Nicholas Meyer
From *Parts IX and X: 2018 Annual* (2018)

There's a cartoon, known, I suspect, to all Sherlockians. It depicts a small boy in bed, staring with consternation and dismay at the last Sherlock Holmes story in the book he holds before him. *What now?* His expression seems to signify.

I was – and am – certainly not alone in identifying with the expression on the boy's face in the cartoon, as well as the feelings to be inferred behind it. When newcomers to the Holmes Canon reach the end of the sixtieth Doyle story, feelings of bereavement typically predominate. None of this is new. It is said that when Doyle killed off Holmes – (apparently!) – in "The Final Problem", young men in London went to work wearing black mourning armbands.

Just as surely, I am neither the first nor the last to have slid into the next phase of grief: Denial. The impulse to write my own Holmes story, to continue the adventures of that unique personage and of his Boswell. Fan fiction. Whether executed as straight-faced pastiche or broad parody, there are far more Holmes adventures penned by "divers hands" than the mere sixty penned by Arthur Conan Doyle, who remained oddly obtuse about the appeal of his creation and his own relations with The Great Detective.

Yet the unconscious plays strange tricks. Doyle, who kept trying to kill off Holmes, nonetheless seems to have expressed a knowing kinship with him. Holmes tells Watson he is descended from the sister of the French artist, Vernet. Being fictional, he is descended from no one. It is Doyle himself whose ancestor was Vernet's sister. One could thus term them cousins. Further, both Doyle and his alter ego bank at the same bank. Even more suggestively – as Holmes would observe – both are offered knighthoods in the same year. Doyle's impulse was to turn his down – he felt it would identify him as an establishment patsy. He relented at the insistence of his mother, under whose thumb he spent much time. By revealing contrast, Holmes disdains his knighthood without a second thought. And we never hear a word about Holmes's mother – only his skittish distrust of women in general.

Finally, and perhaps most tellingly, when Doyle did kill off Holmes, in the memorable struggle with his nemesis, Professor Moriarty, at the picturesque Reichenbach Falls, he conveniently failed to produce the detective's corpse, thus opening the floodgates for . . . the rest of us?

All of which leaves much from for speculation, embroidery, and additional Holmesiana.

In any event, even Doyle couldn't kill off Holmes, who, as we all know, rose from the dead, not on the third day, it may be, but still, there was a resurrection that has been going on ever since – first at Doyle's hands, but later, at ours.

Although cynical folk have argued that these "ripoffs" of Holmes and Watson are conceived with mercenary motives, speaking for myself, I don't think this is either fair or true. The small boy, despairing in his bed, doesn't dream of adding to The Canon as a way of enlarging his purse. Certainly I didn't. Writing my own Holmes story was simply an itch I had to scratch. Sixty stories are not enough! That my books went into profit surprised no one more than their author.

I hazard the guess that the stories that follow were all written out of affection and enthusiasm, not with any thought of piggy-backing on the genius of Doyle for pecuniary gratification. I could be wrong. You be the judge.

Nicholas Meyer
December 2017

Lose Yourself in New Pastiches
by Lyndsay Faye
From *Parts XI and XII: Some Untold Cases* (2018)

Whyen kindly folks ask me to write about Sherlock Holmes, my answer ought to be carved into a woodblock so I can stamp it on every occasion: I would love to. Yes, absolutely! But I do this for a living, weirdly – the writing, storytelling, etc. And it takes me about three weeks to craft a good short story, so I am careful about my *pro bono* projects. I always say, if you're not good enough for poetry, write short stories. And if you're not good enough for short stories, write novels.

I write mostly novels, by the way.

I can recall the exact moment when David asked me to contribute a Holmes pastiche for the first volume to benefit Undershaw. I remember it because I immediately said absolutely yes, turned it in, saw it in print, and then was relentlessly hounded for more pastiches until the point when I said (pretty much) never ever ask me this again.

So he asked me to write a forward.

I'm not telling this story in a negative light, in case anyone was wondering. In fact, David is responsible for a huge amount of new stories existing. He badgers, he cajoles, he solicits, he wheedles, and he cadges. It works. I value very few things more than I value new Sherlock Holmes stories, so I applaud these results.

Let this be a proclamation: David Marcum, and the authors featured herein, have brought more Sherlock Holmes stories into the world. The tales are fantastic. They are traditional, which is tricky. They are labors of love. And David Marcum loves Sherlock Holmes the way I do, never quite forgetting about him as we walk around grocery shopping or vegetable chopping or bar hopping.

Lose yourself in new pastiches. Nitpick them. Love them. Analyze them.

Whatever you do with them, I'm simply glad they exist in the world.

Lyndsay Faye
BSI, ASH
July 2018

Foreword
by Otto Penzler
From *Parts XXII, XXIII,* and *XXIV: Some More Untold Cases* (2020)

Everyone reading this extraordinary series of books discovered Sherlock Holmes in his or her own way. No one wrote of that magic moment more compellingly than Ellery Queen (in this case, Frederic Dannay, one of the two cousins who collaborated under that memorable pseudonym) in his essay collection, *In the Queen's Parlor.*

When I was ten years old, P.S. 9, my elementary school in the Bronx, offered what I imagine was common in those long-ago days but which I fear may be less common now: A library class. Once a week, our teacher would walk us down to the school library, where Miss Gibson would talk about how to use about books. We were shown the proper way to open a book, learned the rudiments of the Dewey Decimal System, and absorbed her cheerful talks about the wonders of reading.

For the second half-hour of the class, we were allowed to take any book we wanted off the shelf and read. I pulled down an anthology (title unknown, now), scanned the table of contents, and was intrigued by the title "The Red-Headed League."

I was instantly captivated by this Sherlock Holmes fellow and by the utterly bizarre notion of someone with a particular hair color being hired to copy the *Encyclopaedia Britannica.* Totally immersed, I was crushed when the bell rang, signaling the end of the class.

No, no, no. Wait. I have to know what this all means.

Mercilessly, the class was herded back to home room. Never was a class so eagerly anticipated as the following week's library hour.

Eventually, I learned that there were more stories like this one. I bought *The Complete Sherlock Holmes,* the Doubleday edition with that magical introduction by Christopher Morley, read it more than once, and lamented that there weren't more stories about that odd but curiously likable detective.

Happily, I was wrong. There *are* more stories, and this volume – all the volumes in this worthy series – prove that life always offers hope.

Otto Penzler
New York
April 2020

43

Foreword
by Nancy Holder
From *Parts XXVIII, XXIX,* and *XXX: More Christmas Adventures* (2021)

Sherlock Holmes and Christmas: Two fixed points in a changing world. The Great Detective, cracking the case with a dramatic flourish (and, often, a somewhat lengthy explanation). His faithful Boswell, marveling at the genius of Our Mutual Friend. Roasting chestnuts, glittering Christmas trees, carolers in hoop skirts and bonnets. A Victorian Christmas in all its holly-and-ivy splendor.

We who know and love The Canon – the fifty-six original stories and four novels written by John H. Watson (with an assist from Sir Arthur Conan Doyle) – wax nostalgic for the traditions of a time and place we will never see. At least I do, and I have spent the majority of my Christmases in Southern California, where guys in flip-flops spray artificial snow onto the windows of taco shops and sushi restaurants, and we watch *A Christmas Carol* with the air conditioning on – as do, I assume, my many friends in Australia, Hawaii, Florida, and so many other pleasant climes. Simply going by the cards I receive in December, Christmas as celebrated in late nineteenth century Britain and Ireland is the Ur of winter celebrations, and we perpetuate its hold on us with wholehearted devotion.

As a dedicated Sherlockian, I usually crack open "The Adventure of the Blue Carbuncle" to usher in Holmes at Christmas. This is the only story in The Canon that takes place at (or very near) Christmas. A review of the beloved tale is pretty much *de rigueur* at any December Sherlock Holmes cookie swap and/or Christmas jollification. How many of us have debated the various fine points of the story – (Why leave John Horner in the clink overnight? Does Peterson reap the reward for the gem?) – while sipping tea, brandy, or mulled wine and munching gingerbread? Nearly all of us – no matter if we celebrate Hanukkah, Diwali, Kwanzaa, or as is the case at my house, more than one winter holiday. For the duration of this one story, we happily transport ourselves to a Victorian Christmas.

But while "Blue Carbuncle" may be the only Christmas story in the Canon, it is, of course, not the only Christmas story featuring Holmes and Watson. MX Publishing, who published a lovely, hefty Christmas assortment in 2016, have done it again – a Santa sack brimming with Yuletide pastiches sure to please the traditionalists among us. Hewing close to the Canon, with no supernatural or fantastical elements, these are the kinds of stories sure to warm the heart (even if it's 98-degrees Fahrenheit outside) and take us back to where we want to be for our winter holidays – with Holmes and Watson, wrapped in gas lamp frost, where it's always (or close to) 1895. Dozens of talented, clever, careful authors have penned wonderful stories tailored to this season of joy, wonder . . . and Sherlock. Whether it's Christmas in July where you are, or snowy with a chance of sugarplums, I urge you to unwrap and savor. What lovely gifts await you.

Nancy Holder, BSI
Near Seattle
July, 2021

Foreword
by Jeffrey Hatcher
From *Part XXXI, XXXII,* and *XXXIII: 2022 Annual* (2022)

I've never written a Sherlock Holmes pastiche. At least not in prose. I've written the plays *Sherlock Holmes and the Adventure of the Suicide Club*, *Sherlock Holmes and the Ice Palace Murders*, and *Holmes and Watson*. I also wrote the screenplay for the film *Mr. Holmes*, based on Mitch Cullin's novel *A Slight Trick of the Mind*. But I've never attempted a classic short story or novel of the sort Arthur Conan Doyle excelled at. The reasons are two-fold:

I've never had the stamina to write prose fiction, be it the short story or a long form narrative. There's something about the density of the words and the requirement to depict a complete world with both exterior action and interior thought that defeats me. When I was in junior high, I started writing a shorty story – maybe it was going to be a novel, I can't remember – and around that time I'd read Dashiell Hammett's *The Maltese Falcon*. Its opening is devoted entirely to a description of what Hammett's private eye hero Sam Spade looks like:

> *Samuel Spade's jaw was long and bony, his chin a jutting v under the more flexible* V *of his mouth. His nostrils curved back to make another, smaller,* V. *His yellow-grey eyes were horizontal. The* V *motif was picked up again by thickish brows rising outward from twin creases above a hooked nose, and his pale brown hair grew down – from high flat temples--in a point on his forehead. He looked rather pleasantly like a blonde Satan."*

So, I figured that's what a writer's supposed to do. Start with your main character and describe him in laborious, infinitesimal detail. So that's what I did. I can't remember who my main character was or if he even had a name, but I was onto my third page and hadn't gotten below his upper lip. And he wasn't going to be the only character in the story. I was going to have to do this with all the characters. Then I'd have to describe the rooms they inhabited, their homes and offices, their cars. Not to mention the outdoors. It came down to this: I don't like having to describe what the tree looks like. I never finished that story or novel or whatever it was supposed to be. It was properly abandoned. Instead, I turned my interest to dramatic story telling: Plays and screenplays, the first fully executed one being a one-hundred-forty page film adaptation of Ian Fleming's *Moonraker*, five years before the Roger Moore movie. (Mine was better.)

The second reason I've never attempted a Sherlock Holmes story is that although the form seems simple enough, schematic even, the content, tone, and style that Conan Doyle mastered with such apparent ease is actually very hard to impersonate. The joy in a familiar form such as the Holmes stories lies in the reader experiencing the changes the writer rings within the form.

I wrote a few *Columbo's* in the 1990's and each classic *Columbo* episode had the following structure:

Act One: *Meet the polished, sophisticated murderer and watch him or her commit the ostensibly perfect crime.*

Act Two: *Columbo investigates, discovers a clue that tells him the perfect crime isn't so perfect.*

Act Three: *Columbo and the murderer play cat and mouse as more mistakes are uncovered and more chess moves take place.*

Act Four: *The murderer finds the means to save himself.*

Act Five: *Columbo tricks the murderer into incriminating himself or reveals the final damning clue that closes the case.*

The fun was in watching the form reenacted in different settings with different characters, clues, twists, and surprises.

Similarly with Holmes, we start a story expecting a scene in Baker Street, the arrival of a client, a mystery posed. "Will you help me, Mr. Holmes?" Then Holmes and Watson set forth into the streets of London or the Great Grimpen Mire to investigate the case. They meet increasingly desperate and malevolent characters. Another crime is committed or foiled. Finally, the culprit is captured. Throughout the story Holmes will reveal his deductive powers, his psychological perceptions, his wit, his courage, his humanity – along with those of Dr. Watson's. Yes, there are occasional departures from the form, but, with rare exceptions, the departures are not what we crack the spine for.

Enjoy the stories you're about to read. Think of them as an old and dear friend who's come to visit you – and he's got something terribly new and exciting to tell you.

Jeffrey Hatcher
March 2021

Poems

Two Sonnets
by Bonnie MacBird
From *Part III: 1896-1929* (2015)

Out of the Fog

When electronic clutter clouds our minds
With trifles, and presentiments of doom
There's always a retreat we know to find
Up seventeen stairs to that gaslit room.

Perhaps a brandy, in our easy chair
We turn the pages of a well-worn book.
Now, there beside the fire, sit our pair.
Two gentlemen, a smile, a knowing look.

And so with pipe in hand, our man unmasks
With reason, knowledge and a touch of art,
A source of horror, which he takes to task
And sets the evil, from us, far apart.

The side of angels and the depths of hell
Emerge from fog; are dealt with. All is well.

The Art of Detection

The world is puzzling, that we know for sure
To tame its mysteries a worthy goal.
For this we turn to science, but the lure
Is to unmask the secrets of the soul.

For Sherlock Holmes, the boundaries are clear.
The facts are clay, and scientists need bricks
To build a solid construct, yet appear
To some like a magician playing tricks.

But inferential logic can go wrong
And fail to parse out motives or mistakes.
The mind of man is like a complex song
And a musician's ear is what it takes.

Holmes uses all – his knowledge, mind and heart,
Because to practice science . . . is an art.

51

No Ghosts Need Apply

by Jacquelynn Morris

From *Part VII: Eliminate the Impossible 1880-1891* (2017)

Modern and medieval,
Practical and fanciful,
The mysteries of the commonplace.
A window with a yellow face,
A spectral hound,
A speckled band,
An intricate suicide, a bridge, a gun,
Three glasses of wine, with beeswing in one.
The cyclist forced to wed,
An anarchist left for dead.
A lodger that's veiled,
A soldier who's paled.
The goose with a crop,
A plaster bust shop.
The dog that did nothing – a curious incident.
A coffin bearing twice its content.
The print of a thumb
And a thumb that was gone.
Tenacious black clay,
A horse with a blaze.
A sinister cripple,
A vial of vitriol.
The typewriter and its relation to crime,
A world which oysters have overrun.
Hair of chestnut or red,
The pig that was dead.
Two ears in a box,
Paregoric's the stuff.

Red to the elbow in murder,
The Cornish horror.
Lowenstein of Prague,
Robert's sister's dog.

The trifles observed,

Reached improbable truth,
Standing flat-footed when the game's afoot.
For the love of his art
Living by his wits
Seeing things as they are is as good as it gets.
To the untrained mind it appears supernatural
When in fact the solution is frankly, discernible.
No vampires nor ghosts will our Holmes accept,
His criminals must be fully-fleshed.

Unrecorded Holmes Cases
A Sonnet
by Arlene Mantin Levy
and Mark Levy
From *Part XI: Some Untold Cases (1880-1891)* (2018)

The master Sherlock Holmes found many clues,
John Watson wrote them up and made them great;
His cases ranged from opal rings and shoes
And stains and smoke, to those of heavy weight;

But really those of most intrigue to us
Are unrecorded tales of quirky guys,
Like Ricoletti with his club foot plus
Abominable wife, or Upwood's lies;

Persano had a matchbox and big worm,
James Phillimore's umbrella disappeared;
A rat (Sumatran giant) took its turn
As did Vittoria, circus belle with beard;

So these and more add fun to Canon lore
We wish Doc Watson would have written more.

Adventures

The Adventure of the Defenestrated Princess
by Jayantika Ganguly
From *Part I: 1881-1889* (2015)

I have often remarked on the variety and oddity of clients who sought the aid of my friend, Mr. Sherlock Holmes, at our shared quarters. More often than not, our visitors would be accompanied by an aura of drama and intrigue. An especially dramatic entrance sprung to my mind when I last visited Holmes in Sussex Downs, and he finally gave his assent to reveal the details of the case. The parties involved are beyond human reach now, and the only sufferer of this narration would be Holmes's own perception of his sentimentality – or rather, the lack thereof.

It was towards the end of autumn in the year 1882, and in the months that I had known Holmes by then, I was truly convinced that he was as coldly logical and unfeeling as he projected himself to be. He had been generous enough to permit me to accompany him on several of his cases, and I was as much in awe of his genius as I was appalled at his apparent lack of empathy. While he was mostly polite to his clients, and unfailingly gentle with the fairer sex, I had come to realise that he did not much care for their plight; it was the puzzle which appealed to him. I know better now, of course, but in those early days, Holmes and I were not as close, and he kept much of his thoughts to himself.

This particular case began with a gunshot at the ungodly hour of three in the morning. The terrible noise roused me from my sleep. I hurriedly threw on my dressing gown, pocketed my bull pup and rushed downstairs to find Holmes similarly dressed and armed.

"What happened?" I enquired, my voice barely a whisper.

"From the sound, I can only tell you that a .476 calibre Enfield Mk I revolver has been fired within twenty yards of our abode, Watson," Holmes replied grimly. "I intend to step out to investigate further."

"I should like to keep you company, if you do not object," I offered.

"Thank you, Doctor. Your assistance may be invaluable. I suspect we shall have an injured person at hand shortly."

We passed an anxious Mrs. Hudson in the hallway. Insistent knocking, growing increasingly desperate with each passing moment, beckoned us to the front door. Holmes waved Mrs. Hudson away to safety, and gestured at me to take up a discreet position, so I could assist him if our late-night guest bore intentions of assault. The detective threw open the door.

A raggedly-dressed young man stood outside, one hand still raised towards the knocker and the other clutching his abdomen.

"Mr. Holmes?" he whispered hoarsely.

To my surprise, Holmes pulled him in immediately and closed the door. The boy leaned against the wall, breathing heavily. His dark eyes were wide as he stared at Holmes.

"Oh, but you are more beautiful than I was told to expect, Mr. Holmes," the boy sighed dreamily. "May I paint you?"

I was rendered speechless. Holmes appeared embarrassed and flabbergasted in equal measures. Then the boy collapsed and I noticed the dark blood coating his fingers, realising he had been delirious with pain.

"Get your medical kit ready, Watson," Holmes said urgently. "I will bring up our visitor."

I rushed upstairs and grabbed my bag and some clean linen. We might not have the antiseptic environment of a hospital, but I would not let an infection take my patient. But where could I perform the required surgery? Our living room did not offer a surface large enough.

"My bed should suffice," Holmes said, walking in with the boy in his arms.

Wordlessly, I followed him to his bedroom and spread the clean linen on his bed. With as much care as a mother would display for her injured child, Holmes laid our visitor on the bed. He proceeded to turn up all the lights.

In the well-lit room, I could see the beauty of that young, smooth, golden face and felt a wave of fury sweep through me. The boy could not have been more than fourteen. How dare a ruffian harm a child?

Holmes's soft voice broke through my anger. "How may I assist you, Watson?"

"Cut away his clothes, if you would, Holmes. I need to see the bullet wound," I told him, pouring alcohol on both our hands.

Holmes nodded and carefully removed a strip of the boy's blood-stained shirt.

"It might be better if you removed the shirt completely," I suggested.

Twin spots of colour appeared on my friend's pale cheeks. "I am afraid that may not be prudent, Doctor," he said. "Our client is a lady."

I could only stare at him in shock. However, as I turned my eyes back to my patient, I realised he was right. The figure under those ragged-boy clothes could only belong to a woman.

As it turned out, she was a rather fortunate young lady. Once I had cleaned the blood, it appeared that the bullet had passed cleanly through her side without touching any vital organ, and there was nothing for me to do except clean up the wound and bandage it. She would be fine. Holmes heaved a sigh of relief when I informed him. He laid a set of spare clothes on the chair and we left the girl to rest. We would get her story when she awoke. I was quite exhausted myself, but curiosity gnawed at me.

"A foreign lady," I said to Holmes.

He nodded. "Indeed, Watson. I was not able to deduce much, but it appears she is from our Indian colonies, belongs to a royal family – or at least a very affluent one, studies at the University of London, is a voracious reader, dabbles in art and the violin, seems to be good at horse-riding, fencing and shooting – and is presently caught in a web of international politics. She was abducted recently, but either escaped or was rescued soon."

"How could you possibly know that?" I asked, amazed. "She asked if she could paint you, so I can understand her affinity for art, but how could you know the rest?"

Holmes gave me a small smile. "Look at her boots and jewellery, Watson – custom made, extremely expensive. Also, the soil is clearly from Gower Street. From the dents on her nose, she regularly uses eye glasses, even at this young age – clearly reads a lot. So, a young, studious and rich foreigner in Gower Street – could it be anyone other than a student at the University College London?"

I nodded, following his observations. "You mentioned she plays the violin, rides, fences and shoots."

"Riding boots, calluses and gun-powder residue," he replied. "And if I am not mistaken, that is an 1874 Chamelot-Delvigne in her pocket."

"Abduction? Did you deduce that from the rope-burns on her wrists and ankles?"

"Bravo, Doctor."

"But why on earth is she dressed as a man, Holmes?"

"I suspect it was to foil an assassination attempt," he remarked. "I shall know more upon an investigation of the contents of her coat pocket and satchel."

My face must have betrayed my thoughts, for Holmes laughed. "Do not worry, my good doctor, I assure you that I have our client's permission." He regarded me thoughtfully. "I suggest you rest while you can, Watson – I shall wake you if your patient has any need of you."

I was too tired to argue, so I took his advice. As it turned out, our visitor did not wake until Mrs. Hudson was sent to help her out of bed. One look at the apparel Holmes had laid out for the young woman and our landlady was kind enough to bring up some of her own laundered clothes. Finally seeing the girl dressed in feminine attire, I realised what an utterly beautiful woman she would be in a few years. Even though the dress was plain and ill-fitting, I could easily believe Holmes's conjecture that she was a princess.

"Good morning, your Highness," Holmes greeted her, and almost simultaneously, I asked, "How do you feel?" when Mrs. Hudson and my patient appeared at the breakfast table. I noted absently that Holmes seemed to be observing the princess rather intensely.

"Much better, thank you, Doctor Watson, Mr. Holmes," she replied softly. "You have all been very kind. And please, you must call me Ada – everyone does. I am afraid my Indian name is not conducive to the British tongue, but 'Ada' is quite close to the shortened version."

I was surprised to note she spoke with an upper-class British accent. She smiled at my surprise.

"I have mostly been educated in Europe," she said. "My father is uncharacteristically modern, and I have been rather fortunate for it."

Mrs. Hudson had thoughtfully set up a third place for breakfast, and Holmes invited our client to join us. She took up the chair gratefully and we ate together in silence.

The Princess was the first to speak when we took up chairs near the fireplace.

"Did you have a chance to look through my papers, Mr. Holmes?" she asked quietly.

"Indeed," Holmes replied.

"And what do you make of it?" she enquired.

"I prefer not to hypothesise until I have adequate facts, your Highness," Holmes told her. "I must confess myself stupefied, though, at the absence of any symptoms of poisoning."

Ada laughed. "Oh, you are right, Mr. Holmes, I have been poisoned. However, in my family, we are inured to most varieties of venom, and for anything more potent, we have a *vaidya* – I suppose you could say doctor – at hand. I have not been seriously harmed."

Holmes nodded, but did not look very convinced. "It might be best for you to give us the facts first," he said instead.

Ada smiled ruefully. "Of course, Mr. Holmes, I shall do as you say. I suppose I was hoping to see your skills of deduction first-hand. Victor was always rather verbose about your talents. And when your . . . ." She paused and glanced at me. "Well, M suggested that I consult you at the earliest."

Holmes frowned and the Princess smiled again. She really did have a rather fetching smile. The M she had spoken of, I learnt several years later, was none other than Mycroft Holmes.

"I apologise, Mr. Holmes, Doctor Watson – my brains are still rather addled. Let me narrate the events that have led me here in chronological order." She paused again. "I am afraid it is a rather long tale, but I shall endeavour to make it as brief as possible."

"My father is the King of Terai, a small Indian territory. Incidentally, Mr. Holmes, your friend Victor has lived in our kingdom for several years now, and I have been friends with him since I was a child. It was he who first spoke of you." She smiled fondly. "But I digress. My father is a great believer in education, gentlemen, and at his insistence, all his children – there are six of us – have been thoroughly educated in various parts of the world. This has also helped us further our international relations. Consequently, our little kingdom has prospered even more. Lately, however, my father has not been keeping very well and desires to see all his children married. My brothers and sisters are significantly older, and therefore, already well-settled. While I would prefer to complete my graduation before I wed, my father's plight does not allow for such delay. As it is, I am sixteen, which makes for a rather old bride in traditional families. It was initially believed that there would be a dearth of suitors for my hand . . . now, however, it appears that the problem is quite the reverse." She paused and smiled sardonically. "I do have a rather significant dowry to my name."

"Currently, I have four perfectly fine men willing to take me for a wife. One has been chosen by my father and our mutual acquaintance M, and the rest by my siblings. The first, Sir Norbert, is a British nobleman of impeccable heredity, tragically impoverished. The second, Rajkumar Vikramaditya, is an Indian prince from a neighbouring eastern state. The third, Prince Pierre, is the heir to the throne of an African kingdom. The fourth, Dokter Diederik, is also a European gentleman of Dutch origin, not titled, but immensely rich. I have met each one, Mr. Holmes, and they are all wonderful gentlemen . . . and I am unable to choose. Ordinarily, I would blindly follow my father's advice, Mr. Holmes – he is the wisest man I have ever known, but recent events have made me wary. The warning letters in my bag started pouring in a fortnight ago. There have been three assaults on my person and two break-ins at my London residence in the last week. I am reluctant to bother my father with this, so I have consulted with M, who has been akin to a guardian to me since I arrived in this country. I intended to visit you at a decent hour last evening, but I was cornered in my apartment by a gang of ruffians. My guards fought them off bravely, allowing me to escape in disguise, while my maid dressed herself in my clothes and fled in another direction as a decoy. The man who followed and shot me on Baker Street must have taken me for a messenger sent to seek your assistance."

"You were abducted two days ago," Holmes said.

She nodded.

"Did you know your captor? How did you escape?" I asked.

"Faithless man," she said quietly. "It was one of my friends from the university. Fortunately, my men caught up with the carriage I was in."

"Where was he supposed to take you?" Holmes asked.

"I do not know, Mr. Holmes. He killed himself before we could take him to the police."

"Are you quite certain you do not have any lingering effects of poisoning? Watson may be able to help."

"Thank you. That is very kind of you."

"May I enquire if any your suitors or their assistants bear the initials K.O.?" Holmes asked.

The Princess stared at him in shock. "None," she said eventually.

"But you are – or were – close to someone with those initials," Holmes said, watching her keenly.

"Yes. Kaarle Olivier is my best friend," she replied defiantly.

"Why did you not go to the police?" Holmes asked.

"M advised against it."

"Does he have any ideas?"

She looked away. Holmes frowned, but before he could question the princess further, Mrs. Hudson appeared with the newspapers. It was unusual for her to bring them up herself; obviously she desired to check up on Ada, whom she now considered to be under her wing.

Holmes pounced upon the papers. The front page declared, "Defenestration in London!" Holmes quickly passed the paper to me and I read out loud:

> *Late last night, a young woman was thrown out of her third-floor apartment window at Gower Street. The girl, who was killed upon impact, has been identified as Her Royal Highness, Princess Advyaitavadini, youngest daughter of the Indian King Abhayananda of Terai. Her entire entourage, consisting of six trained guards, three male servants and three female servants, has also been found to be killed in a violent fight while defending the princess. The deceased, known to her friends as Ada, was well-liked amongst her fellow students at the University. Her friends have confessed that the princess had been threatened and attacked previously as well, but had refused police assistance. This brutal massacre of thirteen people, however, is being investigated by Scotland Yard, under the able leadership of Inspector G. Lestrade, whom the public may remember from the Jefferson Hope case.*

Ada had lost all colour and tears poured down her cheeks. Her hands shook, portraying her distress, and I was reminded that she was still barely more than a child.

"I must go to the university at once, Mr. Holmes," she cried, pushing herself off the chair with some effort. "This news must not travel to my father at any cost."

She staggered towards the door but faltered halfway. Fortunately, Mrs. Hudson caught her.

"Now you listen here, young lady," Mrs. Hudson scolded. "You are to stay here and rest. Mr. Holmes and Dr. Watson will take care of your troubles."

"But . . . ."

"No buts. Look at the state of you, all pale and trembling! What you need is a cup of good, strong tea," our landlady said firmly, and proceeded to press a cup into the girl's hands.

Holmes took a seat next to the traumatised girl and said gently, "I shall attempt to contain the news, barring which, I shall ensure that news of your survival accompanies any notification from the university. However, you must stay hidden here until I return. Watson and Mrs. Hudson will look after you. Do you understand?"

She nodded tearfully.

Holmes turned to me. "Watson, no one must see her. If we have any visitors not accompanied by myself, escort her to my room. I expect Lestrade shall come by at some point. Be ready."

"Certainly, Holmes," I promised, understanding his warning to be armed and prepared.

"Mr. Holmes," Ada called softly. "My people . . . they have to be cremated, and their ashes sent home to be scattered in the holy river. I do not know who the thirteenth person is, but if she is Christian, she ought to be buried here. If you require me to identify my people, I shall accompany you."

Holmes's grey eyes glittered like diamonds as he turned back to the girl.

"Who knew the specific number of people in your entourage?" he asked.

She frowned. "I am not sure. It was not exactly a secret."

"Do you have any idea who the unknown woman might be?"

"It could be the milkmaid, the charwoman or the laundry girl – they were friendly with my staff and often visited socially. In fact, Jane – the laundry girl, and Satyanand – one of my guards, were hoping to marry when we returned to Terai." Ada pursed her lips, eyes bright with unshed tears. "You will find out who did this, won't you, Mr. Holmes?"

"I shall certainly endeavour to do so," Holmes replied.

Ada nodded, visibly assured. "Please spare no expense. No price is too dear to me to avenge the murder of my people!"

Holmes nodded his assent. "How many of your suitors are presently in London?"

"All of them."

"One last question, before I leave," Holmes said quietly. "Could you describe Sir Norbert and Dokter Diederik?"

Ada smiled. "I can do better. I can give you their pictures." She fetched a small album from her dress pocket and handed it to Holmes, pointing out each of her suitors.

Holmes appeared pleased. "Thank you," he said. "I shall be back soon."

Holmes was away for several hours. I changed the dressing on Ada's wound, and then looked through the papers Holmes had spent the night poring over. There were fifteen envelopes, several of which bore stamps from exotic cities. Each contained an insult, scrawled on a torn piece of foolscap in an untidy hand with scarlet ink:

Vile _worm_, thou wast o'erlook'd even in thy birth. (London)

You are not worth another _word_, else I'd **call** you knave. (London)

I wonder that you will still be talking. _Nobody_ marks you. (Madrid)

Here, thou incestuous, murderous, damned Dane, _Drink_ off this _potion_! (Helsinki)

Dissembling harlot, thou art _false_ in all! (London)

I shall laugh myself to _death_ at this puppy-headed monster! (London)

Thou unfit for any **place** but hell. (London)

Away! Thou'rt _poison_ to my blood. (Calcutta)

More of your conversation would _infect_ my brain. (Cairo)

Away, you mouldy rogue, away! I am <u>meat</u> for your master.
(Havana)

O <u>faithless</u> coward! O dishonest wretch! Wilt thou be made a <u>man</u> out of my vice? (Milan)

*<u>Take her away</u>; for she hath lived too long, To fill the world **with** vicious qualities.* (Hamburg)

I shall cut out your tongue. 'Tis no matter, I shall <u>speak</u> as much wit as thou <u>afterwards</u>. (London)

O you <u>beast</u>! I'll so maul you and your toasting-iron, That you shall think the <u>devil</u> is come from hell. (Krakow)

Heaven truly knows that thou <u>art false</u> as hell. (Odessa)

I stared at the scraps in disbelief. When I looked up at Ada, she was smiling sadly.

"Shakespeare. I thought the first few were a joke," she said, her voice quiet.

There was also a small diary filled with neat, feminine handwriting, meticulously noting down the date and time of receipt of each letter, and the Shakespearean play each message was taken from – *The Merry Wives of Windsor, All's Well that Ends Well, Much Ado about Nothing, Hamlet, The Comedy of Errors, The Tempest, Richard III, Cymbeline, Coriolanus, Henry IV, Measure for Measure, Henry VI, Troilus and Cressida, King John,* and *Othello.* Ada had also noted down the bold and underlined words separately.

The underlined words read: *"worm word Nobody Drink potion false death poison infect meat faithless man Take her away speak afterwards beast devil art false"* and the bold words read *"call place Away with I".* Even I could see the barely concealed warning in the papers and the missive to call India. I wondered what else Holmes had deduced from these. How was it even possible to deliver these letters so regularly from such different locations?

Ada had also made a list of her staff members, including the local hires and their contact details. Similarly, she had also listed the London addresses of her suitors.

I recognised the English nobleman immediately. He was at least thirty years older than our young princess! When I made a remark, Ada simply smiled and said, "They all are; at forty seven, your bachelor Englishman

65

is in the younger half. The Indian is the youngest at thirty five – and I am to be his fifth wife. The African is fifty two, and I shall be the second wife; the first died recently. The Dutch is seventy, a famed misogynist until now."

"Would you not prefer to wed someone close to your own age?" I enquired, curious.

She smiled sadly, her bright eyes dimmed. "I have a duty to my kingdom, Dr. Watson; I do not have the luxury of love."

I had a sudden thought. Could it be that the warning disguised as threats were the work of a rejected admirer from a failed love-affair? I did not realise I had spoken out loud until I saw the stricken expression on her face.

"M thinks so, too – in fact, I made the notes under his instructions," she said unhappily. "But I know Kaarle would never do so!"

"I am glad you think so, *ma mie*," came a soft voice from the door.

Ada jumped out of her seat with a cry of "Kaarle!"

Monsieur Olivier strode in and engulfed her in his arms. She sobbed quietly on his shoulder.

I took a moment to regard the rather striking blue-eyed, dark-haired young man before Holmes, who had followed the young man in, cleared his throat delicately.

The young pair sprang apart immediately.

"*Je suis désolée, mon trésor,*" Ada said quietly. She turned to Holmes. "How did you find him, Mr. Holmes?"

"From the letters," Holmes replied. "You had, rather helpfully, written down the Shakespearean references. All foreign places started with the same letter as the play's title, and the bold words were followed by such letters of the alphabet. 'Call MH. Place CCH. Away for MH. I KO.' I paid a visit to the Charing Cross Hospital and found him in the morgue, looking for you. Child's play."

The princess directed her flashing dark eyes at the young Frenchman. "It was you," she spat. "You sent those letters! You killed my people!"

Monsieur Olivier winced. "*Non, ma mie, non,*" he pleaded. "I merely attempted to warn you. There is a great conspiracy afoot. You are in grave danger, *ma mie*."

Ada glared.

"He was with M," Holmes said gently.

Ada turned her furious gaze back to the boy. "How do you know M?" she demanded.

"That ought to be a story for another time," Holmes interrupted impatiently. "We have more pressing concerns."

Ada stepped back, gathered herself and reclaimed her seat. "You are right, of course, Mr. Holmes. My apologies."

Holmes gestured for the young man to take a seat as well. He lit his pipe and I offered cigarettes to the boy.

"Cremation and transit of the ashes have been arranged," Holmes said, his voice quiet and soft. "Notice of your safety is also en route to your family."

"Thank you," Ada whispered. Her eyes shone with grateful tears.

"The additional victim appears to be Jane Miller, your laundry girl," Holmes continued. "She is the only person unaccounted for. Requisite funeral arrangements have been made."

Ada nodded.

"News of your survival has been contained so far. I would like to keep it thus until we are able to locate the perpetrator." Holmes blew out a long spiral of smoke. "Monsieur Olivier has been trying to warn you of imminent danger for the last two weeks. M and I agree with him."

"But why would anyone want to kill me? No one stands to gain anything from my death. Once I am married, my death would undoubtedly benefit my husband, but till then, I am pretty useless." Ada frowned and glared at her young friend. "How do *you* know?"

Kaarle winced. "After we parted in Geneva, I went to meet my father. I accidentally stumbled upon a conspiracy involving Terai. Your father is not on his deathbed. Each of your suitors is a political plant. The British, Dutch and Indian represent their own, and the African is a French agent."

"But Terai is neutral!" Ada exclaimed. "We have always been peaceful."

Kaarle shook his head. "Terai is rich, independent, and possesses a powerful military force. It is strategically located and impossible to avoid for any trade route through Asia. You are surrounded by British, French and Dutch colonies, as well as rebellious Indian states. It is no secret that you are the favourite daughter of your father, and unlike most kingdoms where the crown automatically passes down to the eldest son, your family has been known to be eccentric enough to choose a successor deemed worthy. Your father himself was the fourth son, was he not? And your grandfather the second son-in-law?"

Ada nodded, her eyes wide.

"Your husband would be in the race for the crown of Terai, a most desirable object for each of your neighbours. The French and the Dutch would gain a strong foothold in the east, and will be able to wrest control of several states from the British. The British would become invincible if they won Terai. Any Indian state that has your unconditional support would gain not only a great army, but also a political advantage against

European intruders. Also, even though your father is non-aligned, some of your siblings are very involved in the Indian independence movement. You have been known to sympathise."

The Princess lifted her chin defiantly. "I advocate peace, like my father before me. However, if you saw the brutalities heaped upon my countrymen, you would feel the need to rebel, too. Terai is only safe because we are powerful enough."

"Nonetheless," I interjected. "This does not explain why anyone would wish to harm Ada. Surely it is in the interest of these men to keep her alive and happy with them, so they could win her hand?"

Holmes smiled. "You have cut straight to the heart of the matter, my dear doctor," he said. "While the British, French, Dutch and Indians stand to win, others stand to lose. As such, eliminating the princess is a good way of reducing the risk. One less contender to the throne."

Ada sprang from her seat. "Are you implying my relatives are involved, Mr. Holmes?"

"I do not theorise without adequate data," Holmes replied calmly.

"But you suspect?"

"It is only logical."

"No," Ada declared. "Please cease your investigations. I shall return to my homeland immediately."

"Are you out of your mind?" Kaarle cried. "You will be killed on the way!"

The princess remained stubbornly silent.

Holmes turned his raptor gaze upon the young woman. "There is no dignity in death by betrayal," he said quietly. "If a member of your family is indeed responsible for this assault, would their next move not be to eliminate your father and other dissenting members of your family?"

She staggered. Holmes caught her gently and led her back to her chair. I had always known Holmes to be chivalrous, but he usually disliked women. In this instance, however, I could see genuine concern for the girl in his eyes. Was it because she was barely more than a child, or could it be that Holmes's projection of machine-like imperturbability was false?

"Do not exert yourself, Ada," Holmes said softly. "You have been poisoned, abducted and shot at; you require rest."

Kaarle's eyes widened in shock. "But I warned you! Did you not heed my words?"

"I did," Ada said softly. "I was prepared for the wormwood in the wine and hemlock in the quail."

"Correct me if I'm wrong, your Highness, but were you with one of your suitors each time you were attacked?" Holmes asked.

She nodded. "I had wine with the African prince; it was one of his special vintages from his vineyard in Bordeaux. Quail was served for dinner with your British peer. I was taken from the street right outside the Indian prince's hotel, and the attack last night happened just after I returned from dinner with the Dutch gentleman."

"What happens to your dowry if you die?" I asked.

She shrugged. "I suppose it reverts to my father's treasury." She looked straight at Holmes. "My relatives would not care about that. It is not a significant sum of money for my family."

Holmes nodded.

I turned to the boy and asked, "Who is beast devil?"

"I am unsure," Kaarle replied. "As I said, I overheard two men talking of Terai. I sent out whatever information I had through mail to warn Ada – in parts, so that they would not be intercepted, and *prima facie* nonsensical, so that they would be dismissed as innocuous. I had the two agents arrested and made my way to London immediately. I arrived at Charing Cross last evening."

The bell rang.

Holmes quickly sent our young guests to his bedroom with strict instructions to stay out of sight.

"I have been expecting you, Lestrade," Holmes said, greeting our visitor.

Inspector Lestrade shook his head sombrely. "It's an unholy mess, I tell you, Mr. Holmes. Some foreign princess got herself killed, and the Prime Minister descended upon us." He smiled. "We know who did it, but we need your help to find the fellow."

Holmes arched an eyebrow.

"The princess left everything in her will to a Kaarle Olivier; she was sweet on him in Switzerland, her friends say. We know Olivier arrived in London yesterday. Probably wanted to marry the girl, but she was to wed someone of her own class – must have killed her in a jealous fit."

"And her entourage?" Holmes asked.

"Died protecting her, didn't they?"

"Do you honestly think one man could have killed thirteen people single-handed?" I interjected hotly.

"Accomplices."

"Tell me, Inspector, are you familiar with the brothers Zvíře and Ďábel?" Holmes enquired.

"Beast and devil!" Lestrade exclaimed. "Are they involved?"

"It is likely." Holmes took in my befuddled expression. "Mercenaries, my dear doctor, named for their looks. These two make a most vicious pair of criminals. Their origins are unknown, and they are fluent enough in at least six languages to disguise themselves as natives. I believe they are wanted by several nations."

Lestrade groaned.

"I believe we may be able to capture them," Holmes told the policeman. "However, I shall need full cooperation of Scotland Yard."

"By all means, Mr. Holmes." Lestrade's beady eyes glinted with excitement. "What do you need?"

A devious smile appeared on Holmes's thin face, and, for a moment, I was reminded of a bloodhound catching a scent. "We shall lay a trap, my dear Inspector, and I need bait."

"What bait?"

"I believe you are aware of the shooting here last night?"

Lestrade nodded.

"I would like Scotland Yard to publicly state that valuable information on the perpetrators has been found at Baker Street, and an eye-witness has survived. The police have a solid lead and shall arrest the culprits soon."

"Now, look here, Mr. Holmes, I can't put out false information."

"It is true."

"What?"

Holmes smiled. "We have an eye-witness who was shot by Zvíře last night, presently under the care of Dr. Watson."

"I need to see him," Lestrade said stubbornly.

Holmes glanced at me.

"I'm afraid my patient is not in a state for visitors at the moment, Inspector," I replied. "However, we may be able to set up a meeting later today."

"Rest assured, Inspector, once we have the thugs, your eye-witness will testify if required. Also, as always, I would like you to keep my name out of it." Holmes's demeanour was sombre. Even at that young age, he was quite masterful. Lestrade agreed reluctantly and departed.

"Now we wait, Watson," Holmes sighed.

Lestrade kept his word. The evening papers carried the bait.

Barely an hour later, Sir Norbert, Ada's British suitor, appeared at our doorstep. He looked much younger than his forty-seven years, and was unusually handsome. His long fingers clutched the evening *Times*.

"Mr. Holmes," he said softly. "You must find my Ada; I know in my heart that she is alive."

"What makes you so sure?" Holmes asked sharply.

"This." The nobleman held up the newspaper. "I knew each man and woman that looked after Ada, Mr. Holmes. If only one person survived, it is she. These Indians – *Rajput*, they are called – would protect their charge at any cost. If Ada perished, the rest would commit suicide."

"Interesting," Holmes remarked.

Sir Norbert's response was cut off by the entry of a rather large elderly gentleman.

"Where is *het meisje*?" he demanded.

"Interesting," Holmes repeated. "Dokter Diederik, I assume?"

"*Ja*. Where is she? We will go to Maastricht and be safe."

"Why do you assume she is alive?" I asked.

"I believe it is more surprise than assumption, my dear Watson," Holmes drawled. "After all, our guest here is an excellent shot."

Instantly, in a coordinated move, Diederik grabbed me and held a gun to my head, while Sir Norbert drew a sword from his cane and rested the tip on Holmes's throat.

Holmes appeared indifferent. "It is a .476 calibre Enfield Mk I. I was right after all, Watson. I can confess to a monograph on the subject."

"Clever, aren't you, Holmes?" the Englishman spat. "Now, where is the girl?"

Holmes shrugged nonchalantly. "How would I know?"

The sword pressed in. I could see droplets of blood beading on Holmes's pale neck.

"Would you like me to shoot your friend?" Diederik growled.

Holmes's eyes flashed silver with contained rage. "If you harm Watson, Zvíře, I promise you and Ďábel shall not leave this room alive."

I finally understood. Zvíře and Ďábel had been posing as Ada's suitors!

Ďábel laughed. "You are hardly in a position to threaten," he mocked. "Now tell me where she is and I might let you live." He jabbed the blade further.

Holmes ignored him.

A door opened. "Stop," Ada commanded. "Let them go."

"Do not come out!" Holmes shouted.

The princess stepped out of Holmes's bedroom. Her hand was steady as she aimed her pistol at the scoundrels.

"Now, Watson!" Holmes cried.

Pandemonium ensued. Two shots rang out, followed by a cry of pain and the sound of shattering glass. Holmes knocked the sword off Ďábel and delivered a swift left hook. Simultaneously, I brought up my good leg in a brutal kick and Zvíře staggered, giving me ample time to pistol-whip him. Kaarle dived at Ada and both hit the floor. Kaarle moved quickly to shield her. Lestrade and a dozen policemen burst in.

Holmes and I stepped back, allowing the policemen to handcuff the two rogues. Zvíře was hit in the arm by Ada's shot and his bullet had shattered the framed painting behind her head. Kaarle had saved her life.

"Now, gentlemen, would you care to enlighten us regarding the identity of your employer?" Holmes asked cheerfully, holding his handkerchief to the cut on his neck.

"Go to hell," Zvíře growled.

"What are you willing to offer us in return?" Ďábel asked at the same time.

"That would depend on how valuable your information is," Holmes replied. "If it is good enough, we may forget that you assaulted and attempted to murder the princess."

Lestrade protested, but Holmes held up a hand to silence him.

"The money came from India. We heard references to a Ranjit Singh."

Ada paled. "The royal counsel. We must inform my father."

Holmes nodded. "And who is your British contact?"

"We do not know the principal. He is simply referred to as the professor. We only met with one of his agents, a university student named Horace Bloomington."

Holmes turned to Ada. "Your abductor?"

"Yes," she said softly.

"Very well," Holmes said. "Assault and attempted murder charges will be dropped."

The criminals smirked.

"However," Holmes continued, "You will be charged with the murders of the real Sir Norbert and Dokter Diederik as well as thirteen innocent men and women."

"You cheat!" Ďábel cried, lunging at Holmes. He was restrained by two able-bodied policemen.

"Congratulations, Lestrade, on a case well-solved," Holmes told the shocked policeman. "You will find the murder weapons on your prisoners, and bodies of the two gentlemen at the Highgate cemetery, close to a birch tree, judging from the mud on their shoes. Also, the charred end of Zvíře's sleeve and the soot on Ďábel's trousers betray their presence at the crime scene last evening. I have no doubt that you will be able to extract the names of their accomplices hired for the act."

Lestrade thanked Holmes effusively and departed.

"Thank you, Mr. Holmes," Ada whispered. "You have brought peace to the souls of my fallen compatriots."

"How did you know?" Kaarle enquired.

"It was elementary," Holmes replied. "Zvíře and Ďábel had to be in close proximity to the princess, which indicated the suitors. Fortunately, I recognised them from their pictures. They may not remember, but we have crossed paths before." He looked up at our curious faces. "It had best be discussed over dinner."

After Holmes regaled us with his tales over a lavish dinner at Simpson's, I asked Ada about her future.

"I suppose I shall have to marry either Vikram or Pierre," she said sadly.

I noticed the stricken expression on Kaarle's face. Before I could say anything, though, Holmes announced that he had an errand to run and requested Kaarle to accompany him. Ada and I returned to Baker Street.

Unable to bear the aura of misery surrounding my companion, I finally asked her the question which had been plaguing me. "Is there no way you could escape this unwanted marriage? Your father is not ill, you may be able to buy some time."

"It does not matter, Dr. Watson," she wept. "I would never be permitted to marry Kaarle, even if I renounced my husband's claim to contend for the throne of Terai. We need the political support. If I did not have a duty to my kingdom, I would have happily taken this chance to be presumed dead."

I could only offer her a warm beverage in consolation. Exhaustion crept in upon her, and I sent her to bed. I waited up for Holmes, but at the stroke of midnight, I found myself too drowsy to sit and retired to my chambers.

Holmes and Kaarle finally appeared at breakfast. It was obvious that they had been up all night. Kaarle's cerulean eyes were red-rimmed, as were Ada's. A wave of sympathy coursed through me at the plight of the young couple.

Holmes rested a hand on the boy's shoulder. "Ada," he called gently. "Kaarle would like to have a few words."

Ada looked up apprehensively.

Kaarle winced. "I may not have been entirely truthful about my origins in the past," he began, eyes downcast. "I am not French, though my mother was. I am the crown prince of a small island nation off the coast of Nice. I have been in exile for several years, but I have now been reinstated – and finally in a position to ask for your hand in marriage." He knelt before her and held out a solitaire ring. "*Advyaitavadini*," he pronounced carefully. "*Ma belle, ma petite, ma bichette, ma mie - je t'aime, veux-tu m'epouser?* Would you do me the honour of being my wife? *Kya aap hamari ardhangini banengi?*"

Ada stared at him. "When did you learn Hindi?" she whispered.

73

"You learnt my language for me, the least I could do was to learn yours," the crown prince muttered, his cheeks aflame. "I should also tell you that I have M's blessing, and I have sought your father's approval through him, which, I am assured will be forthcoming. My father sends his regards as well." He looked up at her hopefully. "So . . . will you?"

A beatific smile spread across our young princess' visage. "Yes," she whispered shyly. "*Oui. Haan.*"

The ring was slipped on. The euphoric groom-to-be picked her up and twirled about the room, both of them giggling like schoolchildren.

Holmes and I exchanged an amused glance.

"Mr. Holmes, Dr. Watson," Ada said breathlessly, as Kaarle finally released her. "Would you be our witnesses?"

Kaarle nodded enthusiastically. "Without you, we would be dead. Without you, we would have been torn apart. We owe you our life and our happiness. The traditional ceremonies in our respective kingdoms would be arduous, but we would like to have a small church wedding in London before we depart, and we would be very honoured if you would be our witnesses."

Holmes had a strange look on his face. For an instant, I was afraid he would reply in the negative. He glanced at me and I nodded slightly.

"It would give us great pleasure," Holmes said quietly.

Much to our embarrassment, the young couple flung themselves at us. I patted the boy's back awkwardly while Holmes turned an alarming shade of red in the girl's arms. Then Ada embraced me and Kaarle enveloped Holmes. When we were finally released, the prince laughed.

"*Désolé*," he said, smiling. "We forget how reserved the British are." He took his fiancée's hand. "We shall be in touch, gentlemen. *Au revoir.*"

The young royals departed with a spring in their steps.

I could not contain my curiosity any longer. "Holmes, did you mete out romantic advice to the boy last night? Did you take him to this M you all keep talking about?"

Holmes nodded and refused to meet my eyes. I smiled to myself, preparing to tease my friend.

"Not a word, Watson!" he shook his head. "It was only logical."
He turned dramatically, his greatcoat bellowing behind him like a cape, and, for the want of a better word, *fled* – quite possibly to delete all traces of sentimentality from his brain-attic!

A Child's Reward
by Stephen Mason
From *Part XXII: Some More Untold Cases (1877-1887)* (2020)

As I approached our rooms in Baker Street after a long day of visiting patients, I noticed that the sun was considering once again placing itself into the arms of Morpheus. Late in autumn, the days were becoming noticeably shorter, with a crispness in the air each evening. As I reached the steps outside the front door, it was comforting to see the usual ornaments – the gas lights paired on either side, the fire insurance company emblem from a bygone period, and the hook-rug mat for cleaning one's shoes before entering the domicile. Mrs. Hudson greeted me in the hallway, indicating supper, consisting of soup, beef, and potatoes, would be served in approximately thirty minutes.

Climbing the stairs and crossing the threshold into our sitting room, I found my flatmate sitting in his favorite chair near the fire. A quick glance indicated he had removed several of the sheets stuck to the mantelpiece by the jack-knife, clearing away some of the backlog of requests for his attention.

"Welcome home, Watson. Pull up a chair and tell me about your day."

I hesitated, wondering if I had just stepped into a dream. Never before had he shown much – or for that matter any – interest in my professional duties.

"I would be happy to, but I must admit you've taken me by surprise. You seem to be in an unusually humorous mood. Do you have an explanation for this attitude?"

"I have taken to heart your constant scolding, and have attempted to lessen the load held down by my unique paper weight. I must tell you, many of these missives aren't so much a request to solve a mystery as they're a personal unburdening of one's soul. For example, this particular note is from a respected banker in Nottingham who has been slowly embezzling funds from his institution to support a mistress. He is asking if I believe that he should turn himself to the police, or simply try to pay back the funds over a period of time, now that the tryst has ended."

"Surely at least one of the notes provide a hint at future work?"

"Nothing intriguing enough to whet my appetite."

"Well, Mrs. Hudson gave me notice that our meal will be arriving soon.

"Good," he replied. "Since we have a few minutes, I would like to discuss a matter with you, Please, take a seat."

I did so, puzzled, and he continued. "As you recall, yesterday morning before leaving the house, you asked for your cheque book, as you were planning on purchasing some new equipment to replace those holdovers from your army days – a new medical bag and stethoscope, for instance. As I left before you, I didn't notice until the early afternoon that you had replaced the book on my desk. While I would never consciously impose on your privacy, it was easy to discern you hadn't removed a cheque from the book. Yesterday evening, it was apparent on several occasions you were considering to start a discussion, but each time held your tongue. I felt it best to allow you to choose when the time was ripe for a conversation."

As I positioned myself in my comfortable armchair, I pondered where he was headed. Before I could speak, he continued.

"However, I have since decided instead to force the issue. As we have been in association now for a while, I believe we should discuss our financial positions. I'm aware of your paltry wound pension of approximately two-hundred-pounds-per-year. Your medical services working at Barts and as a *locum* don't add substantially significant funds to your account. I can see how an individual of your standing can sometimes struggle to get by on such a balance."

I was a bit embarrassed, and defensive. "As you know, I have been in discussions to add another source of income – namely monies to be earned from chronicling your cases. I'm hoping to negotiate a solid return for each of those 'stories'."

"I hope that you have made a suitable and profitable arrangement."

"Interestingly enough, I left the bargaining part of the deal to Doyle – he's acting as my literary agent. While I'm not quite aware of the specific amounts that's he's hoping to arrange for each of the stories, which we hope will be soon appearing on the newsstands, it seems as if he'll get the larger percentage of the income for his efforts."

"Hmm. Have you considered finding a new agent?"

"As you know, he is also a medical practitioner, but writing appears to be his true calling, and I'd like to help him to get more firmly established in the field. And to this point, he seems pleased to be involved in bringing your cases to the public. They seem to be a nice diversion from his more serious literary efforts."

Holmes nodded. "Which brings us around to my reason for initiating this discussion. From our early association, our arrangement was that you would share in my fees on those cases where you acted as a consultant – there was no reason that you, as a professional, shouldn't be treated as such. After all, you are often called upon to provide medical services. You regularly do substantial leg work on my behalf, often putting your life and health at risk – not to mention the lack of sleep from my eccentric late-night habits. As my little practice has grown and achieved greater success, I would propose that you deserve a greater portion of that."

I swallowed, not quite sure how to react. "And what," I said, "would you consider to be a fair amount to compensate you for my services?"

"Oh, I'm not prepared to discuss specifics – at least not yet. I simply wanted to broach the subject to determine how you would react to my proposal."

Before I could respond further, both of us noticed footsteps on the landing outside our door, succeeded by knocking.

"It appears that Mrs. Hudson has brought up a visitor, and based on the lightness of the steps, I wouldn't be surprised to find that it's one of the Irregulars to provide an update on a small matter in which I've asked their for assistance. You may enter, Mrs. Hudson."

In stepped our landlady, and as Holmes had correctly predicted, a youngster followed right behind her. But to our surprise, the expected lad turned out to be a lass.

"Mr. Holmes, apparently this young lady has requested an audience."

"Fascinating. It appears that our Wiggins has expanded his pool of helpers. Or else someone has decided to pull a practical prank on me."

"Actually, I believe that she would like to discuss your services as a detective."

"I'm not sure what assistance I could possibly offer her, but as this may be a novel experience, I suggest she come in and take a seat. Mrs. Hudson, would you please send up appropriate refreshments for our young guest."

"Mr. Holmes," said the girl, "I'm your *client* . . . ."

"That is yet to be determined."

"I don't know if I should have anything to eat. It might ruin my dinner, as my mother always tells me."

"I think we can risk a glass of milk. Why don't you sit on the edge of the cane-backed chair and explain why you're here talking to us, in lieu of doing chores or schoolwork."

"I don't have much time, as I'm supposed to be out of the house for only fifteen minutes, visiting my friend, Katie."

"As time is a premium, then, let's start at the beginning, Miss – "

"I'm Elenora Darlington, but my friends call me 'Ellie'. I'm here to hire you to help me with a very troubling case."

"While I'm sure you're sincere in your request, I'm not too sure that can help you to find a lost puppy or repair a broken toy."

"Mr. Holmes, that seems to be a little on the patronizing side," she said, surprising and amusing us both. "I assure you that my request is much more serious, and will test your skills as an investigator."

"Miss Darlington, I apologize for taking your young age for granted. I am curious: How old are you?

The young lady held up both hands, with four fingers extended on each hand.

"So, eight years old."

"Yes. I was confirming you can count." She giggled, and then flashed a huge smile toward Holmes, which then quickly changed to a frown. "I'm sorry. My father says that I'm bright for my age, and that it will get me into trouble. I need your help finding out what has happened to my mother."

I reacted quickly. "Is she missing, or worse?"

"No, she is still with us. But she's not."

Holmes gave me that look which meant to allow time for the client to tell her story. "I don't quite follow," he said. "Start at the beginning, and explain in as much detail as you can."

Mrs. Hudson stepped into the room just then with a small glass of milk, which she handed to our petite visitor. "Mr. Holmes, do you think it prudent for me to stay, lest the girl need something else?"

"Normally I like to interview my clients in private, but in this instance, I believe your presence to be welcomed. Now, young lady, you were saying . . . ?"

"I'm not too sure where to start."

"Let us follow a series of questions and answers that may help you arrange your thoughts better. To begin, what is your father called?"

"Daddy!"

"Actually, Ellie, I meant, do you know your father's first name?"

"Yes, it's Nathaniel. Most of my family call him 'Nate'."

"Including your mother?"

"She . . . used to . . . ."

"And what does your father do?"

"Normally whatever mother and grandmother tells him to do."

"I meant, does your father work at a job?"

"Yes. He's is a teller at a bank several blocks from here. He says that we'll never be rich, but it pays the bills."

"Who else lives in your house? Do you have any brother or sisters?"

"No, it's just mother, father, my grandmother, and our new housekeeper, Mrs. Wiggleston. Mother says that Mrs. Wiggleston helped to bring her into the world."

"Earlier, you said your mother was here, but wasn't. Can you please explain what you mean by that?"

"It's very confusing to me. My Mother, Norah, has always been, as my daddy calls it, a little 'flighty'. But lately, it's been much worse."

"In what manner?"

"She's extremely forgetful. She can't remember where she put things, or events that occurred in the past, and even names of pets that we've had. And doesn't even call me 'Ellie' anymore. It's now 'Elenora'. The same with daddy – 'Nathaniel', and not 'Nate.'"

"Do you believe that your father has noticed these differences?"

"Oh yes. He and I have talked about it. He thinks mother is just upset about something."

It was my turn to join the questioning. "Ellie, while all of that may seem strange, you must understand that when parents come under unusual stresses, it can show itself in different ways. There might temporary loss of memory."

"Oh, it isn't just forgetting things. She acts differently too. Lately she seems to be much more distant to grandmother, who is usually sick in bed, and doesn't have many good days, while being much friendlier to Mrs. Wiggleston."

Here she paused, and a tear began to form in her right eye.

"I don't think she loves me anymore, either."

As Holmes and I sat there, not sure on how to react, Mrs. Hudson saved the day by stepping forward and gently hugging the child, stroking her hair until she had composed herself.

"Miss Darlington," said Holmes, "I'm not sure what Dr. Watson and I can do to solve your mystery, but believe me when I state we won't rest until your fractured world is made whole again, even if we must use all the glue and paste in the universe."

While I may never be blessed with a child of my own, if ever so fortunate, I hope each night to see the same smile which came across this little girl's face. Her entire countenance lit up – but then a serious look once again appeared.

"I'm afraid that I may not have enough money to pay you. But I'll give you every penny that I have."

"Which is how much?"

"Twelve pennies."

"What a coincidence! That just happens to be my fee." With a smile my way, "Watson, per our previous discussion, I feel comfortable splitting it evenly with you."

"I think that I'll waive my percentage for this one, thank you very much."

"Ellie, can you estimate how long this change in behaviour has affected your mother?"

"It started a couple of weeks ago."

"Did anything else happen around that same time?"

"Not exactly, but it was just a few weeks after Mrs. Wiggleston started working in our home." She wiggled forward, now much less upset than before. "So what is our next step?"

"*Your* next step is to get yourself home before you get into trouble with your parents. I have the beginnings of a plan already formulated in my mind. Dr. Watson and I will drop by your house tomorrow afternoon to meet your mother. I'll need you to be a detective-in-training to aid us in solving this case. Can you play-act when we appear, and simply follow along with whatever I say?"

"Oh yes. My daddy thinks that I'll be a stage actress when I grow up, so I can definitely help you."

"Young lady, please leave your address with Mrs. Hudson as you exit downstairs. By the way, how far do you live from here?"

"Three blocks or so, though it seemed much longer when I was walking. I have such short legs. And of course, I'm not allowed to cross the street by myself, so a very friendly woman took my hand at each of the corners."

After Mrs. Hudson had escorted our young client out the door and down the stairs, I smiled over at Holmes.

"I have no idea what is in your mind, but I just can't imagine that there's much of a mystery here to solve."

"You may be correct, but it's just possible there's more to the story than we just gleamed from her statement. Let us have our supper, after which I'll focus on the task at hand. You'll have a part to play in this drama, which I will outline before we sally forth after lunch tomorrow."

Approximately one-thirty on the next day found Holmes and me on a pleasant walk from our lodgings to Miss Darlington's residence. While Holmes is much more familiar with London geography, I was less knowledgable about these nearby blocks, in spite of their nearness to Baker Street. The homes were similar to Mrs. Hudson's structure at 221, but these domiciles appeared to have more families with children located within. We reached the address provided, with Holmes surveying the house for a few minutes before approaching the front door and using the attached knocker.

A middle-aged woman, average in height and appearance, opened the door with a look that I can only imagine was reserved for salesmen and tax collectors.

"State your business and don't tarry, as if I have enough to take care of without listening to your fast talk of gadgets that I neither need nor desire."

Holmes tipped his hat, "Madam, I can understand your feelings toward those of the soliciting profession. I tend to hold the same opinion of many of them. However, our business is with Mrs. Darlington, the woman of the house. I believe that she'll be grateful to see us, once we've stated our intent."

"Please step in – minding that you wipe your feet first. I'm not going to re-clean the foyer because of your carelessness."

The domestic left us the hallway, and two doors opening and closing deeper within the house were soon heard. In the few minutes that we were left to ourselves within the front entry, Holmes observed every object, including the small statuary on the end tables, and a few photographs hanging on the walls. His focus seemed to linger particularly on a family portrait

"Gentlemen, I believe that you requested time with me. May I have your names and purpose of this visit?"

The question was issued by a woman of medium height and build, with brunette hair and a disposition that indicated our presence was a bit bothering. The similarities in facial features made it easy enough to see Elenora Darlington was her offspring. Holmes stepped forward, withdrew from his pocket two visiting cards, one light blue and one teal in color, and waited while Mrs. Darlington reviewed both of them.

"So which one of you is Mr. Jonathan Franklin?"

Holmes slightly nodded his head. "That would indeed be me, my lady. However before we continue introductions and purposes, may I request that you invite your daughter to join us? The impetus of our appearing at your doorstep includes her."

It was apparent Mrs. Darlington was slightly confused by the request, but turned to the servant, who had been slouching against the doorframe to the hallway. "Mrs. Wiggleston, would you fetch Elenora? And please bring tea and biscuits for our visitors. Gentlemen, please take a seat while we await my daughter."

Within a few minutes, our little client sprinted through the doorway, breaking out into a wide grin as she spotted Holmes. However, a slight shaking of his head, which only the daughter could see, was enough to quell her enthusiasm.

"Mrs. Darlington, as the cards indicate, my name is Jonathan Franklin, a sales representative for Kirby Housewares. My line of business doesn't have an impact on our visit. However, my friend here is Asa Billings, and his vocation is important to our task. As his card indicates, he makes his living by his talents for telling a story – thus as a writer for *The Evening News*. I know that your time is valuable, so I'll make my explanation both clear and concise.

"I have a daughter of similar age to your dear Elenora here. I love my little girl to death, but she would leave her head on a park bench if it wasn't attached to her body. Yesterday afternoon, the latest of more times than I can count, she left the front door open after returning from a romp in the park. Of course, our small terrier, Benji, made a break for it, escaping down the street. It would have only been a matter of minutes before he would have become the unfortunate stepping-stone of one of the thousands of horses on our busy city thoroughfare. Miraculously, your daughter happened to see our wandering family member racing down the pavement, and with no thought of her own safety, grabbed our little darling just before she ran out into the street, facing certain peril, if not death."

"Elenora," said Mrs. Darlington with a frown, "when did this feat of bravery happen?"

Ellie spoke without hesitation, immediately playing her part to perfection. "It was yesterday afternoon, Mother, as I was returning from Katie's house."

"To finish the tale of heroism," continued Holmes, "as I was pursuing our adorable little mutt, I soon encountered Benji in the loving arms of your daughter. I offered her a cash reward, which she humbly refused." Mrs. Darlington glanced strangely at Ellie again at that bit of information. "But I decided the story of your daughter's selfless act needed to be told to the residents of London. So this morning, I contacted my good friend, Mr. Billings here, who has offered to write up the story for the next edition of his periodical. And there you have it."

"That is an amazing story. Elenora. Why didn't you tell me about this adventure when you returned home yesterday?"

"Umm . . . if you remember, you and father were in the middle of an argument – "

" – Lively discussion – "

" – and it simply slipped my mind by the time we gathered for supper."

Holmes stepped back into the conversation. "Mrs. Darlington, I believe that this story will tug at the heartstrings of citizens far and wide.

82

Do we have your approval to have the narrative placed in the newspaper tomorrow evening?"

"Yes, I suppose that would be all right."

"Mr. Billings, do you have everything that you need for the story?"

"I have all the details that you provided to me earlier today concerning the actual events, but Mrs. Darlington may be able to fill in some background information concerning the family – particularly of young Miss Elenora."

Mrs. Darlington interrupted, "Oh. I'm so sorry, Mr. Billings, but Elenora and I are overdue for an appointment that we must not miss. I'm afraid that you must rely on Mr. Franklin's statement for the basis of the story. I'm sure that would be sufficient."

Holmes answered, "That it will. However, I do know that Mr. Billings could use a photograph of Elenora to assist in preparing an artist's rendition for the article. May we borrow this one hanging on the wall, as it appears to be a very recent one? I promise to return it within a day or two."

"That should be alright. I'm not one to be too overly attached to such objects of sentimentality. And now, gentlemen, my daughter and I must get ready for our appointment . . . ."

"Certainly," agreed Holmes. "I believe that we have sufficient to our needs. Elenora, again thank you so much for your assistance in the matter."

"You know Mr. . . . Franklin," she said with a twinkle in her eye, "I have had time to think about it, and I believe I will accept that reward you offered me yesterday."

Mrs. Darlington showed her surprise, "Elenora! That is being just a little impudent, don't you think?"

Holmes replied, "Not in the least! It shows that Elenora has spunk – she might even make a good sales lady in future years."

Holmes fished a coin out of his trouser pocket and handed it to the young lass. "Here is a sovereign for you to keep. I would suggest that once you're older, you always keep a sovereign with you, as you never know when you might need it to repay a bet or as a debt of gratitude."

Mrs. Wiggleston led us to the front door, where in my role as a reporter, I asked, "Before we leave, may I ask you one or two questions?"

Looking like a very nervous fox on the morning of a hunt, the lady nonetheless relented.

"How long have you known this lovely family?"

"I have worked as their housekeeper for two months. But I've been informally part of the family for years. I had the wonderful experience of bringing Mrs. Darlington into this world. I worked for Mrs. Darlington's mother then, twenty-seven years ago, was so taken by such a sweet baby I stayed on with the family, acting as both nanny and nursery-maid. I only left their employment once young Mrs. Darlington went off to boarding school. With no other family of my own, I sought out the possibility of once again joining the family to look out for Elenora in the same manner as before."

Holmes didn't seem to have any further questions, and with that, we tendered our thanks and left the Darlington residence, walking briskly back to our Baker Street quarters.

I settled back into my favored chair, but Holmes paced back in forth in front of the fire, occasionally taking a puff on a cigarette, but letting most of it burn down on its own. The picture he'd borrowed was propped nearby.

"Holmes, where do we turn now? I simply don't see a mystery here to solve. Again, I believe that Mrs. Darlington's forgetfulness is due to some stress that we may not have witnessed. Am I missing something?"

"Yes you are. Within five minutes of being at the house, I had observed the key to unlocking this mystery. I now have to determine the best way of resolving it, without having anyone physically harmed."

"You suspect there may be foul play?"

"I suspect that is a possibility, but it hasn't occurred yet. I'm concerned that our little ruse this afternoon may be discovered by the parties involved before I'm ready to move against them. Therefore, time is of essence. I'm off to visit someone whom I've been able to assist in a couple of small issues – in return, he is often willing to help me in my investigations. I believe that the final piece to this puzzle may reside in the general census and birth certificate records."

By the time that I'd retired for the evening, Holmes still hadn't yet returned, which I assumed meant that he might have found another clue to chase, or that he might be pursuing leads for another case of which I wasn't yet aware.

The next morning over breakfast, Holmes gave me a short *précis* of his activities the previous afternoon, and not long after, I found myself standing with him, alongside Inspector Lestrade, outside of the Darlington residence. Holmes had spoken to him yesterday after the direction of his research began to make clear what was going on there.

"Mr. Holmes, once again, I'm in your debt for unweaving this tangle, but I'm perplexed as to why we're taking this route to close out the case."

"Watson will tell you that while I focus on the details of the case and the smallest of trifles, I cannot resist allowing just a little drama. Please knock on the door, and remember to play out your parts."

Response to the summons took longer than expected, with a gentleman that I could only assume was Mr. Darlington opening the door and staring out at the three of us with a questioning look. His dress indicated that he was likely preparing to venture off to work.

"You must forgive my tardiness in answering the door. Evidently our housekeeper hasn't yet arrived for her daily duties. May I help you three gentlemen?"

"Yes, I'm Inspector Lestrade of Scotland Yard. We've had a series of serious crimes on this block in the past two days, including robbery, burglary, assault, and even an attempted murder." The crisp way that he listed the offenses almost convinced me that it was true. "I would like to ask you and your wife a few questions to see if you might be of any help in my investigations."

The man looked surprised. "We would be happy to assist in you in any manner possible, but I can assure you neither of us will have any pertinent information that you might be able to use."

Interestingly, and thankfully, Mr. Darlington didn't question purpose of either Holmes or me being with Lestrade.

We were led through the main hallway to a pair of sliding glass doors at the left of the stairway, revealing a library. "Wait here while I summon my wife."

"And your daughter," added Holmes.

Darlington looked puzzled, but he nodded in agreement and left us.

Many of the room's shelves were sparsely filled with books, but instead were cluttered with frames containing coins of various denominations and origins. Darlington returned and said that his wife would join us momentarily. Then, noticing my interest in the collection, he stated, "I'm the head teller at one of the branches of the Capital and Counties Bank. As you can guess, I regularly come into contact with coins of all ages and from numerous countries on a daily basis. Though my annual salary limits my ability to purchase the most valuable of coins, I'm able to obtain those which catch my collecting fancy before they're turned back into circulation.

"For example, take this frame here," pulling one down from the second shelf from the top. "While none of these coins would be considered extremely valuable by any reputable numismatist, I fell in love with them because of their unusual toning. Most silver and copper coins will turn to various tints over time, while gold coins are the most resistant to this transition. Once the coin turns black or brown, they lose their draw to me, but the various shades of magenta, blue, orange, and even green, have always caught my eye."

Once the frame had been passed to each of us, with Holmes and Lestrade showing polite interest, it was returned to its original resting place. Then Darlington turned back to Lestrade. "Now, how do you believe we can support you in this investigation? As an officer of a bank, is there any chance that my help in solving a crime may ultimately benefit my own employer?"

"So that I don't have to repeat myself," countered Lestrade brusquely, "we'll wait for your wife and child to be present. They may be able to provide valuable input into this inquiry."

We stood in awkward silence while Darlington took a spot behind his desk. Within a few moments, we were joined by Ellie and the woman whom we had met yesterday afternoon. They went to stand with Darlington.

Immediately upon seeing us, Mrs. Darlington expressed surprise. "Mr. Franklin – Mr. Billings! What an unexpected – ! I honestly didn't expect to see you again."

In his element, Holmes then took charge of the discussion.

"Mrs. Darlington, I'm afraid that our visit yesterday was a bit of a charade. In reality, my name is Sherlock Holmes. I'm a consulting detective, occasionally called in by Scotland Yard to consult upon difficult investigations. This is Dr. John Watson, my associate. Your husband has already been introduced to Inspector Lestrade, representing the Yard."

Mrs. Darlington inquired, "Why did you lie to me when you were here yesterday? I'm at a complete loss to what is occurring here."

"Until we had a better grasp of what was happening within a few houses of your residence," replied Holmes, his tone grim, "we didn't want to unduly frighten you or your daughter."

Holmes then glanced over to young Elenora, who had been standing close to the library doors, away from her mother and father. A quick wink that only the young lass and I could witness seemed to give her comfort. He then turned his attention back to the mother.

"I'm afraid that your daughter may be unwittingly involved in a sequence of crimes that could put her life in jeopardy," he lied. "The dog that she rescued yesterday didn't escape from my house, as I fictitiously told you. Instead, it escaped from the clutches of the leader of a major criminal syndicate which operates just a few blocks from here. This villain had paid a substantial fee to import a very exotic breed from the United States as a gift to his wife, and was desperate to recover the pet.

"A source of mine, who is buried deeply within this man's organization, happened to mention last night that the principal of the group has discovered that your daughter was in possession of the canine, and will stop at nothing to regain it."

Holmes spun the tale that we had rehearsed, but even though I knew it to be false, it still gave rise to feelings of concern. I was impressed that Ellie, who knew that she had never recovered a dog – either for Holmes or a criminal – showed no indication that the story was entirely false.

"Why not simply come to our door and ask for the dog's return?" asked Mr. Darlington, looking confused. "And by the way, who does have the dog?"

"He has been turned over to the local authorities for safekeeping," replied Holmes. "Unfortunately, your question doesn't have a simple answer. This particular person is simply evil, through and through. He believes that your daughter intentionally took the dog, and has no intention of ever returning it to the rightful owner. It's my belief that the term 'rightful' is being very generous, as there is evidence this man may himself have had the dog stolen from a wealthy land owner before having it shipped to England.

"While it may seem incredibly cruel to you, this monster has been known to punish those that he believes have 'wronged' him – in very unspeakable ways. It's also entirely possible that not only will he attempt to vindicate his loss upon your daughter, but your entire family. We believe he has also learned of your occupation, Mr. Darlington, which may give him impetus to attempt a kidnapping for ransom."

At this point, Mr. Darlington laughed quietly, but then asked with a very muted voice, "This is simply too amazing of a story for me to believe. What game are you gentlemen really playing?" The tone in which the question was asked indicated that he hoped he was correct in this assumption.

Lestrade responded, "Sir, do you really believe that the three of us have nothing better to do than to waste your time, or to make up such a fantastic story for no purpose?"

"I suppose not," was the man's nervous reply.

"As a matter of fact," continued the inspector, "we have received information, believed to be credible, that the organization we're discussing has planned on moving against your family and this residence as early as this morning. I've posted another inspector outside – inconspicuous of course – to provide further protection for you. I just hope that four of us here in the house may be enough to blunt any type of offensive attack."

"Mr. Darlington," Holmes said, "should the unthinkable occur, and an assault be attempted on this house, what would you consider to be the most defensible room?"

"Good heavens, man! We're not at war here!"

"Trust me, I wouldn't be asking this if I didn't think of this conflict to be most serious. Again – which room would you feel that we could secure?"

"I would assume the basement cellar."

"Where is the entrance?"

"Toward the back of the house, just adjacent to the kitchen."

"Is there more than one exit from below?"

"No, just the interior stairway."

"That wouldn't be safe, then, as they could easily block our sole way to exit. A fire would then seal our fates." Holmes was painting quite a forbidding picture.

"I suppose that the next best choice would be the dining room, which is adjacent to the kitchen. There are two entrances, but both could easily be blocked with the table, the hutch, or the sideboard. There are no windows within that room."

Lestrade stated, "I think that we're safe for a while longer, but I do think that we'll need to consider what we need in terms of supplies, arms, and other items if we're required to make a defense within the dining room."

As one can imagine, by this time both parents looked extremely frightened. Holmes, again only seen by Elenora and myself, gestured for the young girl to move closer to her mother, standing between the desk and hall door. Holmes himself moved over to the one window looking out onto the street, and very gently pulled back the drape so that he could cautiously peer out.

Just then, two shots rang outside on the street. While I was prepared for some type of disturbance, the volume of noise even made me nervously jump. Both Holmes and Lestrade immediately took up position next to each of the library doors.

Mr. Darlington ducked behind his desk, but within seconds, circled around, grabbed his daughter, and pulled her to safety behind the solid piece of oak furniture. After what seemed to be a long minute, but couldn't have been more than a few additional seconds, he glanced over the top and inquired, "Where is my wife? She isn't here."

Holmes was able to provide a response, "As soon as the shots occurred, she bolted out through the doors, down the hallway, and – I must assume – has now sheltered herself in the dining room, as we discussed. It's now time to pull down the last curtain to this little drama.

"Lestrade, if you will be so kind as to recover Mrs. Darlington from her hiding spot, while Watson invites Gregson into the library."

The library had become slightly crowded, with Holmes, myself, Inspectors Lestrade and Gregson (who had waited outside), Mr. and Mrs. Darlington, and Elenora all present. As might be expected, Mr. Darlington was exasperated and more than slightly irritated.

"I demand some answers to what has been going on right under my nose. I'll be damned if I have a clue to what has transpired."

Holmes patted the father on the sleeve. "Mr. Darlington, I know all of this must have been extremely trying to you. But I hope our little charade just now will make everything clear. The explanation to this tale will take a few minutes, so please feel free to get comfortable."

As he spoke, I kept an eye on Mrs. Darlington, who looked as if she would bolt from the room if a path presented itself.

"We start with a visit by your very bright and innovative daughter the day before yesterday. Ellie was very concerned with your wife's behaviour of late, and wished for me to look into the matter to see if I could discover a cause."

Mrs. Darlington opened her mouth as if to chide the child for her impertinent deportment, but Holmes hushed her before a word could be uttered.

"Madam, I would suggest you stay quiet and let the full story be told without any interruptions on your part. To continue, by the end of Elenora's visit, I was still unclear on what was going on within the confines of this residence, but I believed the sincerity of Ellie, and that her instincts were correct that something was amiss.

"Yesterday, Dr. Watson and I visited your residence with a story about a lost dog, concocted to simply get a feel for the mood of the house, and to talk to your wife firsthand. And now, before I continue, Mr. Darlington, I would strongly suggest you take a seat."

"I believe I will remain standing, as I still am undecided on whether one or all of you deserve a rain of my fists for this shocking conduct."

"Such is your choice." Holmes then turned to the library doors, and with raised voiced, called out, "Constable, would you please bring in the other women?"

Though I was prepared, it was still a shock to see Mrs. Darlington walk into the room, standing where she could stare balefully at – Mrs. Darlington. Holmes reached out to steady the father, as it was apparent his knees had just buckled and his eyes gave every appearance of fainting at any moment.

Next to enter was Mrs. Wiggleston, her arm in the grip of a constable. "Watson," asked Holmes, "would you please pour some liquid strength for Mr. Darlington from the decanter on the back shelf? Here, drink this, and now take that seat I offered just a few minutes ago."

Now mild as a kitten, Darlington acceded to Holmes suggestion, staring quietly at both women with a look of complete confusion. In the meantime, Mrs. Darlington – the newly arrived Mrs. Darlington – quickly crossed the room and stood with her husband and daughter.

"Mr. Darlington, yesterday while Watson and I were waiting for your wife and daughter within the front room, I took notice of the family portrait hanging on the wall."

"That was taken just a couple of months ago," said the confused man.

"Yes. A few minutes later, I noticed that your daughter was wearing the same dress as the one in the photograph. Now, as girls of her age tend to sprout up faster than a plant in the spring, I assumed that the picture must have been recently made.

"More importantly, I saw a couple of other interesting items – things that I have trained myself to observe. First, as your daughter was standing next to her mother, it was obvious that she seemed to be a good inch or so shorter than she was in the photograph. Now, one can put that down to the fact that possibly one or the other wearing raised shoes, but since the photograph was a full-length, I could tell that everyone concerned was wearing low heels – as were both mother and daughter yesterday. Their heights then should have been the same in both photograph and here yesterday – or Ellie should have been taller. But somehow daughter had instead shrunk instead of growing in the few months. I also noticed that the Mrs. Darlington that I met yesterday was slightly heavier than the subject in the photo – not significantly, but at least six or seven pounds, I think. Now it's not impossible for someone to gain a bit of weight in that amount of time, but there was a noticeable change.

"With these items, along with your daughter's suggestion at forgetfulness, not using pet names for you or her, and her apparent affection for Mrs. Wiggleston – preferring this woman from her long-ago past over her own invalid mother upstairs, with whom she had markedly decreased her level of contact – a very strange idea began to ferment in my mind. After we left here, I was able to make my way to offices housing the various birth records, where I have friend who is willing to support my vocation with information as I may need.

"Imagine my surprise, Mr. Darlington – actually, I'm sorry. I wasn't surprised – to find that Mrs. Wiggleston here is the proud mother of an adult daughter, who just happened to have been born on the exact same day as your wife."

With a shake of the head, Darlington responded, "That's not possible. I've heard the story over and over again. She delivered my wife on the second of May, 1859, according to both her and Grandmother. How

90

could she have given birth to her own child on the same day when she was assisting in that birth? Wait – ”

Suddenly he glanced quickly around the room. “Where is Grandmother? How could we have forgotten her through this whole ordeal?”

Ellie answered, “When I came downstairs with . . . Mother – ” She glanced nervously at the woman who had accompanied her just a few minutes earlier. “ – Grandmother was knitting in her bedroom. I assume that she’s still up there. Should I go ask her to come down and hear all of this?”

“No,” said her father. “I think that the shock would be too much for her – it may still be too much for me.”

Holmes continued, “I believe that is wise. She’ll have plenty of time later to digest these proceedings. Nonetheless, trust me, Mr. Darlington, when I say that I personally observed the birth certificate which indicates that Mrs. Wiggleston, recently widowed, gave birth to a baby girl named Sheila Wiggleston on the exact same date that your wife was born. I would ask Mrs. Wiggleston to explain this seeming contradiction, but it appears from her flushed colour that discussing this issue would be very difficult for her right now.” All the servant could do was gently nod her head up and down.

“I suspect that it’s really is quite simple, if not a little sordid, of an explanation,” said Holmes. “It seems – ” He addressed the woman who had rushed across the room and was still gripping the hands of her husband and daughter. “ – that Mrs. Darlington’s mother actually gave birth to *twins* on that day twenty-eight years or so ago. Unfortunately, she was led by Mrs. Wiggleston to believe one of the girls had been still-born, and so, while tending to the needs of the remaining live birth, she managed to somehow bundle the other baby out of the room and then the house in order to make the necessary arrangements to keep her.”

“It wasn’t like that,” interrupted Mrs. Wiggleston.

“Indeed. Then how was it?”

“We truly thought that the second baby was dead. It was only later, as I was carrying the poor thing away so that the mother wouldn’t be upset, that I saw her breathing.”

“Then,” said Holmes, “the prudent thing to do would have been to immediately retrace your steps and present the matching baby back to her mother. But sadly, you yourself had lost a child the year before – the records confirm this as well – and earlier that year your husband had passed away from a bout of influenza. Giving you as much benefit of the doubt as possible, you simply walked away, cradling the baby next to your bosom.”

91

"Once I arrived at home," explained Mrs. Wiggleston, "I was obviously not in my right mind. I had decided to raise her as my own, but I had no plan beyond that." She looked toward the real Mrs. Darlington. "I suppose that I felt that if also remained part of your life as your nanny, my dear, that it would somehow remove some of the guilt that I felt for depriving you of your twin sister."

"And so things have remained for the past twenty-eight years," said Holmes. "At some point, Mrs. Wiggleston left your mother's employee, Mrs. Darlington, when her services were no longer required, having some kept the existence of her own 'daughter' a secret through those years. Then, a few months ago, you and Mrs. Wiggleston became reacquainted, and she was hired to work as Ellie's nanny, as well as the housekeeper of the house. She saw the life that you had – a loving husband, and a fine child – and thought that her daughter was being unfairly deprived."

"No!" cried Mrs. Wiggleston. "It wasn't like that!"

"How can you say that?" cried Mrs. Darlington, rising to her feet. Then she turned and looked at her husband. "She lured me to her house one weekend while you were out of town, visiting your parents, and then – ever since, I've been her prisoner! While my . . . while my *sister* was here, trying to take my place." Then she scowled. "And neither of you even noticed the difference!"

"That isn't true," countered Holmes. "Both Ellie and her father had discussed how unusual you were acting, and Ellie took the initiative to hire me to investigate. And you must remember that Mrs. Wiggletson had been careful to coach her daughter in your various behaviors, so that she could fit in as easily as possible. Even so, her performance was far from perfect."

Throughout, Sheila Wiggleston had simply looked toward the floor, offering no comment or response. Holmes glanced at her, and then toward Lestrade and Gregson. "Inspectors? I believe that the rest is up to you."

Gregson moved to speak, but he was interrupted by Mrs. Darlington. "Wait!" she cried. Then, looking toward Holmes, she asked, "What will happen to them?"

"They committed a crime," said Holmes simply. "They will be charged with kidnapping you, plus whatever else that seems appropriate."

The room was charged with silence for a long moment while the lady chewed at her lip. Finally, she shook her head. "If I don't press charges, will they still be arrested?"

"No, ma'am," said Lestrade. "But the charges are serious – not to mention if we can still make anything stick related to that long-ago kidnapping of your newborn sister. I urge you to – "

"No!" interrupted Mrs. Darlington. "No – I want a chance to know my sister. What they did was wrong. I've – I was kept prisoner by Mrs.

Wiggleston, it's true, but she was not unkind to me. I missed my family here terribly, and I could only imagine – " She paused and swallowed. Then, "And . . . and I don't know how this would have ended if . . . if Sheila had been able to successfully replace me. But she is my sister, after all, and I want to know her better. And my mother upstairs deserves to know that she has another daughter as well."

Gregson frowned, and Lestrade threw up his hands in frustration. "Well, then, I suppose that there's nothing for us here." Then he looked at Holmes, with something like a twinkle in his eyes. "Thank you, however, Mr. Holmes, for a most interesting morning. Rather like something from *The Prince and the Pauper*."

When the police had departed, and we were left with the Darlington family, as well as Mrs. Wiggleston and Sheila, Darlington stood, his hand reaching again for that of his wife. If she had been angry at him a moment earlier, it had dissipated.

"Why, then," he asked of Holmes, "all of this drama?" He waved his free hand. "Why not just free my wife and arrest these women?" He glared at Mrs. Wiggleston and her adopted daughter.

"It was in the way of a demonstration – to you and Ellie, as well as to Sheila Wiggleston herself. She needed to understand that she isn't a true mother – at least not yet – and that she had no business trying to take on that role without earning it honestly.

"As you have probably guessed by now," he continued, "the entire story that we told you after our arrival – a criminal with a missing dog seeking vengeance – was complete fantasy, designed to solicit a suggestive response from Sheila when the proper time arrived. That's when I looked out the window, to give a signal to Inspector Gregson, waiting outside. The shots that you heard were courtesy of him, firing his service revolver into a couple bales of hay that we'd placed nearby.

"Sheila," he said, turning to the young woman who looked so much like Mrs. Darlington, "it's my belief that a mother, when she believes danger is about to reach her family, will seek to protect her most valuable and cherished asset: Her children. You, unfortunately, reacted totally differently, running *away* from the danger, only thinking of your own safety. That isn't the appropriate response to take in a moment of crisis for a mother."

Sheila looked up then and nodded before again lowering her eyes.

"But Mr. Holmes," said Mrs. Wiggleston, puzzled. "Why go to that trouble – to give us such a scare, and to let Sheila have the opportunity to learn such a lesson? You must have known that she wouldn't be going to prison. What gave you that idea?"

"Why, from Mrs. Darlington herself." All eyes turned to Ellie's mother. "Yesterday afternoon, while you were here, Mrs. Wiggleston, I reconnoitered your little dwelling in Orde House Street, just around the corner from the Hospital for Sick Children. I have some skill with entries through locked doors, and I found Mrs. Darlington inside, as I thought that I might. I arrived prepared to take her away with me, but immediately after identifying myself, she began to ask me what she had missed. She assured me that she'd been well-treated – but that without a doubt she was a prisoner. I told her why I was involved, and what I'd learned from the birth and death records. She confirmed much of the same from what you'd told her during the two weeks that she was kept locked up, unable to escape, and unheard by the neighbors when she would call out.

"And yet, she has some sympathy for her newly discovered sister, and through our conversation yesterday afternoon, we conceived of this little idea together. I involved the police because their presence leant veracity to the endeavor, but Mrs. Darlington never intended to actually press charges."

With that, the lady herself released herself from her husband's grip and walked across the room to her sister. The similarity between the two was striking. "I wish that we had met under different circumstances, but I would rather know you this way then not at all." She reached out, and after a moment Sheila took her hand with a smile. "Would you like to come upstairs and meet our mother?"

Sheila nodded, and Mrs. Wiggleston gave a small sob – I couldn't tell if it was from happiness, perhaps at the punishment they'd narrowly avoided, or possibly that she was about to irretrievably lose some aspect of the relationship to the girl that she had raised as a daughter. In any case, the Darlingtons, along with Sheila and Mrs. Wiggleston, all left the room together, with only Ellie remembering to look back in our direction, giving each of us a sweet smile.

I'm happy to report that a few weeks ago young Elenora Darlington visited our Baker Street sitting room, accompanied by her newly found Aunt Sheila. It turned out that her grandmother is a woman of stronger constitution than anyone had thought, and once the initial shock wore off, she had gratefully accepted having a second daughter.

And more importantly, Ellie seemed to relish having something of a second mother.

> *"It was all-important. When a woman thinks that her house is on fire, her instinct is at once to rush to the thing which she values most. It is a perfectly overpowering impulse, and I have more than once*

taken advantage of it. In the case of the Darlington substitution scandal it was of use to me . . . ."

– Sherlock Holmes
"A Scandal in Bohemia

Bootless in Chippenham
by Marino C. Alvarez
From *Part XIII: 2019 Annual (1881-1890)* (2019)

I have been privy to many cases which Holmes investigated over the years. None, however, involved an actual historical relic whose storied history is recorded and on display at the Bodleian Library at Oxford University. It began on a cold November evening as rain-hardened drops pelted down against our window, with the proverbial heavy yellow fog limiting our view of the overcast sky. Holmes was reading *The Times* and seemed somewhat perplexed as he turned away, lighting his cherry-wood pipe. Several minutes passed. "Yes, Watson, it is a curious advertisement."

"Curious, Holmes? What do you mean?"

"This entry in the agony column of *The Times* that reads: *"Boot and Pole. Plough tonight. Mendoza."* To himself, he murmured, "Something about this entry brings to mind a past remembrance." Just then, we heard the bell, followed by Mrs. Hudson ushering Inspector Lestrade up the stairs and into our room.

"Ah, Lestrade, have a glass of brandy to warm you from the night's dampness."

Lestrade took the libation that I gave him. "Thank you, Doctor. Mr. Holmes, there is a puzzling situation that may be of interest. I've just returned from Northfield Street in Ealing. We found the body of a Mr. Sidney Selden, a middle-age man, wearing a mac and lying face up in the gutter outside a pub. Seems to be a natural death. But he is known to us as a fencer of stolen goods with a criminal history. His watch, fob, and money pouch were missing. Additionally, these two papers without words, only pictures – one that seems to be a crude drawing showing a shield with three objects upon it – were on his person. You may see them for yourself." Holmes took the pieces of paper, each just a few inches across, and carefully examined both the elaborate pictorial display and the curious drawing before passing them across to me.

"Hmm. The sketch of the shield and boots is on common paper, while the other is much older. Where did you find them?"

"They were sheltered from the elements in an inside pocket, away from the water in which he was lying."

"Surely you noticed that the primitive pictorial representations in the more elaborate drawing are not European in nature?"

"Well, Mr. Holmes, I just glanced at the papers and, knowing Selden's reputation and your interest in such matters, brought them straight to you."

"Yes, of course, Lestrade. I'll keep them for further study. And now, let us go to Ealing and see what else we can learn."

I wasn't anxious to venture out into the cold night air, but with umbrella in hand I joined Holmes and Lestrade as we hailed a cab and made our way to Northfield Street. I was stunned to notice that our destination was The Plough, a pub known for its food and questionable musical performances. Recalling the agony column entry that we had recently discussed, I said, "Holmes . . . ." He noticed my gaze toward the pub and nodded, but narrowed his eyes and shook his head, as if he didn't want the connection to be revealed so soon.

A constable was on the scene when we arrived and had kept bystanders at a reasonable distance from where the body had been found. Although it had already been taken to the morgue, Holmes still made his own painstaking study of the scene. This examination was quite trying, as the area was being continually assaulted with the falling rain. Holmes, however, was not deterred. He used his lens to view closely the markings of the depressions that still remained in the nearby muddied area. When he had finished, he paused and said to Lestrade, "We are finished here. Other than it would be wise to look for a fellow with both boots having cobbled heels, one smooth rubber-soled right boot and the left with a

97

traditional work boot design worn slightly on the instep, there is little more that can be determined. I have a fair idea of the identity of the man we seek, and I'll examine the body in the morning." With that, we said goodnight to a most surprised inspector and hailed a cab, making our way back to Baker Street.

Upon our return, Holmes went directly to the bookshelf and sorted through his scrapbooks, removing three volumes containing the letters *C*, *S*, and *W*. He paged through the entries and stopped to read two items. Carefully he made a few notations, and then sat back in his chair. It wasn't difficult to observe that he was in a brown study, frequently examining the papers removed from the body that had been found lying in the rain-soaked mire. He was still doing so when I went to bed.

The next morning found us eating a breakfast of fresh rashers and eggs, prepared by Mrs. Hudson. I assumed from observing his lens resting on the pictorial representations and the additional notes made from his scrapbooks, lying open on the desk, that Holmes had remained awake through much of the night.

"We have our starting points, Watson."

"What's that?"

"Why, the pictogram of the three boots and shield, and the boot marks in the mud last night. What remains is our examination of the body."

"Pictogram of three boots?" I asked, puzzled. However, Holmes didn't reply and, without another word, we finished our repast and then made our way to the morgue, where we were met by Doctor Whitcomb, the Medical Examiner. He told us that Selden died from an ordinary coronary heart attack. Holmes, always thorough, was given permission to examine the body. After several minutes, he announced that he concurred and thanked the Medical Examiner, and we left the premises to return to our lodgings. After again scrutinizing both papers, he told me that he would be back in time for supper and left with them in hand.

Holmes returned in the early evening and we enjoyed a meal prepared by Mrs. Hudson. Retiring into his chair and lighting his pipe, he told me what had transpired. "Watson, this afternoon was most enlightening."

"Where did you go?"

"First to the British Museum, followed by the British Library. Then I returned to The Plough before making a quick turnaround to Oxford. While at the Museum, I confirmed an interesting bit of heraldry." He held up the sketch of the shield and, as he had informed me that morning, boots. "Did you know that boots were symbolic of mounted riders and used to represent charges – often displayed as riding boots, sometimes with spurs? But of more importance is the elaborate primitive drawing." He handed it to me for further examination. "Upon visiting the Library, I was directed to read specifically about the *Codex Mendoza*, an Aztec document created to give to Charles V, the King of Spain."

"Aztecs!" I examined it in greater detail than I had the previous night. "I say! It does have pictorial designs of an eagle and other artifacts."

"Yes, Watson, it has immense antiquarian value. In Oxford, I visited the Bodleian Library, where I was given permission to examine the actual document, as the head librarian had used my services in the past. They were quite intrigued and concerned to see that ancient slip in your hands – a detail copied from the original – as until this afternoon it was believed to still be stored within the library's collections. At some point in the past it had been stolen.

"The *Codex* itself is a document, hundreds of years old, that contains Spanish explanations and commentaries regarding the tribute paid by the conquered Aztec, as well as a description of their daily life, as represented in pictograms. I learned that the *Codex* was named after the man who likely commissioned it, Don Antonio de Mendoza, a viceroy of New Spain. It was being sent on a ship of the Spanish fleet when it was taken by French privateers. It ended up in the French Court, and it was later sold to Richard Hakluyt – you may know the name. He was the same English writer Hakluyt whose work was used by Shakespeare as the source for writing *The Tempest*. But these Shakespearean associations are of no consequence to the problem at hand. The *Codex* later passed through a number of owners. The entire thing was given to the Bodleian Library in 1659 – five years after the death of one of the past owners – John Selden, an English jurist who originally possessed it at one point."

"Was he related to Sidney Selden from last night?"

"Apparently not, but he was a leading member of the Antiquarian Society for historical research during the seventeenth century. He had written his motto, '*Above all freedom*', on the top right of his copy of the *Codex Mendoza*, adding historical relevance. The document became prominent again in 1831 when Viscount Kingsborough became aware of its existence and brought it to the attention of scholars. That document is certainly a valued piece of Aztec history.

"The historical significance of the *Codex* and its influence cannot be underestimated, and one has to wonder why a known fence was showing an interest in it. Remember this point, Watson: While the detail of the *Codex* was taken and ended up in Selden's possession, the actual document is still safe, and it remains locked in a display case in the Bodleian."

The next day, Lestrade dropped around to our quarters at Holmes's invitation. When he arrived, he informed us that the unusual pieces of paper taken from the body of Sidney Selden were of less interest than first imagined, as there was no evidence of foul play – which we already knew. What he had felt might be a curious fact was irrelevant, as the man had died of natural consequences, and it was of no account that his meagre possessions had been stolen after death.

Holmes chuckled and told Lestrade that there was more to this inquiry than mere stolen items. He then related the details of his travels, explaining the background of the more elaborate drawing in the *Codex Mendoza*. "And we mustn't forget the sketch of the shield and the boots," he added, repeating the heraldic connections for Lestrade's benefit.

After listening to Holmes's narrative, the inspector was puzzled. "What does heraldry and the *Codex Mendoza* have to do with our man Sidney Selden?"

"They have everything to do with what I just recounted."

"But – ?"

"Rest assured, Lestrade, the boots will soon become evident." Holmes then rose suddenly and asked us to join him in catching a train to Chippenham in Wiltshire. Lestrade appeared bewildered at this sudden decision to travel to the West Country, but he and I had learned that following Holmes's lead was the easiest way toward understanding. Without delay, we left the premises and hailed a cab to Paddington Station.

Throughout the journey, Holmes refused to be drawn into making any explanations. Instead, he ranged forth on a variety of topics, and while Lestrade was obviously wondering about the reason for our journey, he seemed to enjoy himself and a chance to leave London for the day.

In Chippenham, we left the platform and began our walk into the town. Prompted by Holmes's earlier discussion and description of the heraldry of boots and spurs, I was suddenly struck by the same symbols shown all around, including upon the Coat of Arms in front of the Council Building. With a start, I realized that the crude sketch that had been identified to me as a heraldic representation of three boots was somewhat duplicated on the colorful plaque. As Holmes and Lestrade continued up the street – Lestrade apparently oblivious of the connection – a local passerby, taking notice of my attention without my asking said, "The Coat of Arms represents two influential local families who lived here in the thirteenth and fourteenth centuries. On the sinister side, looking toward the shield on the right, are the arms of the Hussey family. They were Lords of the Manor from 1290 to 1392. Do you notice the boots?" I replied that I did, although without having had them previously identified as such, I would have likely called them something else.

He continued, "In old French, the name *Hussey* means '*booted*', and the Coat of Arms is a play on their name, showing three boots with spurs. In heraldic terminology, it is described as '*argent three boots sable*'."

The fact that Chippenham made use of a drawing of three boots in in a shield as part of its coat of arms gave me some vague indication of the reason that Holmes had brought us here. Hastily, I thanked the gentleman and hurried up the street in order to catch up with my companions.

Soon after, Holmes was able to summon a wagon and the three of us climbed aboard. Holmes gave the driver a few whispered instructions, and he took us into the countryside. Holmes was silent for much of our journey through the beautiful countryside, until we were approaching a lonely inn. It was then that Holmes turned to the inspector and me and told us the purpose of our quest. "Lestrade, please recall when, at the scene where Selden's body was found, I made a careful examination of the area. The boot prints that I described, along with an entry in that morning's Agony Column stating '*Boot and Pole. Plough tonight. Mendoza*', suggested a specific individual's involvement in the matter. I verified what I recalled about this man, Gideon Walsey –"

"Walsey!" cried Lestrade. "That thief?" He nodded. "The boot marks . . . ." he said with understanding, although I was still in the dark.

Holmes looked my way and smiled. "As I was saying, I verified what information that I had about him in my scrapbooks – you'll recall, Watson, that I examined '*S*' for *Selden*, '*W*' for *Walsey*, and '*C*' for *Chippenham* – and learned that the man in question was serving time in Dartmoor Prison – or so I thought. A wire quickly determined that he was released a month ago. But I learned something much more interesting: His cell mate was also named Selden – the Notting Hill Murderer."

"Another Selden!" I cried.

"Exactly," said Holmes, "a man whom I verified happens to have relational ties with the dead man. In fact, they are cousins.

"So," he continued, "we have Sidney Selden, a noted London fence, lying dead outside a pub that was mentioned in a newspaper entry from that very morning. He undisputedly died from natural causes, and yet there are boot prints in the mud beside where he fell that belong to a man who has recently been released from prison, where he shared a cell with the dead man's cousin. Additionally, in the dead man's coat pocket is a curious sketch of a shield and boots – indicating a connection to Chippenham, where Walsey is from – and also a detail of a rare and valuable document. And anytime that both a thief and a fence have ties to something like that is an indicator of a situation much more complex."

Lestrade questioned the connection to Chippenham, and I was able to provide an explanation of the shield and boots. Holmes raised his eyebrows at my sudden knowledge, but I related how the local man had pointed it out soon after we left the train.

"There is another connection," added Holmes. "The word *Mendoza* in the advertisement has a double meaning – a reference to the *Codex*, and something else, as you will soon see." The inspector nodded knowingly, while I remained confused.

"And now, Lestrade, we have arrived at this inn, where I have it on good authority that we will find our man. Inside, you are going to apprehend Mr. Gideon Walsey."

Lestrade and I looked at one another, both of still in a state of some bewilderment, but Holmes had clearly said all that he intended. As the horse drew to a stop, we heard a strange type of music coming from inside. We climbed down from the wagon and approached the low building. Upon entering, I was astounded to see a man standing on the far side of the room wearing one boot, with the other foot clad only in his stocking. He was playing some odd musical instrument, apparently consisting of a thick pole inserted and affixed into his other boot, resting upon the wooden floor. A series of metal bits and pieces were fastened to the pole. When shaken, they clanged together. The sound was akin to a tambourine, an effect that was enhanced as the man played the instrument by holding and applying a notched stick that combined to produce both a clicking and rattling sound.

"What is this that makes these cacophonic sounds?" I cried.

Holmes simply smiled and said to both of us, "That is Mr. Gideon Walsey, whom I mentioned outside, playing a traditional English percussion instrument – a *Mendoza*."

As we approached the man, he stopped playing and quickly gave a sigh, dropping his head on his chest. "Mr. Holmes. We meet again."

"Still playing the Mendoza, I see. I know how much this instrument means to you."

"Just like your violin does to you, Mr. Holmes."

"And . . . What's this?" he asked, reaching forward and plucking something from the man's waistcoat. "A nice watch."

Walsey swallowed. "An inheritance from my uncle when I was a lad."

"Interesting," said Holmes. He examined the pocket watch carefully with his lens. First on the outside, and then opening the back to view the inner workings. "And the initials – *S.S.?*"

"His name was, um, Samuel Stuart," replied Walsey cautiously.

"I see," said Holmes. "And you say that you were a young boy upon receiving this watch?"

"Yes."

"Did your uncle visit America?"

"I don't know," replied Walsey.

"No matter. I have made a study of pocket watches, as they are often significant in many of my cases. This particular watch was manufactured in the United States by the American Watch Company. Observe the thick glass bezel with a brass chain fob at the top. Notice when I turn the cover." We watched as Holmes unscrewed it as if he were taking a lid off a jar. "As you can see, this watch doesn't have a flip-open clasp and hinge lid."

He again took his lens and examined the inside of the watch. "Just as I thought. The case is engraved . . . " He turned it so that we could see "*SILVEROID A.W.C. Co.*" etched across the metal. ". . . and a serial number. Understanding the serial number provides a precise year when and where this watch was assembled. This particular watch was manufactured in the United States around 1884 and became the official standard for railroad watches to be used by conductors and time-keepers. Notice the winding stem at the twelve o'clock position, the black Arabic numerals on a white dial, a steel escape wheel, the open face, and . . . ."

He paused. "There are other distinguishing features, but these suffice. This watch couldn't possibly have been given to you as a youngster, since it has been recently developed to incorporate the features and the purpose I mentioned. Had you been given a watch dating from your youth, in all likelihood, it would have required a key for winding. The absence of a key on your watch fob indicated to me that this watch is a recent acquisition."

Walsey listened but didn't protest Holmes's explanation. He shrugged his shoulders and withered dejectedly into a nearby seat, waiting for what was to follow. Lestrade looked questioningly at Holmes, who held up the watch. "Selden's," mouthed Holmes silently. Without further explanation, Lestrade took hold of Walsey's arm, putting him under arrest for stealing the dead man's possessions. "Your boot prints were found beside the body," he said smugly. Then he allowed Walsey to put on his other boot and gather his Mendoza before escorting him out of the pub and into our wagon for the ride back to Chippenham, where we soon departed on the train to London.

The only time that Walsey exhibited any reaction during our journey was soon after our departure, when his facial features and his eyebrows rose in response to Lestrade telling him that he was being arrested for being in possession of a watch belonging to Sidney Selden, who had been found dead outside The Plough Pub in London two nights before. Walsey seemed surprised upon hearing that name, but he quickly regained his composure and simply turned his head to look out of the window.

As we settled in for the long journey back, Lestrade demanded further explanation. Holmes nodded, and began to take the pieces of the puzzle and arrange them into a whole. "When I first examined the mud near Mr. Selden's body, I noticed two distinct boot markings belonging to the same person. You know that when I find a matter out of place, it arouses my suspicions. Although both boots had the same heel cobbling, the right boot made a smoother impression in the mud while the left boot showed deeper tread, along with slight wear on the instep. I had already recalled the entry from *The Times*' agony column earlier in the day regarding The Plough as soon as we arrived at the pub."

I repeated the entry: "*Boot and Pole. Plough tonight. Mendoza.*" Walsey turned his head curiously.

Holmes nodded and continued. "When I noticed the odd boot marks in the mud, I recalled such characteristics have an association with certain boot-related entertainments. My thoughts turned in passing to that curious fellow, Little Tich – "

"The little chap known for the Big Boot Dance with very long soles?" I interjected.

"Indeed. The fact that the death occurred at The Plough, as mentioned in the advertisement, and additionally remembering the associated words "*Mendoza*", and "*Boot and Pole*", led me quickly to that curious musical instrument, and subsequently our friend here – a seasoned burglar whose past exploits were well-known to the police, and with whom I once had an encounter years ago when he was stealing some counterfeit plates. Clearly the message implied that Selden was to meet Walsey at The Plough, where

104

he would be identified as the man playing the Mendoza. This fact led to other questions, which were twofold: 'What was the significance of the two papers found on the body?' and 'Why was Gideon Walsey in the proximity of a dead man known to facilitate the exchange of stolen goods?'

"As I explained, my research revealed Mr. Walsey's recent background, as well as his cell-mate, Selden. What were the odds that two Seldens could be involved in this matter without there being some connection – one found dead in the street in Ealing and other a convict in Dartmoor?

"This was a case of unexpected doubles. Two Seldens – not counting the historical John Selden. Two Mendozas – the unusual musical instrument first suggested by the bootmarks in the mud, and then the *Codex Mendoza*, as revealed by the drawing found in the dead man's pocket. The hand-drawn sheet along with it, showing heraldic boots, implied a Chippenham connection – where I learned that the man who played the Mendoza lives.

"Although I doubt that Mr. Walsey will confirm it, I theorize that what must have happened is this: Mr. Sidney Shelden conceived a desire to steal the *Codex Mendoza* – possibly after receiving the smaller related detail by someone in his capacity as a fence. As I mentioned, the Bodleian was unaware that it had been taken. Later, while on a visit to the prison in order to see his cousin the murderer, it was mentioned that Walsey is a high-profile burglar. Perhaps, thought Sidney Selden, Walsey could be commissioned to steal the *Codex* from the Bodleian. Selden the convict then approached his cellmate, who agreed. Walsey was to be released within the month. He agreed to become part of the plot and then give the stolen *Codex* to Sidney, who would then fence the document to the highest bidder. Sidney would take two-thirds of the revenue, to share with his cousin, and Walsey would take his share." He glanced at Walsey. "Perhaps the arrangement was somewhat different, but I expect that I understand the general plan." There was no reaction from the prisoner.

"But Holmes," I asked. "How would the convict who will be in prison for life make use of his share of the money?"

"That question, Watson, is one that I am not prepared to answer. Perhaps he has relatives somewhere who might benefit from his acquirement. With the finish of this scheme, I doubt that we shall ever hear of him again. In any case, a few weeks later Walsey was released.

"Walsey and Sidney Selden never actually met, as it was imperative that they not be seen together in order to avoid arousing any suspicions from the police – Walsey a paroled convict, and Sidney Selden known to the police as having a criminal background of receiving stolen artifacts.

Both communicated only by curt statements appearing in the agony column of *The Times*. But at some point a meeting must take place, so that Sidney Selden could describe what was to be stolen – and more importantly, for each man to take the measure of the other.

"On that fatal night, Walsey alerted Selden in *The Times* to meet at The Plough, and look for a man playing a Mendoza – an interesting and amusing coincidence. I was able to confirm with The Plough's owner that Walsey was performing there that night. He also indicated that Walsey was returning to his home in Chippenham the next day – yesterday.

"Unbeknownst to Walsey, Mr. Selden suffered a mortal heart attack seconds after arriving at The Plough. Somewhat ironic is that within minutes of leaving the pub after his performance, Walsey, upon seeing a strange man lying dead in the street, instinctively grabbed the man's watch and the money pouch and quickly left the premises. That man was Sidney Selden, his faceless co-conspirator, whom he had never previously met. If he hadn't taken time to steal the man's personal possessions, then Lestrade, who had no other suspicions because the man had died of natural causes, would have never involved me in the matter.

"Walsey, believing that Selden simply hadn't shown up, was none the wiser that the plan had gone awry due to the man's unexpected death. He continued on to Chippenham to entertain and wait for developments. Certainly he would have learned that Selden had died, if he hasn't already, and that the plan to fence the *Codex* would need to be revised or abandoned. As it stands now, he is guilty only of robbing the dead man's money pouch and watch – a minor offense, but more serious as the man is on parole.

"I'm sure that confirmation of my explanation, including any planned association with the theft of the *Codex Mendoza*, will be denied. Am I correct, Mr. Walsey?" He glanced at the prisoner, who had no reaction.

"I am curious, however," continued Holmes. "With every other fact serving to reinforce the others, there is one that I cannot reconcile – How did Sidney Selden come to have the sketch of the boots and shield of Chippenham, your home, in his pocket?"

Walsey was silent for a moment, and then he stirred and spoke, while continuing to stare from the window at the passing countryside. "Perhaps, Mr. Holmes, you'll find that – in addition to being simply a fence of stolen goods – he possibly also had other interests, such as heraldry and history. Possibly through his correspondence, he developed a friendship with someone of like interest – and made the sketch for use in a discussion when he was able to finally meet this friend in person."

Holmes looked at the man speculatively for a moment and then said, "I suppose that will have to do. It's as good an explanation as any."

106

NOTES

Places, names, and events in the story pertaining to the *Codex Mendoza* are factual:

> *https://publicdomainreview.org/collections/codex-mendoza-1542/)*

So too, are the Mendoza, an English percussion instrument played with a boot anchor:

> *https://en.wikipedia.org/wiki/Monkey_stick*

The town of Chippenham's coat of arms can be seen here:

> *http://www.chippenham.gov.uk/*

Harry Ralph (Little Tich) was a prominent comedian and Big Boot dancer in the 1880's and 1900's:

> *https://publicdomainreview.org/collections/little-tich-and-his-big-boot-dance-1900/*

The Adventure at the Beau Soleil

by Bonnie MacBird

From *Part IV: 2016 Annual* (2016)

We all have our personal weaknesses, and neither I nor my friend Sherlock Holmes are exceptions. It is easy to note one's friends' idiosyncrasies, but I'm not without my own occasional indiscretions, particularly gambling. As a young man I had not yet developed the fortitude to resist the occasional wager which I could not truly afford. And so it was, in November of 1889, that I found myself, as a result of a single ill-considered bet regarding the lineage of a friend's dog, suddenly and catastrophically without funds.

It was still early in my marriage to Mary Morstan, and I was particularly eager to make up this lost sum quickly and to keep the circumstances of it from my young wife, if not my friend Sherlock Holmes.

It was with great relief, then, that a visit to Holmes launched us on a long and complex case which offered not only a welcome distraction to my paltry medical practice, but the possibility of a sizable reward as well. Mary had been called away to yet another friend's sickbed, and I was free to travel with Holmes to the South of France, where one way or another, I might make up for my indiscretion.

I have recounted this larger case elsewhere in a tale I call "Unquiet Spirits". It took us abroad, first to the South of France and eventually to Scotland in a curious adventure concerning spirits, both of an alcoholic and a spectral nature.

But it was a single incident during this case which I wish to relate to you now, as it afforded one of the clearest, and most remarkable examples of that facility for observation and deduction which was the hallmark of my friend's method.

It was late November when we arrived in Nice on the *Train Bleu*, thankfully escaping the bitterness of an early winter. Enroute I discovered to my surprise that Sherlock Holmes, like myself, had embarked on this journey with practically no cash on hand.

Despite a past year of triumphs, Holmes had somehow managed to accrue little in the way of remuneration. I will not linger on my theories as to why, but will only say that as for many gentlemen, the subject of money was abhorrent to him.

As we arrived at the train station in Nice, it became suddenly clear that we had but one pound and a few pence between us.

"Holmes, I had no idea that you were without funds! Did you suppose that I had enough to sustain us on this journey?"

"Not at all, Watson. I saw your situation immediately when you arrived at Baker Street yesterday."

"How?

"The cuffs of your shirt, and your hair, of course."

"Oh, really, Holmes!" I had begun to sweat in my winter suit, and signaled for a porter.

"No, we will carry our own bags. In answer, Watson, it was the overlooked small ink stain on your right cuff, about which you are normally fastidious, and the self-inflicted haircut – you could not quite reach the back – both of which indicate an effort to save funds."

"Perhaps I have just been busy!"

"You've had few patients, Watson. I know that for a fact."

We struggled with our bags toward the waiting cabs. The bright sun felt blinding.

"Have you been spying on me? How?" I asked, shielding my eyes.

Holmes smiled. "Tut tut, Watson, you know my methods. There is little in London that escapes my view if I choose to attend to it."

"But my practice! Surely that is beneath your notice?"

"Watson, your association with me has brought you to the attention of some unsavory characters. I keep a watchful eye on you for that reason. I hope you will forgive me."

While I later grew to appreciate Holmes's benevolent interest, at that moment it rankled. "Fine," I said, none too amiably, "but what are we to do now? We cannot afford a hotel."

"That, dear friend, is a problem I have solved in advance. Come. We have just enough for a cab and a bite of lunch."

After a brief ride through Nice, we found ourselves shortly at the Hotel Beau Soleil, an establishment which Holmes knew well. There, he said, we would be lodged for free, courtesy of an old acquaintance, one Monsieur Dulac, the hotel detective.

Despite the cheery exterior of pink stucco nestled in palm trees and a riot of bright flowers, the interior of the Beau Soleil was a study in faded grandeur. Its cracked marble flooring, worn sofas, and drooping palms spoke of better days.

As we had to wait in line behind several others for the single, languid desk clerk, I distracted myself by attempting to observe the three in line ahead of me, as Holmes might. At the head were an elderly Russian couple whose proud carriage and once expensive clothing announced they could be of royal blood. Behind them was a well-tailored Englishman with sleekly styled hair and a polite manner. A rising businessman, I inferred confidently, from his highly groomed appearance – and a kind one, as well. I observed him gently directing the older couple toward the elevator after they had received their key.

But at last we were handed our own keys, and soon discovered that our courtesy lodging was to be single, cramped room which we were to share. This contained two hard beds, a broken armoire, and just enough floor space to accommodate our valises. A small, dusty window faced the back of the hotel, and when I finally forced it open, it proved to be situated directly above the rubbish bins. A ripe and fishy aroma assailed me. I slammed the window shut.

Holmes was already stretched out on the bed farthest from the window. He did not move.

"Who is this M. Dulac who has been so 'generous'?" I asked.

"A reasonably competent house detective. I assisted him once and he invited me to stay for free in return for consulting on any matters which may arise during my stay. I have no doubt that such a case will present itself, and soon."

"He should only get half a case for this sorry room," said I.

To appease my grumbling, Holmes suggested lunch, and we pooled our meager resources to visit the hotel restaurant, so confident was he that our fortunes were about to change.

This once grand dining area had tall arched windows looking toward the sea, a profusion of weeping ferns, and pink tablecloths the colour of the stucco exterior. A rather gaudy pink and green Oriental china service covered the tables, and a single, forlorn waiter bustled between the three or four groups of diners.

We ordered and Holmes began to discourse on the merits of the South of France, the village of Èze, Provençal cooking, and particularly the lavender fields nearby which supplied so many cologne manufacturers.

As he rattled on, revealing a remarkable but tedious depth of horticultural knowledge, my attention wandered to a curious tableau across the room. A woman of perhaps fifty, with an enormous bosom, many jewels, and a large feather in her hair was holding court at a table. With her were a small boy, a very old man, and the same handsome younger gentleman who had been in front of us in line at reception.

This suave fellow was energetic and solicitous in the extreme to all three of the others. I now realized he probably was not a businessman, but connected in some way to this family. His attentions to the small boy seemed to be instructive; he gave directions to the child to sit up, place his napkin in his lap, and the like. The boy complied with visible resentment and I smiled, remembering the efforts of my poor mother when I was that tender age.

The older gentleman, however, drew my attention. There was something very peculiar about him. He had a wild mane of vivid red hair, evidently dyed, as white roots were in evidence. He was toying oddly with his meal.

Suddenly, without warning, he started to flip his food across the table, using his spoon as a kind of catapult. The boy found this hilarious, though the other two were appalled.

"Watson," said Holmes sharply. "I perceive that lavender farming is not of interest to you. What is so funny?"

"Haven't you noticed the bizarre little group at the table over there?"

"Of course. Try not to stare."

"What do you make of it, Holmes?"

"A tragedy in the making. Nothing to laugh about."

"Really? How so?"

"I recognize the elderly gentleman. He is the Count of Marne LeCroix. French, but he taught at Camford. He was once a renowned scholar and professor, and is now clearly senile. His wife has ceased to love him, and he is unsafe, even in the bosom of his own family."

"What? Holmes, really!"

"The little boy, however, may yet save the day."

"And how on earth do you deduce all this?"

"Watson, please, it is obvious." Holmes lowered his voice and leaned in to me, to speak softly. "No woman would allow her husband such a public display of bad taste – note the hair – and childish antics if she cared for him. The boy is remarkably observant, and loves the old man who is likely his grandfather – note the similarity of the ears. He's kept the elderly gentleman from spilling his water twice, and retrieved his lost napkin. Now, did that entertain you? Yes? Good. Pray let us eat in silence, as I need to think."

Suddenly irritated, I threw down my napkin. "Well, I need a walk to clear my head," said I.

"Leave a few shillings, please. And by all means, do try to clear your mind," said Holmes, in a tone which implied this would be an impossible task.

I departed in some pique to leave my companion to his thoughts, and relieve my own by a walk along the promenade. A half-an-hour later, spirits suitably brightened by the fresh sea air and bright sunshine, I returned to our room to find a note on my bed. It read:

"The expected case has appeared, Watson. I am summoned by Dulac to the lobby. Join if you wish."

I descended there in search of Holmes and found him in intimate conversation with a stocky, animated Frenchman with dark hair, inverted "V'" shaped eyebrows, and the stooped posture of a praying mantis.

"Ah, Watson, glad you are here. May I present the house detective, Monsieur Henri Dulac? We have worked together before. It seems there has been a major jewel theft within the hour."

"Only you, Mr. Holmes, *s'il vous plaît!*" cried Dulac. "Discretion –"

"Watson is my friend and colleague. It is both or none."

Dulac was taken aback but pressed on bravely. "Very well. But the lady is a Countess," he was saying. "This must be handled with the utmost delicacy. She will not speak to you directly."

"Well, that will not do," said Holmes. "Where is she just now?"

"She has retired to her suite."

"You have suites?" I exclaimed.

Holmes frowned. "When were her diamonds discovered missing?"

"An hour ago."

"And whom does she suspect?"

Dulac next related that evidence pointed to the Countess' private maid, but the girl swore she did not steal the jewels. The maid was found asleep in an adjacent room, and difficult to rouse. They were still plying her with coffee and brandy, hoping to get more from her. All that they had learned thus far was that she was never allowed to touch the jewelry box and claimed not to have done so.

"Two of my men are with the girl now, but the diamonds are nowhere to be found," said Dulac. "They cannot have gone far."

"If she had stolen them, might she not have run away instead of taken a nap?" said Holmes dryly.

"Everything points to the girl. The evidence does not lie."

"Ah, at last you arrive at the facts. *What evidence?*"

"Her fingerprints are clearly on the box that contained them," said Dulac.

"That is quick work indeed," said Holmes. "You are absolutely certain they are hers?"

"I took an impression from her hands, and another from the jewelry case. I have made a comparison." Dulac pulled out a large magnifying glass from his brown coat and grinned at us. "You see, it is not only the famous English detective who carries with him the magnifying glass. In France, we know the fingerprint well."

"I am aware of that."

"We have this method before you in England, I believe," said Dulac, who took delight in this fact.

From across the lobby, I suddenly glimpsed the rotund, bejeweled lady I had observed at lunch, attempting to hide her enormous girth behind a large potted fern. She peered at us through the leaves like a lion in the jungle. When her fierce eye chanced upon mine, she looked quickly away. The boy peeked brazenly around the fronds and was suddenly jerked back. I thought I caught a glimpse of the younger man with them as well.

"Holmes," I murmured, nodding in their direction.

"Yes, I know," said he. "Monsieur Dulac, I presume your victim is the rather ample brunette married to Count Marne LeCroix, of the unusual hair and impaired judgment? And is that not she, standing behind that palm over there with the little boy, and also that younger gentleman, her paramour?"

Dulac gasped. I, too, was taken aback. *Paramour?*

"Yes, that is she. And yes, her husband, the red-haired man, is the Count. But you are mistaken about the other. He is her nephew's tutor, not her, er, how do you say?"

"Don't be so delicate. 'Paramour' is a French word, and you understood me perfectly."

M. Dulac shrugged and looked away. "That is not for me to say."

"Let us continue with the case," said Holmes. "In what kind of container was this necklace stored that would make you so very sure of the fingerprints?"

"An ebony box."

"Excellent. May I see it, please?"

"No one but the Countess may touch it. It is her rule. The box travels in a velvet bag which she herself carries in her luggage. It was found by her bed where she left it."

"Yes, but *you* have touched it. Let me see it now. Is it not there, in the bag by your feet?"

Dulac looked uncomfortable. He glanced back at the Countess who hid again behind the palm.

"All right, then." He lifted up a carpetbag that rested on the floor next to him. From it he removed a velvet bag, and from this an ebony box. Clearly visible near the lock were several oily fingerprints.

Holmes snapped open his magnifying glass and examined them carefully, and then bent in to smell the surface. He smiled.

"I can assure you that these are the maid's fingerprints," said Dulac. "We will arrest her. I think we can make her tell us."

"Then why have you consulted me?"

Dulac looked uncomfortable. "Well, in case we cannot. Perhaps you can make her . . . or perhaps you can . . . find . . . ."

Holmes grunted. "You don't think she did it, do you?"

Dulac looked down at his feet. "I . . . something . . . does not . . . how do you say, feel right." He paused. "Do you wish to see the room or question the chambermaid?" he asked finally.

"Does the chambermaid have a lover? Did you ask this?"

"Of course, I am not a fool! No, she does not. This is true, says the Countess, and her nephew confirms."

"Ah, the little boy," said Holmes.

"Yes. Robin. He is ten but mature for his years. He travels with the Countess and seems to be a very observant little boy."

"Yes, he is. And no, I do not need to see the room or the chambermaid. I will speak to the Countess now. They are there, across the lobby."

We all looked over and again the preposterous little dance was performed as the Countess hid herself. Holmes waved cheerily to them. The little boy waved back, and the Countess jerked him back, roughly.

Holmes started toward them. Dulac put a hand out to stop him. "Please," said he. "She will not speak to me either. Only she will speak to the manager. Perhaps Monsieur Bertrand . . . ah here is Monsieur Bertrand now!"

Bertrand, a barrel-chested, self-important little rooster of a man, moved briskly toward us, waving the air in front of him as if to dispel peons. He spoke briefly to Dulac in French, then turned to Holmes.

"Monsieur Helms. We are grateful for your help. But we cannot have you mixing with – "

"The name is Holmes. You would like this solved?"

"Yes of course."

"What is the name of that rather solicitous tutor?"

"Mr. Richard Carrington. Welsh, I believe."

"No, English," said Holmes. Without a further word, Holmes strode across the lobby over to the threesome. I followed, fascinated. Before anyone could stop him he grasped the woman's hand, bowed deeply, and kissed it with an old world flourish. "Countess!" he purred.

No less surprised than the rest of us, she yanked her hand back in alarm and Bertrand dashed between them. "Ach!" he cried. "*Je vous en prie! Excusez-moi, chère Comtesse,*" said he, fawning his apologies to the woman.

She sniffed, offended. "I have a sudden urge to visit the veranda, Robin," she said to the boy. Her eyes rolled vaguely in that direction as though she had lost her way. The little boy, with a bemused glance at us, took her arm and began to lead her off.

Carrington started to follow but Holmes said "Mr. Carrington, would you be kind enough to stay a moment?"

He turned and lingered reluctantly. "Hadn't you better address the issue of the missing jewels?" he said. "Leave me to my work."

"If you will excuse me?" said Holmes, suddenly touching the man's hair. Carrington reared back, offended.

Holmes smelled his own fingers then laughed. "Of course. It is the same oil on the jewelry box," said Holmes, simply. "Violet Macassar, if I am not mistaken. This is your man."

Carrington sputtered. "What? Why?"

"The maid's fingerprints were on the box, Holmes, not his," pointed out Dulac.

"Wrong clue," said Holmes.

"How are you so stupid!" cried Carrington. "Her fingerprints on the jewelry case? That little strumpet ran her fingers through my hair not an hour ago. I rebuffed her and she was angry. Look, see how messy my hair remains now," exclaimed the tutor, stepping forward and bending his head for us to see. It was true, his formerly patent leather hair was now roughed up in back. There is your proof!" he cried.

"Inventive," remarked Holmes. "But it was the Countess who ran her fingers there. I smelled the same oil on them just now. That formula is highly perfumed. I wager the maid did not touch it willingly."

Next to me I noticed the staunch Dulac smile appreciatively, his head nodding agreement. But the manager Bertrand was not convinced. He leaned in and whispered something to his detective.

Dulac waivered. "*Oui, oui, d'accord.* I will search the maid's room again. Perhaps in a moment or two." He sighed but did not depart.

Bertrand put a hand on Holmes's arm. "Mr. Helms, we must not insult this gentleman – "

"Dulac," said Holmes, "You do not need to search anyone's room. You will not find the diamonds there."

"But why – ?"

With a sudden lunge, Holmes reached into Carrington's waistcoat pocket and pulled out a string of glittering diamonds.

"Because they are here."

There were gasps all around.

Carrington looked poised to flee, but Holmes quickly collared him. Dulac withdrew a pair of handcuffs and instantly had the man under control.

"Thankfully I remained here," Dulac remarked to the manager, one hand clamped on Carrington's arm.

Holmes held the diamonds aloft where a shaft of late afternoon sunlight hit them and they shot rays of light into our eyes.

Bertrand stepped forward and took the jewels into a pristine handkerchief from his breast pocket. He held them out, sparkling against the white linen, then wrapped them and placed them in that same pocket. "I shall return these to the Countess. How did you know the jewels were there, Mr. Heinz?"

"*Holmes!*" said I.

"Two things," said Holmes. "That Carrington is a thief is beyond question. I observed him at reception when we checked in, pickpocketing the elderly Russian gentleman who had been in line before him. The watch, I believe."

Oh, no. How had I missed that?

"But . . . how did you know the diamonds were here?"

"Carrington would have anticipated a thorough search of the rooms, but has had no time to go elsewhere. He gave it away by patting his pocket repeatedly since they entered the lobby."

"This is outrageous," said Carrington. "Those were planted on me. I am a respectable man."

Bertrand cast a stern eye at my friend. "You had better be extremely sure of yourself, Hames," said Bertrand.

"Ah, but I am," said my friend.

"We cannot afford to offend our paying clientele."

"I shall sue," whined Carrington. "Sue!"

Holmes laughed. "I think not. There is more to this. Mr. Carrington and the Countess are involved romantically and – here I'll admit I indulge in conjecture – I believe he harbours the deluded assumption that she may abandon the Count and run away with him."

Carrington spluttered an objection.

"Oh come now," said Holmes. "We have already determined that she ran her fingers through your hair. I observed you passing notes to your lady love at lunchtime, the both of you enjoying this subterfuge in front of her senile husband."

"That is your word against mine," said Carrington.

"Ah, but the little boy is well aware of your intentions, didn't you notice?" Holmes said, and turned to Dulac. "Fetch the child over here and ask him, if you do not believe me."

"Really? Well, how do you suppose I stole the jewels and left another person's fingerprints on the case?" blustered the thief.

"Simple. You presumably drugged the maid. Tincture of opium would have been my choice. I'll wager Monsieur Dulac will find the remains of that or something similar in your room or a nearby trash receptacle. Then you used your own hair oil to anoint her fingers and impress them on the case, an amateur's move and one which gave you away."

"Preposterous. I told you she attempted to seduce me not two hours ago! But I would have none of it! She was simply careless."

"Naturally that is your story."

"It is not a story! Why would I do such a thing? I am well paid, in a position of privilege. I am being framed!" exclaimed Carrington, holding up his cuffed hands in outrage.

"But how can stealing the Countess' jewels endear him to her," asked Dulac, needing one final nail in the coffin.

"Easily imagined, said Holmes. "He might play the hero by 'finding' them when others cannot, thus advancing his plans to win the bigger prize. The Countess will no doubt be a widow soon."

Turning to Carrington, he asked, "Will little Robin and the sedative bottle confirm your guilt? Ah yes, I see it in your face. Give yourself up, Carrington, and you may escape the worst."

"*Mais oui.* Better for you to confess," said Dulac.

Carrington hesitated. The weight of the accusation settled over him, and in the way of the coward, he suddenly broke into tears. "Mercy. Please have mercy on me."

"That is for the courts to decide," said Holmes, "Take him away, gentlemen. You have your solution. And the jewels."

Dulac signaled for assistance. Two men then escorted Carrington away. "*Merci,* Mr. Holmes," said he, shaking my friend's hand with enthusiasm. "We are greatly appreciative."

Behind him Bertrand coughed discreetly. The manager then turned to go, indicating his detective should follow.

I cleared my throat. "Er . . . Monsieur Dulac?" I said. "In the question of remuneration . . . ." I sensed my friend's embarrassment at this but ignored it. Dulac and Bertrand exchanged a look which I did not quite understand. Bertrand waved a hand to dismiss the house detective. Dulac glanced at us with regret as he departed.

The manager stepped forward and addressed the following to me: "Mr. Winston, we are grateful for the solution. But Mr. Helms did not have to actually *do* anything to solve this crime – he did not even leave this lobby! I do not feel obligated in any way. But out of generosity, please enjoy three days more in your room. Good day, gentlemen."

He turned and left. There was a moment of silence, then Holmes snorted with laughter. "Well, once again, *Winston,* observation and deduction seem like child's play when explained. Perhaps I should buy a cape and wand. In any case, do you think you can stand three more days in our garret?"

"Two, at most, *Helms.*" I said. "Now . . . what shall we do for supper?"

The Affair of Miss Finney
by Ann Margaret Lewis
From *Part II: 1890-1895* (2015)

It was in the third week of June, in 1890, that Sherlock Holmes encountered a case the likes of which he'd never before had the misfortune to solve. Women had always been a puzzling topic for Holmes. After my marriage to Mary, he exhibited no overt ill will toward my bride, and yet he made it clear that he was not happy about our nuptials. It is with the Miss Finney affair that I believe he came to see my wife with new eyes.

That day, I'd stayed late into the evening with one of my patients. In fact, I returned home at such an hour that I was certain Mary had gone to bed. The house was dark, save for a solitary gas lamp in the front hall that she left up for me so I could find my key in the dark. I did my best not to wake her, but instead turned the corner and surprised her in the hall, candle in hand. She wore her lavender dressing gown trimmed in white lace, and her hair fell to one shoulder in a single, blonde braid.

She gasped. "James!"

I smiled and kissed her cheek. It was a personal affection of ours that she'd address me in a form of my middle name. "I'm sorry, dear; I didn't mean to startle you."

She placed her hand on her breast and sighed with relief. "That's all right. I wasn't expecting you to be there. My, but you were quiet."

"I thought you were asleep."

"Did you have anything to eat?"

"Yes. The housekeeper insisted on feeding me after the baby was born. Child gave us a bit of a fright, but ultimately it all went well."

"Boy or girl?"

"Girl." I smiled. "Charming little thing."

Suddenly, the bell rang downstairs.

"Who might that be?" Mary asked.

"There's only one person who would ring at this hour." I charged with a stiff gait down the stairs and swung open the front door.

Sherlock Holmes stood on the step. "I'm glad you are here, Watson. I see your wife is still awake. Excellent. May I come in?"

"Of course."

Mary looked askance at me as I led my friend up the stairs. I gestured for her to precede us into our parlour. "Is something wrong?" she asked as I closed the door behind us.

120

"Mrs. Watson," Holmes said. "I came here to find you, especially, in the hope that you might assist me."

"I'm always happy to be of help, Mr. Holmes."

He began to pace the carpet, his nervous energy evident in his stride. He removed his hat, and I realized his hair was mussed as if he'd been asleep. Whatever it was, it had apparently awakened him.

"In my entire career," he said, "I have been fortunate that I have never dealt with a case such as this. I have always known it was possible that something of its ilk might walk through my door, but I'd hoped I'd never see it." He stopped at my fireplace and continued in a hoarse voice. "It is heinous, monstrous, depraved, and vile. It is pure evil."

"Whatever is it, Mr. Holmes?" Mary asked.

"There is a young lady, who waits for me now at Baker Street. I came here, leaving her in the care of the maid. I fear she has been ill-used."

"Ill-used?"

"In a most unspeakable way."

Mary's fingers went to her mouth. "Oh . . . ."

"Good Lord," I whispered.

"She does not know the man who attacked her. He abducted her, rendering her unconscious with chloroform. The man gagged her, put a burlap sack over her head so she'd not know where she was, and later held a knife to her throat as he did . . . what he did. After, that he beat her and left her alone in this fashion for three days in some sort of prison, giving her only marginal food and drink, if any at all. Around ten-thirty this evening, she managed to twist herself free of her bounds and crawl through a coal chute to escape.

"A cabby named Preston, whom I know from other cases, brought her to me tonight believing I might help her. Even so, I have sent word to Stanley Hopkins at the Yard. He is a compassionate sort, someone a woman in this state might find consoling." He shook his head. "Meanwhile, I have tried, in vain, to interview the lady at length, to glean more definitive details about her ordeal, but her upset renders her unable to speak of it coherently. Much of what I've told you I was able to deduce by observation, but when I attempted to examine the blood under her nails, she recoiled from me as if my hands were laced with acid."

"The poor girl." Mary shook her head.

"Mrs. Watson, I have the faculties to help this young lady, but she cannot reveal what she must to me because . . . ." He paused, his lips turning downward in a troubled frown.

"You are a man," she finished for him.

He nodded. "Despite her desire for my assistance, she is not entirely . . . comfortable . . . in my presence, which I understand completely given the circumstances." He continued in a subdued voice. "Mrs. Watson, you've read your husband's narratives and you know that I have not always spoken of the fair sex in the most sympathetic terms. Nonetheless, I would never wish to see such grievous harm done to a woman."

"I know that, Mr. Holmes," Mary said in a gentle voice.

My friend averted his gaze from her and turned to pace the rug again. "The loathsome vermin who did this must be found, but without more data I am in the dark. There is grain powder and saw dust on her dress, along with mechanical oil, indicating she was kept at a mill or some similar place. Where, that is the question. I need her to reveal more. She fears me, though, which, while irrational, is, as I said, understandable."

Mary nodded. "What would you have me do?"

"I would like you to interview her while the doctor and I listen from the adjoining room. Mrs. Hudson may have helped, but she is with her son this evening. Besides, I think someone close to her own age may comfort her. The housemaid would be of little use in this regard, for I need someone with a quicker intellect."

"But, Mr. Holmes, I am not a detective. I am hardly qualified – "

"On the contrary, you are uniquely qualified for what I am asking. You are reserved, but not shy. You are also personable, and what she needs now is a friend. I believe she will respond to you better than I because, in addition to being female, you have a genuine, sympathetic character. And yet . . . ." He leaned on the fireplace mantel and pressed his knuckle to his lips.

"What is it?" Mary asked.

"You have never done this before. Perhaps I am asking too much of you. It is just that I can conceive of no other way."

"If there is no other way that you can think to manage this situation," Mary replied, "then I must do it, must I not? At the very least I should do the very best I can."

Holmes looked from my wife to me, and back again.

"All right, then. If you feel confident enough to try."

"I confess, I am not entirely confident, but I will find my way. What sort of questions must I ask?"

"It is best to concentrate on her senses, what she smelled, heard, etcetera. Anything that she can remember to describe this man, for she could not see him. Also, the location is important. He took her someplace she'd never been before, to her knowledge."

"Did she not come to your rooms from there?" I asked.

"She hid under a tarpaulin in barrel cart that was next to the building and allowed it to take her away, so she was not aware of the path she took. When that stopped, she apparently came upon Preston, who immediately thought to bring her to me. He wondered if he should to take her to a hospital, and in truth, that may not have been a bad idea considering her condition."

"I should examine her, then, Holmes," I said. "She will no doubt have some serious injuries with the treatment she's received."

"I agree, but given her reaction to my touching her hand, doing that may be difficult at first. You should wait until your wife has won her trust."

"Should I write down her answers for you?" Mary asked.

Holmes pursed his lips thoughtfully. "That would be a fine pretence. As I said, I plan to eavesdrop with your husband from my bedroom. I'll make an excuse and pretend to leave the house, perhaps that I am going to find the doctor. She need not know he is even there – you'll wait in my room, Watson – then I'll enter my bedroom from the hall. When I've heard enough, I'll return as if I'd returned from the outside. You may then show me what notes you have, so she does not suspect that I was listening through the wall."

Mary sighed. Her clear blue eyes glistened once more with uncertainty.

"This will certainly be a challenge, Mrs. Watson," said my friend.

"Yet you say you cannot convince her to speak to you."

"No," he said. "I am afraid this case is doomed to failure at my hands alone."

"Very well, then." Mary nodded. "Let me dress and we shall go."

After a few moments, Mary emerged from our bedroom dressed in a simple, emerald green gown accented with ivory, with her hair neatly wrapped in a bun. She carried over her arm two other gowns and personal linens.

"I thought perhaps she might like some clean clothes. These dresses are different sizes."

"Very good, Mrs. Watson," said my friend. "Let's be off."

We summoned a hansom cab. As we made the short drive to Holmes rooms down the street and around the corner, Holmes gave my wife some additional guidance on the sort of questions to ask. He then added, "You should be aware that she is in the condition she was in when she arrived. The maid wanted to clean her up, but I asked her to wait until you have seen her."

Holmes led us up the stairs, gesturing us to be quiet. He directed me to enter his bedroom door, and when I did, I went immediately to the small peep hole Holmes had created in the wall to see into the sitting room. In the room it was hidden by a moulded glass wall decoration that expanded the field of vision so one could see the entire room laid out. As I peered through the hole, I froze for a moment, mortified at the site that met my eyes.

A young woman around the age of three and twenty sat in the chair at Holmes's hearth. Her pale red hair was ratted and dirty, and her fair skin layered in grime. Her dress, a soft pink calico, was ripped in several places and soiled with oil, muck, and dust. She was missing a shoe and her stocking was rent, leaving her foot nearly bare. A crocheted afghan blanket of red and blue had been laid about her shoulders, and yet she still shivered as she lifted a cup of tea to her swollen lips with fingers cut and covered with dirt and blood. Black and blue bruises coloured her right eye and cheeks, the sides of her mouth, her arms, and red, raw burn wounds circled her wrists.

I looked at my Mary, who had preceded Holmes into the room, and I could see alarm in her opened lips and widened eyes.

"Miss Finney," Holmes said in a quiet voice.

The young woman twisted in her chair as if stung. "Mr. Holmes?" Her voice had the lilt of Irish.

"This is Mrs. Watson. She is the wife of my dear friend, Doctor Watson."

"The gentleman who writes of you?"

"Yes. I thought she might keep you company while I find the doctor. I am hoping he will assist me with your case."

"Oh." She blinked at Mary with pale blue eyes that seemed lifeless. "Thank you, Mrs. Watson."

"You are so very welcome." Mary walked across the room and tugged the bell rope. "Why don't I have the maid bring up a wash basin with warm soap and water, and we can clean your wounds a bit? Won't that make you feel a little better?"

"I think that's an excellent plan, Mrs. Watson," said Holmes. "Meanwhile, I shall be on my way. Good-bye, Mrs. Watson, Miss Finney." He nodded his head and stepped into the hall, closing the door solidly behind him. He then entered his room silently from the hall and came to stand beside me near the wall, to listen.

The maid answered the summons and brought Mary's requests. Mary then sat before the young woman on the ottoman to ring out a towel with warm water and soap.

"Thank you, Mrs. Watson," Miss Finney whispered. "You are very kind."

"Why don't you simply call me 'Mary'," my wife said. "We are about the same age, are we not?"

"I am twenty-five," Miss Finney said. "My name is Melinda."

"Melinda is a beautiful name." Mary smiled warmly. "Let me start with your face, dear." She began to clean the young woman's cheeks with gentle touches.

"Mr. Holmes is a good man," my own lady continued as she worked. "On our ride here he told me he wants to help you, but you'll need to tell him more of what happened to you."

"I know," Miss Finney said with a quivering voice. "But . . . it's so difficult to . . . talk about it . . . there's so much . . . ."

"I cannot imagine," Mary agreed. She patted the young woman's face with a dry towel. "But perhaps if you and I break the whole ghastly thing up into tiny, little pieces, discussing it won't be so trying. In fact . . . ." Standing, she went to Holmes's desk and took up a piece of foolscap, pen, and ink. "I shall write some notes, and we can tell him these little pieces when he comes back."

"Little pieces? What do you mean?" Miss Finney's pale eyes were wide.

Mary set the paper next to her on the side table. "Thinking about everything at once is just overwhelming, so we focus on one little thing at a time. For example, when you were in the room alone, I understand your eyes were covered so all you could do is listen. Did you hear anything?"

"Yes."

"What?"

Miss Finney swallowed hard. "The rats."

My eyes shot over to my friend standing across from me. He winced.

"Good God," I whispered.

Holmes again held his finger to his lips and I went silent once more to listen.

"Shall I roll up your sleeves, dear, so I can wash your hands?"

Miss Finney tenuously put forward her arms, and allowed Mary to wash the dirt, blood, and ichor from her arms and fingers.

"Did you remember hearing anything from outside?" Mary asked as she worked.

"Church bells."

"Church bells? You are certain it wasn't a clock tower?"

"Yes. The bells didn't ring every quarter hour, but every few hours. I am sure it was the Angelus. I prayed it . . . ."

Suddenly, the clock on the mantelpiece chimed midnight. Miss Finney started, but Mary soothed her by placing a firm hand on her shoulder. Dropping her face into her wet hands, Miss Finney sobbed.

Mary pulled the young woman to her shoulder and let her cry there. She rocked her gently, stroking her tangled hair. I turned my gaze to my friend, who stood by the door wearing a thoughtful expression.

125

"It's all right, dear," Mary said finally. "It's another little piece that'll help him find where you were imprisoned. It could help lead him to . . . to the one who did this."

"Y-yes. I see." Miss Finney sniffed.

Mary brushed loose hair from the woman's face. "Did you hear anything else that you recall?" Mary asked, she dabbed Miss Finney's tears away with the towel, and returned to bathing the young woman's wrists and fingers.

"A gurgling and swishing, like water in pipes . . . only louder."

"Excellent. That's another thing that Mr. Holmes might find useful. I'll write that down." Mary set aside the rag a moment to write on the paper.

I looked over at Holmes and saw a gleam in his eyes. This had apparently indeed triggered a thought in his mind.

"Now, in this room . . . did you smell anything that stands out in your mind?"

"Oh." Miss Finney rolled her eyes. "That I shall never forget. It smelled so foul there. There was waste . . . some of it my own, I fear. But mostly it smelled like . . . bread yeast . . . only the strongest I have ever smelled. It was mixed with the scent of beer. It was overwhelming. I don't know that I shall make bread or smell beer for an entire year after this."

I saw a slight smile curl at the edge of my friend's lips.

"Did the . . . man who attacked you smell this way, too?"

"Yes, he smelled strongly of it. That, and tobacco. A very acrid tobacco, much like what I smell here. I'm afraid when I entered Mr. Holmes's sitting room, I wanted to retch."

Holmes sighed. He closed his eyes and rested his head against the wall.

"He put a gag on you, I understand," Mary prompted.

"Yes, it was . . . so horrible."

"I don't doubt it," Mary said gently. "Did the cloth he use taste of anything?"

"Oh, it tasted rank. Like stale beer."

Holmes nodded, as if he expected to hear this. "Now the man," he murmured. "Ask about the man."

"Now here's one more thing, and I think this may be the most difficult of all, dear." Mary shifted her seat closer to the young woman and taking the younger woman's hands in her own, held them tightly. "Was the man who did this . . . could you tell if he was large or small in size?"

"He . . . was . . . broad shouldered, average build, I think. But not so tall."

"Were his hands rough, or smooth?"

126

"S-smooth. If I'd not known him otherw-wise, I'd say he was a gentleman. And the way he spoke was educated. He had a rasping voice, not very deep."

"So he spoke to you. Did he say anything that stands out in your mind? Something specific?"

"Not much I'd repeat. He said such foul things."

"But you'd recognize his voice if you heard it again."

"Yes. I don't think I can ever forget it."

"Melinda, you are doing brilliantly. See how much easier it is to take it piece by piece?" Mary wrote these down on the paper she had beside her.

"I feel badly that I could not tell Mr. Holmes this. He asked some similar questions, but I just c-couldn't . . ."

"It's all right, dear. I'm sure he understood. But you see? We have all these notes here that will help him."

"There's one more thing you might write down."

"What's that?"

"He had a beard. A short one. It was very strange . . . coarse, like horsehair. He had a moustache, too, but it was not as rough."

"Very good. I know that will be helpful."

Holmes patted me on the shoulder and gestured with his head for me to follow him. He went out into the hall, walked quietly downstairs and led me out the front door.

Once downstairs, he reopened the front door noisily and walked up to the landing, taking care to walk heavy on the stairs. I did the same. Holmes knocked lightly on the door, and heard my wife say, "Come in."

"Hello again, Miss Finney, Mrs. Watson," Holmes said, entering the sitting room. "I have located the doctor."

"I think Miss Finney is doing better, Mr. Holmes," my wife said. "She shared some things about her ordeal that I recorded for you."

Holmes took up the paper my wife held out to him and glanced over it. "Ladies, this is marvellous. It will help tremendously." He folded the paper and put it in his pocket. "Miss Finney, I assume you live with relatives?"

"Yes. My father."

"Do you wish me to contact him to let him know where you are?"

"Yes, please. He is the proprietor of the Celtic Knot Public House, on Surrey Row in Southwark."

"If I may," I interjected. "I'd like to examine her injuries."

"Of course, Watson. Miss Finney?"

I sat before the young woman, and when I reached out to touch her chin to inspect her bruises, she shied away, pressing against my wife who sat beside her. Mary placed her arm around her shoulders reassuringly. "It's all right, Melinda," Mary said. "My husband is very gentle."

With Mary's reassurance, she allowed me to give a superficial inspection of her injuries. She needed a more thorough exam, but I determined that she would be all right for the time being.

Mary then said to me, "Do you think I could have the maid draw a bath for Miss Finney? Then I can finish caring for her?"

"That is an excellent idea, dear. I can give you some ointment and bandages for her wounds."

"Meanwhile, the doctor and I have some other work to do," said Holmes. "Thank you for your help, Mrs. Watson."

"You are very welcome, Mr. Holmes."

After Mary led Miss Finney from the room, Holmes went to the mantel to fill his long clay pipe from the tobacco slipper. Halfway through this process he paused, set aside the pipe, and took a cigar from the coal scuttle.

"Holmes, this is simply monstrous."

Holmes lit his cigar and paced the floor, puffing and thinking.

"Southwark." He stopped in his tracks.

"Southwark?"

"Anchor Brewery, Watson. It is right next to St. Saviour's Church in Southwark. That is where she was imprisoned. I'm certain of it. The smell of yeast and stale beer. The gurgling pipes, rather loud from her description. A good deal of water, malt, and hops. Clearly a brewery. The Celtic Knot Pub is also in Southwark, and her father would likely order from a local brewer. I believe this monster works for her father's beer supplier. He probably kept her in the brewery's cellar. The closest supplier is Barclay's Anchor Brewery."

"It cannot be that simple, Holmes. Can it?"

"Usually it is. Most victims of this crime know their attackers in some way. Human nature, really. We covet what is most familiar to us. The difficulty lies in finding the man within a brewery establishment that fits her description, but I believe I know where to start."

There was a knock at the door.

"Come in, Hopkins."

The youthful, primly-dressed Scotland Yarder stepped through the door. "How the devil did you know who it was through the door?"

"I was expecting you, and you have thick knuckles."

"Of course." He gave my friend an amused grin. "What's this about then, Mr. Holmes?"

As Holmes explained in delicate terms the situation at hand, Hopkin's expression clouded.

"Dark business," he said. "There was a report this morning of a missing young lady from Southwark. It wasn't my case, so I don't know the details, but I wager it's the same one. I can send word to the Yard." He pulled out a notebook. "So you want to look in at the brewery? No one will be there at this hour."

Holmes went to the closet and took out a dark lantern. "Which is precisely when I wish to go, my dear fellow."

"Now, wait just a moment. There are laws to follow."

"And you should follow them, of course. I place all the legal formalities of entering the building in your capable hands. You shall meet us there when you have papers."

"Meet you there? You mean – ?"

"The rest shall remain unsaid, Hopkins, lest you find yourself in a position of having to lie to your superiors. Here is the address. Join us as soon as you can. Watson, I trust you have your revolver? Right then, let us be off."

As we made our way to Southwark in a hansom, Holmes asked, "What do you make of it, Watson?"

"As I said before – monstrous."

"What of her description of the man?"

"Medium build, I think. With a beard."

"Yes. She said the beard was like horsehair. What does that suggest to you?"

"It was fake?"

"I believe so."

"Then the man would be clean-shaven."

"Most likely. Ah, here we are." Holmes tapped the roof of the cab with his cane.

The brewery loomed dark and large in front of us as we approached it. Holmes lit the lantern in his hand, and began to walk around the building.

"Wouldn't it be better to see what's here in the daylight, Holmes? Why did we have to come at night?"

"Seeing evidence would be better during the day, I admit. Now, however, our quarry will not be here. He took her in the evening, left her alone late at night, and abused her, I would surmise, earlier the next day. She was gagged so she could not be heard as he left her here. That's why she took the late night opportunity to escape, for she knew he'd leave her to herself. I wanted to find this prison now and inspect it before he can return."

"Will you have enough light?"

"I've found clues in less light than this, my friend. Hello, here is a coal chute." He held his lantern over the rusted entryway and crouched. From the edge of the rusted metal chute door, he removed a tiny piece of fabric and thread.

"Hold the lamp won't you, Watson?" I did as he asked, and he examined the fragment closer to his eyes.

"Pink calico. This is where she crawled out of her prison. The room is beyond this wall."

I walked a few steps along the building. "There's a window here, Holmes, but it seems to have been blacked over on the inside."

He looked over my shoulder. "Close the lantern."

"Why?"

"A precaution. Let me see if we can open this window." He bent down in the dark, and I could see his shadow moving in a pushing motion. "Ah, for shame. It is a crank window, locked from the inside. Very well, then, I must break it or find another way in."

"Someone will hear you if you do that."

"Yes, I'd rather find another way." We walked together down the length of the wall, and around the back of the building. There we found a simple wooden door, which was locked with a padlock. I opened the lantern slightly so he might inspect it.

"This Aquire model is not much of a challenge." From his the pocket inside his coat, Holmes pulled out what I recognized as his lock picking tool kit, selected and instrument and went to work. It wasn't long before we were inside and making our way down a set of creaky wooden stairs into an unused portion of the giant brewery cellar. I say "unused" in that it didn't seem to be currently employed for the brewing and ageing of beer. It was, however, filled with old barrels, equipment, bottles, sawdust, and tools which were layered in dust.

Holmes took the lantern from my hand and stood gazing at the slate floor. Footprints were clear in the dust, leading to the end of the room and another singular, wooden door, which was bolted shut.

Holmes slid open the bolt and stepped into the chamber beyond. A foul odour struck me first as we passed into what had been the young woman's prison. I took my handkerchief from my sleeve and pressed it to my nose and mouth to block out the stench. Holmes held up lantern to illuminate the entirety of the grim space.

"Here are her bonds," he said, touching bits of thick rope with his cane. "Being a tiny woman, she wriggled free of them. What have we here?" He handed me the lantern, and bent down. He then lifted up a small glass bottle in his gloved fingers. Opening the top, he sniffed.

"Spirit gum. That confirms the fake beard, Watson."

"He put it on here?"

"I think not. Most likely he carried this small bottle in his pocket to re-affix the hair piece as necessary. They fall off with oil from the skin and perspiration when worn too long. This bottle is not empty, so he probably did not drop it on purpose."

"He then left the premises wearing the beard."

"I think so."

"There doesn't seem to be much else here," I said, walking the length of the room to the coal chute. "Other than that burlap sack, which you say covered her head, and this cloth." I picked it up off the floor. "Her blindfold, I'd assume."

"Yes, and this is the gag." Holmes said, pointing with his cane to another crumpled, stained rag. "No, nothing much else, Watson. He brought her here three days ago, used her, and left her here for his next convenience. Ultimately he would have killed her, I believe."

A slight movement near my boot caused me to jump. "Good heavens. The rats. I'd forgotten. It seems we've startled them." I looked up at Holmes, and saw he was gazing at me with a peculiar glint in his eye. And yet it was as if he was not seeing me. His jaw and fists were clenched tight and his lips were pressed into a firm line.

"Holmes – " I began.

"Let's go, Watson. I have had enough of this atmosphere."

I followed him outside, and, as we returned the way we had come, we encountered Inspector Hopkins with two constables.

"There you are, Holmes. You've been inside?"

My friend described the inner chamber we found, and handed Hopkins the bottle. "You might want to leave a constable here in case he returns."

"Are you off then already?"

"Yes, to the Celtic Knot Pub. The owner is Miss Finney's father, and I suspect he knows who this villain is, though he might not realize it. The villain works for this brewery, and knew Miss Finney already. He knew when she'd be vulnerable, and he followed her. He also knows where that room is, knew it was abandoned, and that he could use it with impunity."

"You don't mind if I come along, do you?"

Holmes smiled. Hopkins was a student of his methods, if an imperfect one.

"Of course, Inspector. Let's hail a cab, shall we? The pub is in Southwark but too far too walk."

When we reached the pub, we encountered the owner turning down the gas lamp outside the shop. He was a small man, whose pale face and shock of white hair betrayed his own Celt heritage.

"Ach, fellows, I cannot help you tonight. As you see I'm closing the doors a bit early. We've had some family trouble."

"We are aware," said Holmes. "That's why we are here. My name is Sherlock Holmes, and these gentlemen with me are Inspector Hopkins of Scotland Yard, and my associate Doctor Watson."

"Sherlock Holmes – Scotland Yard." He nodded. "You are quick, gentlemen. I only submitted a missing person's report today, as they'd not let me do it sooner."

"Shall we go inside?"

"Surely, surely." He led us into the pub, and locked the door behind us once we were inside. It was a clean, bright establishment inside, not as grim or dark as others I've visited. In fact, I'd say that while the establishment was one a man would frequent, it had the prim, orderly touch of a woman's influence, with shining glassware, well-swept floor, and dust-free artwork and lamps.

"Would you like a pint, gentlemen, or anything else to drink?" Mr. Finney ushered us to a large table at the centre of the floor and we sat together. "*Gratis*, of course. You're here to help, and I'll not take a farthing."

"I'm on duty, so nothing for me," said Hopkins. "Though Holmes and the doctor can indulge."

"If I had something now, it may put me to sleep," I said. "Holmes?"

Holmes shook his head. "I think you might want something for yourself, Mr. Finney. What we have to tell you might be a shock."

The barkeep paled visibly and sank into the open chair beside Holmes. "It doesn't serve to drink the profits," he said in a subdued tone. "You might as well tell me what you must."

"First, let me begin by assuring you that your daughter is alive."

"Oh, thank God." Finney rested his face in his hands.

"But there is more," my friend continued. In a gentle tone, he revealed the facts of his daughter's misery, and as he spoke the barkeep's eyes welled with tears.

"Dear Lord in heaven," he muttered, when my friend finished. He wiped his eyes with his fingers. "My sweet Melinda. Where is she now?"

"The doctor's wife is caring for her at my residence. She's sleeping in the guest room now, I hope. We shall bring her home tomorrow, late in the morning."

"Why late?"

"She must identify the culprit, and you also may help with that goal. The man who did this worked for Anchor Brewery and would have been here regularly. Do you know anyone that fits that description?"

The elderly man dabbed his eyes once more with a handkerchief. "There are three that I know. Charles Hamming is the nephew of the owner and the salesman who takes my orders. The delivery driver is Paul Somersfield, and then there is Joshua Gable. He's an odd fellow, a bookkeeper for the brewery, and he comes here frequently after he leaves work. He doesn't say much, but he has a queer look in his eyes."

"Are any of these fellows clean-shaven?" I asked.

"Clean-shaven? Yes, Gable is clean shaven. The other two have moustaches, and Hamming has a beard after a fashion."

"After a fashion?" I asked.

"He's been trying to grow one, it seems. It's not filled in."

"This has been a helpful interview, Mr. Finney," said my friend, rising from his chair. "Let's leave you to your rest, confident that your daughter will be returned to you tomorrow."

"Thank you, gentlemen," Mr. Finney said, shaking our hands. "Thank you so very much."

As Holmes and Hopkins stepped outside, I paused a moment with Mr. Finney. "Sir," I said, "Your daughter will have great difficulty returning to your pub, I think. It is where she was taken, and the memories of her experience will be quite raw. Does she have anywhere she can go to stay for a time to calm her nerves? Somewhere in the country perhaps?"

Mr. Finney nodded. "I have a sister in Yorkshire. I'm sure she'd be happy to have Melinda to stay with her for a while."

"Excellent," I shook his hand once more. "And if there's anything I can do to help in anyway afterward, pray, let me know."

When we arrived at Baker Street, Holmes, Hopkins, and I found Mary in Holmes's sitting room, sleeping in the chair by the fire. I touched her shoulder and she woke with a start. "Oh! You've returned. I am sorry. I tried to stay awake."

"Do not apologize, dear," I said. "Is Miss Finney in bed?"

"Yes. She's clean and her wounds are bandaged. The maid gave her one of her nightgowns and put her in your old room. I stayed with her until she fell asleep."

"I think sleep is a fine idea for all of us," I said. "I don't believe we can do much more until morning. Or, rather, later this morning."

"I'd rather not leave her, though. The maid said there was a room downstairs where I might sleep, but I wanted to wait until you came back before I went to lie down."

"I hope you would both stay if you can," said Holmes. "Tomorrow morning may be a trial for her, and your presence would be a great help to me."

"That room will accommodate both of us, as I recall," I said. "I'll send a boy over to our flat gather some clean collars for me and some things for you as well, Mary."

"Hopkins," Holmes turned to the inspector. "Those three men can be collected when they report for work in the morning. Do you think you could bring them here?"

Hopkins shrugged. "We've done it before, so I cannot see why not. With some good constables with me, I believe we can have them here around ten o'clock."

"Then you should all go get some much needed sleep. I will stay up a bit longer and smoke – " He paused. "A cigarette or two."

I smiled. "Very well, then. Good night, Holmes."

The next morning, I awoke at eight o'clock. Mary had already risen, dressed, and gone to look after Miss Finney. I washed and dressed quickly, and, upon entering Holmes's sitting room, discovered a breakfast laid out for us. Holmes, Miss Finney and Mary were already seated at the table. One of the windows, I noticed, was opened slightly, allowing a fresh morning breeze to billow the curtains.

"The maid has anticipated our needs, Watson," Holmes said. "Come join us."

I did as he suggested, and we ate together in silence for a few moments, until Holmes said, "Miss Finney, there is something I must tell you."

She looked up at him, her right eye more a vivid blue in contrast to the grey-blue bruise that surrounded it. "What is it, Mr. Holmes?"

He placed his napkin and looked around at all of us. "This morning, Inspector Hopkins will be bringing three men here, one of whom is most likely your assailant."

Miss Finney set her fork down on her plate with a *clink*. "Oh."

"Do not fret, dear lady. I will not ask you to face him. However, if you desire justice, you must identify him for the police."

She shook her head. "But I did not see him."

"You heard his voice. Therefore, I will interview the men in this room. You will listen to the conversation from my bedroom, which is adjacent to this one." Her eyes widened at the suggestion of being in his bedroom, but he held up his hand. "Mrs. Watson will stay with you, will you not, Mrs. Watson?"

"Of course," Mary said.

"There, on my chemistry table, you will see that I have an Edison light bulb in a lamp stand. I have attached it to a switch that I'll give to you. When you hear a voice you recognize, you will flip the switch to signal to me."

"Will they not see the light go on?" Miss Finney asked.

"They may, but that need not concern you."

Miss Finney looked to Mary, who, in turn, placed her hand gently on her arm. Miss Finney straightened her shoulders and turned back to my friend.

"I can do it," said Miss Finney. "I *will* do it."

"Capital. There is only one thing more." Holmes leaned forward with his elbows on the table and asked in a voice that was most gentle. "Are you certain that there is no particular word or phrase that the man used, nothing he said that stands out in your mind? Anything he said may be of help to us."

Her delicate lips turned down in a frown. "Patience."

"Patience?"

"The first morning, just before he left me, he said that. He mocked me by saying 'patience is a virtue.' It was horrible . . . he made it sound as if I wanted . . . ." She covered her mouth and wept once more.

Mary rested her hand on her shoulder. "Mr. Holmes – "

"No more, Miss Finney. I have precisely what I need. Watson, would you escort the ladies next door? I have set some chairs in there so they may be comfortable. I'll ask the maid to clear these dishes, then I'll prepare the light switch."

I did as he asked, and when I opened the door to his room, I was surprised at the site that met my eyes.

It was tidy to the point of being pristine. Holmes had, no doubt, spent a better part of the night cleaning it. The window was also cracked open like that of the sitting room, allowing in the fresh air. He'd set two padded chairs near the wall where he and I had stood the night before to listen to Mary's conversation with the young lady. There was also a small side table with a pitcher of cool water and drinking glasses.

"Well, then," I said. "Here you are, ladies. Is there anything else you think you might like?"

"I may close the window later if there's a chill, but I think we're fine for now."

"I'd recommend a book," I said. "But reading the detailed lives of criminals might be a bit much."

"I think we'll be all right," Mary said with a smile. "What time do you expect Inspector Hopkins to arrive?"

I glanced at my pocket watch. "Any time now. He said he would be here around ten o'clock."

"Then we haven't long to wait."

Suddenly the door to the closet opened, and Holmes stepped into the room.

"Good Lord, Holmes," I said. "What . . . how did you . . . ?"

"I'm sorry, ladies. Watson." He held up a bit of rubber-coated wire linked to a small black box with a switch. "This is for Miss Finney. I had to pull the connection through."

"But your closet . . . what did you do?"

He glanced over his shoulder. "Oh, that. After you married and moved, I knocked a hole in the back of my closet, and another in the sitting room which is covered by those additional drapes. Having a hidden way into my room is useful, especially when one must string wire." He smiled and placed the box in Miss Finney's hand. "Simply flip this switch. Watson, let's you and I go in the other room and test it. We have little time."

I followed him back to the sitting room. There he stood in the centre of the room and called out, "Miss Finney, flip the switch please." The lightbulb on Holmes desk lit. "Excellent, you may turn it off now."

"Will you interview all the suspects at once, Holmes?"

"Of course, Watson. If a man is interviewed alone, his voice isn't natural. Put him in a conversation with three or more people, and he'll speak normally. That is what we want. Ah, I believe that is Hopkins' ring downstairs. Watson, sit over at my table near the lamp, won't you?"

Holmes then paced back and forth as we heard several men tramping up the stairs. "Come in, Hopkins," Holmes called out, before the officer's knuckles had struck the door.

Hopkins entered followed by three men and two constables.

"Sit, gentlemen, please," Holmes said, gesturing to the chairs at the dining table. "I fear I haven't much time. I have more pressing matters to attend to today, but I promised the inspector I'd assist him with his case, so let's get on with it."

Hopkins raised an eyebrow at Holmes, then turned his gaze to me. I shrugged my shoulders, wondering what this meant.

"Now, gentlemen, you have been asked here by the inspector because a crime has been committed, and we wish to know if you were involved." Holmes paced around the table, not looking at the suspects. It appeared to me as if he were not interested in them at all. "You sir, are a bookkeeper are you not?"

This question was posed to the man who sat at the end of the table. He was not overly tall, but his eyes were squinting and his mouth turned in an awkward scowl. Clean-shaven and of middle years, he did not meet my friend's gaze.

"I am. How would you know?"

"I was told one of you was a bookkeeper. You seemed most likely, with the mark of a pen on your thumb and forefinger, ink stain on your cuff, and the wear on your sleeve. You also have indentions from a pair of spectacles which are currently in your breast pocket. Your attitude is also lacks the confidence of a salesman. Therefore you are Joshua Gable. This man here," he pointed to the bearded young man who sat beside Gable, "has that confidence. You are Charles Hamming, are you not? Nephew of the owner of the Anchor Brewery?"

"I am. But I fail to see – "

"Of course you do. And that means you," he said to the third, moustached, muscular fellow, "are Paul Somersfield, the delivery driver. Your build belies that line of work."

"Aye, that'll be what I do, but I have no idea why I am – "

"You are here because a young woman was abused and assaulted in the brewery basement."

"Good God," said the bookkeeper. His scowl softened. "Who would do that?"

"One of you three. All of you have association with the Celtic Knot Pub, and all three of you work at the brewery. It can only be one of you. To be frank, I'd rather one of you simply confess and spare me the agonizing tedium of working it out of you. I swear, Hopkins," he turned to the inspector suddenly. "Could you have brought me a less interesting case?"

"I . . . bring it to . . . you?" Hopkins repeated. He crossed his arms. "What do you – ?"

"I grow tired of having to solve the simplest little problems for Scotland Yard," Holmes interrupted. "Is there not one that you could puzzle for yourselves? Why must I be the one to labour for you when the answers are always so obvious?"

"Well if the answer is so obvious," said Hopkins, his voice dropping to a growl, "why don't you just give it to us now?"

"I think you should be patient," Holmes snapped in return.

The salesman snickered.

"Why are you laughing?" Holmes said.

"You're asking him to be patient. You are the one who needs patience."

"I need *what*?"

"Patience. You do most of the talking, you cut others off, and do not let them finish. Who do you think you are?"

I felt heat on my left hand. Glancing next to me, I saw that the bulb was lit.

Holmes did not appear to notice. He leaned over Hamming as if examining a bug under a microscope. "Tell me, Hamming. What happened to your cheeks?"

"My cheeks? What do you mean?"

"There are small abrasions on your skin, just above the line of your beard. It looks to me like the skin has been ripped away."

"I'm not used to shaving above the beard line and I scraped it by accident."

"No, no, that is not from shaving. That injury happens when one pulls off a fake beard affixed with spirit gum. If you remove it after a short time without solvent, it hurts like the devil. I know what that injury looks like, as I've done it to myself a few times. When did you do it? Two, three days ago? It's not quite healed. Do you see it, Hopkins? I must admit, hiding a real beard under a fake one shows some cleverness, but if you're going to use a disguise, you might at least learn how to remove it properly."

As Holmes spoke, the light went on and off several times next to me, then finally remained lit.

"Here now," said the delivery driver. "What the deuce is wrong with that bulb there?"

Suddenly the door burst open and Miss Finney entered, followed by a rather anxious looking Mary.

"Mr. Holmes, did you not see the light?" Miss Finney cried with some exasperation.

"I did," Holmes replied. "I was merely confirming your identification."

Jumping to his feet, Hamming spat a word toward the young lady that I shall not record in this memoir. It was so vulgar that everyone froze with shock.

Everyone save Holmes, however. He sprang forward with a solid right cross that sent teeth and blood shooting from the man's lips. There was also a loud *crack* when he connected, and I surmised he'd broken the man's jaw. Spinning from the force of the blow, Hamming crashed to the floor in an unconscious heap.

Releasing a contented sigh, Holmes straightened his jacket, then turned to the women in the doorway.

"I apologize for that, dear ladies. Though I must admit it did give me tremendous satisfaction. I hope it did for you as well, Miss Finney?"

She gave him a slight smile. "It did, indeed."

"Well, there you are, Hopkins." He waved at the unmoving lump on the floor as if it were a fly. "Pray, have your men drag this vile refuse from my sitting room."

138

"With pleasure," said Hopkins. "I admit I thought you'd lost your mind for a moment there. All that about bringing you boring cases . . . ."

"It's often true," said Holmes said with a smile. "But not in this instance."

Hopkins gave Holmes a wry grin as he followed his constables and the others out the door.

"Holmes, Mary and I would be happy to take Miss Finney to her father," I said. "If there's nothing else you'll need from us . . . ."

"No, Watson. We are finished here."

Miss Finney went to my friend and, with a slight hesitation, laid her hand on his forearm. Holmes's eyes widened slightly at the gesture. He did not shrink away, but remained still at her touch.

"Mr. Holmes, I know that I wasn't the easiest client for you – "

Holmes shook his head. "It is all right."

"Yes, but, I want you to know. You've helped to restore my faith in men and you have given me hope. Thank you."

"You are welcome, of course. Be well."

As we helped Miss Finney into a carriage outside, I heard Holmes's violin playing a sweet, melancholy melody. From that day, I noticed he seldom made negative references to women or marriage in my presence. I wonder now if seeing Mary's effectiveness in this case amended his point of view, not only of her but of all women, or if seeing Miss Finney's strength in her suffering made him less apt to deride them. If it is either, I can only say that he's has become, and always will be, a better man for it.

Doctor Watson's
Baffled Colleague
by Sean M. Wright
and DeForeest B. Wright, III
From *Part XXXV: 1889-1896* (2022)

READERS PLEASE NOTE: A large envelope was recovered from the double-drawer of an old rolltop desk in 1977. Within was found a completed manuscript of a novel, (later published in 1979 as Enter the Lion *1979). Another large manilla envelope contained some partial manuscripts, apparently abandoned attempts at novelization, along with notes outlining those narratives. In company with these were found other memoranda and carbon copies of several letters. All were discovered to be the work of Mr. Mycroft Holmes. One letter in particular is of more than casual interest to Holmesian devotees, concerning an event which took place while Sherlock Holmes was thought to have died.*

Diogenes Club
20 October, 1894

D ear Doctor Watson,

Your letter, delivered to me here at the Club, formed the final course, so to speak, of an enjoyable dinner of roasted chicken, steamed Brussels sprouts smothered in Béarnaise Sauce, and creamy mashed potatoes. To this was paired a luscious, and no less buttery, chardonnay.

Herr Yosep Schmidt, our club's chef for barely two years, continues to delight our palettes. He recently introduced for the dessert course a confection popular amongst his Dutch relations living in the mid-Atlantic area of the United States. It is a pie but, unlike most of our own varieties, the crust is quite short, light and flakey, filled with thin slices of pumpkin and apple, layered one over the other, the top dusted with cinnamon and nutmeg.

Your letter thus finds me in an expansive mood.

Should I suspect your request to know more about the period from 1891 to 1894 and the part I played in Sherlock's absence during those three years is prompted by a desire to replenish your stock of sensational stories for *The Strand*? If so, I cannot begrudge you your oft stated desire to share examples of my brother's singular gift for solving difficulties – especially seeing how thoroughly your charming and homely sketches demonstrating Sherlock's wit and industry are anticipated by an enthusiastic readership.

I therefore regret being unable to assist you in this regard. Diplomatic considerations constrain me from sharing details of my brother's sojourning through Persia, Tibet, Arabia, and especially his audience with the Khalifa at Khartoum. These must, at present, remain the exclusive possession of Her Majesty's Foreign Office.

Still, I am obliged to find a way of thanking you for the superlative snuff and the box of fine *habanos* with which you gifted me. [1] My brother's return allows me to more fully acquaint you with certain details relating to the incident which left Doctor Jasper Anstruther so utterly baffled. I still insist that my part in clearing up the affair was quite negligible, little more than calling the bluff of an *agent provocateur*.

It was my intention to offer this explanation upon my brother's return from his self-imposed exile but I did not wish to trespass on your grief at the time of your own sadness and loss. [2] Time has been a tonic, I see, and, now that you have resumed your old rooms in Baker Street, I am glad to give fuller clarity to the case.

You'll recall, my dear Doctor, that you sent your colleague to the club to consult me, but I was not there. Having no duties in Whitehall that afternoon, I decided myself to forego my normal schedule: Entering the Diogenes at precisely a quarter-before-five to dine. Lingering over the newspapers while enjoying a good cigar, I allow the quiet to aid my digestion. At twenty minutes past the hour of eight, I always depart the club, cross the street, and enter my own front door.

To my deep chagrin I have learned to suspend my routine on the fifth of November to escape being accosted by swarms of high-spirited children roaming the city, carrying buffoonish effigies of Guy Fawkes and Pope Leo hanging on poles, and gaily insisting, "Penny for the Guy, sir! Penny for the Guy!"

Having had an audience with the late frank, outspoken Cardinal Manning, I pondered whether would he might still share the same fate as Cardinal Vaughan surely will. [3] The tradesmen join in the clamour selling bangers, eels, chestnuts, and other comestibles as, to the cheers of the throng, the bonfires are touched off and the effigies burnt. *Panis et circensis, per omnia secula seculorum.* [4]

Re-reading the previous paragraph, I sound like a sour, old cynic, do I not? In truth, I've not entirely forgotten the frivolities of youth. I encourage Mrs. Crosse, or the maid, or the tweenie to deal with the youngsters' raucous merriment by gifting them with pennies taken from the pile I leave each year on the side table in the foyer. [5]

In her continuing quest to keep me apprised of all things Catholic, Mrs. Crosse had arranged the newspaper on my luncheon tray, so I could not fail to notice a story about the Oratorian Order of priests and brothers. It regarded completion of the façade over the south door of their church in Brompton. Construction had begun two years earlier and was nearing completion.

Consternation had arisen within their ranks after it was announced that the statue of St John the Baptist appearing in the original design of the promising young architect (and recent convert), Herbert Gribble, had been supplanted by a statue of the Virgin. The reporter found it worthy of note to identify both devices as Gribble's work. A final decision was expected within the fortnight. It seemed a tempest in a Holy Water stoup to me.

The rest of my afternoon was taken up reading about the high-minded, conscientious Queen Anne. The biography was somewhat less than accurate, based as it was, on the Duchess of Marlborough's malicious memoirs. [6]

It was near tea-time when the front doorbell rang. The setting sun cast long shadows across the floor. Surely it was too early for the urchins to begin making their rounds?

In the event, Florinda, the tweenie, brought a calling card on her salver announcing my visitor to be a Doctor Jasper Anstruther. Wondering how I might assist a medical professional. Doctor Johnson's gentle wisdom came to mind: *"Curiosity is, in great and generous minds, the first passion and the last."* I instructed Florinda to let the gentleman know that I was in.

Rising from my chair. I watched the doctor in the foyer remove hat, overcoat, and gloves. A tall, well-formed gentleman, Doctor Jasper Anstruther, walked with a slight stoop, leaning heavily on a silver-headed walking stick. His Brilliantined hair was severely-cut and prematurely greying.

The doctor's well-tailored clothing, gleaming silk hat, and chamois gloves of the finest make, not to mention his boots, the best found in Bond Street, proclaimed him a physician catering exclusively to the carriage trade. Milords and ladies, the landed gentry, men of property – these were the patients who met within the confines of his consulting room.

No expectant fathers pounded on his door hours before sunrise. He would never be called on to cross town in a mad dash to dose a Kensington doxy or patch up a fumbling Whitechapel cutpurse.

In treating ailments afflicting the affluent, Doctor Anstruther was less concerned with leeching black eyes than with preaching the benefits of banting. [7] Any broken bones he set came from patients playing cricket or leaping a tennis net. In short, he treated gout, never scurvy.

Behind his silver-rimmed *pince-nez* was a friendly, open face. Have you noticed, my dear doctor, how the puffiness surrounding your friend's watery blue eyes offsets his obvious intelligence with an air of dissipation? He seems anemic. Has he a kidney disease?

Doctor Anstruther offered his hand and begged my pardon in a friendly yet distracted manner. He told me he had first gone to the Club but was directed to find me at home.

Asking me to forgive his intrusion upon my time, he then explained that having spoken to his "professional neighbor in Paddington," you – my dear Doctor Watson – about an odd situation having taken place the day before which was preying on his mind. [8] You, in turn, having "great confidence" in my abilities, suggested he seek my help.

I told Doctor Anstruther that my contact with you was irregular, but I was aware of how highly esteemed you were by my late brother, and I would do what I could to be of some help. [9]

I rang for the maid and informed Nora that there would be another for tea.

"I hope I can live up to Doctor Watson's expectations," I said. "Allow me to point out that you were previously in Her Majesty's Navy – I would suggest as a commissioned officer?"

"Indeed, that is so!" Doctor Anstruther admitted, a note of astonishment in his voice "How could you know?"

"The tip of an anchor tattoo appears on your wrist, just below your shirt-cuff. Your demeanor suggests that of an officer. And you have clipped your moustache with precise military fastidiousness."

The doctor's brow knotted. "Could not a decent barber have done as well?"

"Too be sure," I agreed, "Yet, despite pomading your hair, it is obvious that it could stand a cutting. A good barber would never have allowed you to leave his establishment without attending to both your tonsorial needs."

"Well, sir," said Anstruther with a dry snort, "that's putting your brains to good work. Very well, I'm convinced that you're the man who can solve my problem."

At the sight of his obvious prosperity, I recalled, dear doctor, our first chat in the Stanger's Room—telling me how impressed you had been by Sherlock's inference that you had the more lucrative practice since your steps were worn down three inches more than your neighbor's. After meeting Doctor Anstruther, I realized my brother's deduction was so much twaddle. [10] Despite his oft-stated warnings to the contrary, Sherlock occasionally falls victim to making bricks without clay.

Getting back to my visitor, I waved him into the barrel chair opposite my own and asked him to tell me his tale.

"Since our practices adjoin each other," the doctor explained, "we alternate as each other's occasional *locum*. [11] An incident I found quite baffling occurred this week as I sat in my consulting room."

Nora returned with tea and cakes. As she poured, the doctor reached into the breast pocket of his frockcoat and took out a small Bible bound in soft, pebbled, black leather. Between its pages was a small white envelope. He handed me both.

I inspected the envelope. In an almost illegible scrawl was written the word "*Doctor*" above the Paddington address. The same hand had printed the following words:

> *From the sole of the foot even unto the head there is no soundness in it; But wounds, and bruises, and putrefying sores: They have not been closed, neither bound up, neither mollified with ointment.*

> *Isaiah I:VI*

The envelope was of ordinary bond. The address and message had been written with a double broad nib by a person using his off-hand. The Biblical citation was written on a page of yellow, lined paper torn from a pad, such as used by solicitors. Holding up the paper to the light, I noticed two circular marks, presumably left by a pair of pint glasses set down on the pad before the message was written, indicating the likelihood of its being written in a pub.

"How came you by the Bible and message?" I asked.

He cleared his throat, "Well, yesterday morning one of those Roman chaps – a priest, you know – made a call at my practice. He gave his name as Father Genesius O'Toole, belonging to the Oratorian order."

I immediately recalled the story from the morning paper.

"Truly? That's certainly of interest."

I rose from my chair, crossed the room to sit at my heavy oaken desk, and opened its rolltop reaching for a sheet of foolscap and a pen.

"Pardon me but I should like to take down your description of this man."

"He is, I would say, about twenty-five years," recalled the doctor, "a shortish young man, perhaps five-feet, six-inches in height. He had close-set blue eyes, a round head, with straight, light-brown hair brushed down over his forehead.

"May I ask the reason for his visit, if it is not a breach of ethics?"

144

The doctor shrugged. "Oh, I can't see any harm in it. Said he'd felt done in for several weeks and hoped I might suggest a good tonic to bring him back up to snuff for all his religious duties."

"Can you describe his attire?"

"Well, let's see," Doctor Anstruther began after taking a sip of tea. "He wore a black low-crowned hat with a circular brim. He also wore one of those long black gowns with a fringed sash around the middle into which he had thrust this very Bible, which he wore on his hip."

"I believe the gowns are called *soutanes*," I interjected as I started writing on a second piece of paper. "You examined him, of course. What else was he wearing?"

"He wore a pair of black trousers and a white shirt with that backward-style collar Roman clergymen prefer. I noticed that his shoes were a little down at the heel, if that is of any help."

"And your diagnosis?"

"Oh, definitely anemic. Told him to get out in the sun more. See if he could arrange to eat more red meat and liver," he said, picking up his plate with two small tea cakes on it.

"I prescribed ferrous sulphate tablets of 5.02 grains. To be taken twice per day," he added before taking a bite of cake.

Looking up from my desk and turning round to Doctor Anstruther, I asked, "Getting back to this message, did he hand it to you when he paid?"

The doctor's brows knotted again.

"Well, that is the odd part. As he was dressing, I wrote out a prescription and handed it to him. I then made out a receipt for two pounds, telling him I was remitting one pound since he was a man of the cloth. Having rebuttoned his, ah, *soutane*, he looked up and said, 'Gold or silver have I none but such as I have I will give thee.' [12]

"So saying, he drew his Bible from his sash, flung it at me, and bolted out of my consulting room and into the street. I attempted to give chase, but he was a good fifteen years younger than me, and my legs aren't the best, anyway. By the time I reached my front door, he had vanished. Not knowing what else to do, I burst out with a hearty laugh and yelled after him, 'Pon my word, sir, this is the first time some blighter has used the Testament for the purpose of avoiding a payment!'

"Returning to my inner chamber I retrieved the Bible, discovered the unsealed envelope still within, opened it and read the citation from Isaiah. This is what I told Doctor Watson and why I am now here."

I considered his story for a moment.

"Your practice is close by Saint Mary's Hospital in Praed Street, I believe?"

"Yes, quite close."

"You acted as *locum* for Doctor Watson this week, I dare say."

"Why, yes, on Monday and Tuesday."

"This is Thursday and Mister O'Toole visited you on Wednesday."

"Father O'Toole you mean."

"Mister," said I. "The man you describe was not a priest, Roman or otherwise."

He blinked three times, rubbed his eyes, and said, "Forgive me Mr. Holmes, but I – I saw the *soutane*."

"Oh, I have no doubt of that," I said. "but alas, certain anomalies within your strange but detailed narrative leave no doubt that this man took advantage of your unfamiliarity with Catholic customs and practices for his own purposes.

"He very likely read the same article I did about the Oratorian Order finishing up a church. But real Oratorians do not wear the Roman collar. They wear a soft, *revers* collar over the black tops of their *soutanes*. That was the first anomaly.

"The second was that they do not carry small Bibles in their sashes. Their Latin prayerbooks, called *breviaries*, resemble Bibles to the untrained eye, but they contain daily readings and chants: Psalms, prayers, parts of the Gospel, and tales about various saints which all priests are bounden to chant or read at certain hours.

"And the third anomaly is that even if they did carry Bibles, they certainly would not carry the Anglican Authorized Version. Catholics have their own English translation, you know. The Authorized Version is forbidden for Catholics to read, having been put on The Index long ago." [13]

Looking again at the quote from Isaiah, it seemed that might be a connection.

"On Monday or Tuesday, while acting for Dr. Watson, had you a patient seeking a cure for with an open wound, running sore, or some skin disease? Perhaps something on the order of *tinea pedis*? Something which the patient claimed to have suffered from for a period of time?" [14]

"Why, yes, I did!" my visitor exclaimed after a moment's recollection. "A pretty, though tartish young woman, perhaps five-feet-two-inches tall, with curling, blonde hair, very blue eyes, a short nose and freckles. Her breath, however, was extremely odiferous. The name she gave, I believe, was Henrietta Jenkins."

"Excellent! Thank you for the description," I nodded, adding the particulars to my note. "Now, tell me what occurred during her call."

I examined her feet and wrote a prescription for an ointment which she disparaged, saying she had used it before to no avail. She then removed a one-pound note from within her blouse, slapped it on the desk, then flounced out of the office."

I put the sheets upon which I had been writing in an envelope. Ringing for Florinda, I gave her with a five-pound note, bidding her take the message to the corner telegraph office to be sent to the address on the front.

"Well, Doctor," said I, "this Miss Jenkins is working with the O'Toole creature.. Since you were acting for your neighbor, first the woman, then the man, believed you were actually Doctor Watson.

"Meeting in a nearby pub, Jenkins told O'Toole what had happened in your office. They seem to have some knowledge of Scripture and found the text from Isaiah concerning putrefying sores being left unalleviated by ointment as fitting the situation, As you had prescribed the same ointment other doctors had without success, the two thought up this prank as an extravagant Guy Fawkes Day charade with O'Toole playing a sham priest. The ruse was concocted simply to taunt you."

Doctor Anstruther considered my explanation a moment or two then gave a short laugh. "Why, yes, that must be the answer. As you explain it, all the puzzle pieces fall into place."

Finishing his cup of tea, my visitor stood up and, taking my hand, was most effusive in his thanks. Waiving away his offer to pay for my time, I let him know I found his tale a pleasant diversion of an afternoon. He graciously invited me to stop by his practice should I ever have some medical need.

Collecting his habiliments, Dr. Anstruther walked out the door and into the crowded streets as the frolicking and merriment of Guy Fawkes Night commenced.

This is where the tale ended originally, Doctor Watson, and I dare say that you and Doctor Anstruther shared some laughter over the Biblical scorn for poor doctoring. In fact, the situation was not quite finished at this point.

The citation from Isaiah was certainly aimed at you, Doctor, but it had nothing at all to do with disease – it was a deadly threat.

With Sherlock supposed to be dead, the Government's hands were tied in some respects. In my story, I tell of sending Florinda, my tweenie, to the telegraph office. The telegram she sent for me, concerning Doctor Anstruther's descriptions of his two visitors, was sent to the Home Secretary.

You recall I mentioned the marks of two pints of beer being set on the paper containing the quote from Isaiah? With your and Anstruther's medical practices so near Saint Mary's Hospital in Praed Street, I suggested the Home Secretary wire the Commissioner of Police. with instructions to send two of his men to the Fountains Abbey pub, also in Praed Street. They were to be on the lookout for O'Toole and Jenkins. The day had not ended before the two were apprehended and detained by Scotland Yard.

A telegram from Inspector Athelney Jones identified the young man and woman as "for hire" to anyone with the money to pay for burglary, smash and grab, and other minor crimes. They have yet to be caught in the act, but have been seen in the vicinity where a crime has occurred.

I was unable to explain at that time, Doctor, but Colonel Sebastian Moran, Mr. Moriarty's lieutenant, had been spying on your movements, having taken it into his head that you knew where my brother was concealing himself. I believe he came to this conclusion when your accounts of Sherlock's cases began appearing in *Strand Magazine* two months after my brother's disappearance and reported death. [15]

A custom has grown up among some of London's criminal gangs to send veiled threats to each other using curses, imprecations, and maledictions found in Holy Writ. Moran paid the Jenkins woman to come to your office with a real medical complaint. That done, O'Toole, in the guise of a priest, was sent with the threat culled from Isaiah. Moran's intent was to threaten you so that, when he confronted you demanding to know of Sherlock place of concealment, you would comply without putting yourself or your good wife in danger.

Unfortunately for the Colonel, Jenkins and O'Toole bungled it. You, Doctor Watson, were gone and they mistook Doctor Anstruther, who obviously never identified himself as acting as your *locum,* for you.

Since you had no idea that Sherlock was alive, let alone where he was travelling, this persecution had to be brought to a quick end. I thus fought fire with fire, so to speak, by using O'Toole's Bible to convey to Moran a message from the Foreign Office, not mentioning myself at all.

The way I sent my message was to use a double-broad nib to write a series of Biblical citations from Genesis, in order, in an envelope marked *Moran*. The words I wanted Moran to read I had underlined with pinpricks thus:

> Genesis 19:17: *stay*
> Genesis 2:10: *out of*
> Genesis 2:23: *my*
> Genesis 3:24: *way*
> Genesis 13:9: *or*
> Genesis 2:9: *evil*
> Genesis 2:18: *will*

Genesis 42:4: *befall*
Genesis 3:11: *thee*

Scotland Yard returned the Bible to O'Toole with directions to give it and the envelope to Colonel Moran, and make no mistake about it.

The old hunter understood the threat, and that it was backed up with the might of Her Majesty's Government. He left you alone from then on. He was unable to trace Sherlock until that fateful night earlier this year, when you and my brother were able to bag him as he attempted to shoot my brother.

I hope, my friend, that the true details of the problem which baffled Doctor Anstruther may somehow find their way into your adventures.

And now, the calendar shows that, come three weeks, the strains of *"Remember, remember, the fifth of November, Gunpowder Treason and Plot!"* shall again be heard across London.

We have come full circle. And I shall again keep to my rooms. Yet I shall continue to regard you, Doctor Watson,

With sincere best wishes,
Mycroft Holmes

NOTES

1. Non-cigar aficionados will want to know that *"habano"* refers to the dark colored leaves cut from the top of tobacco plants. These are used to wrap the filler tobacco in cigars, imparting a strong, slightly sweet, flavor.

2. *"In some manner he had learned of my own sad bereavement, and his sympathy was shown in his manner rather than in his words."* and *"Work is the best antidote to sorrow, my dear Watson."* (From "The Empty House".) We see that Sherlock Holmes's source for this knowledge was very likely Mycroft. This sadness is often taken to be the death of Watson's first wife, the former Mary Morstan, heroine of *The Sign of Four*.

3. Henry Edward Cardinal Manning (1808-1892), along with Herbert Alfred Cardinal Vaughan (1832-1903), were successive Archbishops of Westminster following the reestablishment of the Catholic hierarchy in England by Blessed Pius IX in 1850. Nicholas Cardinal Wiseman was the first to hold the office, dying in 1865, succeeded by Manning. The Catholic hierarchy begun by St. Augustine of Canterbury in 597 ended when Queen Mary died (1558). The reestablishment was not popular. The attitude taken by *The Times* (14 October, 1850), labeling the site in London for the archbishopric as either a *"clumsy joke"* or else *"one of the grossest acts of folly and impertinence which the Court of Rome has ventured to commit since the Crown and the people of England threw off its yoke,"* reflected the feelings of many in England.

4. Mycroft's Latin lament is translated *"Bread and circuses, world without end"* (literally, *"through all ages of ages"* – sometimes rendered as the more banal phrase, *"forever and ever"*).

5. The merriment of Guy Fawkes Night is similar to the U.S. celebration of Halloween as observed in former times, as a boisterous festival for children without the month-long assault of candy adverts. The annual event in England celebrates the failed Gunpowder Plot of 1605. A group of English Catholics, tired of persecution and the loss of basic human rights, hoped to assassinate Protestant King James I and substitute a Catholic monarch in his place. On November 5th, Guy Fawkes was arrested while guarding a great pile of explosives ready to be touched off beneath the House of Lords as soon as the King arrived.

6. Anne, younger daughter of James II and last reigning monarch of the House of Stewart in 1702, followed the joint monarchy of William and Mary. An assiduous ruler, Anne was, by the Acts of Union (1707), the first to reign over the kingdoms of England, Scotland and Ireland united as a single sovereign entity known as Great Britain. The Duchess of Marlborough was Sarah Churchill, one of Sir Winston's forebears. She had been Anne's closest friend. They fell out over policy. Until the mid-twentieth century, Sarah's spiteful memoirs have colored opinions of Queen Anne among less critical historians.

7. *Banting*: William Banting (1796-1878) wrote a booklet detailing the first known low-carb, high-fat diet. He eliminated all grains, granular sugar,

vegetable and seed oils, and grains, specifically wheat. His booklet became so popular "banting" became another word for dieting.

8. In "The Boscombe Valley Mystery", the now-married Watson, invited to join one of Holmes' investigations, hesitates, citing a long list of patients to be seen. "*Oh, Anstruther would do your work for you,*" says Watson's wife, the former Mary Morstan.

9. Watson's short accounts of the Holmes adventures began appearing in the pages of *The Strand Magazine* in June 1891, garnering great acclaim after a very short time.

10. Holmes's deduction about Watson's practice by looking at his front steps, was included by the doctor in the opening of "The Stockbroker's Clerk".

11. The seasoned Sherlockian likely will not need to know the definition. For others, *locum tenens* is a Latin phrase meaning, "*to hold the place of*". In other words, a professional who is called on, for a generally short length of time, to take the place of another in the same profession, used especially regarding a doctor or a clergyman. Watson's wife's remark about Dr Anstruther has already been noted: In "The Stockbroker's Clerk", Watson declares, "*I do my neighbor's when he goes. He is always ready to work off the debt.*" And when Holmes asks for his friend's company in "The Final Problem", Watson replies, "*The practice is quiet,*" said I, "*and I have an accommodating neighbor.*"

12. Acts 3:6. Simon Peter's reply to a lame beggar seeking alms before raising him up and bidding him walk, the Apostle's first miraculous cure following the Ascension of Jesus.

13. *The Index of Forbidden Books* (*Index Librorum Prohibitorum* in Latin) began informally with Pope Gelasius I, c. 496 who recommended some books to Catholics and forbade to read others that he found malignantly harmful to their faith and morality. During the Council of Trent (1545-1563) the first printed *Index* was published in 1559 by the Sacred Congregation of the Roman Inquisition (precursor to the Sacred Congregation for the Doctrine of the Faith). The Authorized "King James" Version was on the *Index*, not due its translation, but because of its pernicious footnotes attacking, denying, mocking, and even misstating aspects of Catholic belief.

14. *Tinea pedis*: The medical terminology for "*athlete's foot*".

15. Sherlock Holmes and Professor Moriarty fought in May 1891. The following July, the first of Dr Watson's short accounts appeared, "A Scandal in Bohemia".

The Riddle of the Rideau Rifles

by Peter Calamai
From *Part II: 1890-1895* (2015)

As I write these lines, a dreadful darkness is descending over the civilized world. In Europe, only Britain, Ireland, and neutral Sweden and Switzerland remain free from the Nazis, and yet the United States of America remains on the sidelines as Herr Hitler extends his mailed grip around the Mediterranean and North Africa. Canada and the other self-governing Dominions are doing all they can to help our Mother Country. But without the industrial and military might of America on our side soon, I fear for the future of humanity.

This is not a propitious time to make public the tale which I recount here. Its publication now could arouse further those isolationist and anti-war sentiments already too evident among our neighbours to the south. But it is a story which the world should hear someday, and while I am still able I must record how brilliant detective work averted what would have been a calamitous international incident between Canada and the United States.

Yet I am getting ahead of myself. In writing this narrative I have drawn upon my personal diaries and other original documents in my possession. Once I completed my task I destroyed those documents, lest others reveal matters that I believe must remain forever secret. To my nephew Jonathan – or indeed to his progeny – I leave the decision about when to publish this account of the wisest man I have ever known.

Bartholomew Evans
Ottawa, November, 1940.

The little water remaining in the Rideau Canal was still frozen solid that March Tuesday in 1894 when the Private Secretary informed me that the Prime Minister, Sir John Thompson, wished to see me. I hurried along the corridor in the Centre Block where I, a very junior aide, was privileged to share a cramped office with several other young men. To my surprise, I was instantly ushered into the Prime Minister's office.

"Evans, I have an important task for you," Sir John said without preamble. "Read these."

152

From a pile on his desk, the Prime Minister handed me what I recognized, even at that early stage of my career, as a sheaf of state papers. Or more precisely, fair copies of those papers. They revealed an astonishing development.

That great Liberal, William Gladstone, then Prime Minister of Great Britain for the fourth (and final) time, had written my Prime Minister, soliciting his support publicly for a movement called the Anglo-American reunion, which sought the ultimate federation of the entire English-speaking world.

"We would thus repair the ruction with America caused by the folly of George III and the blundering of Lord North," Gladstone wrote.

Sir John had replied (no doubt also by diplomatic bag) that he was well disposed toward the idea, but domestic circumstances forbade any public show of support. His letter then marshalled facts of which I had been utterly unaware.

My Prime Minister said mysterious elements in Ottawa had begun fomenting anti-American sentiment within the past year, and their machinations had found favour in his own caucus and, indeed, even within his cabinet. Despite discreet yet concerted inquiries by Colonel Arthur Percy Sherwood of the Dominion Police, the source of this campaign remained unidentified.

"Until it is known and scotched, my hands are tied and I dare not act as you request," Thompson had written.

The third and last letter was the response from Gladstone. He well understood Thompson's predicament, he wrote, and had a possible solution to offer. With our approval, the British Prime Minister would dispatch a personal representative to investigate the anti-American phenomenon. Although the investigator was as yet unknown to the wider world, his detecting talents were highly recommended by Mr. Gladstone's closest advisor, a man who sometimes constituted the entire British government because of his unparalleled knowledge of every portfolio.

"I agreed, of course, Evans. What else could I do? I have just had a cable saying that this man is arriving by train in an hour. Apparently his name is Sigerson. Your task is to offer him every assistance, acting with my full authority. But keep me informed as well."

So overwhelmed was I by this sudden revelation of domestic unrest and secret prime ministerial investigations that it was all I could manage to stammer my assent and retreat from Sir John's presence, clutching the sheaf of papers. A quick consultation with the Private Secretary revealed that a suite of rooms had been booked at the Russell Hotel for Mr. Sigerson.

I met Gladstone's representative at the station what seemed like mere minutes later. My first impressions were favourable. Mr. Sigerson carried himself with a quiet authority beyond his years, which I judged to be about forty. Spaced widely above an aquiline nose, his grey eyes darted constantly, taking in details. When we shook hands his grip was firm, and his figure, while slight, was wiry. He stood perhaps an inch or more taller than my five-foot-ten. I judged that Mr. Sigerson would be a good fellow to have beside you in an altercation, should our mission come to that. Just as I completed this surveillance, he spoke:

"I am going to address you as Evans and you should call me Sigerson, now that you've taken my measure," he said with a wry smile. "Our first order of business must be to gather data. I cannot make bricks without straw."

I was to discover in our short time together that Sigerson (as I indeed came to call him) was given to uttering such homilies leaning heavily toward Biblical and classical allusions. From this habit and his precise manner of speaking, I judged that he was a university man like myself, although a product of the English system and a decade my senior. Yet I failed utterly during the next few days to draw from him whether he had attended Oxford or Cambridge.

My own university connections from Queen's, however, could serve us well for this sensitive mission. Many of my fellows were now placed within the federal government as I was, not yet exercising great authority, but in positions where their fingers rested on many quivering strands of information.

We agreed that we would conceal Sigerson's real mission in Ottawa, telling people instead that he was an academic from Norway making a study of Canada-U.S. relations as a possible parallel to Scandinavia. We left his bags at the Russell and took the chance of calling on two of my Queen's connections without making appointments.

In the first of what turned out to be continual surprises, not only did Sigerson immediately begin to speak English with what sounded to my ears like a Norwegian lilt, but he also somehow contrived to *appear* Scandinavian, if not actually Norwegian.

Unfortunately, the first interview with a university contemporary elicited little more than some embarrassing sobriquets by which I had been known in certain undergraduate circles. The second classmate, however, suggested it might be worthwhile for us to talk with a friend of his, Jack Wells, who was with the detective service of the Ottawa city police.

"I will send a note saying that you will call this afternoon. If there have been any day-to-day incidents arising from tensions between Canada and the U.S., Jack is the fellow to know," said my classmate.

154

After a modest lunch, we walked to the police station and were quickly shown into the office of Detective Inspector Jack Wells. Events intervened even as we took our seats.

"I apologize if I seem somewhat distracted, gentlemen, but I received information of the most distressing nature only hours ago," said Wells. A few questions from Sigerson drew out the whole story.

A promising young detective constable named O'Reilly had been killed in a fall early that morning, apparently after a bar room brawl. His battered body, reeking of liquor, had been found on the stone bottom of a drained lock of the Rideau Canal, adjacent to an old government building known as the Commissariat.

"It's a black eye for the force, sure enough, but worse than that, his family won't be eligible for any pension because he wasn't on duty when he died. And the wife has two small children to rear by herself."

"What ought O'Reilly to have been investigating, Inspector?" I asked.

"Smuggling, Mr. Evans. We have reason to believe that someone is attempting to smuggle explosives into Canada. It could be some latter-day remnants of the Fenians."

I quickly informed Sigerson about the rag-tag Irish-American nationalists who had sought thirty years earlier to "capture" Canada and hold it hostage until Britain granted independence to Ireland. With the exception of one raid, their military forays into Canada had been failures and, by the early 1870's, the Fenian Brotherhood had vanished.

"I should like to examine the constable's body," Sigerson said without preamble. "My knowledge of advanced forensic techniques has proven useful to authorities in the past."

Wells replied, "I don't see that any harm can arise from that. We will do anything to get to the bottom of this tragedy."

In the station's basement mortuary, Sigerson drew from an inner coat pocket a magnificent brass-bound magnifying glass. Not that one was needed to see the terrible bruises, mottled yellow and purple, which covered almost every part of the constable's body. Instead, Sigerson studiously applied his glass to the man's hands, wrists, forearms and ankles. From one wrist he plucked something with a pair of tweezers, placing it in a small envelope. He did the same with a scraping from the sole of one of the constable's shoes.

"Your constable didn't die as a result of a bar room brawl or even a tumble onto the lock bottom, Inspector," Sigerson announced as we mounted the station stairs. "He was beaten to death by several men who used clubs and also their feet, and they delivered the fatal blows when he

155

was bound and unable to defend himself. It was homicide, likely deliberate murder."

"You astonish me, Mr. Sigerson. How can you possibly know this?" asked Wells.

"Because the constable himself told me, or rather the evidence of his body did. The backs of his hands and forearms are cut and battered, the classic wounds suffered by someone trying to defend himself against a superior force which overwhelmed him in an initial assault.

"Rope burns around his ankles and wrists indicate he was struggling against restraints. I would hypothesize that he was beaten while bound in an attempt to extract some information. When your police surgeon performs an autopsy, he will likely discover many broken ribs, and possibly tibia and fibula as well. Those would not result from your standard drunken brawl."

The Inspector was beside himself with excitement.

"If this is true, it will be a capital piece of good news in this sorry affair, Mr. Sigerson. Not only would it remove the stain from the constable's character, and from the force's, but it would go a long way toward convincing the commissioners to award a service pension to O'Reilly's widow. Is there no way to obtain some evidentiary proof?"

Sigerson replied: "I took the liberty of removing a small sample of the rope fibre that was adhering to the constable's skin. With access to a dark-field microscope, I expect to identify its origin. I have written a small monograph about distinguishing fibres of the seventy-three most common ropes."

As luck would have it, another of my Queen's contemporaries had recently been seconded as an assistant to George M. Dawson, the second-in-command of the Geological Survey of Canada, which was Canada's oldest scientific agency. The survey was housed in a former hotel on Sussex Street and would have the latest in microscopes. I undertook to get in touch with my colleague and arrange access to the specialized equipment for a "distinguished scientific visitor from Norway." Sigerson and I agreed to reconvene Wednesday at the hotel.

That morning we called first upon Jephro Clarke, also a friend from college. He turned out to possess an ample supply of the sort of "straw" sought by the British/Norwegian investigator to form the "bricks" of his case.

"Yes, I myself have noticed anti-American sentiments about town, and not just the letters to the editor in the *Free Press*, *Journal*, and *Citizen*. They are particularly strong in a society to which I belong," Clarke confided.

156

"Pray tell us more, Mr. Clarke. Omit no detail, no matter how trivial it may seem to you," Sigerson urged.

"There is not much to relate, Mr. Sigerson. I am a member of the Hibernian Debating Society, an assemblage of good fellows who convene every Thursday evening for invigorating discourse about matters of topical concern. We normally gather in a meeting room of an inn on Duke Street and then adjourn downstairs afterwards to the public bar where the discussion continues, usually becoming somewhat more animated.

"Yet animus has never been a feature of our discussions, at least not until these past months. A few members began voicing opinions antagonistic towards our American neighbours, and the sentiment seems to have gained a hold, certainly among some of the more vocal members."

"Is there anything which distinguishes these particular men?" I asked. Sigerson shot me what I imagined was a look of approval.

"Not really, Bart. They're relatively new here in town but mostly from up the Valley, so there's the usual touch of Irish somewhere in their background. You hear traces of it when they talk. But they're solid fellows. I had occasion to recommend two of them, a father and son, to my superior for employment when we were faced with a sudden double vacancy at the Commissariat."

At the second mention in two days of this building, Sigerson raised a quizzical eyebrow, and Clarke elaborated. Like me, he was a personal aide, in his case to the Deputy Minister of Militia and Defence. The department was responsible for the Commissariat Building, a substantial stone edifice beside the lowermost locks of the Rideau Canal. Dating from 1827, the building had originally stored tools and equipment during the canal construction. For the past four decades, it had served as a storehouse for military goods, with an armourer and carpenter actually living on the premises. The current holders of those posts had been recruited from the Hibernia membership after the previous incumbents were discharged by the Clerk of Military Stores, the official with day-to-day responsibility for the building.

"I am heading over that way myself on a small errand, gentlemen. If you would like to accompany me I can show you around and introduce you to the Pattersons, father and son."

It was but a short walk to the west side of the locks and a gentle descent from Parliament Hill (formerly Barrack Hill) to the Commissariat. Somewhat to my surprise, Sigerson cross-questioned Clarke about the changing uses of the building and the various structural additions and subtractions. This inquisition continued as we toured the three floors, with Clarke throwing open doors to reveal stores of tunics, boots, infantry greatcoats, serge trousers, forage caps, braces, brushes for hair, shoes and cloth, button sticks, eating utensils, and all else necessary to keep a battalion of soldiers well shod, well clothed and well fed.

On the second floor, Sigerson opened one door himself. "This is far neater than I would have expected," he murmured.

"I believe that room is used for training purposes," responded Clarke, who did not look in. My quick glance revealed a dozen or so unmatched wooden chairs arrayed around three walls, while windows in the fourth gave a view out to the Ottawa River. Several coils of heavy rope were piled in a corner, leaving most of the floor unobstructed, probably for training demonstrations as Clarke had said. This interpretation was reinforced by the spotless nature of the floorboards, which were obviously scoured regularly.

On the main floor, a storeroom held rows of wooden crates of Snider and Martini-Henry breech-loading rifles, plus metal ammunition cases. Here Sigerson again withdrew his magnifying glass and proceeded to examine the rifle crates minutely, even dropping down onto the floor to look more closely at some detail.

He paid the same close attention to the work spaces used by the armourer and carpenter. As he was finishing that inspection, the Pattersons walked in and were introduced by Clarke. He and I moved off a few paces as Sigerson engaged the father and son in animated conversation.

"Well that was two hours very profitably spent," Sigerson said, rejoining us.

As we climbed back to street level, I informed Sigerson that he could call at the Geological Survey at his convenience to use the microscope, and he decided to go at once.

Meanwhile, I pursued my own line of inquiry. At Sigerson's request, I was to uncover everything I could about the Clerk of Military Stores, the official who had summarily dismissed the previous armourer and carpenter at the Commissariat.

This proved a more difficult task than I had imagined. Ottawa was then (and is even now) really a very small town, despite being the national capital. All persons of note are known to one another and information circulates quickly about their character and any particular foibles. But although several of my coterie could name this shadowy figure as Benjamin Saunders, none could provide any other details. Finally, through the friend of a friend of a friend, I was able to glimpse the personnel file of the man who effectively commanded the Commissariat and maintained an office there. Brimming with fresh information, I rushed back to the Russell Hotel.

Sigerson was curled comfortably into a basket chair in front of the blazing hearth in his sitting room, a darkened cherrywood pipe in one hand. From the opacity of the room's air, I hazarded that he had smoked more than one pipe.

"Yes, this is fully a three-pipe problem, my good Evans. Please tell what your inquiries have uncovered."

Restraining my excitement I marshalled and summarized the facts as logically as I knew how, for Sigerson seemed to prize ratiocination above all other virtues.

"The Clerk of Military Stores is Benjamin Saunders, although perhaps I should say Colonel Saunders, for it was his military service in the British Army which secured him the post only last year. One of his letters of recommendation came from his superior, the commanding officer of the Irish Guards.

"But the most interesting fact lies in Colonel Saunders' outside activities. My friend Clarke confirms that the clerk is an active member of the Hibernian Debating Society. Clarke also now recollects that it was Saunders who first drew the Pattersons to his attention as possible replacement artisans at the Commissariat, whose hiring Clarke in turn recommended to his Deputy Minister."

"Did you discover anything further about the two men who left so precipitately?" Sigerson asked casually, blowing out a smoke ring.

"They have disappeared from town so I could not talk with them. But from all accounts, they had given satisfaction right up to the time when they were summarily dismissed by Saunders."

Sigerson appeared to be digesting this information and for a minute his eyes strayed toward a violin case on the window sill. With a shrug, he turned again to me.

"My own inquiries were also productive, Evans. The Survey indeed possessed the requisite microscope and I was able to identify the fibres which I took from Constable O'Reilly's wrist. They come from a particular type of tarred rope manufactured exclusively for the Royal Navy, although it is sometimes also supplied to Britain's colonies if they are raising their own fleets, as I understand Canada is.

"Making use of this information requires us to have been especially observant. Would you please provide me with a description of the empty room we saw at the Commissariat, my dear Evans?"

It was a test, and I strove to come up to the mark, repeating the details mentioned earlier.

"Have I missed anything of importance, Sigerson," I inquired.

"Only everything," he replied with a sigh. "You see, Evans, but you do not observe. In contrast, I immediately noticed a ladderback chair along the west wall which showed rope wear on the lower portion of the front legs. And in that pile of ropes, the top coil was a tarred hemp which I wager will match the fibres from the constable's wrists.

"As well, the spotless nature of the floor is suspicious in a room devoted to training. I fear the floor had been only recently scrubbed to remove blood stains, and that it was in that room that Constable O'Reilly received his fatal final beating. Despite poisoning myself with three pipes, however, I am no closer to understanding how he got there and why someone thought his death was necessary."

I was beginning to lose patience with this self-indulgent performance. "Is there anything else I should have noticed at the Commissariat, Mr. Sigerson?" I asked with some asperity.

"I draw your attention to the curious use of nails in the end pieces of the gun crates. Also worth a second look are the stocks of wooden dowels beside the carpenter's bench."

He could not be drawn further on that point. Over dinner in the hotel dining room, he instead expounded knowledgeably about an astonishing range of subjects, from the bimetallic question of Montreal to the great herd of bisons of the fertile plains and the breeding cycle of the stormy petrels of British Columbia.

"I have some private inquiries to make during the day tomorrow, so perhaps we can meet here in the late afternoon and partake of some more of the hotel's excellent cooking. As well, it would be best if you could acquire a set of clothes suitable for a labourer."

"What sort of labourer?"

"Oh, nothing too exotic, someone along the lines of a beamster, wheel tapper, drayman, pot burner, or knacker. Even a guard lacer would do, although it might be too early in the year for their activity."

I am positive that Sigerson was hiding a smile behind his hand as he ran through this list of occupations, still common then toward the end of the Victorian era but likely unknown to many as I write.

Late the following afternoon, dressed as a drayman, I called at Sigerson's rooms. Instead of the investigator, I was greeted by a fellow of coarse appearance, the lower part of his face obscured by a black beard and his stout body contorted from some sort of arthritic condition. His blackened fingers and stained vest front suggested daily toil with greasy machinery.

"Do you think I will pass as a plate-maker, Evans?" the apparition asked. His accent sounded like a kinsman to the Pattersons, father and son.

I was so completely deceived by Sigerson's disguise that it was some few seconds before I replied in the affirmative.

"We are bound for the Couillard Hotel, an establishment in one of the less salubrious parts of your nation's capital, an area called LeBreton Flats,

I believe. The Hibernian Debating Society will be holding its weekly discussions upstairs and then adjourn to the public bar. We will watch them from a quiet corner. If there is any talking to be done, pray let me do it. As you may have noticed, I have some small facility with accents and dialects."

The new Ottawa Electric Railway did not yet service that area, so we took a hack and had the driver let us off a short distance from the Duke Street location. As local residents, a drayman and a plate-maker obviously would arrive on foot. There was time only to settle ourselves at a secluded table with our pints before a dozen or so men descended the stairs. Among that number were the Pattersons and Colonel Saunders, but not my friend Clarke. Equally fortunate, I had been in the background when Sigerson spoke with the Pattersons at the Commissariat.

Just as I was congratulating myself on the success of our covert observations, Sigerson poured the remains of his bitter into my glass and approached the bar for a refill. While there, he made a point of talking with the Pattersons, who seemed to have no inkling of his true identity.

"Well, Evans, at last I am beginning to see the light," he said as he returned.

"I fear the case is still all dark to me," I replied.

"It is not my custom to divulge the outcome of my investigations until they are complete, a practice which sometimes causes distress to a regular companion in London." Sigerson paused and gazed briefly into the distance. A smile flickered across his bushy face.

"But matters stand differently with you, who have not had the opportunity to become inured to my difficult moods. So I will tell you the key to the whole puzzle. Those men are not, as you think from their speech, natives of the Ottawa Valley. They are in fact Irish Americans."

Not another word of explanation could I wrest from him that evening, as we sat and watched for another two hours until all the Society members had departed. As we stepped outside, Sigerson gave a triumphal cry and bent down to scoop up a finger's worth of the muddy clay protruding beside the boardwalk.

"The last piece of the puzzle," he ejaculated in triumph.

All I learned, however, was that I was to call at his rooms the next morning and also arrange through my friend Clarke for a ten o'clock rendezvous at the Commissariat to include the Pattersons, Colonel Saunders, and Clarke himself.

I remember that I did not get much sleep that night and called so early that Sigerson had only just completed his toilet. He insisted on ringing for breakfast, and shortly we were joined by Detective Inspector Wells. Yet

Sigerson's only reference to the case was to ensure that three constables from the Ottawa force would be present at the Commissariat.

On our walk to the Canal, he spoke of Archibald Lampman, a poet who was a public servant in Ottawa and whose work appeared in *Atlantic Monthly*, *Harper's*, and *Scribner's*. Both the Inspector and I confessed that we had never heard of Lampman or his book, *Among the Millet*. But Sigerson was an admirer and had called upon the young poet at the Post Office Department, offering praise and encouragement.

"Art in the blood is liable to take the strangest forms," he remarked enigmatically.

At the Commissariat, a choleric Colonel Saunders and a brace of truculent Pattersons awaited us.

"What is the meaning of this? Why am I being mustered like this on the say-so of some pettifogging youngster," the Colonel demanded, glaring at Clarke and then at the three uniformed constables hovering in the background.

Sigerson took charge masterfully, abandoning his Norwegian persona. He led the group to the room containing the workbenches and crates of rifles. There he explained that he was acting on behalf of Sir John Thompson, and indicated me as the Prime Minister's private secretary (a post I would, in fact, occupy later but with a different man.) His remit was to investigate the origin of recent anti-American feeling and discover how deep it went.

"And I can now answer those questions," he announced in a restrained tone. "The anti-Americanism is an elaborate hoax, a ploy to camouflage a much more sinister purpose. That goal was to stage an inconsequential armed attack against the United States, one in which no one was harmed, which would appear to have been carried out by forces from Canada, acting with official sanction. And the Commissariat served as the planning and training centre for all this."

Bedlam erupted. Who was behind such a plot? What was the intention? When would it be carried out? How? And did he have any evidence for this fantastical suggestion?

"You are looking at it," said Sigerson, pointing to a crate labelled as containing a dozen Martini-Henry rifles. "Rifles have been removed and cached for the putative assault, after which they will be abandoned as evidence of Canadian involvement."

"This is preposterous," Colonel Saunders exclaimed, stepping forward. "Try to lift that crate with the rope handles on the ends, and the weight will prove the rifles are there."

Sigerson continued in the same quiet voice. "Yes, I concede that the crate feels heavy enough to suggest nothing is amiss. The men behind this plot, although in my opinion seriously deluded, are at least cunning. Yet they were undone, as in that old adage, by something as common as a nail."

He tapped the end of the crate with his walking stick.

"I tried to draw Mr. Evans' attention to the peculiar nails in these endpieces. They are of a larger size than the nails used elsewhere in the crates. That is because the original nails have been extracted to remove the endpieces, which were modified and replaced. If you look carefully, you will also notice a few holes from the original nails in which someone failed to properly place the larger nails."

Sigerson offered his magnifying glass and the Inspector took a look.

"I dare say you are correct, Mr. Sigerson, but I don't see how this proves the rifles are missing, much less the serious plot you have alleged," he said.

"You have to ask yourself, Inspector, why nails were substituted in the endpieces. The most rational explanation is that longer nails were necessary to contain something extra added to the ends of the crates. My surmise is that this something extra is lead which Patterson senior, the armourer, crafted in sheets to fit. This additional weight was necessary to compensate for rifles which had been removed."

At this repeated allegation, Colonel Saunders erupted.

"This is a farrago of absurd suppositions and theories and I intend to expose it. Patterson, open this crate at once," he ordered the carpenter.

"Yes, please do," added Sigerson.

The cover was quickly off, revealing a top layer of three neatly arranged bundles. Despite the thick cloth swaddling, we could discern the tell-tale shape of a rifle.

"Go ahead, take one out and unwrap it for this gentleman," the Colonel told Patterson.

In a moment, the young man held out for inspection a Martini-Henry rifle still shiny with protective grease from the factory.

Sigerson stepped forward. "Mr. Clarke, would you be so kind as to remove a bundle from the second layer and unwrap it for us."

The Colonel moved so quickly that he eluded the outstretched arms of the Inspector and two constables. The third brought him down with a classic rugby tackle. When we looked round, Clarke was holding out a wooden replica of a Martini-Henry. Further investigation revealed that the crate had contained three actual rifles, nine replicas and sheets of lead in the endpieces.

"Copying the rifle stock in pine was a simple matter for a carpenter," Sigerson said. "But he needed something ready-made in the shape of a barrel. I attempted without success to interest Mr. Evans in the absurdly large supply of wooden dowelling here."

Inspector Wells was motioning his constables to take away the Pattersons and Colonel Saunders. "We will get the details of this plot from them back at the station, Mr. Sigerson."

"I have no doubt that you will, Inspector. But there is something much more serious about which you will also want to question these men than theft and this half-baked plot, as it would be called in Devon."

Without another word, Sigerson then led the entire company to that mostly empty drill practice room on the next floor.

"Here is where Constable O'Reilly was beaten to death, and these are some of the men who did it," he announced with more emotion than he had shown previously. This was the story he then unfolded.

The constable was indeed on the job Monday night and he had followed one of his smuggling suspects to the Couillard Hotel. Sigerson matched soil from O'Reilly's boot to the mud sample from outside the inn. ("I have written a small monograph about soil identification," he said.) Somehow the "Society" members drinking there concluded, erroneously, that the constable had tumbled to their plot. They overpowered him and took him to the Commissariat, where they roused the Pattersons in their living quarters.

Sigerson walked over to the wall and lifted out a ladderback chair. Then he gathered the top coil of rope from the corner.

"The constable was tied to this chair with that rope and systemically beaten to discover how much he knew. But it was all a terrible mistake. By the time the conspirators realized O'Reilly was following another trail altogether, it was too late. He now knew they were up to something even more diabolical. They felt they must kill him, which they did with blows to the head. They then doused his body with liquor to make it look as if he had been in a bar room brawl. After that they dropped him head-first onto the stones on the bottom of the empty lock in an attempt to conceal the true cause of the fatal head injuries. The inference would be that O'Reilly had stumbled into the lock in a drunken stupor – which is in fact the conclusion leapt to by his superiors."

From the looks the constables gave the Colonel and the Pattersons, I feared it would go much harder for them now back at the station.

Before going our separate ways, we had agreed to meet later for a final summing-up. It was a sombre group which gathered that afternoon in a conference room attached to the Prime Minister's office.

Sir John himself was present and listened with great attention as Sigerson recounted the events at the Commissariat and explained his deductive trail. Inspector Wells then reported that three other crates of rifles had been similarly tampered with, and that the missing rifles, along with numerous articles of official Canadian army gear and uniforms, had been recovered from a cache. Under vigorous questioning, the three men had confessed their participation in the plot and implicated others, including many members of the Hibernian Debating Society.

All but a few were American citizens, of Irish ancestry, who had been posing as Canadians from the Ottawa Valley. Colonel Saunders, however, insisted he was British, although of Irish sympathies, and denied any part in the fatal beating of Constable O'Reilly.

"I still can't quite fathom what they hoped to accomplish by all this," said the Prime Minister.

"Their plan contained far more passion than reason," Sigerson replied. "As latter-day Fenians, they were looking to thwart Britain at every turn. A strong federation of English-speaking people could only delay Irish independence, in their perverted view. So they came to Canada a year ago and began what amounted to a whispering campaign to make it seem that Canadians were becoming increasingly anti-American. The raid across the border would be the culmination, with your army's rifles and uniforms abandoned to implicate the Canadian government. No matter how strenuous the denials, there would be no way that the American public would accept stronger ties between our two countries under the guise of the proposed federation."

"What first alerted you to this plot, Mr. Sigerson?" asked the Prime Minister.

"The Pattersons' accents. It was obvious at once to my trained ear that the overlay on their Irish background was American, likely Eastern Seaboard, not from the Ottawa Valley. That started me along the line of investigating why Irish Americans might be trying to pass themselves off as Irish Canadians."

"I assume you will be heading back to London to report."

"Not for a few weeks, Prime Minister. My report to Sir William will be sent by diplomatic pouch. I have a good acquaintance who suggested that I visit his farm out West. But first I must stop in Toronto."

"Why is that, Mr. Sigerson," asked the Prime Minister as he rose.

"My acquaintance urged me to get shod there. His bootmaker is Meyers. Perhaps you've heard of his establishment?"

POSTSCRIPT

It was to be seven more years before Meyers the Bootmaker achieved immortality through publication in 1901 of The Hound of the Baskervilles, *an adventure that actually took place in 1889, five years before our Ottawa story, according to Dr. John Watson's account. A reader of this tale today may well marvel how I could not have recognized an investigator who spoke of a "three-pipe problem", yearned to play the violin, employed a magnifying glass to such effect, and appeared to have written monographs on every aspect of criminal deduction.*

In my own defence, all I can say is that the whole world believed that the Master Detective had died that terrible day in May 1891 when he plunged over Reichenbach Falls in a fatal embrace with his arch-enemy Professor Moriarty. In reality, he was to reappear to Watson's astonished eyes the month after the visit to Ottawa, but his return did not become general knowledge until October 1903, when The Strand *magazine published a story entitled* "The Empty House."

You can imagine my astonishment while reading that tale to learn that while Sherlock Holmes roamed the globe between May 1891 and April 1894, he often assumed the persona of a Norwegian explorer named Sigerson.

Ottawa References

- *The Dominion Police* – Organized around 1870 to monitor and infiltrate the Fenian movement and protect cabinet ministers. Later responsible for security on Parliament Hill and for most federal policing services east of Lake Superior. Colonel Arthur Percy Sherwood became head in 1885 and held that post for a generation. In 1919, the force was merged with the Royal North West Mounted Police to form the RCMP.
- *Russell Hotel* – Built in 1865 on the east side of Elgin at Sparks, the Russell was the fashionable hotel in Ottawa until the Chateau Laurier opened in 1912. It was first building in the city to boast bathrooms and steam heat. Prime Ministers John A. Macdonald, Charles Tupper and Wilfrid Laurier all lived at the Russell during their terms in office. The hotel suffered a fire in 1901, was rebuilt, but closed in 1925. It stood derelict until April 14, 1928, when another fire gutted the building and the land was cleared for the War Memorial.
- *George M. Dawson* – Director of the Geological Survey from 1895 until his sudden death in 1901.

- *An inn on Duke Street* – The Duke Hotel, later the venerable Couillard, was at 101 Duke Street.
- *Commissariat Building* – Now houses the Bytown Museum.
- *Beamster, wheel tapper, drayman, pot burner, knacker, guard lacer, plate-maker* – Tannery worker, railway worker who checked the wheels of locomotives, goods carrier by horse cart, pottery worker, dealer in old/dead horses, someone who laces up ladies' bicycles to prevent dresses getting caught in the mechanism, engraver of printing block plates.

Sherlockian References

- *Sometimes constituted the entire British government* – The phrase "sometimes the British government" was applied to Mycroft Holmes, older brother to Sherlock and a senior public servant.
- *Attended Oxford or Cambridge* – A contentious and unresolved issue in Sherlockian scholarship.
- *Have written a small monograph* – Holmes wrote monographs about the identification of tobacco ashes, tattoo marks, the tracing of footsteps, ear shapes, the effect of trades upon hands, and ciphers. He planned ones about the use of dogs in detection, malingering and the typewriter in crime.
- *You see, Evans, but you do not observe* – A recrimination Holmes directs at Dr. Watson more than once.
- *A three-pipe problem* – A classic Sherlockian description.
- *The bimetallic question, the great herd of bisons of the fertile plains*, and *the stormy petrels* – The names of three Sherlockian scion societies in Canada.
- *Meyers* – The title given to the leader of Canada's premier Sherlockian society, the Bootmakers of Toronto.

ACKNOWLEDGEMENTS: This story could not have been written without the plot advice and editing skills of J.A. ("Sandy") McFarlane. Valuable assistance was also provided by librarians in the Ottawa Room of the Ottawa Public Library, Gideon Hill, BSI, and Rideau Canal enthusiast Ken Watson.

The Adventure of the
Willow Basket
by Lyndsay Faye
From *Part II: 1890-1895* (2015)

"An artisan of considerable artistic skill," Sherlock Holmes answered in reply to my latest challenge, pulling a thin cigarette from his case. "A glass-blower to be specific, although I nearly fell into the rash error of supposing him a professional musician. Shocking, the way the mind slips into such appalling laxity after a full meal – I'll be forced to fast entirely tomorrow in case my wits should happen to be called upon."

Staring, I marvelled at the man before me, who scowled at his now-exhausted supply.

"Dear me, I shall have to stop for tobacco on our – "

"No, I won't have it!" I lightly slapped the white linen tablecloth between us, causing our whiskys to shiver with a sympathetic happy thrill. "Eight in a row is quite too many, Holmes! Even you cannot pretend to clairvoyance."

"You wound me, my boy." He lit the cigarette, suppressing an impish expression. "I have never pretended to clairvoyance in my life, though I have placed eleven such repellent creatures in the dock for swindling the credible out of their hard-earned savings. One, a Mr. Erasmus Drake, defrauded over a dozen widows using only a mirror, a pennywhistle, and a cunning preparation of coloured Chinese gunpowder. He won't be free to roam the streets for another three years, come to think of it."

"Well, well, never mind clairvoyance then, but you have just identified the professions of eight individuals at a single glance! I shall have to commence approaching complete strangers and demanding they give us a full report of their lives and habits in order to corroborate your claims."

"My dear fellow, surely you know by now that you needn't trouble yourself."

"All right – how do you know he is a glass-blower?"

The detective's eyes glinted as brightly as the silver case which he returned to his inner coat pocket. We sat at our preferred table in the front of Simpson's, before the ground-glass windows where we so often watched the passersby; but despite the glow bestowed upon London minutes before by her army of gas-lighters, the illumination beyond the wavering panes no longer sufficed for even my friend's keen gaze to pick out those details by which he had built his reputation, and thus we had shifted in our seats to examine the restaurant patrons instead. Holmes's turbot and my leg of mutton had long since been whisked away following our early repast, and we sat in a small pool of quiet amidst the throng of hungry journalists and eager young chess players, their sights fixed upon sliced beef in the dining room or cigars and chequered boards up the familiar staircase. There seemed not a man among them my friend could not pin with the exactitude of a lepidopterist with a butterfly; and, while his remarkable faculty always gives me as much pleasure as it does him, on that evening we reposed with the more luxurious complacency of two intimate companions who had nothing more pressing to do than to order another set of whiskys.

"I know he is a professional glass-blower because he is not a professional trumpet player," Holmes drawled, gesturing with slight flicks of his index finger. "His clothing is of excellent quality, only a bit less so than yours or mine, suggesting he is neither an aristocrat nor a mean labourer, but rather a respectable chap with a vocation. His cheeks are sunken, but the musculature of his jaw is strongly developed, overly so, and there are slight indications of varicose veins surrounding his lips. His lungs are powerful – I don't know if you heard him cough ten minutes ago, but I feared for the crystal. He has been expelling air from them, with great strength and frequency. At first I nearly fell into the callow error of supposing him an aficionado with some brass instrument, possibly playing for an orchestra or one of the better music halls, for which failing I blame the exquisite quality of Simpson's seafood preparations. However, when I glimpsed his hands, I instantly corrected my mistake – his finger-ends display no sign of flattening from depressing the valves, but they do evince a number of slight burn scars. Ergo, he is a glass blower, one I would wager ten quid owns a private shop attached to his studio if the cost of his watch chain does not mislead me, and you need not disturb his repast, friend Watson."

I was already softly applauding, shaking with laughter. "My abject apologies. I was a fool to doubt you."

"Skepticism is widely considered healthy," Holmes demurred, but the immediate lift of his narrow lips betrayed his pleasure at the compliment. My friend is nothing if not gratified by honest appreciation of his prodigious talents.

For some forty minutes and another set of whiskys longer, we lingered, speaking or not speaking as best suited our pleasure, and I admit that I relished the time. My friend was in a rare mood – for, while he is tensely frenetic with work to energise him, he is often brooding and silent without it. The extremities of his nature can be taxing for a fellow lodger and worrying for a friend, though I suspect not more so than they are burdensome for Holmes himself. It was a pleasure to see the great criminologist at his ease for once, neither in motion nor plastered to the settee in silent protest against the dullness of the world around him.

I was just about to suggest that we walk back to Baker Street when we wearied of Simpsons's rather than flag a hansom, for it was mid-June and the spring air yet hung blessedly warm and weightless before the advent of summer's stifling fug, when my friend's face changed. The languid half-lidded eyes focused, and the slack draught he had been taking from his cigarette tightened into a harder purse.

"What is it?" I asked, already half-turning.

"Trouble, friend Watson. Let us hope it is the stimulating and not the unpleasant variety."

It was then I spied our friend Inspector Lestrade casting his dark, glittering eyes around the dining room, turning his neatly brushed bowler anxiously in his hands. His sharp features betrayed no hint of their usual smugness, and his frame, already small, seemed to have shrunk still further within his light duster. When I raised a hand, he darted towards our table with his head down like a terrier on the scent.

"By Jove, there's been a murder done!" Holmes exclaimed, as usual failing to sound entirely displeased by this development. "Lestrade, pull up a chair. There's coffee if you like, and – "

"No time for coffee," Lestrade huffed as he seated himself.

Holmes blinked in urbane surprise, and I could not blame him. I, too, suspected that beneath the inspector's obvious anxiety lurked another irritant – while Lestrade is often officious, he is never curt, and he had not bothered to greet either one of us.

Musing, I took in the regular Yarder's rigid spine and brittle countenance. My examinations drew a blank, save for the obvious conclusion that his nerves had been somehow jangled. I could not imagine what the matter might be, for the year was 1894 and I had not seen the inspector since April and the arrest of Colonel Sebastian Moran, a dramatic event indeed, but one which paled significantly in comparison to the fact of Sherlock Holmes being alive at all. Following my friend's return from his supposed death at the grim plunge of Reichenbach Falls, I had wrestled briefly with powerful conflicting emotions, the pain of abandonment and the joy of an unlooked-for miracle foremost among them – but by June of that year, the occasional haunted, hunted looks in Holmes's eyes, which even he could not conceal, combined with the rueful courtesies he showed me when his natural impatience ought to have driven such considerations clean from his vast mind, had convinced me he could not have done otherwise than he did. Excluding the deep pangs caused by my recent marital heartbreak, I felt as ebullient as any shipwreck survivor, and only wished our old friend Lestrade the same felicity.

"Tell me about the murder," Holmes requested, "since you decline to be distracted by coffee."

"Beg pardon?" Lestrade growled, for he had fallen into a reverie with his fingertips pressing his temples.

"Report to me the facts of the homicide, since you refuse the stimulating effects of the roasted coffee berry."

"I do speak English, Mr. Holmes." Lestrade tugged at his cuffs in fastidious annoyance, recovering himself. "It's a bad business, gentlemen, a very bad business indeed, or I should not have troubled you. I applied at Baker Street, and Mrs. Hudson said you were dining here."

"That much I have deduced by your – "

"Shall we skip the parlour tricks, Mr. Holmes?" Lestrade proposed with unusual asperity.

Holmes's black brows rose to lofty heights indeed, as did mine, but he appeared more curious than offended. As I had not observed the pair interact other than a terse welcome back to London from Lestrade at Camden House in April, followed by some professional discussion of the charges Colonel Moran would face, I sat back against the horsehair-stuffed chair in bemusement which verged upon discomfort.

"It is a murder," Lestrade admitted, clearing his throat. "Mr. John Wiltshire was discovered in his bedroom in Battersea this late morning, stone dead, without a trace of any known poison in his corpse, nor a single wound upon his body to suggest that harm had been done to him."

"Remarkable, in that case, that you claim a murder has been committed."

"He was drained of blood, Mr. Holmes. His body was nearly free of it." Lestrade suppressed a shudder. "It disappeared."

A chill passed down my spine. As it has been elsewhere mentioned in these chaotic memoirs that Holmes rather admires than abhors the macabre, I shall not elaborate upon this quirk of his nature – I must mention, however, that Holmes's entire frame snapped into rapt attention, while Lestrade's bristled in what I can only describe as animosity.

"There's some who would think that horrible, but you're not to be named among them, I suppose." The inspector levelled a challenging stare at Sherlock Holmes.

"I readily admit to thinking it varying degrees of horrible based upon the character of the deceased," Holmes replied with a yawn, reverting to his typical supercilious character. "The facts, if you would be so kind."

"The facts as I have them in hand are these: Mr. John Wiltshire dined with his wife and an old friend on the night of his death, and later Mrs.

Helen Wiltshire called for a bath to be drawn for her husband. The housekeeper asserts that the ring occurred, the water was heated, and nothing else of note took place. The upper housemaids all confirm that Mrs. Wiltshire slept in her own room that night, afraid to upset her husband's apparent need for quiet and solitude. Other than the fact a man has apparently been bled to death by magic, you'd not find me disturbing your supper."

"You know very well that we would hasten to come whenever you have need of Holmes," I asserted, only noting in retrospect my grammatical error.

A glass of whisky appeared before the inspector. Nodding subtle thanks to the jacketed waiter, Holmes ordered, "Do have a sip – it seems as though the circumstances merit it."

Lestrade's countenance dissolved into what might – save for his own restraint – have been a sneer even as he tasted the drink. "Another deduction?"

"You have clearly been much taxed," said Holmes, as dismissive as ever. "Pray, what would you have us do? I require an invitation or a client, and presently I have neither. Shall I look up *vampires* in my commonplace book and wire you upon the subject, or test your patience so far as to accompany you to the crime scene? Has the body been moved?"

"No. I came straight to you," Lestrade retorted, taking another swallow, "whether I liked it or not."

My mouth fell open, and Holmes's deep-set eyes widened fractionally. I fully expected a scathing retort to follow close upon this subtle hint of dismay. To my great surprise, he merely rose, however, nodding at the quaint tobacconist's shop nestled inside the restaurant, and said coldly, "I am at your disposal, Lestrade, after buying more cigarettes. You are giving me the distinct impression I shall have need of them. Watson, settle the bill if you would be so good."

Never will I forget that crime scene, for it occurred after what had been so casually glad a day for me, and the shift into horror was as swift as our cab ride. John Wiltshire lay dead in his tastefully appointed bedchamber, its heavy emerald draperies thrown wide to let in the sunlight and now forgot under the shrouded gaze of invisible stars. He reclined in a bath over which a muslin cloth had been draped, the atmosphere in the room stale with police traffic and tense with revulsion, and a still-damp rubber tarp on the rug nearby informed me he had been examined by the coroner and then returned to his original attitude. Mr. Wiltshire's head and upper torso were visible, his mouth slack and lips white as chalk. The setting and the centerpiece were utterly jarring, with the stately furnishings

172

surrounding a body that appeared horribly – nay, obscenely – withered. Should I have reached out and touched the late Mr. Wiltshire's skin, I could picture it crumbling to dust like paper left to desiccate for centuries. He had in life been a slender man, with deep pouches beneath his eyes and a thin, downturned mouth.

The coroner was finishing his notes wearing a grim expression and, after a gesture from Lestrade, he stepped aside to allow Holmes and myself to view the deceased. My friend whistled appreciatively, which garnered a dark look from Lestrade.

"Skin white as that cloth and utterly parched, vessels drained, form shrunken, as if he had shriveled into a husk," I summarised. "But are we *certain* there were no epidermal wounds inflicted which could have caused this? He was examined on this tarp, I take it."

"Indeed, Doctor. A minute examination was made in this room, but Inspector Lestrade insisted the deceased be replaced lest his original positioning or the water itself provide a clue for Mr. Holmes here," the coroner answered, nodding politely.

"By the Lord," Holmes said mildly, "and here I supposed the circumstances of the killing itself the only miracle which took place today. Admirable, Lestrade."

My friend appeared to be getting a bit of his own back at last, and the official detective ground his teeth as Holmes dipped his torso towards the bath. Avid as the most passionate connoisseur, he lifted the dead man's dripping hand from the water and examined the ivory cuticles, checked the underside of the limb draped over the lip, made a minute study of his dark hair and his unmarked scalp, even lifted the wizened eyelids to reveal his unseeing pupils. I watched, eager to help if I could, but all I beheld seemed the stuff of nightmare and not medicine. Holmes next drew his delicate fingertips along the copper rim of the tub, going so far as to touch the now-tepid water and bring it to his nose.

"For heaven's sake," Lestrade muttered in my ear – but at me there was directed no pique, merely the casual camaraderie of old.

I half-drew a hand over my moustache to hide a smile, but added under my breath, "If Holmes weren't the most thorough investigator the world has ever known, I doubt he would be here."

"More's the pity," Lestrade sighed as my companion pushed upright again.

"I have exceptionally keen hearing, you realise," Holmes mentioned tartly. "Fascinating. As I happen to trust in your thoroughness, coroner – Adams, was it? Yes, Mr. Adams, I suppose you correct in stating that the body lacks superficial wounds. They should have bled into the water if he was killed here, in any event, and this liquid is far too pure to indicate a

173

man's entire life-force could have possibly been drained into it. I can see no trace of blood at all. Testing it for minute traces may prove necessary, and I have that ability, but more urgent matters demand our attention, supposing we can keep this evidence intact? Very good. I detect no more sign of poison than you do, but anyhow poisoning is a medically impossible means of sapping a fellow's blood, unless we are dealing with a substance altogether unknown to science. So here we have a man whose blood was somehow siphoned, and the water is clear. Supposing the corpse had been moved, that would have proven nothing whatsoever, but . . . ."

"But the corpse was not moved," Mr. Adams obliged when Holmes paused expectantly, "because the deep depressions upon the back of his neck and the other on his forearm – there, where it was resting – indicate he was robbed of his blood here somehow, and left to die."

"Capital!" Holmes exclaimed.

"Yes, we worked that one out on our own, Mr. Holmes," Lestrade groused.

Sherlock Holmes did not deign to reply, instead turning his attention to the crime scene as Mr. Adams excused himself, intending to help the constables make arrangements to remove the remains. Holmes made every effort, as he always does, diving into corners and walking with his slender hands hovering before him, seeking any aberration which might bring light where all was dark. After some fifteen minutes of studying carpeting, framed photographs, a mahogany bedstead, and every crevice of every object in the room, however, he tapped his fist against his lips and turned back to Lestrade.

"Will you be so good as to deliver me this unfortunate fellow's biography?"

"Readily, Mr. Holmes. Mr. Wiltshire is employed at a banking firm in the City and has been for some six years hence. We've had scant enough time to question anyone, but this afternoon his direct superior sent me a good report of him. The servants seem to think him a somber man, but altogether a satisfactory employer. He has no outstanding debts and no known enemies – he lives in a quiet fashion with his wife, Mrs. Helen – "

Holmes snapped his fingers. "I hadn't forgot the detail, but was admittedly distracted by so very dramatic a corpse. They entertained an old friend last night – the wife, take me to the wife," he commanded, and quit the room.

Lestrade followed, and I matched my stride to the shorter man's. "I cannot help but sense that our presence on this occasion distresses you, Inspector."

He glanced backwards in surprise. "Oh, I could never be distressed by your help, Doctor. It's always a pleasure to see you. It's merely that

174

Mr. Holmes – well, never mind, Mr. Holmes has never cared a fig what I think, and I don't see why he should start now, so I'll say no more. He'll be waiting for us, and he's right to want interviews at this stage. There *was* a visitor, and it was the wife who rang for the bath to be drawn. I've not been able to question Mrs. Wiltshire yet – she fainted dead away at the sight of her husband and only recovered whilst I was fetching you. Never mind Mr. Holmes's quirks when there's a murderer to run to ground, I always tell myself."

Still mystified for multiple reasons, I could do nothing save accompany him downstairs. We waited in a pretty parlour with all the lamps blazing, a room full of light and colourful decorative china, its walls masked by potted greenery. Something about its coziness unnerved me, and the chamber seemed all the more garishly cheerful when my imagination flashed upon the ghastly events doubtless taking place upstairs, as the shrunken rind which had once been a man was taken out the back through the servants' entrance and at last to the morgue.

When Mrs. Helen Wiltshire entered, she naturally appeared greatly disturbed in mind – her comely complexion was ashen with dismay, her full lips a-tremble, her green eyes red at the edges, her pale blonde hair disarrayed from clutching it in the extremity of her emotion. She was of an age with her late husband, midway between thirty and forty, and was a lovely woman despite her distress. My friend was up in an instant and led her with easy courtesy to the settee, where she perched as if about to take flight.

Holmes smiled gently as he regained his own chair, displaying the almost mesmeric softness he only ever expends upon the fair sex, and only when he desires information from them; but then, I am not being quite just when I say so. My friend may not seek the company of women, but he genuinely abhors seeing them harmed.

"Are you quite comfortable, madam? Should you like a little refreshment to strengthen you? My friend here is a doctor, and he will be happy to locate something fortifying."

"I . . . I don't think that would be . . . ." Mrs. Wiltshire shifted, attempting to smile with little success. She was silent for so long that Sherlock Holmes continued, face alive with encouragement.

"You are of Scottish origins, I observe. In the vicinity of Paisley, Renfrewshire, unless my ears deceive me."

A wash of colour infused Mrs. Wiltshire's dulled cheeks. "Aye, Mr. Holmes, though I've lost a good deal of that manner of speaking."

"Yes, it's extremely subtle. You went on a long stroll this morning, Mrs. Wiltshire? It must be pleasant, living so close to Battersea Park and its walkways, especially at this time of the year – though I discern from your boots that you wandered alongside the Thames on this occasion."

She glanced up, twisting her fingers in her coral skirts. "Why, yes, Mr. Holmes. I was out walking. That is the reason I only learned at around noon that – oh, I can't, I can't," she said upon a small sob. "I very often take long constitutionals. I've never regretted the habit so much as I did this afternoon, when I arrived home and discovered the house was in an uproar and the police had already been summoned over . . . over . . . ."

"Quite."

"I was most unwell afterward. I've only just found a tiny store of strength – I hope you will forgive my weakness, but . . . ."

Again she trailed off, and again Holmes continued. "Will you please tell me about your caller of last night?"

Helen Wiltshire nodded, more tears forming. "His name is Horatio Swann, an explorer of some note."

"Indeed!" Holmes exclaimed. "Yes, I have heard of him. He has made quite the name for himself in scholarly monographs."

"Yes, that is the man," she agreed with another weak twitch of her lips. "My husband and he were acquainted years ago, but Mr. Swann has been traveling in Siam, studying indigenous wildlife. We passed a most pleasant meal, and afterward John seemed fatigued at having spent so much time over vigourous conversation and plentiful claret. I ordered him a bath and left him to himself. He could grow . . . melancholy at times, Mr. Holmes. But for such a fate to befall him . . . ."

Mrs. Wiltshire at this point dissolved entirely and ran from the room.

Lestrade exchanged a glance with Holmes, all pique forgotten in the peculiarity of the moment. He leant forward with his elbows on his knees. "She must have been quite devoted to him."

"It would seem so," Holmes replied without inflection.

"The poor woman must be wrought to her highest pitch of nerves over such a ghastly shock. We must seek out this Horatio Swann," I conjectured, "and ascertain whether he has anything to do with the affair."

"As usual, Watson, you have hit upon the obvious with uncanny accuracy," said Holmes dryly. "But I wonder . . . well, there may be nothing in it after all."

"Nothing in what, Mr. Holmes?" Lestrade questioned, a furrow forming above his narrow nose.

"It's only a whim of mine, perhaps a trivial one at that. But why one should walk along the Thames, noisome as it is, when one could walk through Battersea Park?" Holmes mused, rising and ringing the bell.

A maid appeared within seconds. "Show in the housekeeper, please – what is her name?" Holmes inquired.

"Mrs. Stubbs, sir."

"Mrs. Stubbs, then. Thank you."

Lestrade nodded absently, stretching his legs out before him as if in agreement over Holmes's choice of witness, and I dared to hope that whatever mood had plagued him had been a fluke, and that all would henceforth be well again. Mrs. Stubbs, when she entered, proved a broad woman with neatly arranged curls, the flinty spark of extreme practicality in her eyes, and a direct manner. She stood upon the Turkey carpet with her hands clasped placidly before her, the slight slump of her shoulders the only indication she had been sorely tried that day.

"Yes, gentlemen?"

"Mrs. Stubbs." Holmes remained standing, pacing as he questioned. "My name is Sherlock Holmes, this is my friend and colleague, Dr. John Watson, and this is Inspector Lestrade of Scotland Yard. We wonder whether you might help us in clearing this matter up. You have been the housekeeper for how long?"

"Six years, sir. As long as the Wiltshires have lived in Battersea."

"You find the position amenable?"

"I do."

"Would you describe for me the nature of your late employer?"

"John Wiltshire was a good provider, and I hadn't much cause to speak with him. At times, he seemed a bit wistful perhaps, but he never lashed out or gave me the impression such spells were anything more serious than fatigue."

"Then you would say Mr. and Mrs. Wiltshire were happy together?" Holmes pressed, selecting a cigarette.

Mrs. Stubbs sniffed, seeming more impatient than offended. "As happy as anyone, I hope. They never quarreled, and when banking cost him long hours away, she never begrudged him the time."

"Did she not?" Holmes threw the spent Vesta in the fireplace. "Have you any theory as to what happened last night?"

This at last seemed to move her, but she maintained a neutral expression, swallowing. "That'll be for you gentlemen to decide, I'm sure."

"Was there sign of any intruders this morning?" Lestrade put in.

"No, sir. Well, not precisely."

Both Holmes and Lestrade paused at this, tensing. "What do you mean by 'not precisely,' Mrs. Stubbs?" Lestrade urged.

"It's a silly thing, but the new scullery maid has misplaced the marketing basket." Mrs. Stubbs shrugged. "She's more than a bit simple, and everything is so tospy-turvy today – I'm sure it will turn up. Last week she managed to put the cheese wheel in the breadbox after clearing the servants' supper."

Lestrade sagged, disappointed.

"Would you describe this basket, Mrs. Stubbs?" Holmes requested.

Our eyes flashed to the detective in disbelief.

"It's a plain split willow basket, about a foot-and-a-half long though not so wide, with a handle for the shoulder, lined with a cotton kitchen towel," Mrs. Stubbs answered readily, though her tone was skeptical.

"Thank you," said Holmes, whirling a bit as he strode in tight loops before the fireplace. "One question more, I beg. What was Mr. Wiltshire's mood like after Mr. Horatio Swann had departed?"

"Morose, sir," the housekeeper replied flatly.

Sherlock Holmes stopped, quirking an agile brow. "The usual affliction?"

"Worse, sir. Perhaps he'd a premonition." Mrs. Stubbs set her lips grimly. "To die in such a way . . . God knows he deserved warning of it. Do call for me if you need aught else, but I've plentiful extra tasks to see to and would fain take my leave," she concluded.

When she had departed, Lestrade slapped his knees and hopped to his feet, his unexplained ire fully returned. "This is a serious investigation, Mr. Holmes!"

Holmes swiveled to face the inspector, his high cheekbones dusted with colour, for the first time visibly vexed at the criticism. "I assure you I am treating it as such."

"Oh, yes, I'm sure the *exact* description of this misplaced potato basket is going to greatly assist us in tracking down the killer! Why don't *you* solve that mystery – question the scullery maid, that'll be a good start – and *I'll* catch a murderer. I need to see whether my men have finished," Lestrade growled, storming out.

"What on earth can be the matter with him?" I wondered, regarding Holmes in amazement.

My friend pulled in smoke with a vengeance before crushing the cigarette in a tray for the purpose and shaking his dark head. "I had six theories at the beginning of the evening. I've eliminated five of them," he confessed, striding in the direction of the outer hallway.

"Then what is wrong?" I repeated as we donned hats and gloves.

"A conundrum even I cannot solve."

I opened my lips to protest but found Sherlock Holmes's face as stony as I had ever seen it; he pivoted away from me, thrusting his hands into his pockets as we made to quit the blighted Wiltshire residence.

"But the murder, Holmes! Hadn't you better question more of the ser – "

"That conundrum I *can* solve," Holmes interrupted me. "As a matter of fact, I just did solve it, about five minutes ago. There was never any difficulty in the matter. Come, Watson. We must see what Mr. Horatio Swann has to say."

As circumstances had it, we could not call upon Mr. Horatio Swann until the next morning, as Lestrade had not found us at Simpson's until well past seven after travelling from Battersea and stopping at Baker Street, and Mr. Swann lived some miles distant, in a grand house near to Walthamstow. Lestrade supplied us with a four-wheeler and a pair of constables lest matters take a dark turn, and the journey would have been pleasant enough, passing through the small brick towns with their peacefully crumbling churches and snowlike dusting of white petals from the blooming Hawthorne bushes, had the inspector not been sullen and Holmes coolly silent. I, meanwhile, was abuzz with anticipation, desperately eager to discover what my friend had made of the dreadful affair.

When we three at last stood before the stately structure in question – walled round with charming grey stone, a little lane leading up to a curved set of steps, mullioned windows all sparkling as they reflected the dancing shadows of the white willow branches – Holmes hesitated upon the gravel. Lestrade and I by habit likewise slowed to see whether he would deign to share any of his thoughts.

Then Holmes froze entirely, his spine quivering. We waited, with bated breath, for him to speak – or at least I did.

"Well, what the deuce is the matter?" Lestrade queried, every bit as waspishly annoyed at my friend as previous.

Holmes chuckled, rubbing his hands together. "It's all too perfect. I told you I had heard of Mr. Horatio Swann yesterday, did I not? I have followed a few of his monographs upon the subject of certain freshwater wildlife with particular care."

"And what of it?" Lestrade demanded, exasperated.

"Rather an outlandish residence for a scientist, wouldn't you say?" Holmes replied, winking. "Call for the constables. We'll want them."

Brown eyes widening in astonishment, Lestrade at once did as he was bid, returning a few yards up the lane and gesturing for the Bobbies to follow. By the time they had done so, Holmes had cheerily knocked upon the door and been admitted, I at his heels.

The taciturn butler led us – and, after some persuasion, the Yarders – into Mr. Swann's study. From the instant I entered it, my eyes knew not where to light; the place was a splendidly outfitted gentleman's laboratory, replete with chemical apparatus and walls of gilt-stamped leather books

179

and specimen jars. Of these last, there were dozens upon dozens, lining the shelves like so many petrified soldiers at attention. When my friend saw them, he smiled still wider.

Mr. Swann, surprised, emerged from behind his desk. He was a strongly built man, with a shock of ruddy hair and a ruggedly handsome visage, still wearing a dressing gown and house slippers, as we had begun our journey as early as possible. He appeared merely intrigued at the sight of Holmes and myself – but when he glimpsed the uniformed constables behind Lestrade, his expression shifted to a grimace of pure rage.

"Gentlemen, allow me to introduce Mr. Charles Cutmore, the mastermind behind the infamous Drummonds Bank robbery which so confounded the Scottish authorities, the renowned author of no less than twenty scientific articles of note, and likewise the cunning author of the murder of Mr. John Wiltshire – whose name is actually Michael Crosby, by the by, and who some seven years ago aided this man in making off with six thousand pounds sterling. The pair of them had a female accomplice, to whom you have been introduced under the alias of Mrs. Helen Wiltshire. A pretty little bow to top this strange affair, would you not say so, Lestrade?" Holmes rejoiced.

The inspector stood there stunned for an instant; but a howl of fury and a charge for the door on the part of Mr. Charles Cutmore ceased all rumination. The set of brawny constables hurtled headlong into action, and the pair wrestled their frenzied captive into a set of derbies.

"You've no right!" Charles Cutmore spat at us. "After all o' this time, by God, how d'ye think ye've the *right*?"

"Precisely my question, Mr. Cutmore," said Holmes. "After all of this time safe in Siam with your plunder, why return?"

A steely shutter closed over the bank robber's face even as he renewed his violent efforts to break free. He was dragged, spitting curses at the lot of us, into the adjoining parlour as the men awaited instructions.

"What the devil was that?" Lestrade cried. "A clearer confession I've never heard, but that doesn't explain – "

"No, but this does," Holmes said almost reverently, turning as he lifted one of the glass jars from its shelf.

A miniscule red creature swam within, suspended in pale green-tinged water. It was no bigger than my thumbnail, and the shape of a repulsive maggotlike larvae. I felt my skin tingle with disgust when I saw that, though eyeless, one end of the tiny worm was equipped with a gaping sucker-like mouth.

"Behold the Siamese red leech," Holmes declaimed grandly, presenting it to us. "Not our murder weapon, Lestrade, but one of its kindred. Some of my own studies regarding blood led to a side interest in

180

leeches, and this is one of the only deadly specimens in the known world. It possesses biochemical enzymes in its mouth which render its victims numb and dazed when attacked – and, after having bloated itself upon its unsuspecting meal, expanding to hundreds of times its size when unfed, the same chemicals shrink the wound until it is practically invisible."

"My God, that's hideous!" the inspector breathed, echoing my own thoughts. "But how did you – "

"Charles Cutmore and Michael Crosby were known to be the culprits in the Drummonds affair, but they went deep underground," my friend explained, setting down the deadly specimen. "Crosby had never been photographed, though his description was circulated – he was the faceless banker who enabled the inside job to take place at all – but Cutmore was already making advances in his studies of marine animals, marsh grasses, freshwater habitats, and the like when the theft was discovered, and his photograph was published by the Scottish authorities, which is how I came to know of him. The pair were at school together in Edinburgh. Much more was known about Cutmore than Crosby and, at the time of the robbery seven years ago, Cutmore was affianced to one Helen Ainsley, with whom we spoke. I never dreamed that Charles Cutmore and Horatio Swann were the same biologist until yesterday."

"It still isn't clear to me," I interjected. "You yourself asked him why he returned. Whyever should Cutmore murder Crosby, and after all this time?"

"There we enter the realm of conjecture," Holmes admitted, "and shall only know all after Cutmore is questioned. But here is what I propose: after the robbery, Cutmore made off with considerably more than his share of the profits – note comparatively the residences of the conspirators, after all. So. Cutmore fled to Siam, publishing under an alias and waiting until such time as he could return to the British Isles without his features being so recognisable. Crosby, meanwhile, disappeared into the great cesspool of London and took Helen Ainsley with him, marrying her in Cutmore's absence and continuing to practice banking, from time to time mourning his lost fortune. They may well have believed that the man who betrayed them would never return. But suppose that Cutmore still harboured affections for Helen Ainsley and regretted the loss of her? The reunion last night may have purported to be a friendly one, and Cutmore may even have vowed to restore what he owed them – we have seen the results, however."

"You think this was a crime of passion?" Lestrade drew nearer, glowering.

"Of a sort. Of a very premeditated sort. You have met Charles Cutmore," Holmes reminded him, half-sitting on the desk. "He and Mrs.

Wiltmore were once engaged. He does not seem to me the type to remain in hiding forever, supposing he desires to return to someplace, or someone for that matter."

"But what of her husband?"

"Surely you can see that her marriage to the man calling himself John Wiltmore was a matter of expediency – they knew one another's worst secrets and were very much thrown together. I do not claim to have any practical knowledge of the matter, but who ever heard of a married couple who *never* fought, as Mrs. Stubbs claimed? If they seldom fought, I should only have suspected a happy union, and the same goes for an unhappy one if they fought often. But never? It wasn't a union at all. In fact, I should lose no time arresting her."

"On what charge?" Lestrade demanded.

"That of ordering a bath for her freshly unsettled husband and placing a Siamese red leech in it," Holmes replied, his piercing tenor grown grave. "You don't suppose that Charles Cutmore marched up the stairs and dropped it in unnoticed? When I asked him why he returned, he refused to answer, though he had already given himself away – he was trying to shield his former fiancée. The urge was an honourable one, though she shan't escape the law. I haven't evidence enough lacking her confession to prove my findings in the mystery of the missing willow basket, but judging by her behavior at the house, she'll crack on her own once Cutmore is charged. The pair of them have been in contact for far longer than a day, I believe, probably since shortly after his return to England and his purchase of this estate."

"The missing willow basket? Make some sense, by George!"

"Where is the leech now, Lestrade?" Holmes spread his hands in a dramatic show of longsuffering.

"Good heavens," I gasped. "Holmes, you're right – you must be. They planned it together. You said she had been walking by the Thames and not in the park. She took the leech, wrapped it in the cloth, and made off with it in the marketing basket. It must be in the river now."

"Managing to make the most disgusting body of water in the history of mankind still more repugnant." Holmes chuckled, clapping once. "Well done, my dear fellow."

"To think that he left Helen Ainsley behind and then never forgot her, only to lose her again," I reflected. "It's a terrible story."

"And you claim," Lestrade hissed, advancing still further on my friend, "that you knew all this *yesterday*?"

Holmes glared down his hawklike nose at the inspector. "Can you be serious? Are you suggesting you would have believed me if I told you last night that John Wiltmore was killed by a Siamese leech?"

182

"I might have believed you."

"You might have laughed in my face. This relentless persecution grows tedious, Lestrade."

"Persecution?" Lestrade snarled. "I'm persecuting *you*? Oh, that's rich, Mr. Holmes. Very funny."

"Oddly, I don't find it the slightest bit amusing."

"Gentlemen – " I began.

"Let's have it out in the open then, shall we? Man to man?" Lestrade's shoulders hunched above his clenched hands as if he longed to express his emotions with pugilism.

"By Jove, yes, let's," my friend hissed, standing to his full height.

"Perhaps I had better give you some privacy." Fearing nothing for my friend's safety but feeling dreadfully awkward, I took a step backwards only to find that Lestrade was pointing at me furiously.

"That man," Lestrade snapped, "would – no, don't leave, Dr. Watson, you'd best hear my mind on the subject. That man there, Mr. Holmes, would have taken a bullet for you, I'd stake my own life on it."

Holmes said nothing as I gaped at them.

"And what do you do?" Lestrade was turning crimson with fury. "Instead of seeing it through together, you leave the doctor out entirely, and then you make him think you were *dead*. You stood up there at the altar with him on his *wedding day,* for the love of all that's decent, and do you suppose he enjoyed being written out of the picture? For that matter, how do you suppose *I* felt when I learnt about your demise from a common news hawker? Or when I discovered down at the Yard that Inspector *Patterson* was dashing about rounding up the scoundrels you had apparently been trying to capture for three long months? I should have thought we deserved better from you, Mr. Holmes, and you ought to know it."

Sherlock Holmes, always remarkably pale-complected, had turned absolutely pallid during this speech, though his face betrayed no expression whatsoever otherwise. Meanwhile, my heart was in my throat. I had hardly begun to speak when Holmes held up a perfectly steady hand demanding my silence and said frostily, "You want to know why I left the papers needed to destroy the Moriarty network with Patterson and not with you?"

"I'd find the subject of interest, yes," the small inspector seethed.

Holmes towered over him with that air of aristocratic mastery only he can assume. "I selected Patterson for the task because he *was not* you."

"Of all the . . . ." Lestrade spluttered in outrage.

My friend commenced idly examining his fingernails. "Professor Moriarty was proven to be directly or indirectly responsible for the murder of no less than forty persons, though I suspect the true death count to be fifty-two. Patterson is above the common herd, for a Yarder anyhow, but I had previously worked with him twice. You and I, Inspector," he continued, pretending to struggle for the exact accounting, "have worked together on . . . let me think, dear me, thirty-eight cases, today marking the thirty-ninth. Now, I realise that so many figures in a row must be difficult for a man of your acumen to grapple with, but I shall add one more and have done. Ask me how many times I was shot at during the course of this very interesting little problem we are discussing."

"How many?" Lestrade inquired rather faintly.

"Nineteen," my friend reported, though this time fire underlay the ice of his tone. "And if you think I am not aware of the fact *that man*, as you referred to him, would take a bullet for me, then you are still denser than I had previously supposed."

So saying, Holmes checked the time on his pocket watch and swept out of the room.

We were silent for a moment.

"Oh, good lord," Lestrade groaned, rubbing his hand over his prim features. "I'm the biggest fool in Christendom. That was . . . God help me."

"I'm going to . . . ." said I, gesturing helplessly.

"Yes, yes, go!" the inspector urged, pushing my shoulder. "I'll just confer with the constables while I reflect on the fact that Mr. Holmes is right to call me dense. Go on, quick march."

Hastily, I gave chase. Not imagining my highly reserved friend had any wish to remain in a house where such a scene had just been enacted, as his levels of detachment border upon the mechanical, I dove for the entryway and the faintly blue atmosphere of the mild spring morning beyond.

I found Sherlock Holmes some thirty yards distant, leaning against the ivy-draped stone wall. He seemingly awaited my arrival, although he confined his eyes to the smoke drifting skyward from his cigarette. When I had reached him, I halted the words which threatened to leap from my tongue, knowing this situation required more careful handling. Several tacks were considered before I settled on the one likeliest to succeed without causing further harm, and immediately, I breathed easier.

"Well, my dear fellow?" Holmes prompted in a strained voice when I said nothing. Crossing his sinewy limbs, he lifted a single eyebrow although he still failed to look at me. "Have you any salient remarks to add to this topic? Come, come, I am eager for all relevant opinions upon – "

"Holmes," said I, gripping him warmly by the forearm. "Everything I have to say has already crossed your mind."

184

He did peer at me then, searching my face with the sort of razor focus he ordinarily devotes to outlandishly complex and inexplicable crime scenes. After what seemed an age of this scrutiny, a sorrowful smile crept over the edges of his mouth.

"Then possibly my answer has crossed yours," he continued to quote in an undertone. "You stand fast?"

"Absolutely," I vowed.

A flinch no one save I would ever have caught twitched across his aquiline features; he then clapped my hand which still grasped his arm and broke away to stub his cigarette out against the wall.

"The inspector is sorry over – "

"He needn't be. As Charles Cutmore seems to have learnt to his detriment, the returning can be harder than the leaving."

"Holmes – "

"Do you know, as many features of interest as this case held, I find I tire of it dreadfully, my dear Watson," he announced, wholly returned to his proud and practical self. "A ride back to London with our friend Lestrade and his men and our quarry I think is in order, then a pot of tea at Baker Street and a complete perusal of the morning editions on my part, whilst you work upon whatever grotesquely embellished account of our exploits you plan to inflict on the world next, followed by a change of collar and an oyster supper before Massenet's *Manon* at eight."

So it came about that the good Inspector Lestrade, whose opinion of Holmes's dramatic demise had been such a low one, came to look upon the matter in another light. Whether he ever again spoke to my friend of that impassioned conversation, neither man was gregarious enough to inform me; I highly doubt they broached the topic afterwards. To this very day, however, when Holmes requires a stout colleague or Lestrade has need of England's greatest detective, they call upon one another without hesitation. The horrible death of Crosby the banker was determined a murder by the Assizes and will be tried as such; though the fates of Charles Cutmore and Helen Ainsley have not yet been determined, they belong to that enormous criminal fraternity who have such ample cause to bemoan the existence of my fast friend, the incomparable Mr. Sherlock Holmes.

The Adventure of the Purple Poet
by Nicholas Utechin
From *Part V: Christmas Adventures* (2016)

I am a light sleeper in normal circumstances, but I must have been in a deeply unconscious state when first I felt a hand pulling at the eiderdown upon my bed. As I gradually roused myself, I became aware of Holmes's eager face.

"What the blazes is going on?" I asked, fully awake in an instant as befitted my military training years earlier. "Are we on fire, or is it another of your demanding clients appearing at an ungodly hour?" Holmes smiled.

"Neither, Watson, but it is eight in the morning on Christmas Eve and we are summoned to Oxford. Do prepare yourself and throw some clothes in a bag: Mrs. Hudson has laid out a basic breakfast and we should be able to reach Paddington for the half-past-ten."

It took but a few minutes for me to be down at our hearth. Sherlock Holmes was pacing up and down, his chin upon his chest in thought. I busied myself with the dishes and coffee.

"What is going on at your old University city," I ventured at last, "especially in the depths of the holiday period?" Holmes tossed a telegram to the table in front of me. I picked it up and folded down the creases.

"'*Univ in uproar*,'" I read, "'*Please attend. Baffled by Shelley. Macan.*' Holmes, what on earth does this mean? How can the university be affected by a poet who died seventy years ago?" My friend laughed.

"I know as much or as little as you do, Watson. But Macan is an old acquaintance of mine and he would not waste my time, especially at Christmas, if the matter was entirely unimportant. And, by the by, *Univ.* is not the whole University. I shall telegraph to tell him when we shall arrive."

Fresh snow had fallen in Baker Street, and the relative earliness of the hour meant that the white blanket had not yet been ruined by too many passers-by and dirty traffic. There was a peace and a calm about the place which I enjoyed for a moment before a cab was hailed and we were on our way to the station, barely a ten-minute ride away.

On our arrival at Paddington, Holmes crossed to the telegraph office, and within a few minutes, we were ensconced in a first-class carriage.

Only when the steam was up did Sherlock Holmes finally relax, lying back upon the thick embroidered cloth of his seat. He lit his pipe.

"One or two background facts, Watson. *Univ.* is the shortened form for University College, the oldest college at Oxford. Macan I have known since the '70s, when he was a scholar there and our paths occasionally crossed. He is now a college fellow and a classicist, with an expertise on, if I am not mistaken, Herodotus. As I told you in Baker Street, Reginald Macan is not going to worry about a trifle, and so I am prepared to travel to Oxford on what must be one of the last trains to venture out before the line is closed before tomorrow's full holiday. I fancy we shall be staying in the rather attractive city of spires for two nights. And we shall see what we see and hear what we hear."

Holmes closed his eyes and I could see that conversation was at an end.

The view from the carriage window as we travelled was as picture-perfect as one could have wished. Snow-covered fields spread to the horizon, occasionally interrupted by slight hints of cottages and church towers. There was a wonderful country calmness, lit by a sun blazing down through a crisp blue sky. It was a glorious December morning and I could only guess at what lay ahead.

We drew to a halt at Oxford Station at midday and a cab took us quickly into the city's main street, where we alighted across from the college. A be-gowned gentleman was waiting at the great oaken door, and I was somewhat surprised to see how Holmes and the man greeted each other, in the highest of spirits. I crossed the street, dodging my way through the heavy traffic.

"You are Dr. Watson, I presume," said the scholar, shaking me firmly by the hand. "It is a delight to meet the man whose tales of my old friend so often interrupt my tedious studies. I am Reggie Macan. Come into Univ., both of you, and let me explain why I have asked you to be here."

The three of us passed into the front quadrangle of the college. There was a wide pathway running straight before us, the snow impacted by the passing of feet; but on each side lay lawns untouched by any stray mark, a pristine white. At the far end were two old adjoining buildings, which I took to be the chapel and hall. Gnarled bare wisteria vines twisted their way along the stonework of the four sides of the quadrangle, with arches cut into the walls that led to student staircases.

Sherlock Holmes stood quietly, taking in the view. He was not by nature an emotional man, but I could see that he embraced the atmosphere of peace and quiet.

"It is some time, Macan, since we stood on this spot as undergraduates. But Watson and I are intrigued as to why you think it so

187

vital that we break into what was going to be an exuberant Christmas celebration in Baker Street?" My friend smiled slyly at me. "And what is baffling about Percy Bysshe Shelley? I have always found his poems most congenial." Macan slapped Holmes upon his shoulder.

"Time enough, Holmes. Let us first go to the common room. I shall ask the porter to have your bags taken to your rooms." He signalled to the servant, who had been hovering behind us, and gestured us to follow him over to the right side of the quad.

A moment later we had passed beneath the lintel of one of the stone arches and were hanging our coats upon pegs provided for the purpose. The scholar opened a door and ushered us into a most beautiful panelled room. A festive tree stood at the far end, covered with coloured balls hanging from pieces of twine which caught the flickering light from the candles that stood upon the central oak dining table, on which places were already laid. A fire already glowed gently in the grate and a cluster of decanters shone in the corner

"This is where we shall be dining later, but for now there is a cold collation in the summer common room on the other side of the corridor."

There was a less formal style to this second chamber, with a variety of comfortable looking sofas and armchairs, upon which a number of what were clearly senior college fellows were spread. Macan waved an arm in our direction.

"Gentlemen, may I present my guests Sherlock Homes and Dr. Watson, who I have invited to try and shine some light on our poet's problem. I shall introduce you all properly in due course. A glass of burgundy, Holmes?" he asked, already holding a bottle. A general murmur from the assembled fellows implied that my friend's name was immediately recognised

I felt that Holmes was restraining himself from speaking out, but that he was unwilling to impose himself too quickly upon the sedate traditions of the academic common room. We settled ourselves around a small table in the corner of the room and only then did he show some impatience.

"Macan, I ask again: I enjoy a Christmas puzzle as much as anyone, but . . . ." and he left the obvious question hanging in the air. Our host leaned forward.

"I apologise, Holmes. I shall show you the evidence after lunch, but let me explain what has occurred."

"I should be more than obliged," my friend replied drily.

"You may be aware that Percy Bysshe Shelley came up to this college as an undergraduate in the year 1810. You may also be aware that he left, and was indeed sent down from the university, but a year later, having published a pamphlet extolling atheism. It was a famous story and one that, perhaps, did not redound well on the reputation of University College when, in ensuing years, Shelley became one of this country's finest romantic poets. It took many decades, but we seemed to right some kind of wrong two years ago when almost all of us accepted the offer of a fine memorial – a figurative statue of the man, then only twenty-nine, when his drowned body was washed up on an Italian shore. It had been commissioned by Shelley's daughter-in-law to stand at his grave in Rome, but its plinth was considered of too great a weight to lay upon the churchyard soil, and thus last year – while you, Holmes, were still missing presumed dead yourself – it found a proper resting-place in a special domed structure in the college. It is a glorious sculpture in pure white marble by Onslow Ford, an example of the most superb delicate design and workmanship. In a sense, it demonstrates that Univ. has accepted that an error was made too quickly so many years ago."

Sherlock Holmes responded in some exasperation.

"An informative, but hardly vital, history lesson, my dear Macan."

"Then it will interest you that Shelley's head is entirely purple today."

The others in the common room heard Macan's words clearly, and newspapers and wine glasses were lowered in anticipation. Holmes glanced across at me and raised an eyebrow.

"At last!" Our host's face remained serious.

"Holmes, I suppose this is indeed some sort of Yuletide puzzle, but it is an extremely serious matter. A major work of art has been despoiled and it would be far too tedious, I fancy, to involve the local police force – a force which, it must be said, tries to involve itself in college and University affairs as little as possible. No, there has been no murder or other serious deviltry done, but the story will undoubtedly come out, which will be highly detrimental to the college and could contribute to an element of distrust, and thereby fewer young men choosing to attend here for their further education."

"When you say his head is purple," I ventured, "what exactly do you mean?" Macan was about to answer, but Holmes intervened decisively.

"I cannot but be intrigued, as you thought I would be, old friend. I think you had better show us the scene of the crime – a phrase which is almost certainly a touch too serious in this case. But, come, Watson, we are relaxing in Oxford: let us see how white has turned to purple. Gentlemen," he said, addressing the others in the room, "while you do not exactly appear to be in the uproar that Macan indicated to me in his wire, I hope that by the time you sit down for your Christmas repast on the morrow, there will be no further shilly-shallying over Shelley." With that, he motioned me to follow Macan.

We stepped back into the quadrangle, and our guide led us back towards the lodge, then turned to his left through a corner archway, kicking the snow from his shoes. A short corridor suddenly opened out into a domed area of perfect dimensions, dominated by an ornately carved block of black marble upon which lay the life-size, pure white sculpture of the great poet, of such subtle shaping that it seemed nigh on impossible that it could have been hewn out of Carrara.

Yet, as we approached it, it became apparent that something was badly amiss, for there were blotches and streaks of a deep purple and crimson colour upon the face and head. Holmes descended the two steps and went up to the sculpture.

"Some sad student prank, no doubt," I suggested to Macan, who immediately shook his head.

"Under normal circumstances, Dr. Watson, that is precisely what I should have assumed. But it is Christmas Eve: we have not had an undergraduate on the premises for nearly a month. And there are few of us dons in college at this time of year."

"Seven, including yourself, I should say," came from Holmes, now busy sniffing the sculpture. "Nine places are laid for dinner, I think. This is most interesting, Watson. I should value your opinion." I approached the tainted sculpture in some surprise.

"I am more used to dealing with live bodies, actually," I retorted. My friend smiled, almost impishly.

"Tell me, Macan, when you found the sculpture in this state?"

"After dinner yesterday evening. My rooms are up this staircase, and so I have to pass Shelley."

"Did you tell the other fellows of your discovery?"

"Yes. I hurried back to the dining room, where I found Dr. Rowley and Professor Teasdale. They were appalled, of course. I naturally waited until early this morning to send you a telegram."

"Quite so. Well, Watson, what do you think?"

I had been examining the purple portions closely.

"I don't know what you want me to say, Holmes," I replied, in some exasperation.

"Sixty-three or seventy?" I think the set of my eyebrows must have indicated that I had no idea of what my friend was talking about.

"Macan, I presume the college has a good cellar?"

"Of wines?" the academic asked, uncertainly.

"Well, of ports, to be precise. Watson, did you not smell? Even after a good few hours, there is no doubt that it is port that has settled into the marble. I merely wondered if you recognised the vintage."

190

"I am more of a Madeira man myself, as you well know," I said to Sherlock Holmes, as a few minutes later we settled ourselves once more in the college common room. We were the only occupants, the other dons having disappeared, and Dr. Macan having held back to ask staff about cleansing matters.

"I don't think we must take this affair too seriously, Watson," Holmes remarked languidly, "but it is a decided waste of Ferreira sixty-three – for that is what I fancy it was. Why should any man hate Bysshe Shelley enough to desecrate such a wondrous sculpture?"

I was about to express agreement when the door flew open and Macan appeared as if shot from a cannon.

"I don't believe it! I simply don't believe it!" he cried, as he slumped into an armchair. "They have done it again, and it is worse, so much worse." He tapped his fingers in exasperation and a vein stood out upon his forehead. "Now it is brandy."

"Surely not spirits as well as vintage wine?" I said. Macan stared at us in agitation and then drew a deep breath.

"There is the most delicate tinge of light brown across the toes. They certainly had not been assaulted thus last night, and I had not noticed this disgrace when we were there just now." Holmes furrowed his brow.

"Nor had I," he admitted with some chagrin. "Show me. Watson, you need not come: relax and think of the Malvasia grape."

I busied myself with the pile of newspapers that lay upon the central table and helped myself to another small glass of white burgundy. Some fifteen minutes later, Holmes and Macan returned, my friend holding a handkerchief.

"Here, you can smell cognac quite clearly, and Macan thinks it must have been done during the few minutes he was waiting at the college gate onto the High Street for our arrival before lunch. Oh, and, Watson, I have just checked: there is a half-filled decanter of the Ferreira in the adjacent dining room."

"I had wondered if it might be a college staff member who could have perpetrated these outrages, if it were not a student," I said. "But perhaps we need to investigate the fellows, if port and brandy are involved." Homes intervened suddenly.

"What was that word you used one moment ago, Watson? What is brandy?"

"A spirit, Holmes," I replied, a touch wearily. "One of many."

"Of course: thank you, my friend. Macan, tell me of the six other Univ. fellows at present residing in the college over this Christmas period."

191

"Well, we are a college strong in the arts and classics, as you know. Wilson is a historian of the first order, who concentrates on the Whigs of the last century. Teasdale and Kerr are classicists, Rowley and Seton specialise in ancient and more modern literature respectively, while Dix has been immersed in Goethe for as long as I myself have been a Fellow here. All of us are of broadly similar age, in our fifties and sixties.

"By the by, gentlemen, we shall dine early this evening, to permit the steward and the other servants to leave the college at not too late an hour, to be home with their families for the start of Christmas Day. You are both in rooms on Staircase One, and the porter will show you to them. May I suggest we gather here again at half-past-six? Perhaps, Holmes, by then you may have some theories as to what we are facing here, bizarre as it may seem?"

Holmes looked up at Macan from his chair in relaxed fashion.

"I already have one very specific theory. But I need to know what liqueurs you have available? And I should like to see the College Register – would that be possible?"

"It is held in the Master's Lodgings, but he is away at present and there would be no harm in my bringing it over this evening. And all available drinks are over there in the walnut cabinet – apart, that is from the decanters you have already seen in the dining room."

Holmes crossed the room and swung open the doors of the chest, quickly surveying the contents. "I thought so," he announced triumphantly. "An entertaining evening lies ahead for us, I fancy, Watson."

"Do please share some of your thoughts. Which drink has particularly caught your eye?"

"Don't worry, my friend: you will be present at the *denouement*. I must pay one further visit to the sculpture, smoke a contemplative pipe in my room, and be back down here at the time proposed." With that, Sherlock Holmes strode from the common room, whistling, somewhat to my surprise, a jaunty version of "God Rest You Merry, Gentlemen".

"Oh, and by the by," he said, turning abruptly, "hail to thee, blithe spirit!"

I was somewhat surprised at this exhortation, but was glad to see that, however complex the matter of Shelley's head and feet appeared to me, Holmes seemed confident.

Having spent a restive half hour rambling through the snowy streets of Oxford and watching myriad last-minute Christmas gifts being purchased by anxious-looking townspeople, I changed in my room and was down in the common room at the appointed hour. Holmes and Macan were already seated at a side table, poring over a volume, while fellows drifted about with glasses of sherry in their hands. I crossed to my friends.

"Ah, Watson, we were just going over the Register from eighty-three years past. Here is the relevant entry." said Holmes, swivelling the great leather-bound tome towards me and pointing a thin finger at a written entry. "This is why Shelley left University College."

I peered at the ancient scratchy writing: "At a meeting of the master and fellows held this day it was determined that Thomas Jefferson Hogg and Percy Bysshe Shelley, Commoners, be publicly expelled for contumaciously refusing to answer questions proposed to them," I read slowly, "and for also repeatedly declining to disavow a publication entitled 'The Necessity of Atheism'." I looked up at Holmes and was about to speak.

"Stubbornly, or perversely, Watson."

"Hogg was a close friend of Shelley's," Macan explained. "They were both what you might call intellectual rebels and, with the publication of this pamphlet in March 1811, were frankly mocking the very foundations upon which the University – let alone this college – rested at the time. Another student, a contemporary of the miscreants, reported that the two of them had made themselves as conspicuous as possible in the days leading up to their expulsion – walking proudly and blatantly up and down the centre of the quadrangle."

I could see that one or two of the academics were trying very hard to hear what was being said. Holmes intervened:

"Interesting, my dear Macan, that you yourself have just used the word 'miscreants' to describe Shelley and his confederate?"

"It is, of course, another world today, and I used the term lightly. But the fury at their actions apparently ran very deep at the time, Holmes, and certain of the fellows held much rancour against Shelley for years. It would seem that the Master might have had mercy if the young man had been, er, less contumacious, but was livid when he gave no ground. The Dean said that the student could never ever be forgiven for having brought the college into such disrepute, and apparently even forty years later, eyebrows were raised if any undergraduate expressed an interest in the poet's works."

"And yet the college did indeed forgive in the end," I suggested, "as the acceptance of the monument indicates."

"Indeed," replied Holmes. "Yet troubled waters run just as deep as those that are still, as we see from the desecrations of that monument we are investigating, the source of which I expect to be discovered before the dawning of Christmas Day. Aha, dinner is being called. And Watson, by

193

the way, I should have drawn your attention to the names of the college fellows in 1811."

I was naturally slightly thrown by this aside, but forbore to reply as the nine of us filed across into the dining room, where three college stewards waited. There was a low murmur of gossip as we took our allotted seats around the long oval table. Holmes was in deep conversation with his friend Macan, and I exchanged words with the classics scholar Professor Teasdale to my right, a man of thin features and a nose upon which a pair of wire spectacles was loosely balanced. He was intrigued by our presence and wanted to know what lines Holmes and I were following, especially since only he and one other don had been present when Macan reported the first discovery of Shelley's ruined head. Since I understood so little of the case myself, we moved on to other topics as a splendid fillet of fish was placed before me, and something rather special was poured into my wine glass.

As the evening wore on and two further festive and fascinating courses came and were consumed, Sherlock Holmes became the centrepiece of the dinner. Macan could but shrug his shoulders and grin in my direction as my friend held court. Truth to say, I had heard some of the tales before and his extraordinary summing-up of the recent and intriguing correspondence between Florence Nightingale and William Rathbone came as little surprise to me. But it was a most enjoyable repast, and by the time the port and Madeira decanters had circled for the final time – the table having already been cleared and the servants departed – we all agreed that it had been a most delightful way to spend a Christmas Eve.

The air in the dining room was thick with cigar smoke and the embers in the fireplace were just beginning to die down when Holmes was suddenly at my side.

'Come, Watson, now, and do not appear surprised," he whispered urgently, then passed from the room. I downed my glass in contemplative fashion, rose and bid my friends a good night and compliments of the season. As I too left, I saw Macan giving a slight nod in my direction.

Holmes was outside in the quadrangle, shifting his weight from foot to foot in anxious fashion as a light fall of snow wafted down. He laid a hand on my shoulder and near pushed me to the left and thus, I surmised, towards the corner archway that would lead to the Shelley sculpture. There was only the light of the moon to guide us the few yards before we ducked into the complete darkness of the short corridor.

"Holmes, what are we doing?" I whispered. His grip on my shoulder tightened.

"You have correctly surmised that this is not an important case, Watson," he replied in a low voice, "but it is Oxford, it is Christmas, and it is fun. I should like to see that matters turn out as I predict. Here, now, is the statue, and there is room for the two of us in the right-hand corner of this space in front of the Shelley to wait and see what may transpire. I have a shaded lamp here and am trusting to have a poetic outcome tonight. Silence, please."

Over the years, I have shared with Sherlock Holmes long waits during the watches of the night, the cases involving the infernal spotted snake and the league of red-haired men springing immediately to mind. Despite his words, however, that he believed this case not to be one of the most serious he had entertained, no pitch black wait can ever be entirely relaxed if one has no idea of what to expect; and thus it was that I sought some refuge in the fact that Holmes had not asked me to bring any weapon from Baker Street to Oxford.

Perhaps twenty minutes had passed when suddenly Holmes tautened. I became aware of the slight flickering of a candle from our left, the light brightening as it advanced upon the statue area. A dark figure stepped down towards the plinth.

In a second, Holmes released the lamp shutter and moved towards the form. I heard a strangled epithet and the sound of smashing glass, a sweet and somewhat sickly odour immediately suffusing the enclosed space. There was, however, no resistance from our quarry, a man revealed immediately to be the white-haired Doctor Rowley. He quickly collapsed in Holmes's arms, seeming to sob.

"Back to the common room, old man," said Holmes. "It's a sad story and too many decades have passed for you to make such foolish gestures. He's a broken man, Watson. Could you go ahead to the common room? Reggie Macan should be waiting."

"My goodness, two generations pass, and still the affair rankles," said Holmes, as the gas lights came on and the four of us sat back in comfortable seats, Rowley cowed and shivering. "Can your family never forgive?" The old man pursed his lips and remained silent.

"It was the green Chartreuse tonight, was it not?" Holmes persisted. The broken man nodded. Macan smiled, as if he had begun to understand what had occurred. Holmes addressed his words to me.

"What we have here, Watson, is a story of intractable unforgiving, lasting over too many years. It is a tale of misplaced familial loathing, with a trite and alcoholic end. Dr. Rowley, it is a pathetic tale, would you not agree?" Rowley winced.

"I am at a loss to know how you discovered it was me," he said in limp fashion.

"A simple linking of surnames. You are the grandson of Dr. George Rowley, Dean of this college at the time of the Shelley scandal, and later

195

to become its Master. Your grandfather signed his name in the register on the date that Hogg and Shelley were thrown out. A deeply religious man, he loathed the concept of atheism and anyone who promoted it. This carried through to your father and then to you. Macan tells me that you alone of the fellows voted against accepting the offer of the sculpture to this college.

"And then, once it had been installed, having lost the intellectual and historical argument, you began to concoct a bizarre plan of desecration. For a man of your distinction in the university – you are, I believe, one of the leading experts on ancient literature here at Oxford – you made one flawed decision and one psychologically interesting one. For some reason, you chose to make your mark, quite literally, when the undergraduates were out of college during this vacation: had the attacks on the sculpture been made in term time, they would undoubtedly have been put down to student high jinks. You also decided to play what you thought was a pretty little game, by running to a work by the very man you loathed. Watson, how well do you recall Shelley's lines in his poem 'To a Skylark'?"

"A question I regard as striking somewhat below the belt at this hour, after all we have been through, and indeed imbibed, this night," I responded. Holmes laughed.

"A fair enough answer, Watson! Let me, then, draw to your attention the first lines of the fourth verse. *'The pale purple even melts around thy flight'*. The purple of port, perhaps? I even gave you earlier a hint of the direction of my thoughts, when I gave you part of the opening line of the whole poem – and one of the most famous in all poetic history: *'Hail to thee, blithe Spirit'*. See what Rowley was doing? Brandy is as good a spirit to hurl at white marble as any. That is what we were already faced with by this evening.

"What further alcoholic beverage might be chosen next? There is mention by Shelley, of course, of *'the blue deep'*, but I am not aware of any drink of that hue. And I discarded for the same reason, his use of the words *'that silver sphere'*. But eventually the line *'In its own green leaves'* led me to ask Macan here what liqueurs are held in the common room, and when I saw a full bottle of the superb drink created by monks in their Chartreuse monastery near Grenoble, I was fairly sure of Dr. Rowley's next weapon. And it turned out to be so."

Rowley was a pathetic sight, his thin body almost fading into the folds of his academic gown and his hands clasped in anguish. Macan stood up with an air of finality.

"What you have done is despicable, Rowley. The Master will be told on his return to college, and I have no doubt that he will call a meeting of

196

fellows – just as that held in 1811 to decide on Shelley's fate. The result, I fancy, will be the same."

Sherlock Holmes leaned forward in his armchair.

"I wonder, Macan, whether you are perhaps being a touch severe on your colleague? Despicable his actions have certainly been, and I sincerely regret the uses to which fine port, cognac, and liqueurs have been put. But I fancy your college authorities will provide funds towards Shelley's cleansing, with no lasting damage done, unless it be to Dr. Rowley's own conscience. I have no powers in this matter, but Christmas Eve seems to me to be a time for forgiveness and understanding."

Macan smiled and shrugged his shoulders, his anger clearly receding. Holmes turned towards me.

"What a very curious Christmas we are spending, my dear Watson, when events of nearly a century ago have returned to haunt this ancient seat of learning. I think we shall allow ourselves to enjoy a festive day tomorrow in this lovely city and then return to Baker Street and hope for less bitter, twisted tales to come before us.

"So far as you are concerned, Rowley, you should have considered the closing two lines from another of Percy Shelley's poems: '*The world is weary of the past. Oh, might it die or rest at last!*'"

The Adventure of the Grace Chalice

by Roger Johnson
From *Part IV: 2016 Annual* (2016)

This script has never been published in text form, and was initially presented as a recorded performance in 2011 by the Old Court Radio Theatre Company. *It can be listened to or downloaded on the* Sherlock Holmes Society of London*'s website at* www.sherlock-holmes.org.uk.

This script is protected by copyright. For permission to reproduce it in any way or to perform it in any medium, please apply to *www.sherlock-holmes.org.uk.*

THE CAST

ANNOUNCER – Roger Johnson

SHERLOCK HOLMES – Jim Crozier

DR. JOHN H. WATSON – Dave Hawkes

HENRY STAUNTON – Brian Adrian

INSPECTOR G. LESTRADE – Matthew Elliott

MUSIC	OPENING THEME (*Fauré: Après un Rève*)
ANNOUNCER	*Sherlock Holmes.* We present *The Adventure of the Grace Chalice* by Roger Johnson.
MUSIC	FADE THEME OUT UNDER

SCENE 1

FX	221b BAKER STREET AMBIENCE, WITH A FIRE IN THE GRATE AND A CLOCK TICKING QUIETLY AWAY. HOLMES IS OVER AT THE

198

WINDOW, LOOKING DOWN INTO THE STREET.
WATSON IS RATHER OSTENTATIOUSLY
READING A NEWSPAPER, OPENING IT,
FOLDING IT BACK, TURNING THE PAGES.

WATSON
(A BEAT. HE CLEARS HIS THROAT AND READS) The new Emperor of Germany has dismissed Bismarck and appointed a new Chancellor . . . (A BEAT) Holmes? (A BEAT, THEN, SOTTO VOCE) "Knowledge of politics, feeble . . . ."

HOLMES
(A QUIET DISMISSIVE GRUNT)

FX
MORE BUSINESS WITH THE NEWSPAPER.

WATSON
The Prince of Wales has officially opened the Forth Bridge. (A BEAT) Apparently it's a remarkable structure in itself, and the view from the train is very beautiful on a good day . . . (A BRIEF PAUSE)

FX
MORE BUSINESS WITH THE NEWSPAPER.

WATSON
Samuel and Joseph Boswell are to be executed at Worcester on Tuesday for the murder of a gamekeeper . . . Hmm. The fatal shot was actually fired by their accomplice, Alfred Hill . . . (A BEAT) Hill's sentence has been reduced to penal servitude for life – and yet the Boswells will hang for a crime of which they are innocent! Holmes, this is a disgraceful miscarriage of justice. Even the local gentry have protested to the Home Secretary . . .

HOLMES
(A WEARY VOCAL SHRUG)

WATSON
(A BEAT) No, it's a matter for the lawyers and the politicians, I suppose – not for a private detective. A pity that English justice should come to this. (A SHIVER OF DISTASTE)

FX
MORE BUSINESS WITH THE NEWSPAPER.

WATSON	Ah! Pinero has a new play opening at the Court Theatre – er – *The Cabinet Minister.* (A BEAT) I've always enjoyed his comedies, Holmes . . . Holmes?
FX	WATSON PUTS THE PAPER DOWN.
WATSON	Brrr! This wretched damp weather does my old wound no good at all. (A BEAT) I have a medal somewhere – That's my official souvenir of the second Afghan War, but the bullet in my shoulder is a more effective reminder. (A BEAT) There's no clasp. Did you know that? The battle of Maiwand was such a disaster for our forces that no clasp was issued – just the medal . . . (A MOMENTARY PAUSE, THEN –) For pity's sake, Holmes! Do you really have nothing better to do than to stand at the window, glowering down at the street?
HOLMES	(A QUIET UNCOMPREHENDING GRUNT)
WATSON	(A TOUCH OF BITTERNESS) What was it you said when we first met? "I get in the dumps at times, and don't open my mouth for days on end. You must not think I am sulky when I do that." *Not sulky . . .?*
HOLMES	(HE HASN'T BEEN LISTENING) Watson, unless I am much mistaken, we have a client!
WATSON	(SOTTO VOCE) Thank heaven for that.
HOLMES	Plump – well-dressed – middle-aged – purposeful – and not without self-esteem. (A BEAT) Ah! He has paid off the cab and is approaching our door. Let us hope that he brings something of interest.
WATSON	Let us hope so.
FX	THE DOORBELL CLANGS IN THE DISTANCE. HOLMES GOES AND OPENS THE DOOR OF THE SITTING-ROOM.
HOLMES	(CALLING FROM THE DOORWAY) Mrs. Hudson! Please show our visitor in!

MUSIC	A SHORT BRIDGE
FX	THE VISITOR ENTERS THE ROOM AND CLOSES THE DOOR BEHIND HIM.
HOLMES	Good morning, sir. My name is Sherlock Holmes. This is my friend and colleague Dr. Watson. Now, which of us have you come to consult?
STAUNTON	It is you, Mr. Holmes – you!
HOLMES	Capital! Then please be seated, sir. The basket chair is comfortable, I think. (A BEAT WHILE STAUNTON SITS) And now, if you please, consult!
STAUNTON	Thank you, sir, thank you. My name is Henry Staunton. Perhaps it is familiar to you?
HOLMES	Ah, yes. Surely I have seen you at Christie's and Sotheby's? You have a reputation as a connoisseur of *objets d'art*, I think.
STAUNTON	It is true, sir. I am a man of somewhat retiring, and I might even say refined, tastes. I like to surround myself with elegance and beauty. I do not live extravagantly but I may perhaps call myself a patron of the arts. It is my weakness.
HOLMES	But what is it that brings you to Baker Street, Mr. Staunton?
STAUNTON	Sir, I am the victim of a most audacious theft!
HOLMES	Indeed? This is really most grati – most interesting.
WATSON	What has been stolen, Mr. Staunton?
STAUNTON	It is nothing less, Doctor, than the Grace Chalice!
WATSON	The Grace – ? (A BEAT) Holmes?

HOLMES	It was made for the monks of Melcarth Abbey sometime in the fifteenth century. The records say that it is made of Welsh gold, elaborately chased with biblical symbols. When the monastery was dissolved, the chalice was not among the valuables appropriated by the Crown, though Thomas Cromwell's commissioners made a thorough search. It came to light more than a century later, after the Civil War, when the Grace family acquired the property. (A BEAT) I was not aware that the chalice had been sold.
STAUNTON	It was a private transaction, Mr. Holmes, entirely private. I bought the chalice from Sir Cedric Grace just ten days ago. Thanks to some unfortunate investments, the old gentleman was obliged to sell some of his more valuable possessions – discreetly, of course, most discreetly – and it was my good luck to purchase that particular gem. I may say that it cost me a very considerable sum – a pretty penny, sir! But I do not grudge it, for the chalice is unique, quite unique.
HOLMES	Since you have come to me instead of the police, Mr. Staunton, I take it that the precious object was not stolen from your bank, but from your own house.
STAUNTON	You are correct, sir. I wished to make a proper study of the chalice before depositing it with my bankers. Ah! I had, of course, taken out an insurance policy upon it.
WATSON	Where do you live, Mr. Staunton?
STAUNTON	The house is called Holly Trees. It is not large, but it suits my needs, and the situation close to Highgate Ponds is very charming. I am a bachelor, you see, and I live a simple life.
HOLMES	Pray continue, Mr. Staunton.
STAUNTON	Ah, yes. There is a safe in my study, securely built into the wall, and hidden behind a looking-glass. That, of course, is where I kept the chalice. You may imagine

my distress – my utter distress, sir – when, this very
morning, I discovered the safe unlocked and the
chalice gone!

WATSON   You would be well advised, I think, to give the police
              a description of the chalice.

STAUNTON   I should rather not have to deal with the police, Dr.
              Watson. I value my privacy, and I do not relish the
              thought of large clumsy boots tramping through my
              house and garden. No, I prefer to call upon the skill
              and discretion of Mr. Sherlock Holmes.

HOLMES   That is very good of you, Mr. Staunton. You will
              appreciate, however, that I must have all the details, no
              matter how trivial they may seem.

STAUNTON   Of course, sir, of course. Well, my housekeeper, Mrs.
              Elliott, called me at seven o'clock this morning,
              slightly earlier than usual, and she was in a most
              agitated state. Rather than trust to her somewhat
              incoherent account, I went myself directly to my
              study, where I found the safe door standing open and
              the study window broken. Here, plainly, the miscreant
              had gained entrance, inserting his hand through the
              broken pane and unfastening the latch. I observed also
              a double line of footprints running across the bare,
              damp earth from the high garden wall, and returning
              thither.

WATSON   One moment, Mr. Staunton. Are we to understand that
              your study overlooks bare earth?

STAUNTON   (A PAINED CHUCKLE) It does seem odd, sir, put
              like that, but the matter is simply explained: the
              ground has been prepared for a new lawn, but my
              gardener has strained his back, and the turves have not
              yet been laid. A fortunate thing, as I am sure you will
              agree, sir! Most fortunate, for now we have the
              clearest clues as to the thief's means of entrance and
              egress. Naturally, I have left strict instructions that the
              footprints are to be left untouched.

WATSON	Very sensible.
HOLMES	Yes, indeed. Well, Mr. Staunton, I think that we had better come at once and investigate the scene of the crime. I shall just gather a few essential items of equipment. Watson, will you call a cab?
MUSIC	BRIDGE

SCENE 2

FX	STREET SOUNDS, THE CLIP-CLOP OF HORSE'S HOOVES, AND THE SOUND OF WHEELS ON THE HARD ROAD (THE WHEELS HAVE SOLID RUBBER TYRES) – WE'RE IN A FOUR-WHEELER ON OUR WAY TO HIGHGATE.
HOLMES	Now, Mr. Staunton, you have mentioned your housekeeper. What other staff have you at Holly Trees?
STAUNTON	Besides Mrs. Elliott, there are the maid and the gardener – that is all. I live very simply, as I have told you, sir.
HOLMES	And there is no one else in your immediate household? You have no guests, no lodgers?
STAUNTON	No, indeed, sir. I am not what you would call a sociable man. I have no family and very few friends. I do not wish for more.
WATSON	Your study is on the ground floor, Mr. Staunton, but is it at the front or the back of the house?
STAUNTON	It is at the front, sir.
WATSON	So a passer-by could see the study window from the street?

STAUNTON	Oh, dear me, no! No indeed. The entire property is surrounded by a high brick wall. There is a gate, of course, but that is as high as the wall, and made of solid oak planks. As I told you, sir, I value my privacy.
FX	THE STREET SOUNDS GRADUALLY FADE OUT, BUT THE HOOFBEATS AND THE SOUND OF THE WHEELS CONTINUE.
HOLMES	No doubt there is a gate at the back as well?
STAUNTON	There is, Mr. Holmes, but it is kept locked. The only person who ever uses it is the gardener, Albert Lowry, who comes and goes that way. He rents a cottage in Bacons Lane. (A SUDDEN CHUCKLE)
WATSON	Mr. Staunton?
STAUNTON	Lowry thinks himself a wit, sir, but he has only one joke. His room overlooks the cemetery. He calls it the dead centre of the village. (A BEAT) It is not a very good joke, I fear.
HOLMES	(A BEAT) So the gardener does not live in. Where do the other servants sleep?
STAUNTON	Ah, yes. Mrs. Elliott's two rooms occupy the second floor back. She can almost see Hampstead Heath from her sitting-room window, I believe. The maid, Sarah Gilbert, sleeps in the attic at the back of the house.
WATSON	And where is your own bedroom, Mr. Staunton?
STAUNTON	I also sleep at the rear of the house, Doctor, and I sleep the sleep of the just. Like the servants, I was quite unaware that my property was under attack last night. It is a wicked world, gentlemen, a wicked world. (A BEAT) Ah! But here we are!
FX	THE CAB STOPS.
STAUNTON	Welcome to Holly Trees, gentlemen.

205

MUSIC	BRIDGE

SCENE 3

FX	OUTDOOR AMBIENCE. IT'S A COLD, DAMP DAY, SO THERE'S NOT MUCH IN THE WAY OF BIRDSONG. HOLMES, WATSON, AND STAUNTON ARE WALKING ON A GRAVEL PATH.
WATSON	The gate and the wall are quite as formidable as you suggested, Mr. Staunton. The wall must be at least nine feet high.
HOLMES	Ten-and-a-half feet, I should say, Watson.
STAUNTON	The ground is quite bare, as you see, right up to the front of the house, and there are the stacks of turf, just waiting for Lowry to lay them. You will wish to inspect the footprints, of course?
HOLMES	All in good time, Mr. Staunton. Now, Watson, how far would you say it is from the house to the garden wall?
WATSON	Not more than twenty yards, Holmes. On a good day, this garden must be a pleasant spot – or it will be once the new lawn is laid – but the property is not extensive.
HOLMES	Just so.
FX	THE FOOTSTEPS COME TO A HALT.
HOLMES	Your study is on the right of the front door, Mr. Staunton.
STAUNTON	So it is, sir. But how – ? Ah! The broken window, of course. Yes. And the parlour is on the left.

206

HOLMES	Very good. Now for the footprints. I don't wish to trample on this flower bed, Mr. Staunton, but I see a way through just ahead of us.
FX	THE FOOTSTEPS RESUME AND SHORTLY FADE DOWN.
WATSON	(A MOMENTARY PAUSE) Thank goodness we've had no rain today! Your intended lawn would be a sea of mud, Mr. Staunton, and we might well have lost the burglar's footprints.
HOLMES	Instead, the ground is just firm enough for us, and the prints are perfectly preserved. How very fortunate! Well, before the weather does take a turn for the worse, we should take a cast of these prints. Watson, will you please fetch me a bucket of water? There must be a bucket and a tap in the scullery. I'm sure Mr. Staunton will show you.
STAUNTON	Water, sir?
WATSON	To mix with plaster of Paris, Mr. Staunton. Didn't you notice how heavy Holmes's bag is?
STAUNTON	Oh . . . Yes. (A BEAT) Come with me, Doctor.
HOLMES	Don't be too long, Watson.
MUSIC	BRIDGE
HOLMES	Capital! I have rarely seen such clear prints. Our man has a long stride – perhaps he was eager to cross the garden as quickly as possible without running. The night was rather dark, was it not?
WATSON	These impressions are quite remarkably sharp. It looks to me as if the boots were new. They're large, too. What size would you say, Holmes?
HOLMES	Size eleven, Watson – no doubt about it. (A BEAT) The preservation of the footprints is fortunate, but the

	newness of the boots is not. There has not been time for their owner to impress his personality upon them.
WATSON	The burglar could hardly have left plainer traces if he had intended to.
HOLMES	Indeed.
STAUNTON	(CALLING FROM SOME YARDS AWAY) Will you not come and examine the study, Mr. Holmes? That is where the theft took place, after all.
HOLMES	(CALLING BACK) By all means, Mr. Staunton. (TO WATSON) You know, there are two very singular features here, Watson. For instance, our man seems to have let himself down from the wall with commendable delicacy.
WATSON	Yes, I noticed that. There's no indication that he jumped, and I see no sign that a ladder was used. * Still, it's not impossible that he dropped delicately on to the ground, is it . . . ?
FX	* FADE DOWN WATSON'S VOICE.
HOLMES	(A MOMENTARY PAUSE) Well, our burglar certainly knew what he was doing. This window has been broken in a most efficient manner. The pane was smeared with (HE SNIFFS) treacle and covered with a sheet of strong brown paper. There would have been very little noise, and the broken glass could just be pulled away to leave an opening. (A BEAT) Hmm. The thief removed just the one pane and reached through – like – this – to undo the latch.
FX	HOLMES UNDOES THE LATCH AND RAISES THE SASH WINDOW.
HOLMES	And here on the sill is the print of his left boot – muddy and indistinct, as one might expect. No matter. Let us enter the room.

WATSON   Holmes! Not that way, surely!

HOLMES   Oh, very well. The front door it is, then.

FX   GARDEN BACKGROUND OUT.

SCENE 4

STAUNTON   (A MOMENTARY PAUSE) As you see, gentlemen, I choose the company of art and literature over that of my fellow men. That landscape is by Madame Vigée-Lebrun, and the portrait is the work of Godfrey Schalcken. Both are genuine. I have my doubts about the Fragonard on the far wall, but you will admit that it is very charming.

WATSON   We are digressing, Mr. Staunton. Mr. Holmes is –

HOLMES   (FROM THE FLOOR) Just examining the floor, Watson. (HE STANDS UP) These muddy marks tell us nothing more, I fear. Let us look at the safe. Behind the looking-glass, I think you said, Mr. Staunton?

FX   A CLICK AS STAUNTON RELEASES THE CATCH AND SWINGS BACK THE MIRROR.

STAUNTON   That is correct, sir. I have the key here –

FX   STAUNTON INSERTS THE KEY IN THE LOCK OF THE SAFE AND TURNS IT. HE TURNS THE HANDLE AND OPENS THE HEAVY IRON DOOR.

HOLMES   Ah, yes. Chatwood. A good make, though perhaps you should have invested in something more sophisticated. (A MOMENTARY PAUSE WHILE HE EXAMINES THE LOCK) A really competent burglar would have no great difficulty in picking this lock . . . Hmm. It appears to have been opened with a key, however. It has certainly not been forced. (A BEAT) And nothing was taken except the chalice?

209

STAUNTON	Nothing except the chalice, sir. I begin to suspect that I have harboured a spy in my house, but I cannot think how that could be. The servants are certainly innocent. Both the maid and the gardener have been in my employ for at least fifteen years, and the invaluable Mrs. Elliott has worked for my family since I was a young man. I trust them all, sir, trust them implicitly. Besides, I am quite sure that none of them knew of my purchase. Even the housekeeper never enters this room without my express permission.
WATSON	Is there only one key to the safe?
STAUNTON	There are two, Doctor. I carry this one upon my watch-chain at all times.
HOLMES	And the other?
STAUNTON	It is with my bankers, Holder and Stephenson.
HOLMES	Very good. Now, you have cleared your servants of suspicion. Have you entertained any visitors during the past ten days?
STAUNTON	No. Oh, yes – yes, there has been one visitor. In fact he has spent two evenings here – but you need not suspect him, Mr. Holmes. The idea is quite absurd! I have told you that I am not a sociable man, but once a week I play Ecarté or Piquet with my cousin, Walter Ruskin. Sometimes we meet here, and sometimes at Walter's house at Mill Hill. He is a bachelor, like me, with no other close family.
WATSON	Ruskin? Is that Ruskin the gunsmith, with the shop in Jermyn Street?
STAUNTON	That is correct, Doctor, though Walter retired six months ago. He is a good fellow. We have been friends since boyhood.
HOLMES	Did you tell him about the chalice, Mr. Staunton?

210

STAUNTON   Er – yes. Yes, I did. All he said was that I ought to deposit it in a bank-vault as soon as possible.

HOLMES   Your spare safe key is secure, but your cousin might perhaps have had the opportunity to take an impression of the key on your watch-chain. Such things can be done quickly and discreetly.

STAUNTON   It – it is – possible, Mr. Holmes . . . Physically possible, I mean. I cannot believe that Walter would stoop to such a thing! Besides, he would have no cause to steal from me. He is my creditor, not my debtor, thanks to our weekly gaming. I owe him a substantial sum, as it happens.

WATSON   Nevertheless, Mr. Staunton, we must examine every possibility. Can you give us a description of your cousin?

STAUNTON   If I must, Doctor! Walter is quite as tall as Mr. Holmes here, but more heavily built. He is fifty-nine years of age, with thick dark hair and a heavy moustache. His eyes are light brown – hazel, I think, is the word.

HOLMES   Do you know what size he takes in boots?

STAUNTON   Really, Mr. Holmes! I – I am not sure . . . Walter is much taller than I, and his feet are larger than mine. Larger than yours too, I should say. Size ten, perhaps, or even size eleven.

HOLMES   Well, Mr. Staunton, I think we have done all that we can do here – for the time being, at least. My next move must be to call upon Mr. Walter Ruskin, if you will kindly give me his address. I have a curious feeling that this is one of those straightforward cases that turn out not to be quite so straightforward after all.

STAUNTON   Walter's address is Kingsland, Wiseman's Lane, Mill Hill. But I assure you, Mr. Holmes, that you are barking up the wrong tree.

HOLMES	Thank you, Mr. Staunton. I shall let you know as soon as I have something to report. Come, Watson.

SCENE 5

FX	THE GARDEN BACKGROUND AGAIN. HOLMES AND WATSON ARE WALKING ON THE GRAVEL PATH.
WATSON	Holmes, you said that there are two odd features here in the garden. What is the second?
HOLMES	You didn't notice it? Why, it was simply that the two lines of prints are quite separate: at no point do the footprints leaving the house overlap those made in going to the house. Now, old fellow, I shall endeavour to make my way to Mill Hill. I think perhaps you should return to Baker Street. You'd probably do well to have some lunch on the way. I know how grumpy you can get if you miss your lunch.
WATSON	Whereas a problem like this is meat and drink to you. Very well, Holmes.
FX	THE FOOTSTEPS FADE OUT UNDER.
MUSIC	BRIDGE

SCENE 6

WATSON	(HE'S ON THE OTHER SIDE OF THE DOOR, CALLING FROM THE TOP OF THE STAIRS) Thank you, Mrs. Hudson!
FX	HE OPENS THE DOOR OF THE SITTING-ROOM AND ENTERS, CLOSING THE DOOR BEHIND HIM.
WATSON	Lestrade! How are you? Mrs. Hudson told me you were here. You've not been waiting long, I hope?

LESTRADE	Only a few minutes, Doctor. It's good to see you again. Mr. Holmes not with you?
WATSON	No. He's off on a case. Gone to Mill Hill. I can't say what time he'll be back. Do sit down again. (A BEAT) Er – would you care for a cigar?
LESTRADE	Thank you, Doctor. I don't mind if I do.
FX	BOTH MEN TAKE CIGARS FROM A BOX. WATSON STRIKES A MATCH AND LIGHTS LESTRADE'S.
LESTRADE	(HE DRAWS ON HIS CIGAR, THEN –) Thank you!
FX	UNDER LESTRADE'S REMARK, WATSON LIGHTS HIS OWN CIGAR.
WATSON	(HE DRAWS ON HIS CIGAR, THEN –) Well, Inspector, is it good news or bad? What brings you here this afternoon?
LESTRADE	Good news, in a way, I think. Do you remember Esmond Northcote?
WATSON	I do indeed! A very nasty piece of work. Card-sharp and blackmailer. Murderer too, I think.
LESTRADE	We could never prove the murder, but we did get Northcote sentenced to five years' hard labour on the blackmail charge. He was sent to Maidstone.
WATSON	Five years? Then he must have served his time by now. You surely haven't come just to tell us that Northcote has been released?
LESTRADE	No-o-o. That's not the whole story, Dr. Watson – but I think I shall save the important part until Mr. Holmes returns. You don't mind if I wait here, I hope?
WATSON	My dear fellow, I shall be delighted.

LESTRADE	Thank you, Doctor. Er, can you tell me something about the case that Mr. Holmes is investigating?
WATSON	Yes. Yes – why not? Have you ever heard of the Grace Chalice, Inspector? No? Neither had I until this morning. * I don't need to say any anything about the chalice itself except that it's made of gold and it's worth more money than you or I could ever hope to own . . .
FX	* FADE DOWN WATSON'S VOICE.
FX	FADE UP LESTRADE'S VOICE.
LESTRADE	Retiring nature! Clumsy boots! These people are their own worst enemies. He should at least have reported the theft at the local police station, and given the duty officer a good description of the stolen item.
WATSON	That's just what I said, but he wouldn't hear of it.
FX	WE HEAR THE DISTANT SLAM OF THE FRONT DOOR.
WATSON	Ah! Here's Holmes now.
LESTRADE	(A BEAT) He doesn't sound any too happy, does he?
FX	THE DOOR OF THE SITTING-ROOM OPENS.
HOLMES	(APPROACHING FROM THE DOORWAY) I don't like it, Watson. I don't like it at all. Walter Ruskin hasn't been seen since yesterday evening. The only positive information to emerge is that Ruskin does take size eleven in boots. (A BEAT) Ah, Lestrade. To what do we owe this visit?
WATSON	It's about Esmond Northcote, Holmes.
HOLMES	Northcote? He was released three days ago from Maidstone Prison. What about him?

LESTRADE	He disappeared from view almost immediately, Mr. Holmes, but we think we've found him again.
HOLMES	You *think* – ?
LESTRADE	I put it like that because the man we have is dead and rather horribly mutilated.
HOLMES	(HE'S REALLY INTERESTED) Oh?
LESTRADE	It's not a nice thing, sir. The man's face has been quite burned off with acid. He was killed by a savage blow to the head, and then . . . . Well, there's not enough of his face left to identify him, but all the rest fits. He's a big man, muscles well developed from rowing, a good head of hair. We found him this morning in Abney Park Cemetery, of all places, behind one of the tombs. I don't suppose many decent people will mourn him, but we are still bound to search for his killer. (A BEAT) Anyway, Mr. Holmes, as you took such an interest in Esmond Northcote's arrest and trial, I thought you might wish to come and see the body.
HOLMES	Why not? There are no threads in my current investigation, or none that I can follow today. By all means let us visit the mortuary. Watson, will you come?
WATSON	Certainly, Holmes.
LESTRADE	Thank you, Doctor. There'll be a post-mortem, of course, but I may be grateful for your medical knowledge. I shall go and hail a cab.
MUSIC	BRIDGE

SCENE 7

FX	THE MORTUARY, A LARGE COLD BARE ROOM WITH TILED WALLS. A DOOR OPENS, AND LESTRADE, HOLMES, AND WATSON ENTER.

LESTRADE	(APPROACHING FROM THE DOORWAY) Here we are, gentlemen – Stoke Newington Mortuary. (TO AN ATTENDANT) Thank you, Jackson. We shan't need you. (A BEAT) Over here, Mr. Holmes. This is the one.
WATSON	(A BEAT, THEN, QUIETLY AND SERIOUSLY –) If I were a squeamish man I should not have taken up medicine as a profession. Even so, I have to say that this is one of the most appalling things I have ever seen. Not even in Afghanistan –
LESTRADE	Man's inhumanity to man, eh, Doctor? I'm no philosopher, but something like this, well, it almost makes me despair for the future of the country.
HOLMES	That will do, Lestrade! We must look upon the dead clay before us, not as the mutilated shell of a fellow man, but merely as an object of professional study.
LESTRADE	(PULLS HIMSELF TOGETHER) Quite right, Mr. Holmes. Well, the post-mortem will begin at half-past-six this evening – Dr. Barnes can't be available before then – but there's no doubt in my mind that death was caused by a blow or series of blows to the back of the head.
WATSON	Two blows at least, I should say, with a heavy and very hard object. You can feel where the occipital and parietal bones have been shattered.
HOLMES	It's a brutal business, but it would not be reason enough in itself to bring us all the way from Baker Street. The complete obliteration of the facial features is decidedly unusual, however.
WATSON	Thank heaven! All I can say in mitigation is that the destruction of the victim's face was carried out after death.
HOLMES	So I read it, Watson. How long has he been dead?

WATSON	You know very well that I can't give you a definite answer, Holmes, particularly as the body was found out of doors. (A MOMENT WHILE HE CHECKS THE CORPSE) Hmm. The flesh is elastic. Rigor mortis has passed. (A BEAT) My estimation puts the time of death at twelve to twenty-four hours ago.
HOLMES	(A BEAT) What of the man's clothes, Lestrade?
LESTRADE	They're at the police station, Mr. Holmes. You can examine them if you like, but I don't think they'll tell you much. The body was dressed only in good quality woollen long johns. No hat, no boots, no outer clothing at all.
HOLMES	And no jewellery either, I suppose.
LESTRADE	None.
HOLMES	Whoever killed this man was determined to eradicate his identity entirely. (A BEAT) Esmond Northcote has disappeared from view, so you think that this is he. There is a superficial resemblance, but I think I can prove to you that you are mistaken.
LESTRADE	Oh?
HOLMES	Feel the muscles of the forearms, Watson.
WATSON	(HE DOES SO) Yes, they're very well developed, just as the Inspector said.
HOLMES	They are indeed. But, if I take the hands in my own and close the fists . . . Feel those muscles again!
LESTRADE	Good Lord!
WATSON	(SIMULTANEOUSLY) That's astonishing! Even without touching it I can see that the muscle of the left forearm is far more highly developed than the other. It stands out like an egg!

LESTRADE	Well, that rules out Northcote! He's right-handed, but this man must have been left-handed – and remarkably strong.
HOLMES	No, if he had been left-handed then we would be marvelling at the muscular development of his right forearm. I know of only one activity that can cause the muscle to swell like that. It happens through years of taking the recoil of a rifle.
WATSON	(A BEAT) Then you think this is – ?
HOLMES	I do.
LESTRADE	(ALMOST TO HIMSELF) Tall, well-built, thick dark hair, large feet . . .
HOLMES	Ah! Watson has told you of our current investigation, has he? Yes, Lestrade, this can only be the retired gunsmith, Walter Ruskin.
LESTRADE	Another fugitive! But who would want to kill him, Mr. Holmes? And who, in heaven's name, would want to do *that* to his body?
HOLMES	Who indeed? Lestrade, I must ask you to restrain your natural impatience. There are some further enquiries to be made, but I shall not be able to get the answers until tomorrow morning. Meanwhile, can you arrange for a constable to keep watch overnight on Mr. Henry Staunton's house?
LESTRADE	You think he's in danger, then? From the person who murdered his cousin? Very well, Mr. Holmes. We'll go straight to Highgate Police Station, and I'll make sure that it's done.
HOLMES	Excellent! Now let us gather our belongings and allow the good Jackson to lock up here. I am sure you will not refuse another cigar when we return to Baker Street, and perhaps a glass of brandy – to help keep out the cold, of course.

LESTRADE	Thank you kindly, Mr. Holmes. That would be most welcome. And on the way back, maybe you'll fill in the details regarding this very nasty business.
WATSON	Yes, please do, Holmes! * The picture is almost complete in my mind, but there are still some pieces missing. I'm not entirely sure of the connection between the death of Walter Ruskin and the theft of the Grace Chalice . . . .
FX	* FADE WATSON'S VOICE AND MORTUARY BACKGROUND UNDER.
MUSIC	BRIDGE

SCENE 8

FX	OPEN AIR BACKGROUND. A FOUR-WHEELER APPROACHES AND STOPS. HOLMES AND WATSON GET OUT.
LESTRADE	Ah! There you are, Mr. Holmes! Dead on time – er, if you'll forgive the expression.
WATSON	(AN AMUSED CHUCKLE)
LESTRADE	Afternoon, Doctor.
WATSON	Good afternoon, Inspector.
HOLMES	You're quite prepared, Lestrade?
LESTRADE	All ready, sir.
HOLMES	Have you brought just the one constable?
LESTRADE	There are two, Mr. Holmes. PC Mayne here has come with me from the station, and PC Rowan has been inside guarding the house since the small hours.* Rowan is expecting us, of course, and he'll unlock the gate at – well, right now!

FX	* WE HEAR ROWAN'S FOOTSTEPS APPROACHING ON THE GRAVEL PATH – RATHER MUFFLED, AS HE'S ON THE OTHER SIDE OF THE BIG HEAVY WOODEN GATE. HE STOPS AT THE GATE AND INSERTS THE BIG KEY IN THE LOCK, TURNS IT AND OPENS THE GATE.
LESTRADE	It's like a fortress, this place. (TO ROWAN) Thank you, Constable. (A BEAT) Well, in we go . . . .
FX	THE FIVE MEN WALK ALONG THE GRAVEL PATH TOWARDS THE HOUSE. THE SOUND FADES OUT.
HOLMES	May I ask you and your men to stand back a little, Lestrade? Thank you. Now –
FX	HE TUGS ON THE BELL-PULL. WE HEAR THE DISTANT RINGING OF THE DOORBELL.
WATSON	(LOW) I wonder what he'll say.
FX	THE DOOR OPENS.
STAUNTON	(APPROACHING ALONG THE HALL) Thank you, Sarah. I shall take care of this. You may go.
HOLMES	(BLANDLY) Good afternoon, Mr. Staunton.
STAUNTON	Good afternoon, fiddlesticks! I have a bone to pick with you, Mr. Sherlock Holmes. I specifically told you that I did not wish to call in the police, yet almost immediately you send a uniformed clodhopper to my house . . . . (HE NOTICES LESTRADE, MAYNE AND ROWAN) And, bless my soul, here are yet more policemen! What is the meaning of this, sir?
HOLMES	Yesterday, Mr. Staunton, you commissioned me to investigate the theft of a rare and valuable mediaeval

chalice. Dr. Watson advised you, if you recall, at least to report your loss to the police.

STAUNTON   Well, sir?

WATSON   Mr. Staunton, can we not pursue this conversation indoors? We have some rather shocking information for you.

STAUNTON   Oh, very well – if you insist. Come through to the study.

HOLMES   Come, Inspector. You men will remain here until you are needed.

FX   THE THREE MEN ENTER, CLOSING THE FRONT DOOR BEHIND THEM AND SHUTTING OUT THE GARDEN BACKGROUND.

SCENE 9

STAUNTON   (OVER THE ABOVE: SOTTO VOCE) Policemen in the house now! What is the world coming to?

FX   STAUNTON OPENS THE STUDY DOOR.

STAUNTON   In here, if you please.

LESTRADE   (LOW, TO WATSON) Just like a Bond Street gallery, isn't it, Doctor?

STAUNTON   Well, sir, what information could be so shocking that it requires the presence of a police officer?

HOLMES   You told us yesterday. Mr. Staunton, that the only person, apart from yourself and your insurance broker, who knew that you had the Grace Chalice in this house, was your cousin, Walter Ruskin. You also told us that he was above suspicion.

STAUNTON   I did, sir, I did. But the matter has been much on my mind since we spoke, and I confess that I am less

221

certain now of my cousin's innocence. I told him about the chalice just the day after I bought it. That was nine – no, ten – days ago. We next met just six days later. That was our last evening together, and there was at least one occasion during the course of that evening when he had the opportunity to take an impression of my key. Dear me, what a wicked world it is, to be sure.

HOLMES   When I went over to Mill Hill, your cousin's man Perkins informed me that he had left his house at seven-thirty the previous evening and had not returned. As he was punctilious in his habits, the servants were becoming decidedly uneasy. Perkins suggested that I make enquiries here, Mr. Staunton, or at your cousin's club. Of course, I assured him that his master was not here, and you will not be surprised to learn that he had not been seen at his club for several days. In short, it seemed that Walter Ruskin had disappeared.

STAUNTON   Dear me! Well, that seems to settle the matter. Walter Ruskin, a thief! Stealing from his own cousin. Who would have thought it?

WATSON   But you can see now that the case has become a matter for the police, Mr. Staunton.

STAUNTON   To think that Walter of all people should prove a villain!

HOLMES   (GENTLY) But there is more.

STAUNTON   Oh?

HOLMES   Late yesterday afternoon, Inspector Lestrade here asked us to go over to Stoke Newington to examine a body that had been discovered there. The man had been battered to death. Then his body was stripped, and the facial features disfigured beyond recognition. Nevertheless, I was able to identify the deceased as your cousin, Walter Ruskin.

STAUNTON   (DISCONCERTED) Oh! Er – oh, dear! Is – is it possible that my suspicions were mistaken? (A BEAT. THEN, WITH QUIET DESPERATION –) Can there be a madman at large? Er – is the same person responsible for both crimes, do you suppose?

HOLMES   I fear that that is the case, Mr. Staunton.

STAUNTON   Then I must insist on police protection! Mr, er, Inspector – I really must insist on police protection!

HOLMES   It won't do, you know. Really, it won't. We have the cabman who brought you back from Abney Park. He distinctly remembers the large leather bag that you carried. I've no doubt that it contained your cousin's clothes – and, most importantly, his boots. You had a use for those boots, I think.

STAUNTON   Lies! All lies!

HOLMES   Your cousin had agreed to meet you by one of the tombs in the cemetery. I don't know what reason you devised for the meeting, but it was really very careless of you to leave his body so close to that particular monument. It marks the resting place of Walter Ruskin's maternal grandfather, Marcus Staunton – whose second son was, of course, your own father.

STAUNTON   Lies!

HOLMES   I made other enquiries this morning. The results were very enlightening. It seems that in recent years you have been gambling heavily upon the stock exchange, and losing heavily too. You have taken out a substantial mortgage upon this house, a mortgage which is in peril of foreclosure. The considerable debt that you owed to your more wealthy cousin must have been the final provocation, even though it is unenforceable in law.

STAUNTON   Dr. Watson, I appeal to you –

HOLMES	You resented your cousin's wealth, and I think you resented the fact that he had bequeathed it to the Royal Humane Society and not to you. The opportunity to buy the Grace Chalice suggested further opportunities to you. You made certain that your cousin, and only he, knew of your purchase, so that when the chalice was removed suspicion would inevitably fall upon him. At the same time, of course, you ensured that the money you owed him need never be paid.
LESTRADE	Ingenious, really.
WATSON	Too clever by half.
HOLMES	You yourself removed the precious object from the safe. I have no doubt that it is carefully hidden somewhere in the house. Your object, plainly, was to claim on the insurance while retaining possession of the chalice. You may even have intended to sell it. Such illicit transactions are not, alas, uncommon. Then, wearing your cousin's boots, which are at least three sizes larger than your own, you planted those incriminating footprints in the garden, taking long strides to give the impression of a taller man. It was unfortunate for you that the boots were new and could not be easily identified as his, but that could not be helped.
WATSON	The notion of a thief climbing over that wall was not wholly satisfactory. But how were the footprints managed? They lead from the garden wall to the study window and back.
HOLMES	You are looking at things back to front, Watson. Do you remember the second curious quality of those prints?
WATSON	Ah, yes. Yes, of course! The two lines of prints are close but quite separate.
HOLMES	Just so. What burglar would ever tread so artistically?

224

WATSON	We were told that an intruder had walked from the wall to the study window and back. Consequently, the footprints appeared to us to confirm our client's story, whereas –
HOLMES	In fact, the person who left those prints had walked from the study to the garden wall and back, taking great care on his return not to tread on any of the impressions made on his outward journey. Had he not stepped so carefully, the fact of an inside job would have been plain to the meanest intelligence. In all probability, then, our client himself was responsible for this charade.
STAUNTON	Lies, I tell you! Lies!
LESTRADE	Henry Staunton, I arrest you for the wilful murder of Walter Hugh Ruskin. I must warn you that anything you say will be taken down and may be used in evidence.
STAUNTON	(AN INARTICULATE CRY OF RAGE)
FX	STAUNTON RUSHES FOR THE DOOR BUT IS HELD BY HOLMES AND WATSON.
LESTRADE:	Hold onto him, gentlemen, while I get the derbies on him!
FX	AFTER A SHORT STRUGGLE LESTRADE HANDCUFFS HIM. THEN HE OPENS THE WINDOW AND BLOWS HIS WHISTLE TO SUMMON ROWAN AND MAYNE.
LESTRADE	(CALLING OUT OF THE WINDOW) Rowan! Mayne! Come in here. I have work for you!
HOLMES	Capital! First, I think, Rowan must take our friend here to the police station.

FX	BEHIND THE FOLLOWING, WE HEAR STAUNTON BEING FORCED OUT OF THE ROOM BY ROWAN.
HOLMES	Then we should set Mayne to work searching the house for the chalice. It is here: I am certain of it. While the good constable is thus occupied, we three shall speak with the housekeeper and the maid. The kitchen is the proper place for that.
WATSON	I have rarely felt so relieved at seeing a criminal taken into custody.
HOLMES	Envy and resentment have gnawed away at his soul, I fear. He hated his cousin as only a mean man can hate a generous and contented one.
LESTRADE	Our case will be complete if we can only find the boots, you know, but there's little chance of that, now, is there?
HOLMES	I am not so sure. For all his elaborate planning, Staunton has been singularly careless. It would not surprise me if Mayne uncovers the boots as well as the chalice.
MUSIC	UNDERCURRENT
WATSON	(NARRATING) In this, as in so much else, Holmes was correct. The precious cup had been concealed under a flagstone in the wine cellar. Walter Ruskin's boots were found among Staunton's own footwear. They proved to fit exactly those clear, sharp prints in the garden of Holly Trees. A few days later came word that the Edinburgh police had apprehended Esmond Northcote and charged him with common assault. He was able to prove an alibi, and left the court a free man. No such conclusion was possible for Henry Staunton. He was hanged at Pentonville Prison, and it seems that the loyal Mrs. Elliott was his only mourner.
MUSIC	CLOSING THEME (*Fauré: Après un Rêve*)

226

The Adventure of
St. Nicholas the Elephant
by Christopher Redmond
From *Part II: 1890-1895* (2015)

It was a mild day near the end of March, in the year 1895, when Mr. Thomas Sexton appeared at the Baker Street rooms which I shared with my friend Mr. Sherlock Holmes. Holmes and I were lingering over one of the fine breakfasts provided by our landlady, whose imposing figure as she appeared in the doorway of our sitting-room to announce our visitor was promptly followed by the much smaller figure of Mr. Sexton himself. There was something a little comic about his old-fashioned and threadbare black suit, the jacket and waistcoat stretched to contain his rotund belly, with a smear of some greasy substance near the cuff of his right sleeve, while the firm jaw and solemn countenance above his double chin gave warning that, although he might be small of stature, he expected to be treated with some deference. And yet he was clearly in the grip of an intense agitation, as his writhing hands made evident.

"Come in, come in," said Holmes at once. "Pray have a seat, and perhaps your nerves will be no worse for a cup of Mrs. Hudson's not unsatisfactory coffee. What can be amiss in the affairs of the church to bring you out so early on a Saturday morning, Mr. – ?"

"Sexton, sir, Thomas Sexton. But how do you know I come from the church? I've heard of your wonderful guesses, Mr. Holmes, as we all have, but I have not said a word yet about the church – St. Nicholas the Elephant it is, sir, out in Lambeth, past Elephant and Castle. How could you guess that I was a churchman?"

"I did not guess," said Holmes. "When the available data justify no more than a guess, I remain silent and I observe. In this case, Mr. Sexton, I have observed a spot of what must be candle-wax on the sleeve of your coat. Your attire is otherwise immaculate, so that the stain has come there very recently, and you would hardly have been lighting and extinguishing candles for any household purpose on so bright a morning. Further, I recognize the distinctive if somewhat dull typography of the *Church Times* on the sheaf of paper protruding from your pocket. I conclude that you have been in church this morning, and that your name reflects your calling: that you are, in fact, a sexton."

"It's true enough," our caller replied, gratefully sipping the coffee that Mrs. Hudson had brought for him, "although the word *sexton* is one I don't

228

care to have used, if it's all the same to you, Mr. Holmes. *Church-officer* is the right name nowadays, and church-officer at St. Nicholas is what I have the honour to be. Still, it's true that my grandfather and his fathers before him called themselves sexton. I dare say that may be why my family bears the name it does. Church-officer I have been at St. Nicholas for nineteen years this Whitsun, and never have I seen anything like what has happened this week. Witchcraft, I call it, witchcraft!"

"Tut, man, you call it nothing of the sort," said Holmes. "If you believed that it was witchcraft, you would hardly be here in Baker Street. You would be seeking help within the church itself, from the bishop's chaplain, or whatever the proper dignitary is called. You know very well that whatever has happened is the result of human agency, and so you rightly turn your steps to Baker Street. Or rather, not your steps, but the wheels of the Metropolitan Railway, if your journey is from far-off Lambeth. And so I ask you again: what is amiss, and what have you to tell that might be of interest to me?"

"Well, it may not be witchcraft in the end, but Mrs. Brickward calls it witchcraft," the little man replied, "and what else might anyone call it, with blood on the very steps of the church, and a page of the Bible burned there on the stone beside it?"

"Beside what, Mr. Sexton?" I interjected. "Beside the bloodstain?"

"Beside the body, sir!" he shot back. "Beside the body, there on the pavement. A page taken from the church's own Bible, that sits on the lectern for Mr. Brickward to read each Sunday. Now if there is no witchcraft in it, why would somebody have burned a Bible page, and a chapter of the Holy Gospel at that?"

Sherlock Holmes, who had shown some impatience when our visitor began to describe his problem, was now leaning forward in his chair, his long bony fingers rubbing together rapidly. "Why indeed, Mr. Sexton," he said. "Why indeed. I could suggest six, no, seven possible reasons at once, but without data I can hardly be expected to choose one. But you interest me much more when you speak of a body. What body?"

"That's just it," was the reply. "A body, a young woman, lying there dead, at the side door of St. Nicholas, in Moss Road. We didn't know who she was, not any of us, and nor did the police."

"Ah, the police?" said Holmes. "Of course, they would take an interest in the matter. For all the deficiencies that the police sometimes demonstrate, they can at least be relied upon to take note of a woman's body found at the door of a suburban church. Found when, Mr. Sexton?"

"On Sunday last, at twelve o'clock. We were coming out of Matins and we found it. Mrs. Brickward found it first, as she went round into Moss Street on the way to the rectory, and Mr. and Mrs. Wallace said she was crying and weeping beside it when they saw her. Mrs. Wallace was the first to see the Bible page there, burned so that all you could read were a few words at the bottom of the page. 'Cometh in his glory' it said, and that's all that was left that wasn't blackened, 'cometh in his glory'."

"I see," said Holmes, "and this Mrs. Wallace no doubt summoned the police? But no, she will have been fully occupied with comforting Mrs. Brickward – I take it that is the rector's wife? – and doubtless it fell to Mr. Wallace to go in search of a constable."

"Exactly."

"And when the constable came?"

"Well, Mr. Holmes, he told all the people to go home, all the people who had gathered round I mean, and he sent a messenger for an inspector to come. I waited to see if I could be of any assistance, but there were enough police to do everything, and after they took the body away in a waggon I locked up the church as I always do, and I went home to my dinner."

"Where, no doubt, Mrs. Sexton was all agog to hear every detail of the affair?" I put in.

"I am sorry to say that there is no Mrs. Sexton," said the little man quietly. "She died last year of a fever."

"A careful observer could have seen as much from a glance at our visitor," said Holmes. "I will not insult you, Watson, by mentioning the clues that you might have seen, had you only looked for them. Tell me, Mr. Sexton, as you waited in case your assistance might be required, what did you in turn observe?"

"Observe, Mr. Holmes?"

"Yes, man, observe! Mark, learn, and inwardly digest, to put it in words you must often have read in your Bible. What did you see? There was blood – was there a wound? How was the girl dressed? What did she look like?"

"As to that, I can't rightly say," was the response. "She seemed a fair enough girl, and dressed well enough. She did have a wound, for certain, for her shoulder and side were all wet with thick blood, such as I never saw but once, when a lumber-waggon overturned in Moss Road and there was a man crushed to death."

"Just so," said my friend. "If this woman's death on Sunday last made such an impression upon you, why have you waited until Saturday and then come in such haste to see me?"

"It was the Bible, Mr. Holmes. When we saw the burned page beside the body, we all knew it was from a Bible, of course, but it was only today, when I went into the church to make the candles ready for tomorrow and do my other Saturday tasks, that I glanced at the Bible on the lectern and saw the page had been torn from there. Of course I went straight to the rectory to tell Mr. Brickward, and Mrs. Brickward screamed out that it was witchcraft. When I came away and thought it over a little, I determined to come and see you at once."

"Hmph," said Holmes. "Well, Mr. Sexton, your story is an interesting one, and I do not object to looking into it briefly, for I am rather at loose ends since we put old Carstairs and his not-so-prepossessing son behind bars. Tell me, and then I will detain you no longer: what was the name of the police inspector who took charge of the case?"

"Hopkins, sir," said Sexton, and Holmes gave a brief nod of satisfaction, for I knew that he esteemed Stanley Hopkins more highly than any of the other official detectives. Thus I was not surprised when, as soon as our pompous little visitor had taken his leave, he rang for the pageboy and scribbled a telegram to be sent to Scotland Yard.

"Hopkins will not object to dropping round," he said, "and it may be that he can offer us transportation to south Lambeth this afternoon, as well as the benefit of whatever information the police have failed to overlook. We can at least be confident, I think, that they will have a better theory than witchcraft to explain matters – although, sad to say, little explanation may be needed, for a body at the side door of a church on a Sunday morning is the natural consequence of a quarrel or attack outside some nearby public house on the Saturday evening."

"But the Bible page?" I asked.

"I admit that is a little out of the ordinary," said Holmes. "What do you make of it, Doctor?"

I was flattered that my friend, who had spoken slightingly of my deductive skills just a few minutes earlier, was now eager to hear any suggestion I might be able to make. "I suppose," I said judiciously, "that we may disregard the words left visible at the bottom of the page, since whoever took the page and set it alight cannot have been able to guarantee how much would remain unburnt. 'Cometh in his glory' is hardly a very illuminating message in any case. But might the whole page be some sort of message? It should not be difficult to find out what else should have appeared there."

"Indeed," said Holmes. "Then your theory would be that someone wished to point out a connection between the dead woman, or perhaps the reason for her death, and some incident or moral in Holy Writ? I have known something of the sort once or twice before. The difficulty in this case is the burning. If you seek to leave a written message, Watson, do you generally set fire to it and watch it shrivel to ash before it can be read? No, I think the explanation must be a little different – although I do agree that a message was sent, and indeed received."

231

He would say no more, and I was left to turn the matter over in my mind, and to occupy myself as best I could, while Holmes leafed through the day's newspapers and cut out two or three items with his black, long-bladed scissors, for later pasting into his steadily growing commonplace-books. I glanced at the cuttings later, but could make nothing of them: one was a report on glue manufacturing in some Midlands town, while another discussed the anticipated marriage of a Member of Parliament to the daughter of a Professor of Poetry.

Shortly after luncheon, however, Stanley Hopkins was announced, and both Holmes and I greeted him as the old friend he had become through a succession of odd and once or twice dangerous adventures together. "So it's the Lambeth case, is it?" said the inspector with a smile, as he sat easily in the chair where we had seen him so often before. "Well, you won't find much in your line this time, Mr. Holmes. A dead girl in south Lambeth is nothing so unusual, you know. I say a 'girl' by habit, for so many of those we find dead on the streets are very young, as you know, but this one can't have been less than thirty."

"The girls you find dead on the streets are not so often on the doorsteps of churches, or marked by torn pages from a Bible," Holmes observed. "And I note that you speak of this particular girl as 'the Lambeth case', although there is, as you say, never any lack of cases in Lambeth."

"You have me there," Hopkins grinned. "As a matter of fact, the matter has been on my mind all this week, although I have not been able to spare so much as a constable to look into it since Sunday afternoon. There was something just a trifle odd about the matter."

"The lack of a weapon, for example?"

"I see you know a little about it already," said the inspector. "That was certainly a striking feature, although it may mean nothing, for a knife is a valuable thing to some of the roughs who can be found on the streets thereabouts. I have a little time to spare this afternoon; would you care to ride down to Lambeth with me and see the place for yourself? I can't offer to show you the body itself, for we had it buried on Wednesday in the usual way."

Holmes and I accepted the offer with alacrity, and as we rode through London and across Westminster Bridge, Hopkins gave us, in response to my friend's request, a brief sketch of the personalities at the church of St. Nicholas the Elephant, apart from the church-officer, our caller of a few hours earlier. Ambrose Wallace, the churchwarden, Hopkins dismissed as an elderly busybody, and his wife as a nonentity. "The rector and his wife are another thing altogether," he said, "and I gather that there has been a good deal of talk about them, although it may be no more than the usual gossip in any church, or any pub for that matter, when a young man comes to take the place of an old one. Mr. Brickward is no more than five or six-and-twenty, fresh from the theological college up in Durham, and of course a London parish is a difficult place for a man from the north. Then his wife is a northerner too, and she is said to be a sulky young woman, with a dark eye and a hot temper, who has been slow to seek friends and slower to find them. If Mrs. Wallace had not been nearby to take a motherly interest, she would be entirely without female company."

"An admirable thumbnail sketch," said Holmes. "And she is the one who discovered the body, our client told us. I should be very glad to meet Mrs. Brickward."

However, when the carriage stopped in Moss Road and we rang the bell at the rectory, it was the Rev. Mr. Brickward himself who answered the door. I wondered at the lack of a maidservant, but Hopkins murmured to me that the girl who had been employed at the rectory had left the previous week with Mrs. Brickward's screams of fury ringing in her ears. "A matter of burnt toast, I was told," he added.

"I may have a question or two for you, and also for your wife if she is at home," Holmes told the rector, "but first, it would be a great kindness if you would allow us to see the interior of the church. I dare say these modern bricks conceal stonework and woodwork of some real antiquity and artistic merit, do they not?"

Mr. Brickward, who at first had appeared far from gracious, brightened at once, and in a moment had snatched up a key and was escorting us to the north door of the church, chattering all the way about mediaeval tracery, Elizabethan carvings, and Georgian re-pointing. Inside the building it was so dark, even on a bright spring afternoon, that my eye could distinguish little, and when Mr. Brickward pointed into the gloom and spoke ecstatically about the foliated rood-screen, I nodded mutely. Holmes made even less pretence of taking an interest in the architecture, but made a beeline for the brass-and-oak lectern, where he pulled out his thick magnifying lens, struck a match, lit a stub of candle, and bent to peer closely at the great Bible which lay there. As he moved the flame from side to side, then up and down the open page of the book, I heard a gasp from the back of the church, and realized that the church-officer, our client, had joined us. I chuckled at his anxiety, knowing the care with which Holmes avoided so much as touching, let alone scorching, anything that might yield a clue to his extraordinarily keen eye.

"Thank you, I think that will do," he called, joining us again near the doorway. "Now if Mrs. Brickward can spare us a moment, her clarification of one or two points might be most illuminating."

Mr. Brickward led us back along the path we had taken from the rectory, stepping carefully to avoid the stone flag on which I could still detect a pale brown stain that doubtless represented the dead woman's blood. "Jennie!" he called as we entered the rectory. "Jennie, these gentlemen would like a word with you."

We took seats a little awkwardly in the parlour, all of us save Holmes, who propped his lean frame against a bulging bookcase beside the mantel and surveyed the heavily furnished little room with a keen eye. In a moment the rector's wife appeared before us: a slight, dark woman, as Hopkins had said, neatly though inexpensively dressed in a pale blue costume. Dark shadows beneath her eyes reminded me of the strain this mysterious bloodshed, with the curious and even sinister desecration that had accompanied it, must be imposing on a young couple not yet much tried in the fires of life. It crossed my mind that the young rector, through his ecclesiastical training and no doubt an innately religious cast of mind, must have resources for facing the proximity of death that were not available to his more delicate wife. Seated together on a horsehair sofa, her little hand resting gently on her husband's arm, they seemed a picture of courage in time of sorrow.

Hopkins introduced us, Thomas Sexton adding with a note of pride in his voice that as church-officer he had taken the responsibility of asking Mr. Holmes to look into the affair. Holmes murmured a soothing word or two to Mrs. Brickward, then asked her to tell how she had found the body on Sunday morning.

"I had slipped out of church during the last hymn," she explained. "I know it seems dreadful of me, and I always do stay long enough to listen to John preach, but I do feel so alone in the middle of the congregation sometimes, and suddenly I thought, 'I can't bear to listen to *Alleluia! Alleluia!* one more time. I'll just leave quietly and have a few things started for luncheon before Mr. and Mrs. Wallace arrive, since I don't have Mary Ann to help me any longer.' So I did that, and when I came round the side of the church to the rectory path, I saw the woman lying there on the stone step, with the blood splashed out around her like – oh, like a red cape!"

Her low voice rose in pitch and her dark eyes seemed wider than ever; I saw her husband's protective arm reach around her. "Mr. Holmes," he said, "I hope you will forgive me if I say that my wife is overwrought; she is really not able to discuss this dreadful affair."

"I have only one other question of importance to ask," said Holmes. "Mrs. Brickward, when did you first recognize Ellie?"

The rector's young wife stared at Holmes in horror, rose to her feet, gave a little shriek and crumpled to the floor.

"It was obvious from the first that someone closely connected to St. Nicholas had killed the young woman," Holmes explained as he, Hopkins and I rattled homeward in the inspector's cab. "If you will forgive me for saying so, friend Hopkins, street brawls that end in sordid bloodshed are most unlikely to take place on a Sunday morning, when the public houses are closed and their denizens asleep in their lodgings or under Lambeth Bridge. As soon as I saw the place, I recognized that if there had been a body in Moss Road before the service began, someone among the good people of St. Nicholas would certainly have seen it, perhaps the diligent Mr. Sexton himself. It followed that the murder was committed during the time of the service itself.

"The most important indication, however, was the page from the church's Bible. We may dismiss witchcraft – a suggestion which, I strongly suspect, Mrs. Brickward put forward as a desperate attempt at misdirection. Likewise it was apparent from the beginning that there must be an excellent reason for someone to have ripped a page from the great Bible in the church itself, when so many other copies of scripture are easily at hand.

"You spoke, Watson, of a message being conveyed by the page. Indeed it was, but through no work of the printer or any divine hand. Asking myself why that particular page was torn from the volume, I looked in the volume itself to see what remained, and in the margins of the next page after the torn stub, my candle revealed deep and irregular impressions. It was not difficult to tell that words had been scrawled on the missing page, and I was able to read them: 'John, I have returned. Meet me in Moss Road after the service ends. Ellie.'

"Evidently it was a message for Mr. Brickward, which he was to find when he looked at the Bible during the service on Sunday. The writer, this Ellie, cannot have anticipated that he would find it beforehand, presumably when he came in to see that all was in readiness for Sunday morning, or that he would tear it out, for fear that others might see it – still less that he would confide in his wife. On the contrary, she must have assumed that he would keep his wife in darkness, and even abandon her for the sake of the one who had 'returned'.

"Of course we do not yet know exactly what had been the relations between Mr. Brickward and this woman, but it is clear that despite her husband's remarkable willingness to show her the letter, Mrs. Brickward perceived Ellie as a serious threat and was prepared to take drastic action to keep her from ever meeting her husband.

"Taking the page from the Bible is not, of course, the same thing as murder, but the one led to the other. Again, the opportunity to be in Moss Road during the service is the vital indication. Mr. Brickward himself was, if I may say so, under close observation by the entire congregation throughout the service. Much the same must be true of Mr. Sexton, the church-officer.

235

"Mrs. Brickward says that she left the service early, and that in itself might have given her the opportunity to find Ellie. It must have taken some little time, however, to have words with her, stab her dead, and conceal the knife somewhere. I dare say, your constables will find it in the cellar or kitchen-garden about the rectory if they take the trouble to search. More than that, however, she also needed a moment to burn the Bible page beside Ellie's body."

"I cannot see why she took the trouble to do that," Hopkins remarked.

"I should think," said Holmes, "that she intended her husband to recognize the remains of paper and to realize what had happened. Her heart told her that he would feel himself as much to blame as she, and the secret of Ellie's death would bind them close together. Burning the page, of course, would also ensure that no stranger could read the pencilled message.

"Doing all these things must have taken more than the few seconds by which Mrs. Brickward preceded other churchgoers into Moss Road, and for a moment or two I wondered whether the young woman had, in fact, been killed earlier than I thought. But then Mrs. Brickward herself gave us the explanation. You will recall her remark that the service had included the words '*Alleluia! Alleluia!*' again and again.

"It is many years since I was compelled to attend Sunday School classes as a boy, but I do recall being told with determination, as a matter of great importance in the mind of the maiden lady who instructed me, that in the austere season of Lent, those words are never used in the liturgy. Here we are in March, a fortnight before Easter, and so it is Lent. Mrs. Brickward cannot have heard the congregation repeating *Alleluia!* this Sunday morning – because the prayer book told them not to say it, and because she was not in church at all. I knew that she was not telling the truth, and the matter was settled. Unnoticed by the other churchgoers, for she had no friends to look for her, she was not in the church, but in Moss Road, where she waited for Ellie, killed her, and burned her last message to John Brickward."

"It seems very straightforward as you set it out," said Hopkins. "If only I had had a few minutes to consider the case, I should have come to the same conclusion on Monday last, and you need not have been troubled."

"Ah," laughed Holmes, "and so my hours have made good your minutes. It was a trivial matter, certainly, and yet not without interest, particularly for the novelty of the message written on a leaf of the Bible. Watson, I recall hearing that some device of the sort was used in one of the romance novels of your friend James Barrie. I must look into it one of these days, although I understand that his works are written in a Scots

236

dialect which is perhaps more congenial to you than it is to me."

Murder at Tragere House
by David Stuart Davies
From *Part IV: 2016 Annual* (2016)

I returned late to Baker Street one evening in the autumn of '95 after dining at my club and indulging in a game of billiards with my friend Thurston. And as I approached our sitting room door I could discern voices within which informed me that, despite the lateness of the hour, Sherlock Holmes was engaged with a client. With some diplomacy, I entered with the intention of going straight to my room, but Holmes waved me to my chair by the hearth.

"Ah, Watson, just in time," he cried. "When there is a *crie de cour*, I am quite lost without my Boswell," he said, addressing his remarks to his visitor who sat in the shadows on the chaise longue. He was a young man, somewhere in his early twenties with tousled sandy hair, and was leaning forward in a crouching fashion which indicated his emotional discomfort.

"This is my friend and associate, Dr. Watson, who takes an inordinate interest in my investigations," said Holmes.

The young man rose, gave a nod of acknowledgement and shook my hand.

"And this," continued Holmes, "is Mr. Andrew Sinclair, who has travelled all the way from Ayrshire in Bonnie Scotland to elicit my help."

"Aye, sir," the young man said, with some passion. "My train just got in about an hour ago. I'm hoping I can persuade Mr. Holmes to return with me to Tragere House. It's a most urgent business." He leaned further forward lowering his voice. "It's murder."

Holmes gave a brief cackle and rubbed his hands with pleasure. "That is just the point we had reached in the matter when you so conveniently joined our company, Watson. Now you can be in at the beginning. You know how much I value your opinion in these cases." The veneer of sarcasm in this utterance was so fine that I doubt if Mr. Sinclair noticed it, but I did.

"Would you be so good as to supply us all with a glass of brandy, Watson? I'm sure Mr. Sinclair would welcome such a restorative after his long journey, and then he can tell us all about this story of murder."

Moments later, we were all seated by the glowing embers of the fire with brandy glasses in hand. "Now, sir," said Holmes, relaxing back in his chair, "let me have the facts and please be precise as to details."

"As you know, my name is Andrew Sinclair," began the young man in a clear and confident voice. "I am engaged to be married to Morag Cameron, the daughter of Alan Cameron, the Laird of Tragere. That's a large estate not far from Ayr. The tragedy occurred only last night. I was dining at the big house with my intended and my future in-laws, Mr. Cameron and his wife, Anne. It was the first time I had been treated in this fashion. Morag and I have only just become engaged and there was a certain reluctance on her parents' behalf to accept the match. As wealthy landowners, they viewed me as something of an upstart fortune hunter, keen to get my hands on their wealth through their daughter. They did not want the marriage to take place. You see, I am only the son of the local cobbler, and at present I am merely an articled clerk to Smithson and Wylie in Ayr. But I have prospects, Mr. Holmes, I have prospects."

"I am delighted to hear it," observed my friend, "but could we concentrate on the matter in hand?"

"Aye, sir, I am sorry to digress. It's a wee sore point with me, that's all. I arrived at Tragere House at the appointed time and was met with stilted civility by Mrs. Cameron. Mr. Cameron apparently was attending to business elsewhere, in his study, I was told. But if you want my opinion, Mr. Holmes . . . ."

"Indeed I do," said Holmes.

"I believe he was putting off socialising with me as long as he could. Anyway, Mrs. Cameron was polite enough, I suppose, although I could tell it was a strain for her. Matters became worse for me when Morag had to leave the room to attend to a nose bleed. She had managed to stem the blood in her handkerchief, but needed some cold running water. She insisted that she needed no assistance to deal with this minor problem." The young man gave a dry humourless cough. "So, I was left alone with my prospective mother-in-law. It was a trial, I can tell you. I know I am worthy of Morag's hand and I will make her a good husband, and I fully intend to be successful in my legal career, but of course I could not express these sentiments with any force to my beloved's mother. I knew such claims would suggest a sense of desperation on my part.

"Thankfully, before long the other dinner guests arrived, Dr. Eustace Pavlow and his wife Victoria. They are a gentle couple somewhere in their sixth decade, I should guess. Pavlow has retired from practice now, but is still called upon from time to time by some of his old patients for assistance. We have a nodding acquaintance. On their arrival, I was glad to take a back seat as it were in the general conversation. Then Morag returned and I felt a lot easier. The Pavlows expressed concern about her nose bleed, but Morag assured them that it was a minor matter and had been dealt with successfully. At this juncture, the butler, Rogers, shepherded us through into the dining room. Still, Mr. Cameron had not made an entrance. At first, his wife did not seem dismayed at his absence, but, when the soup was served, she gave an expression of annoyance. 'That man,' she snapped. 'Sometimes he irritates me greatly. No doubt he will have become engrossed in his wretched paperwork and lost all sense of time. He does this quite often and it drives me to distraction.'

"'Oh, Mother,' said Morag, 'I am sure he isn't doing it deliberately. Why don't you go to his study and bring him down?'

"Mrs. Cameron flashed us an uneasy smile and rose from her chair. 'I will. I'll go to his room and drag him here by the scruff of his neck like a naughty schoolboy.' It was quite an embarrassing moment but we all nodded with false smiles. My darling Morag seemed the least perturbed. No doubt her father's errant behaviour was a common occurrence. Mrs. Cameron instructed us to carry on dining so as not to let the soup grow cold and then disappeared. We obeyed her request and indulged in uneasy sporadic conversation until we heard a loud scream. Both Doctor Pavlow and I were on our feet in an instant, quickly followed by Morag.

"'That came from my father's study,' she said, and with speed led us from the dining room up the central staircase to a room immediately at the top of the stairs. The sight that met our eyes is one that will be forever etched in my memory.

"There, lying in a slumped posture, face down on his desk, his arms outstretched, was Alan Cameron. There was a broad red stain on the back of his jacket. It glistened in the gaslight. I could see that it was blood. The result of a series of terrible wounds. It was quite clear that the man was dead. What increased the horror of this scene was that standing by him was his wife, holding a vicious looking dagger in her hand which was covered in gouts of blood. She seemed frozen with shock. She did not move or say a thing as we entered the chamber, and her face registered no emotion whatsoever."

The young man paused in his narrative to take a sip of brandy. I glanced over at Holmes and saw that his face was alive with interest and anticipation.

After a moment, our visitor resumed his narrative. "The doctor gently took hold of Mrs. Cameron and, relieving her of the knife, walked her from the room and administered a sedative. Meanwhile, I coped with Morag who, on realising that her father was dead, became hysterical. I did as best I could, but Mrs. Pavlow took her from the room to comfort her, leaving me with the dead body. I looked closely at it. Mr. Cameron had clearly been stabbed several times in the back. His position sitting at the desk suggested that he had no notion that he was about to be attacked. To be slaughtered." Sinclair shivered at the recollection.

240

"The police were summoned, and a rather brusque Inspector called Crabtree from the Ayr constabulary took charge and promptly arrested Mrs. Cameron for murder. She was carted away, much to the extra distress of my darling Morag."

"Presumably Mrs. Cameron protested her innocence," said Holmes.

"Indeed she did."

"How did she explain the fact that she was holding the murder weapon and standing by the dead body?"

"She said that she entered Mr. Cameron's study and discovered her husband slumped forward on the desk. At first she didn't see the knife protruding from his back. The room was dimly lighted. On approaching him, she realised the horror of the situation and instinctively grabbed the dagger, pulling it out of her husband's back, and then she screamed. After this, she froze with the shock of it all."

"Do you believe this story?"

"Well, yes. The alternative is too unpleasant to contemplate."

"And yet, the man was murdered, and the culprit must be one of the people in the house at that time. And Mrs. Cameron was found with the body and holding the weapon. I can understand Inspector Crabtree's motives in arresting her. But of course the official police always jump to the obvious conclusions."

"It seems too fantastic that Mrs. Cameron should commit such a deed, Mr. Holmes. As far as I know, they were a happily married couple. I am desperate for this mystery to be solved, not so much for myself, but for my darling Morag. Someone else – I have no idea who – must have committed this deed."

"A pretty little problem, eh, Watson?" said Holmes rising and taking his cherrywood pipe from the mantelpiece and stuffing it with tobacco.

"Either that, or no problem at all: the lady is guilty."

"I cannot accept that," cried Sinclair hotly. "I appeal to you, Mr. Holmes, come back with me to Tragere House and see what you can make of the matter."

Holmes puffed meditatively on his pipe, his sharp lean features obscured by smoke for some moments. "It is a pretty little problem," he repeated, "I grant you. What do you say, Watson, do you fancy taking in some lungfuls of bracing Scottish air?"

It was early the following evening that Holmes, Sinclair and I found ourselves travelling in a dogcart from Ayr Station to Tragere House. Holmes had spent most of the journey from London in profound silence. I knew this behaviour of old. I was aware that he was weighing up the evidence that had been provided by our client and considering the various possible scenarios which might lead him to a successful conclusion of the case.

He had discussed the matter with me briefly after Sinclair had left our rooms to find lodgings for the night. "The evidence is certainly damning," he said. "If the lady is guilty, it is certainly the most extreme case of *crime passionel* I have encountered. If you mean to do away with your husband, you do not do it in the middle of a dinner party with a set of guests in attendance."

I agreed. "However," I added, "Sinclair did suggest that Mrs. Cameron was irritated with her husband, and this could have been the culmination of years of frustration – a sudden breakdown of reason."

Holmes shook his head. "It would be a very strong form of irritation that could lead you to stab your husband many times in the back. No, I am sure that it is not as simple as that. Well, we do have the basic facts, but as yet these do not provide us with enough straw to make bricks. We shall have to wait until we get to Scotland and learn more."

Although Sinclair did not comment on my friend's apparent rudeness in his lack of communication during the train journey, it was clear from his behaviour that he was surprised and offended by it. As usual, it was left to me to indulge in trivial conversation with him as the train steamed us north. Luckily, after lunch in the dining car, our client fell into a quiet doze.

Sinclair had wired ahead that we were coming. Doctor Pavlow and his wife had remained at Tragere House in order to comfort and look after the distraught Morag while Sinclair had travelled to London to engage Holmes's help. The dark veil of dusk had already settled itself on the countryside which was ablaze with autumn colours, and the wind was stiffening, causing us to wrap our coats tightly around us as the dogcart rattled along the country lanes and tracks. The Tragere estate was very large, and once we had passed the ancient gateway, it took us some ten minutes before the house itself loomed into view. It was a large, impressive, gothic style structure with fairy-tale turrets. A dull light shone through the heavily mullioned windows, and from the high chimneys there sprang a single black column of smoke.

A tall well-built man stepped from the shadows of the porch to greet us. This was Rogers the butler, who attended to our luggage and led us into the grand hallway.

"Rogers will show you to your quarters," said Sinclair.

Holmes shook his head. "To begin with, I would like to see the room in which the murder took place."

Alan Cameron's study was a small oppressive chamber, panelled in dark wood. The walls were adorned with pictures of Highland scenes, and a stag's head glowered at us above a small fireplace. The desk at which he had been sitting when he was assaulted was splattered with blood. The room was now cold and dank, and even when Rogers turned up the gas, it was gloomy. Holmes threw off his Ulster and, like an eager bloodhound, began patrolling the room, examining carefully each square inch of the surroundings. At one point, he dropped to the floor and crawled about, magnifying glass in hand, muttering quietly to himself. He even examined the wastepaper basket, extracting something that looked like a white cloth. This performance was by now a familiar one to me, but I could observe that Andrew Sinclair and Rogers the butler were both fascinated and amazed at my friend's behaviour.

He spent a great deal of time examining the surface of the desk and the chair in which Cameron had been sitting. He retrieved a penknife from his coat pocket, and then he produced two small envelopes and commenced scraping portions of dried blood from different areas of the desk. After scrutinising them carefully for some moments under the magnifying glass, he placed the scrapings into the envelopes.

He then opened the two drawers of the desk and quickly rifled through the contents. One document in particular arrested his interest, and he spent some time studying it. Meanwhile, we watched in silence as though we were the audience entranced by some remarkable dumb show, baffled and fascinated by what we saw. Eventually, he stood before us, with a smile on his face. "There are some interesting indications here, but nothing yet to fully clear the mist that surrounds this crime," he announced briskly. "However they do provide a basis for some further thought."

The investigation of the room concluded, we were then shown to our quarters to refresh ourselves after the long journey. Before going downstairs for dinner, I went to Holmes's room to see if he would confide in me what his investigations had revealed.

"Look at the two samples of blood I retrieved," he said, casually, as he adjusted his evening tie.

I did so, but saw nothing of obvious consequence and admitted as much.

"See," said Holmes, "the scrapings from this envelope are quite clearly dried blood. How often have we seen such débris, eh, old friend?"

I nodded in agreement.

"However, the flakes from the second envelope are of a different consistency and darker hue. They are not blood at all."

"Not blood . . . !" I exclaimed in amazement. "Then what are they?"

Holmes shrugged. "Without my chemical apparatus I cannot be sure. It is certainly a manufactured substance. I should guess cochineal."

"Great heavens. What does this mean?"

My question prompted one of Sherlock Holmes's enigmatic smiles. "All in good time," he said.

I tried another approach. "What was that document that caught your attention?"

"Ah, that was Alan Cameron's Last Will and Testament. Most illuminating."

"In what way?"

Holmes pressed a finger to his lips. It was an alternative expression to, "All in good time."

"You know my methods, Watson. It is foolish to reveal one's developing theory until it has fully blossomed. This is a paradoxical case. On one level, the solution seems simple, but dealing with all the clues to make a coherent narrative is more challenging. Come now, we shall be late for dinner."

On entering the dining room, Sinclair introduced us to the Pavlows. Morag was absent, however. Sinclair informed us that she was still too distressed to be in company but would be happy to talk to my friend later that evening.

Dr. Eustace Pavlow was, to my mind, the epitome of an old country doctor. He was grey-haired, slight of build, with a pale kind face which seemed to bear a permanently serene expression. Gentle blue eyes stared out from behind a pair of gold *pince-nez*, and his whole manner radiated trust and reliability. His wife, Victoria, was a plump cheery-faced lady who seemed overcome by the tragic event that had occurred the previous evening and had little to say for herself. Indeed, conversation was stilted during the course of the meal, and Holmes, as was his way, remained virtually mute until the coffee arrived. It was then that he turned his attention to Dr. Pavlow.

"What do you make of this matter, Doctor?" he said in an almost casual manner. "Have you any alternative theories concerning the murder?"

Pavlow shook his head sadly. "I am afraid not, Mr. Holmes. It is all quite baffling to me."

"I assume you believe that Mrs. Cameron is innocent."

"Certainly. It is not in the lady's nature to carry out such a heinous crime. I have known Alan and Anne many years, and they were a loving and devoted couple."

"And yet Mrs. Cameron seemed inordinately angry at her husband's non-appearance at the dinner table last evening . . . ."

Pavlow gave a wry smile. "Husbands and wives often get irritated with each other, Mr. Holmes. That is the nature of marriage, but it does not lead to murder."

"You examined the body?"

"I checked Alan's pulse and looked closely the wounds. There were three in all; they were quite vicious and administered with great force."

"With great hatred?"

"I suppose you could say so."

"There is no means of concealment in the room, so the murderer must have entered by the door. It is clear to me that whoever administered the blows was someone that Alan Cameron knew well, since he was sitting at his desk and had no concerns about his assailant being behind him."

"You cannot think that dear Anne did such a thing," said Victoria Pavlow suddenly, with some passion.

"The superficial evidence points in that direction, but I admit I am not fully convinced that she did. Tell me, when you and your husband arrived for dinner, did you go straight into the dining room?"

This enquiry seemed to discomfort Mrs. Pavlow. "Why . . . no, not straight away. I went to the bathroom on the first floor to freshen my toilette, and Eustace waited for me in the hall. This is the usual practise when we come to dinner at Tragere House, which we do at least half-a-dozen times a year."

"You did not encounter Mr. Cameron on your journey there and back?"

"Of course not," she replied with some heat, deeply irritated by my friend's question. "If I had, I would have informed the police."

Holmes nodded gently, apparently unaware of the lady's sharpness of tone.

"Would you mind describing the gown you were wearing at dinner last evening?"

"Really, Mr. Holmes," snapped Dr. Pavlow, "what has this to do with your investigation? It seems a puerile and very personal enquiry."

"It may have much to do with my investigation," Holmes replied lightly, waving his hand airily. "But, of course, Mrs. Pavlow is under no obligation to answer." With a quick swivel of the head he turned his gaze upon the lady in question and she shrank visibly from it.

"It was a long blue taffeta gown," she said quickly. "A very simple outfit."

"Not adorned with seed pearls?"

She shook her head.

"Do you now require to know what I was wearing?" sneered the usually placid doctor.

245

Holmes chuckled. "I think I can guess. Now then, Mr. Sinclair, I wonder if I could have those few words with your fiancé."

This suggestion seemed to unsettle the young man. "Well," he said, hesitating, "I suspect she is resting still."

"I have no wish to disturb her, but there is a certain amount of urgency in this matter. You did say that she would grant me an interview. If we are to prove Anne Cameron's innocence we must act with alacrity. I only require a few moments conversation with her."

"But why? I am sure there is nothing she can add to the report I have given to you."

"Are you sure? Sometimes we see things, are aware of things, that appear to have no relevance, without realising their crucial importance. I have trained myself to use such apparent inconsequentialities and identify any key factors that may otherwise rest unnoticed. To put it another way, sir, we must turn over every pebble on the beach in order to discover the truth."

Holmes and I, led by Sinclair, made our way up the central staircase and along a gloomily lit corridor to Morag Cameron's room. On reaching it, the young man turned to us with a flushed face held in a rigid earnest expression. "If you would bear with me gentlemen, I will appraise my fiancé of your desire to speak with her, and ascertain if she is well enough to cope with being questioned about this dreadful tragedy."

"Certainly," said Holmes, adding when Sinclair had entered the room. "Our young friend has certainly mastered the circumspect nature of the legal language."

A few minutes later, Sinclair ushered us into the room. Morag Cameron was sitting up in bed. She was indeed a pretty young thing with startling hazel eyes and luxurious blonde tresses, but her complexion was pale, and dark shadows under her eyes gave evidence of the strain and distress she was suffering.

Sinclair introduced us and drew up a chair so that Holmes could sit by the bed. "I apologise for this intrusion, especially at this most difficult time," Holmes said in his most solicitous tone. "I just want to clarify a few details concerning the death of your father, so that we can get to the bottom of this terrible tragedy."

"I understand, Mr. Holmes. I am so desperate to uncover the truth, so that my mother is proved innocent and can be released from prison."

"I notice the long black dress hanging on the wardrobe over there. Is that the gown you wore last evening?"

Miss Cameron's eyes widened in surprise at this question. "Why, yes."

Holmes rose from his chair and moved to the wardrobe to study the garment at close quarters. "Most charming," he said softly as he peered at it carefully. "Most charming."

Miss Cameron shook her head in bewilderment.

"Surely you digress from your purpose here, Mr. Holmes," observed Sinclair, somewhat coldly.

"Do I?" remarked my friend casually as he resumed his seat and turned his attention to Morag Cameron once more. "You suffered from a nosebleed the other evening. Is this a regular affliction, Miss Cameron?"

"No."

"But I understand you dealt with it calmly and efficiently."

"I believe so."

"When you excused yourself from the sitting room, what did you do?"

"I came back here, to my room, bathed my nose, and stemmed the flow of blood. Then I returned to the sitting room."

"I see."

"You do not seem content with my answers, Mr. Holmes."

Holmes gave Morag Cameron a cold grin. "I am afraid I am not. I always react in this fashion when someone is telling me a series of lies."

"What the devil do you mean by this effrontery?" roared Andrew Sinclair, rushing forward. I feared for an instant that he would assault my friend, but Holmes raised his hand and stopped in him in his tracks. "I am afraid the truth can often be hurtful, Mr. Sinclair. I am sorry to inform you that your fiancé was responsible for her father's death."

Colour drained from Sinclair's face and he sank down on the edge of the bed. By contrast, Morag Cameron seemed quite unperturbed by this revelation and merely smiled.

"You must be mad! It can't be true," groaned Sinclair, his head sunk upon his chest.

"You will have great difficulty in proving your theory, Mr. Holmes," said Morag.

Holmes shook his head. "You have left a few tracks along the route of murder, Miss Cameron, that should convince a jury to consider the matter with great scrutiny." He pulled out a handkerchief from his pocket. "This is yours, I believe. It has your initial on the corner and it is stained with blood. I found it in the waste paper basket in your father's study where you dropped it, no doubt before you carried out your murderous deed. Although, it isn't actually stained with blood, just something that replicates the colour and consistency – like cochineal. I observe that there is a little bottle standing on the shelf above your dressing table. You used it to fake a nose bleed, which would allow you to leave the sitting room on the evening of the crime and visit your father's study in order to murder him."

Miss Cameron's smile faded now, but she did not respond to Holmes's claim.

"You were wearing the black dress over there, and in the violence of your action, some of the tiny seed pearls became dislodged. I found four of them under your father's chair."

"But why should I want to kill my father?"

"Because he changed his will. I saw a copy of it in his desk drawer. No doubt the original is lodged with his solicitor. He was so opposed to you marrying a man of such lowly financial status, whom he took, quite wrongly, I believe, to be a fortune hunter, that he left you with only a small allowance on his death. He had warned you to cease your relationship with Mr. Sinclair and choose a man whom he believed was more worthy of the daughter of the Laird of Tragere. He was so angry at your insistence in continuing with this alliance that he meant to teach you a lesson for disobeying him. Isn't that the case?"

"He was a stubborn, foolish old man."

"But what good would killing him do?" asked Sinclair, his eyes now moist with tears.

"It wasn't as simple as that. She planned the murder in such a fashion as to implicate her mother. That is why she encouraged Mrs. Cameron to visit her father's room during the course of the dinner the other evening. She knew that her mother would be discovered with the dead body, and thus implicated in the murder. With both her parents out of the way, she would become mistress of the Tragere estate. Isn't that true, Miss Cameron?"

The girl giggled and it was then for the first time I saw the madness in her eyes. They were wild and gleeful, and lacked any sign of contrition.

"Is all of this really true, Mr. Holmes? It's not a trick?" asked Sinclair, the depths of his despair resonating in his voice.

"Of course it's true, you idiot!" cried Morag, her features alive with excitement, and she gave another of her mad giggles. "My father had no right to block my inheritance. And so he paid the price for being so intransigent," she snarled.

"I think we should get Dr. Pavlow to give Miss Cameron a sedative, and then the police must be informed," said Holmes softly.

"Go to hell!" screamed the girl, twisting her body in a paroxysm of impotent anger.

I just stared in pity and horror at the tormented creature, as did Andrew Sinclair, before he quietly turned on his heels and, like a sleepwalker, left the room.

Despite our traumatic experiences of the previous day, as we travelled on the morning express from Edinburgh to London, my friend Sherlock Holmes tucked in to a hearty breakfast in the dining car.

"Fuel for the long tiring journey ahead," he grinned facetiously, and then added in a more serious tone, "And an antidote to the bleak tragedy we have left behind us."

I nodded. "It is Andrew Sinclair I feel the most sorry for. That young man has not only had his dreams of marital happiness cruelly snatched away from him, but it is a blight on his life that will live with him for the rest of his days."

"There are no winners in this matter. One must remember the father cruelly murdered and the widow who has not only lost her husband but her daughter also. The whole case has elements of a Greek tragedy. I wouldn't have missed it for the world." His eyes twinkled mischievously, knowing I would be appalled by such a statement.

"When did you begin to suspect Morag Cameron?"

"Well, the nose bleeding incident struck me as odd, and then when I found her discarded handkerchief in the wastepaper basket, that raised my suspicions further. Why should the girl wish to fake a nose bleed unless it was for a nefarious purpose? It was then that I began to see my way through the mist. Her presence in the murder room was assured, aided by the discovery of the seed pearls, but what puzzled me initially was the motive. Why should this young girl wish to kill her father? And then I discovered the copy of the will, recently dated, which indicated that the bulk of the estate was not going to Morag, as no doubt had been the case previously. Typical of the official police to overlook this piece of damning evidence. But the girl will never see the gallows. Her mental structures have crumbled under the weight of her obsession. It is clear that a kind of madness overtook her. She will end up in some institution for the rest of her life. Strangely, old boy, I feel rather sorry for her. A woman should be able to marry whomever she wishes without constraints and penalties. Don't you agree?"

"Of course," I nodded, with a smile. I was always fascinated when Holmes expounded his views on romance and matrimony.

"Now then," he said cheerily, "be so good as to pass me the toast and butter."

The Perplexing *X*'ing
by Sonia Fetherston
From *Part XX: 2020 Annual (1891-1897)* (2020)

My longtime friend, Mr. Sherlock Holmes, is not a pious man. He is not an habitual church-goer, nor does he count men of the cloth among his close circle. Yet never suppose that my friend is uninterested in religion. Indeed, I have often heard him refer to his great brain, and his deductive powers, as being "God-given". He has performed several discreet favours for a certain prince of the church, as well as for the Holy See itself. Holmes once served as the personal representative of two Coptic Patriarchs for the purpose of negotiating the return of a stolen relic, the value of which was said to be beyond price. On one occasion he disguised himself in the garb an aged ecclesiastic, a costume which allowed him to elude Professor Moriarty. And Holmes is the only Englishman I know who ever spent a week as a guest of the Head Lama in Tibet. So it should not come as a surprise that my friend agreed to take the case of one of the most singular religious persons ever to appeal for our help.

According to my notes, this particular adventure unfolded one Tuesday evening during the spring of 1897. A rainstorm was splashing across the city, and we could hear the wind whistling like a passer-by frightened of a dark burial ground. Under the lamps outside in Baker Street, a lone man struggled to keep his umbrella aloft against the chilly raindrops. We, on the other hand, were warm and dry in our cosy sitting room. Mrs. Hudson gathered the remains of our supper onto her tray, gently tut-tutting over Holmes's uneaten meal. As his friend and sometimes-physician, I was alert to this early sign of *ennui*. My suspicions were seemingly confirmed when I observed Holmes, a few moments later, standing before the fireplace, his right hand twitching reflexively and his eyes raking a nearby table where rested the black case containing his favourite syringe. I gently cleared my throat. "A little violin music just now would be a treat. Will you play?"

He cast an annoyed look in my direction. "Your powers of observation improve, Watson, but as usual your conclusion landed wide." Then he shook his head ruefully. "Yes, I am bored. Yes, a distraction would be welcome. But you are sufficiently acquainted with me to know that when I am working I eat very little so that my blood can pass over my stomach and race instead to my brain. As for the thing which interests me upon the table, it is not my needle but that wire beneath it, which arrived this afternoon." His sinewy arm reached across and he seized a yellow telegram from under the needle case. "Read it yourself."

Must urgently consult you regarding a perplexing matter. Shall arrive in Baker Street to-night at 9 o'clock.

L. Binney

I looked across at my friend. "Holmes, you have a case!"

As if in answer the downstairs bell rang, then almost immediately rang again. "Ah!" Holmes sighed. "One ring means a little something to while away an evening. Two rings promises brainwork." He vaulted into his habitual chair, and arranged his long limbs. Within a minute our door opened half way, and to our surprise our friend Stanley Hopkins peered around the edge, his shoulders glittering with raindrops. Hopkins was a Scotland Yard inspector who had associated with us on several recent cases. Like Holmes, he was an admirer of science, and of following facts to wherever they might lead. He frequently expressed awe at my friend's methods and he sought to apply them in his own work, though with varying degrees of success. Holmes thought Hopkins was capable and talented, and he took what might be considered a fatherly interest in the young man. "Care for a visitor?" Hopkins twinkled.

"Most certainly you are welcome," I replied, rising from my place at the table to greet him.

"Would you mind two visitors: Myself and one other?" he asked, and the door swung open to reveal a slender woman of about thirty years who stood beside Hopkins. Her dark eyes darted around our sitting room, taking it in with equal parts intelligence and curiosity. A mass of rich, brown curls threatened to explode from beneath her remarkable hat. It was an enormous, round black bonnet, lined with tight, ruched pleats, and secured at the side with a huge satin bow.

"Dr. Watson, Mr. Holmes, may I present Major Louise Binney, an officer in the Salvation Army?" Hopkins announced. "She came to me with what she described as a 'perplexation'. It seemed the sort of thing which might appeal to you, Mr. Holmes, so I suggested that she wire you in advance of our arrival."

"A lady Major?" I ejaculated, not entirely sure what to make of this development. "Good heavens, ma'am, you outrank me! I was in Her Majesty's service myself, regular Army, though a mere surgeon." I glanced at the black, belted tunic she wore over her full skirt, its stiff collar standing at attention, epaulettes on her shoulders, along with other insignia which bore the unmistakable mark of a commissioned officer.

"How do you do, Dr. Watson," she said with a slight nod. If her appearance was brisk and military-like, her voice was low and musical. "Yes, I'm a Major. You may know that the Salvation Army is a church, founded right here in England. We officers are ordained ministers, while our lay members are called soldiers. General William Booth established the Salvation Army shortly before I was born. [1] Offering one's heart to God and one's hand to mankind is a rigourous calling, so General Booth drew inspiration from the discipline of the regular Army. We wear uniforms as a witness of our service." Both of her gloved hands rose to her high collar, where, on either side of her chin, were two round pins, each bearing the letter *S*. "We are *Saved*," she said, touching first the pin on the left and then its counterpart opposite, "so that we might *Serve*."

"Sit beside the fire, Major," Holmes invited. "Watson will fetch you a glass of sherry, and some whisky for Hopkins."

"Liquor? No," the Major shook her head. "Salvationists thirst only for the word of our Lord. We abstain from alcohol."

"I see." Holmes held up his pipe. "Would you object if I were to smoke? I find that it concentrates and refines the deductive faculties."

"I prefer that you do not, sir," she quietly replied, and he obliged by placing his old briar in a small dish on the table at his side. He turned his gaze on her.

"Then pray tell me how I can assist you," he said quietly. "Save what you've just revealed about your rank and beliefs, the only the other obvious facts are that you are a single woman, an ardent cornet-player, are preparing to undertake a journey to America, and studied Paul's *Epistle to the Corinthians* just prior to coming here. Beyond that, I know nothing whatever about you."

"Why, Mr. Holmes!" she exclaimed. "How on earth did you – ?"

"May I?" I interjected, handing the whisky to Hopkins and motioning him to a chair. I drew my own seat nearer the fire and settled there. "I have had the pleasure of associating with my friend on a number of cases, and am somewhat acquainted with his methods. Beneath your left glove there is no outline of a wedding ring. Your cheek muscles are high and rounded, indicative of blowing into a horn such as those I've seen Salvationists use in street corner services. A cornet is smaller than a trumpet, so it is better suited to a woman's hands. The edge of a steamship ticket, second class, is protruding from your pocket. I can just make out the word 'Hoboken'. If I'm not mistaken, that is the port immediately west of New York City. As for your evening's reading material, I am in the dark as much as you are."

Holmes smiled and lifted his chin a bit, with that self-satisfied air he sometimes exhibited. "There is a nearly imperceptible dusting of gold on

252

your skirt, where rested the gilt edge of a book. Since you are an ordained minister, a Bible is the sort of book you might choose. From the slimness of the imprint, it could only be a New Testament. You had it open slightly past the mid-point, I perceive, which suggests *Corinthians*. Child's play."

"How easy it is!" said she, folding her hands on her lap. "There is no mystery, then, save for the one I bring to you."

"Tell me more about yourself," Holmes invited, "and then pray let me know how I might help."

"When I was a babe, Mr. Holmes, my own mother was dying of consumption, and so she left me at the Army's foundling home in Spitalfields. There I spent my early years. 'Mrs. General' – General Booth's dear wife, Catherine – frequently worked in the home, and she was always kind to me. She taught me to sew, and to read, and to speak properly. From her I learned to trust the Lord in all things. I would often play with her own daughter, Eva. As a young girl I longed to be just like the Booths! When I reached my teen years, I preached on street corners, and laboured for our Lord in blighted neighbourhoods. Eva and I were what they called 'Sallie Slum Sisters', visiting the sick, helping women and children, and advocating temperance. We studied, and eventually we became officers, beginning our ascent through the ranks. Now Eva is a Colonel and commander of our Marylebone Centre, while I command the Whitechapel Corps."

"Quite enthralling," he said, waving his hand while staring at the ceiling. "Is there some specific way in which I may I assist you?"

"Perhaps I can explain," Hopkins interjected. "I find it helps me to restate a case." I silently blessed him – he knew as well as I the dangers of a bored Sherlock Holmes. Hopkins thrust his hand into his pocket and extracted his notebook. Turning the pages, he began to recite the facts which were known to him.

"The Salvation Army is fortunate to have several generous friends who supply against its needs. One such individual was the late Mrs. Thomas Peppercorn who, with her husband, built a prosperous watch and clock shop in Peter Street, just north of the Gloucester Road. For many years, Mr. Peppercorn was both shopkeeper and repairman, while Mrs. Peppercorn kept the inventory and ledger books. She also was an ardent volunteer and financial helper of the Salvation Army.

"The couple were childless. Having no son or daughter to succeed them, the problem became: What to do with the business? When Mr. Peppercorn died a little more than two years ago, his wife sought to continue their work. She hired a Mr. Edward Spool, who has some skill in repairing timepieces. Mrs. Peppercorn also added a bookkeeper to take over many of her own duties. His name is Tim O'Donnell. He is a

253

Salvation Army soldier – a member of the congregation at the Whitechapel Corps – whom Mrs. Peppercorn met in the soup kitchen during her volunteer service."

"We found him living rough, on the streets," Major Binney said. "A tall man with a pronounced curve in his spine, so he has a crooked appearance. His temperament is a bit coarse at times. Excitable, according to his Irish ways. But I believe his faith is genuine. His skills are good. He helps us a few hours each week with our church finances."

"How did he go from keeping ledgers to living on the streets, and back again?" Holmes enquired.

"He lost his previous position due to drink," she said very simply. "Several years ago, General William Booth published a book, *In Darkest England*. Perhaps you've read it? It contains personal stories of some of the men and women with whom we are privileged to work . . . even to save. Many suffer from the effects of drink. The General estimated there are at present one-million people in England who are completely under the domination of alcohol. It is a wicked, ruinous thing, as Tim learned. He lost his livelihood and friends."

"The Sallies cleaned him up and converted him," Hopkins added.

"Now Mr. O'Donnell is a decent, God-fearing man," Major Binney said.

"You trust him?" I asked her. "You don't worry that he will lapse and drink again?"

She was pragmatic. "There's always a chance, Doctor. And there is always forgiveness."

Hopkins looked at his notes once more and continued. "Mrs. Peppercorn finally wearied of her business responsibilities and sold her shop to Spool last summer. He retained O'Donnell as bookkeeper and Mrs. Peppercorn settled into retirement. She lived with her maid and cook. Mrs. Peppercorn's charitable instincts kept bringing her back to the Salvation Army. She continued as a volunteer in the organization's Whitechapel Corps. Mrs. Peppercorn survived her husband by about eighteen months."

"She was Promoted to Glory ten weeks ago," Major Binney said.

"Promoted to Glory?" Holmes exclaimed.

"That is how we Sallies refer to death," she replied.

"Upon her passing," Hopkins resumed, "Mrs. Peppercorn's estate, approaching four-thousand pounds, was to be transferred as a gift to the Salvation Army. The money came from the sale of the Peppercorn's business, and from the auction some days ago of Mrs. Peppercorn's house and its contents." He paused and drew a single sheet of paper from his notebook. "Here is the Salvation Army's copy of the will, signed by Mrs. Peppercorn on the twenty-third of November of last year." Hopkins handed it across to Holmes. "That is the lady's signature, witnessed by two men employed by her solicitor, Mr. George Besbury-Dubbs."

Holmes scanned the document quickly, then handed it to me. "It seems straightforward. enough," he remarked. "Thirty pounds apiece to her housemaid and cook, then the remainder shall go to the Salvation Army. I am not seeing a 'perplexation' clause, Major Binney."

"Indeed, there is one," our uniformed guest offered. "Mrs. Peppercorn loved the Salvation Army. She often said that we inspired all that was good in her. She worked shoulder-to-shoulder with us, serving soup, distributing bricks of soap, and reading the Gospel aloud in our day room. Could you love the unloved, Mr. Holmes? She most assuredly did. She told me several times over the years that in due course her estate would come to us in order to help the poor. That's why her abrupt change of heart makes no sense. You see, there is a second will."

Holmes suddenly leaned forward like a hound catching a scent on a breeze.

"Dated?"

"The twenty-sixth of November last year."

"Where?"

"At her solicitor's chambers, same as this previous will."

"Witnessed?"

"By the same two who witnessed the first signing three days earlier."

"The benefactors being?"

"Gifts of thirty pounds apiece were made to her servants. But Mr. Spool is now the sole beneficiary of the remainder. The new will goes on to state that '*not one penny*' is to go to the Salvation Army!"

"Legally done?

Our Salvationist visitor shrugged her slim shoulders. "Well, that's the thing, Mr. Holmes." She regarded him quietly for several seconds. "The newer will, the one which eliminates the Salvation Army, was properly drawn up by her solicitor and duly witnessed. That second document, however, was signed with an *X*."

This development sent an immediate shiver through me. "But why?" I asked. "Why would a perfectly literate woman sign her will with an *X*?"

"My dear Watson, you shimmer with pure intelligence. Why, indeed?" Holmes purred. "That her own hand made the *X* cannot be doubted – there were witnesses to her having done so. Yet we know Mrs. Peppercorn to be literate from her business duties, and from her Gospel readings at the Whitechapel Corps. By her previous will we can see that the lady was perfectly capable of signing her full name. Her ability to read and write are facts. So is her unexplained *X* on this second version: It is

255

another fact. And yet – and yet – It is, Major Binney, just as you say. It's a *perplex*."

"It is inexplicable!" she cried. "The Mrs. Peppercorn I knew for many years would *never* cut the Salvation Army from her will, and if by some chance she did, she would never write into that will the vindictive words that '*not one penny*' should come to us. To do so would be cruel, and she was not a cruel woman. Why, on the day before she was Promoted to Glory, Mrs. Peppercorn stopped in at the Corps. She told me how much she loved the Salvation Army. She said that she considered Salvationists to be her family, and that I was like a daughter to her. Then she gave me a present, a clock which Mr. Peppercorn himself built. Her great heart gave out the next morning and I never saw her again."

As she spoke, Hopkins extracted a second paper from between the pages of his notebook. It was a true copy of the second will, which he explained was provided by Mrs. Peppercorn's solicitor to the Salvation Army when that organization came forward to claim its inheritance. We handed it amongst ourselves for a moment, silently reading the pitiless words the Major had described, and examining the *X* near the bottom.

"It does not rise to a police matter," Hopkins asserted. "It is rather a matter for a probate court – or perhaps better, a tangle for you to unravel, Mr. Holmes."

"In the morning I shall undertake to learn more," Holmes said with finality. "I shall look into this matter for you, Major Binney, and offer my expert opinion."

"You have just answered my prayers," Major Binney declared, much moved. "You, and the Lord who works through you. But Mr. Holmes," she continued, "I'm afraid I have but little money to pay you for your services."

"Having and solving your puzzle are payment enough," he told her. "Consider it my contribution to your ministry."

"My gratitude is boundless, sir!"

We said goodbye and they returned to the rainy street, where their hansom waited. "What do you make of her, Watson?" Holmes asked, lighting his neglected pipe.

"An extraordinary woman," I replied.

"An extraordinary client," he corrected. "A client is to me a merely a problem-bearer, a means to an end, an escape from the perils of boredom. Major Binney's perplex helps fill the empty hours, and because it is unusual – the mystery of the *X*, the giver who suddenly withdraws a gift – it should keep my mind nicely occupied for a day or two."

"Have you any theories?"

"No theories as yet," he replied. "I do, however, have a working hypothesis that has to do with the *X*. Rather, with the precise *nature* of the letter. Consider that an *X* consists of two contrasting impulses that meet in a crossing point, then continue on their separate ways. When we find that intersection, we will find the facts necessary to solve Major Binney's perplexing problem."

"We?"

"If you would be so good, Watson? I find a chronicler to be handy, but a friend and able companion is invaluable."

Here was his heart! I've sometimes called Sherlock Holmes a thinking machine, or an automaton – an orphan-like being devoid of emotion. Yet there were times when the mask slipped and he revealed human feelings. "I will be honoured to assist you in any possible way," I told him.

"Thank you, my dear Watson."

Next morning, as we finished our ham, boiled eggs, and toast, the stately figure of Mrs. Hudson glided in, a fresh pot of tea in one hand and a salver bearing a calling card in the other. "A gentleman to see you, Mr. Holmes," she reported.

"I'm expecting him," Holmes replied, brushing a crumb from his lapel. "Show him up, if you please." As she went to the door and began her descent down the steps, he stood and crossed to our hearth, where he proceeded to jab at the glowing coals with a poker. "There's a chill in the air," he said. "Today's weather is almost colder than the heart that changed that will."

"You believe it to be altered, or possibly forged?" I enquired.

"No, I didn't say that – the lady's mark was made and properly witnessed, so it's not a case of was it changed. Rather, it is a case of why that change occurred. We stand on the brink of learning more." The poker clattered to the floor, as Holmes suddenly turned around. "Do come in and be seated, Mr. Besbury-Dubbs."

Mrs. Peppercorn's solicitor was a short, slight, startled-looking man of middle years. His eyebrows rode high on his creased forehead, a condition perhaps aided by a hairline in full retreat. He handed Mrs. Hudson his hat and overcoat, revealing attire a baronet might choose for a Sunday in the park: An impeccable gray wool suit, enlivened by a jaunty, striped silver-and-red tie that was pinned at his throat with a large pearl. "Of course I've heard your name, Mr. Holmes. It was the talk of the Temple when we read Dr. Watson's account of the marriage of our colleague, Godfrey Norton, to that American." [2] His voice was high and reedy. "If I remember correctly, you played a role in that drama – or was it a comedy?" He seated himself and chuckled. "Imagine my surprise when

257

I received a telegram from that same Sherlock Holmes, asking me to call at Baker Street this morning. How might I be of service, sir? Perhaps you wish to consult me regarding legalities because you yourself are to marry?"

"Ha!" barked my friend, as he subsided into his usual chair, elbows on its arms, and long fingers steepled before him. "That is more likely to be the eventual fate of our resident ladies' man, Dr. Watson!"

"I lost my wife several years ago," I explained, wistfully, to our visitor.

"No, Mr. Besbury-Dubbs, I wish to consult you about something even more perplexing than Dr. Watson's love life," Holmes continued. "It is an estate in which you were instrumental. In November of last year you prepared a will for a Mrs. Thomas Peppercorn."

"I did, sir."

"And she signed it?"

"She did indeed, sir" the solicitor agreed. "I saw her sign it, as did two of my clerks who served as witnesses to the act. She affixed her signature to the document in my own chambers. She took the original, and we retained two signed copies of her will in our office safe, as is our usual practice."

"The Salvation Army was the primary beneficiary of that will?"

"It certainly was," the little solicitor replied. "She was very generous to them. As I recall she did 'give, devise, and bequeath' the vast majority of her estate to that organization."

"Just a moment," I interrupted. "I have always wondered why wills use those three words together: 'Give, devise, and bequeath'. They mean the same thing, so they simply repeat themselves."

"So one might think," Mr. Besbury-Dubbs explained. "Though there is an actual difference. In legal terms, to 'devise' is to make a gift of real property, such as land, or a house. To 'bequeath' is to leave behind one's personal property, such as jewelry, china, or a book collection. Both devising and bequeathing constitute an act of giving. Use of the different words dates back nearly a thousand years when it was necessary to include Anglo-Saxon, French, and Latin in our English legal documents so that there could be no misunderstanding of intent."

"I suppose that 'will' and 'testament' are different words, too?"

"Under the law, yes," he told us, "though they are now normally combined for the sake of convenience. However, in times past they could exist as two separate documents, with the will standing for real property and the testament for personal effects. The words '*last* will and testament' indicate that it was to be the will-and-testament maker's final word on the subject."

258

Holmes cleared his throat to let us know that my lesson in the legal lexicon had come to an end. "Several days after the first will was signed, did you not prepare a second will for Mrs. Peppercorn?"

"I did."

"But she did not sign the second will. Rather, she marked it with an X."

Mr. Besbury-Dubbs nodded in the affirmative. "The second will was marked with her X. I saw her place her mark on it, as did the same witnesses, my two clerks. As before, we gave her the original, retained her X'd copies in our safe, and presented another X'd copy to Mr. Edward Spool, to whom she had recently sold her business and who was now to be the main beneficiary of her estate. He accompanied her to my chambers."

"How did she appear?" Holmes enquired. "Her bearing and demeanor? Was she sensible and businesslike, or did she seem upset in any way?"

"Now that you mention it, Mrs. Peppercorn was rather introspective. She read through the changes, and so did Mr. Spool. Truth be told, it was he who put forward that 'not one penny' should go to the Sallies. At first she was reluctant to sign. She complained to us that her hand hurt, and that she couldn't possibly hold the pen properly. She asked to set the second will aside to sign at a later date. At Spool's insistence she finally placed her mark on the document, the X of which you spoke. The X is perfectly legal, just like a signature, as long as it is properly witnessed. It was. She then departed."

"But why proceed with the X, given that her hand would eventually recover and she could come back, as you say, at a later date?" Holmes mused. "What was so important about that will that she had to get the thing done, rather than come back another day?"

"Ah!" The little solicitor's brows inched higher than ever. "I'll wager you are wondering why she marked the second will with an X, when both the first and the third wills were inscribed with her full name?"

Had he fired a ship's cannon across Holmes's deal table he could not have startled us more. "Mr. Besbury-Dubbs!" Holmes exclaimed. "I am all attention. Pray tell me about this third will." My friend leaned back into his chair and closed his eyes, a satisfied smile playing across his lips.

"Two days after affixing her X, Mrs. Peppercorn returned to my chambers, alone. She desired me to make a third will. That one was intended to cut out Mr. Spool and reinstate the Salvation Army as the primary beneficiary. At her insistence I had it drawn up in a hurry, while she waited, and she signed it with her full name. Her hand certainly did not hurt that day! My two clerks witnessed it, as before, so the thing was legally done. She directed that no copies were to be made. She took the

259

one and only version of that third will away with her. That was the end of it."

"How very curious," Holmes said. "And if I am not mistaken, that third will, signed and witnessed as it was, would supersede the second will?"

"Indeed, if it can be produced. Unfortunately, I do not know where it is, so I cannot present it to the court."

"And if I can recover that third will, and bring it to you?"

"It can proceed to a judge, and much joy to the Salvation Army."

Once the little solicitor left us, Holmes reached for his hat and overcoat and made for the door. "Hurry into your things, Watson. Not a moment to lose! We have an appointment with a lady and we must not keep her waiting." In a moment we were seated in a cab, flying through the fog that had settled on the Marylebone Road, making our way toward Bayswater. At ten o'clock Holmes was rapping with his stick on the door of a townhouse located on a quiet side street. Large pots planted with bright red geraniums stood at either side of the shiny black door, their spicy scent filling the air. We were admitted by a butler of perfunctory habits who guided us into a sitting room and told us to wait. "Mrs. Rosalind Baugh is the pre-eminent expert in the field of handwriting analysis," Holmes explained to me. "As respected in her particular field as – " He was cut short when the eminent expert herself stepped into the room.

On first glance, Mrs. Baugh appeared delicate. Even with a rope of thick, white hair coiled atop her head, she was small of stature and thin almost to the point of frailty. She appeared to be near the age of sixty, her face being gently lined, yet her complexion retained the colour which I believe is called Healthy English: Clear and pale, with a delicate pink tint. Her morning gown was indigo, with a rich froth of lace and ribbons at the throat and wrists. As she stepped across the room to greet us, I noticed that her movements were energetic. "Mr. Sherlock Holmes! I've had your telegram, sir!" she cried in a cheerful, girlish voice. "And Dr. Watson! This is indeed an honour, one author to another. Do you know that on one occasion a little treatise of mine appeared in the same edition of *The Strand* as your own account of one of Mr. Holmes's cases? It's delightful to finally meet you both!" Her hands fluttered as she spoke, like twin white moths.

She paid us the compliment of asking us to sign a large autograph album, though we quickly realized she was less interested in having souvenirs of ourselves, and more interested in collecting written specimens of us for study. She carefully fitted a silver pince-nez to her face and peered at our names. "Ah, Mr. Holmes, your capital 'S' will never be surpassed!" she exclaimed, studying the page we had inscribed. "The position of the letter reveals prodigality devoid of pretension. Your upslope indicates a certain clearness of mind, while the shoulders of the subsequent letters affirm an absolute rectitude of character. And Dr. Watson, see how the angular bases of the vowels in your name reveal your intuitive nature. The looping capital 'W" of your second name asserts kindliness and initiative. These are fine attributes for a physician."

"You are able to infer all of that from our signatures?" I asked.

"Of course I can," she insisted. "Handwriting reflects the personality and condition of the writer: His intelligence, his character, his emotions, his tendencies. A determined person writes with a masterful hand. A happy person writes with a lilting hand. One who is ill writes with a weakened hand. The writing of a troubled person loses energy as each letter and line escape his pen. Writers who are in the throes of passion – joy, anger, grief, and the like – betray those sensations to a skilled graphologist. Graphology is superior to its sister pursuits of phrenology and palmistry. The seeker need not submit his head or hand to a practitioner, merely a sample of his writing. The expert scrutiny of handwriting is much more reliable than trying to understand an individual through observation, or even interview."

"Indeed?" Holmes said, with a trace of asperity, as if his ability to "read" a visitor was on par with a mere parlour trick. Holmes was the keenest observer of humans and human nature that I have ever encountered but, as noted elsewhere in my accounts of his cases, egotism was also a strong factor in his singular nature. I wondered whether Mrs. Baugh had discerned this as well from his signature, and was attempting a little jest at his expense.

"Graphology is an exact science, Mr. Holmes," she continued. "Though its roots are ancient, it was the Italians who, three-hundred years ago, refined it to the extent that it became possible for them to detect spies and enemies from writing samples. But it was the French, of course, who introduced romance into graphology – practitioners in the household of Louis *Quatorze* were able to discern the true intent behind notes sent between men and women of the Royal Court." She waggled her raised index finger at us. "Sprightly, Mr. Holmes, sprightly!"

His face assumed a solemn aspect. "Well, I mean to test the limits of your abilities, Madam. Can you, for instance, make meaningful conclusions from a single letter of the alphabet?" He drew the will, signed with the *X*, from his pocket and handed it to her.

Mrs. Baugh dropped into a chair and bent her head over the document. "A very commonplace Copperplate," she began, then looked at

Holmes with a shrewd expression. "But you have no interest in the clerk who copied this document, have you? Neither do I. But see this *X* at the end? That is quite interesting." She reached for a large magnifying lens which lay atop her chairside table, then concentrated the full force of her attention on the single letter. Holmes and I stood patiently before her. And then she lifted her head, her eyes set thoughtfully on the window opposite.

"One prefers to have a paragraph, so as to compare the penmanship against itself. A signature is next best, as writing one's own name is such a personal and revelatory thing." Mrs. Baugh gently shook her head and turned to my companion. "But a single letter, composed of two lines intersecting at roughly the mid-point! You either flatter me, Mr. Holmes, or you come to tease me, asking me to interpret such a little thing!"

To my astonishment Holmes dropped to one knee before her seated figure, and looked directly into her clear blue eyes. "In my career, my dear Mrs. Baugh, I have found that it is often the little things which are the most important." An encouraging look played across his features. "Tell me something most important about that little *X*."

She studied it half a minute more and then rose from her chair, offering her hand to my friend and bringing him to a standing position. "The letter *X* is widely considered to be the most eccentric in the English language, Mr. Holmes," she began, handing the will back to him. "It is a letter rarely used, and therefore brimming with evocation. We shall begin with the downstroke on the left, which travels diagonally to the lower right position. You may have observed it was made first. It is not straight, but contains a hint of a jag. So slight is that jag that one must scrutinize it under a powerful lens, as I did, in order to see it. Think of a river, Mr. Holmes. Rivers always take as their course the route of least resistance – that is why they are crooked. I find it is the same with people. This downstroke was made by a person who is seeking an easy way, the easiest available means to an end, and so the hand has twitched ever so slightly. On the right is the second line of the *X*. It commences on the upper side and moves diagonally toward the lower left. It extends slightly higher than its counterpart, hinting strongly at dissimulation. Candor, you see, is invariably indicated by a certain evenness of each stroke – in other words, for an honest person the lines would be equal. Therefore, this *X* was made by an individual who is trying to deviate, or to trick. Taken together, these two strokes confirm that the *X*-writer is insincere. She – for the mark contains other characteristics that lead one to conclude it was made by a woman – was being dishonest."

"Mrs. Baugh, you are a wonder," Holmes said, and he bent to gently kiss her hand.

We hurried to a lane in West London, near a small park of that name, where the Peppercorns had lived. As Hopkins told us the previous evening, their home had just been sold. A wagon sat before it laden with rugs, tables, and other household goods. A driver tying down the last of the home's contents directed us to a door at the back. After a moment a thin, careworn woman appeared and admitted us. At my companion's enquiry she told us her name was Florrie Budd, housemaid. It seemed the cook, Mrs. Hixson, had already departed for a new situation, while Florrie was left to see to the emptying the house. "I go to my cousin the day after to-morrow," Florrie said. "She's housekeeper of a hotel in Scarborough, and I'm to work with her."

"And you leave here with thirty pounds in your pocket," Holmes commented.

"Mrs. Peppercorn were good to me," Florrie confirmed. "I were housemaid to her and Mr. Peppercorn going on fifteen years." Her face crumpled and tears spilled down her cheeks, which she mopped with the corner of her apron. Holmes steered her toward an old stool, settling her onto it. He patted her arm gently. His manner was invariably kind in situations such as this. "Pray compose yourself, Florrie," he said to her. "Tell me, was Mrs. Peppercorn generous with others, too?"

"With Mrs. Hixson, same as me," Florrie said.

"How about with the Salvation Army?" Holmes asked.

"Oh, yes sir, she loved the Sallies!" Florrie told us. "But there was questions later."

"What kind of questions, Florrie?"

"Mr. O'Donnell come by one day. He has a temper, that one. He were shouting, and Mrs. Peppercorn began to cry."

Holmes glanced over at me, then back at the maid. "He was shouting at Mrs. Peppercorn? Why?"

"No sir, not at her," Florrie said. "He were shouting about Mr. Spool – that's the man that has the Peppercorn's clock shop now. He said Mrs. Peppercorn were careless, and she must do as Mr. Spool wants. Do it. Make it right."

I spoke up. "Tell me, Florrie, did Mrs. Peppercorn leave behind any papers – anything official-looking? Anything that might have come from her solicitor's office? A will, perhaps?"

"Oh yes, sir," she replied. "A lot of papers, in her desk. I can't read. I don't know what they was. But I put 'em in boxes."

I leaned toward her. "Where are those boxes?"

"The dustman took 'em. Ten days ago, likely," she said. "Those papers are gone. And the last of the furniture goes today."

"But is the desk still here? It's possible you overlooked something."

263

"Maybe I did. Maybe the desk is in the wagon."

Holmes and I sprinted out and around the house. The wagon-driver was about to leave, but after Holmes parted with a half-a-crown he was willing to wait. We climbed on the back and moved some dining chairs aside. There, under a square drugget, was Mrs. Peppercorn's desk. We quickly opened its drawers, even checking for false bottoms and tapping for concealed panels, but to no avail. Florrie had done her job well. There was no sign of any will: First, second, or third. Defeated, we climbed down and the wagon went on its way.

We were still brushing the dust from our knees and hands when Holmes turned to me, wearing a bemused expression. "But for the intervention of 'Mrs. General' Booth, our friend Louise Binney might well have had a life like Florrie's," he observed. "They are similar in age, and it's probable their backgrounds are much the same. Thanks to the Salvation Army, today Louise is a high-ranking officer. Florrie didn't have that advantage, so she remains in a lowly state. Notwithstanding, they have hard work in common."

The sun was labouring to break through a fog that lingered into the afternoon. Holmes and I stopped at a stall for sandwiches and tea, then pressed on to the Peppercorn's former place of business. We stood on the pavement across from the shop, trying our best to look like two acquaintances who'd met there by chance. From the corners of our eyes we each stole quick glances across the street. In a large front window we could see a jumble of clocks and watches displayed for the benefit of passersby. Over the door protruded the round face of a real clock, its skeletal workings throbbing with each passing second. Presently, I felt Holmes's hand on my wrist. "I say, Watson," he said with quiet urgency. "The pocket watch that belonged to your brother – the one I once examined and told you of his having descended into poverty and drink. Have it with you?"[3]

I clapped my hand to my pocket. "I do."

"May I?" He held out his hand, and I gave it to him. I observed, dumbfounded, as he seized the stem and wound it forcefully until the spring snapped. He broke it! "Alas, Watson, your watch needs attention," said he, returned it to me. "See if they'll tend to the injury while you wait. Now off you go to learn a great deal."

"Learn a great deal about what, Holmes?" I asked with annoyance.

He snarled impatiently. "You know my methods. Put them to use! What is particularly noteworthy about the shop? Its contents? Its workers? Its condition? Is it prosperous, or fallen on hard times? What of Spool himself? His appearance and character? Data, Watson – bring me data!"

I suppressed the urge to tell him to do it himself. I remembered the solicitor, Besbury-Dubbs, and how that individual was already well-versed, as a result of my published accounts, on the subject of Sherlock Holmes. My friend was well-known and might be recognized, whereas I was merely his invisible chronicler, his "Boswell", his interpreter, his companion. No one knew me. I shrugged and waited for the traffic to lighten so that I could cross the street.

The bell over the door tinkled a welcome as I entered the shop. It was small, though neat and attractively arranged. After being in the chilly street it felt warm and cheery. A sharp tang of oil and metal hung in the air, and underneath it, from somewhere in the unseen back of the shop, came the smell of coffee. A portly man in shirtsleeves, wearing thick glasses, peered at me across the counter. I'd interrupted his work – the dismantled gears of a large clock lay spread on a piece of cloth before him. He was of middle years, medium height, with dark hair and beard after the Van Dyke style. He took off the glasses and reached for his coat. Drawing it on, the man greeted me and asked how he could help me.

"I say, is Mr. Peppercorn in?" I enquired. "My pocket watch has stopped, and he has always looked after it beautifully."

"I'm very sorry to say that Mr. Peppercorn died two years ago," the man replied. "I'm Mr. Spool, and this establishment is now my own. I've a skilled hand with watches. Perhaps I may be of assistance?"

I handed over my watch. He removed the crystal and face, and peered inside. "Why, it's just the spring needs replacing. I've three others ahead of you. Will you leave your watch overnight and return for it to-morrow? Four pence for the repair, and no charge for cleaning." He smiled – here was a pleasant, capable man at home in his establishment.

"All right. If you would be so kind as to prepare a ticket so that I might claim it?" I said to him. "My name's Hudson. And perhaps I might have some of that coffee I smell? Just the thing to warm me up before I return to the cold and damp outside."

"Of course! Just you wait."

As I hoped, he pulled back a curtain and vanished into the rear of his shop. As he did so I had a glimpse of a little stove, cups on a table, a whisky bottle, and a plate with a half-eaten meal, and then the curtain fell. I quickly seized my chance, and, in a paroxysm of activity, I darted behind the counter. I scrutinized that morning's post, as well as several bills which were opened. I memorized names on a couple of accounts that were past due. Heart pounding, I had just resumed my former position when I heard an angry unpleasantness from behind the curtain.

"We are in this together." This was Spool!

"We are not." It was a harsh, accented voice I didn't know.

265

"I'll inform them you're clutching a bottle again." Spool again. "You'll be ruined."

"That's blackmail, you cur," the mysterious voice replied with a snarl.

"You're finished here. Out, and never come back!" Spool hissed.

The curtain flew aside and a man I'd never before seen – a tall man with a twisted spine matching the description Major Binney had given us for Tim O'Donnell, the Sallie soldier and bookkeeper – stalked out. Though dressed in shabby clothes, he placed a smart Salvation Army cap on his head and looked over his shoulder to the back room. "I took another drink or two, but there is healing for that," he declared. "No such cure for the likes of you, Spool!" He departed, slamming the door so hard the bell dropped to the floor.

After a few seconds of silence the curtain twitched again, and a smiling Spool came out with a cup of coffee in his hand. He was unruffled, though his colour was high. "Here you are, sir. Now about a ticket so you may claim the watch . . . ."

"Thank you kindly, but I have pressing business elsewhere," I told him. I snatched my broken watch from the counter, returned it to my pocket and hurried out the door. O'Donnell was nowhere in sight, and neither was Sherlock Holmes. After several minutes of searching, I gave up and went back to Baker Street.

Holmes was already there when I returned, and to my amazement he was seated before our fire with none other than Tim O'Donnell. They were deep in conversation. It seemed Holmes, too, had recognized the man by his malformed spine and had persuaded the bookkeeper to accompany him. According to O'Donnell, Spool was perpetually short of cash – he'd bought the business from Mrs. Peppercorn, but he was in trouble because of his many other expenses. "That accounts for the past-due bills I saw," I told them.

"There are several more like it," O'Donnell confirmed. "Spool has to raise cash, and do it quickly. He remembered Mrs. Peppercorn – she was an old woman, and her heart was failing. Clearly, she didn't have much time left. That's how he came up with a plan to frighten her into making him her heir.

"He began to leave bottles of whisky in the back room," our visitor continued. "I wasn't able to withstand the temptation. When I started drinking again, he threatened to blackmail me, saying he would go to the Sallies and get me sacked. I risked losing my position at the shop, and at the Salvation Army, if I didn't support his unfounded claims." Spool confronted Mrs. Peppercorn with the old ledgers she'd kept for many years. He maintained that she'd exaggerated the shop's value, thereby cheating him. She hadn't, but in order to bolster his complaint he produced O'Donnell to support the accusations. "I had to lie to protect myself. I told Mrs. Peppercorn there were problems with her books, that she must do as Spool said, and repay him. I did that, and I am ashamed. I even caused her to weep!"

"So we were informed," Holmes commented.

Spool threatened the widow with legal action if she didn't re-write her will, leaving him the portion previously set aside for the Salvation Army. According to O'Donnell, the words, *"not one penny"* were suggested by Spool as a sort of cock-a-doodle.

"So, Mr. O'Donnell, you are the *X*," Holmes exclaimed. "He represents the crossroads of this case, Watson, where Spool's greed intersected with Mrs. Peppercorn's intentions. No wonder Mrs. Peppercorn told her solicitor that her hand hurt. The second will was made under grave duress, after the warning of a professional bookkeeper. Marking it with an *X* was the only avenue of protest she had."

"And Spool seemed like such a nice, jovial man," I said.

"We want the third will so that Spool cannot profit from his scheme," Holmes concluded. "Unless the third version is produced, the *X*'d will is the one that the court must accept. Mrs. Peppercorn's money will be released to Spool."

O'Donnell said in future that we could find him at the Whitechapel Corps, and he left us with his promise to give the police a full statement. "He will give evidence against Spool. For that the judge will show Mr. O'Donnell a measure of mercy," Holmes predicted after our visitor was gone. "Maybe that's more than he deserves, but I think that O'Donnell has taken this valuable lesson to heart. Major Binney will forgive him. She's already told us there is forgiveness for drunkards." He looked at me and shook his head. "You still think Spool is 'nice'? You must learn a lesson, too. *'O villain, villain, smiling, damned villain!'*"

"Shakespeare, I suppose?" I queried, and my friend nodded.

A half-hour later we were on our way again, stopping only so that Holmes could send Hopkins an urgent telegram explaining what had transpired, and requesting that he come immediately to the Whitechapel Corps. Our cabby deftly navigated the East End with its pungent, badly congested streets. The inspector was waiting when we arrived. We found the Corps to be a much-repaired old building not far from the Liverpool Street Station. It consisted of a large, clean central room with a kitchen and a couple of offices at the rear. Here was where daily bowls of soup were given out to hungry persons of all ages. Here also was where poor souls could find refuge from the elements. Here, too, was where noontime Christian services took place, amid considerable singing, shaking of timbrels, and preaching. I never heard Louise Binney preach, but if her kind manner was any indication, then I am certain her sermons were less about brimstone and more about practical goodness. She was Christianity with its sleeves rolled up.

When we arrived it was nearly half-past-six, already growing dark outside. Inside, we found Major Binney handing around mugs of sweet tea and pieces of buttered bread to the ragged mass of humanity huddled on benches placed throughout the room. Though she noted our arrival, she continued to push her tea cart until it was empty, then turned it over to a young associate and stepped forward to greet us. We shook hands and she motioned us into her small office located behind the kitchen. It felt chilly. The tiny grate was empty, as coal would have been an extravagance for this woman who placed the comfort of others before herself. A folded military-style cot was tilted against one wall. On her writing table lay a battered silver cornet, an oil lamp, a neat stack of correspondence, a tray for a fountain pen, her gilt-edged New Testament, and a chipped saucer containing several pennies and some postage stamps. Holmes, Hopkins, and I sat shoulder-to-shoulder on a short bench placed against the wall. Major Binney settled on a hard chair in front of her table. She untied the bow at the side of her chin and lifted the stiff round bonnet from her head. "Please excuse the informality," she told us. "It has been a tiring day. I helped deliver two babies, one of whom won't survive this night. Then I ministered for several hours outside an opium den near the river. Afterward, I nearly came to blows with the Devil himself in Aldgate. I must admit, though, that I'm happy."

She listened solemnly as Holmes explained about the three wills, and how Mrs. Baugh suspected the *X*-mark was made under duress. He finished by relating our adventures: The visit with Florrie, the sacrifice of my pocket watch, and O'Donnell's shame. Hopkins added that the will with the *X*, the version which left "*not one penny*" to the Salvation Army, would necessarily be accepted into probate court, as no trace of the third will could be found.

"I'm terribly sorry for Mrs. Peppercorn," the Major finally stated. "She must have been frightened by the spectre of two angry men claiming she'd cheated Mr. Spool. No wonder she looked so sad when I last saw her."

"But why didn't she come to the police for assistance?" Hopkins asked. "We could have helped her."

"Put yourself in her place," Holmes advised. "The police would have questioned her. Beyond that, she faced the prospect of arrest because of

Spool's accusations. Mrs. Peppercorn was old and alone, in failing health, and, as the Major has noted, she was likely very frightened."

"At this very moment my men are bringing in Spool for questioning," Hopkins said.

"Will he be charged?" I asked.

"Interfering with a witness – O'Donnell – at present," Hopkins replied. "If we had that third will, I could easily add fraud and attempted theft."

"Well, I'm most grateful for your having shed a lot of light on my case, Mr. Holmes," Major Binney said. "I'm appreciative of Dr. Watson's help, too. I'm so glad that Inspector Hopkins arranged for me to meet you. You've been very gracious toward me and my church."

Just for a moment, the only sound in the room was the steady ticking of a small mahogany mantel clock located above the fireplace. Holmes turned toward it.

"Is that by chance the clock Mrs. Peppercorn gave you the day before she was, as you say, 'Promoted to Glory'?"

"Why, yes, Mr. Holmes, it is." She rose, took it in her hands and placed it on her table.

Holmes regarded it curiously. "Of all things: The clockmaker's clock is not very good at keeping time. See? It's thirty-five minutes behind. May I?" He reached across, released the latch on the back, and opened the small door that provided access to the clock's movement. Wedged inside, amid three pulsating brass wheels, there was a slip of white paper. He extracted it, and unfolded it on the table. "Major, I believe this is the *final* last will and testament of Mrs. Thomas Peppercorn: Behold the third will."

And so it was. The document, dated the 28th of November last, stated Mrs. Peppercorn's clear intent to revoke all previous wills and leave her entire estate to the Salvation Army, less thirty pounds each to her cook and maid. It was signed, not with an *X*, but with the full signature of Mrs. Thomas Peppercorn. Rosalind Baugh had been correct: The will signed with the *X* was completed under stressful conditions, against Mrs. Peppercorn's wishes, but done to prevent Mr. Spool from further harassing her. This third will was dated two days after the will with the *X*. Clearly, Mrs. Peppercorn left this final will with those she trusted most: The Salvationists, and Major Binney in particular.

Hopkins reached for the will. "At first light, I will stand before a judge in company with Mr. Besbury-Dubbs," he told us. "If the circumstances are bit irregular, this will is perfectly legal. The Salvation Army will inherit after all."

"No more perplexes," Holmes said.

269

Major Binney smiled her thanks to us, and for an officer of superior rank I thought she blushed quite prettily. Then she insisted on giving me the clock in honour of my broken pocket watch.

"You've found that will at a fortuitous time, Mr. Holmes," said she. "Eva Booth and I have just received orders to leave in two days' time for America. Our schedule is moved up! Eva has been promoted to Brigadier. She will become the Salvation Army's commander for the Eastern United States. I am to be a Colonel and her second in command!" We congratulated her and then rose to go. As we filed out through the kitchen, I happened to glance back over my shoulder – a gold sovereign glinted atop the pennies and stamps in her chipped saucer! The sight of it must have caused me to stumble, for Holmes's strong hand steadied my shoulder and directed me through the central room and outside.

Our uniformed friend remained with us on the pavement as Hopkins hailed a cab. A misty evening rain was falling, and a single gas lamp illuminated the wet cobblestones and damp passersby. At that moment, Holmes and I saw an inebriate topple into the watery gutter, and to our horror he suddenly vomited on himself. We looked on in amazement as Major – now Colonel – Binney knelt beside him and with her own clean linen gently wiped his chin and breast. The cabby called down to her. "Miss, I wouldn't do that for a million pounds!"

She looked up at him, the raindrops sparkling on her face and hair. "Neither would I," she replied. "But I'd do it for love." She helped the drunken man to his feet, watched him toddle away, and went back inside her Corps as we three departed for our supper in Baker Street.

I settled into the cab between my friends, cradling the clock in my hands. "A most remarkable client," I stated.

"No," Holmes corrected me. "A most remarkable woman."

NOTES

1 – Booth founded the Salvation Army in 1865.
2 – Norton married Irene Adler in "A Scandal in Bohemia".
3 – *The Sign of the Four*.

The Case of the Plummeting Painter

by Carla Coupe

From *Part VI: 2017 Annual* (2017)

The early November morning dawned cold and blustery, and from the frosty earth a damp chill rose that settled in one's bones. Grey clouds gave the world the monochromatic cast typical for the season. We breakfasted late and moved to the fire as Mrs. Hudson cleared the table. She bustled out with the laden tray, closing the door firmly behind her.

After a quarter hour, Holmes flung *The Times* and stretched his long legs to the hearth. I looked up from my medical journal.

"Nothing of interest?" I asked.

His reply was a grunt.

I was not surprised, for he had been in a dark mood several days now. Bereft of a case to capture his interest and occupy his mind, Holmes was prone to these periods of depression. I was just grateful that he had not succumbed to the dubious charms of the needle that rested, seemingly innocuous, in its morocco case in his bedroom.

I returned to the journal, and Holmes continued to stare into the dancing flames.

Half an hour later, I finished a fascinating article regarding new surgical techniques and was lighting a cigarette when the sound of rapid footsteps alerted me to the advent of a visitor.

A quick knock on the door, and the boy in buttons entered and held out a note to Holmes.

"From Inspector Hopkins, Mr. Holmes," he said.

Holmes blinked twice and, as if galvanized by the flutter of paper, leapt to his feet and snatched the note from the boy's hand.

I sat upright and dismissed the boy with a nod as Holmes tore open the message and scanned the brief missive.

"Well? What does Hopkins want?"

Holmes turned to me, eyes alight, delight etched on his austere features. "He requests our assistance with a case." He shed his dressing gown, threw it over the back of a chair, snatched up his jacket, and with a bound headed toward the stair. "Come, Watson!"

Stumbling in my haste, I flew down the staircase and caught up to Holmes at the front door. He tossed me my coat and we quickly donned coats, gloves, and hats while the boy flagged a cab.

Once inside the vehicle, Holmes gave the direction and we settled back.

"Is it theft?" I asked.

He shook his head, his thin lips pressed together, as if he was suppressing a smile of excitement.

"Murder?"

"Death, certainly. As to whether it is murder . . . ." He tapped his forefinger to his chin thoughtfully. "At least the good inspector called me in from the first. Perhaps he has learned the benefit of prompt action. But we must pause now, and wait to speak with him before making any further assumptions."

So I curtailed my impatience and gazed at the passing buildings as we traveled to a narrow street near Notting Hill Gate, where we alighted at one of a long row of nearly identical brick homes, all suffering from benign neglect. A constable stood outside the door, nodded brusquely at our approach, and allowed us inside. In the dim foyer, polished but shabby woodwork and worn cocoa-nut matting greeted us. To the left, a small parlor maintained a brave pretense of gentility, while the room to the right sported a dining table and chairs, as well as a sideboard. Atop the sideboard stood a tantalus, with an empty space where one of its decanters would usually be placed.

Inspector Hopkins, looking rather more rumpled than usual, hurried toward us from the rear of the house.

"Thank you for coming, Mr. Holmes, Doctor."

"Have you moved the body?" enquired Holmes after shaking the inspector's hand.

"Not yet. I knew you would want to see it."

He escorted us down the narrow passage and through a baize door into a compact, surprisingly modern kitchen. In the distance I heard soft weeping: A housekeeper or maid, no doubt. A door led directly to the back garden, most of which was taken up by a large outbuilding. Mossy slate pavers covered the ground between the kitchen and outbuilding. A covered form lay about halfway between the two. Hopkins removed the covering to reveal the supine body of a heavy-set man of early middle years. The cause of death was obvious, for the pavers beneath his head were stained with blood and brains.

"This, gentlemen, was Edgar Tice, artist and homeowner," said Hopkins. "He was discovered around six this morning by Annie Cusak, his maid, who stepped into the yard to dispose of the ashes from the kitchen grate. Neither she nor the housekeeper-*cum*-cook heard anything out of the ordinary during the night, and the last time either set foot out here was around eight in the evening. The coroner puts the time of his death at sometime before midnight."

The inspector and I stood to one side as Holmes contemplated the scene. The outbuilding appeared to be reasonably maintained and well-used, and I wondered if it housed Tice's studio. After a few moments Holmes knelt and bent over, his face a bare inch from the man's jaw. He studied Tice's waxen face for a long minute before straightening, his gaze sweeping over the rest of the body. Pausing at Tice's upper chest, he examined the lapels of his dressing gown and the rumpled shirt beneath. Narrowing his eyes, Holmes stood and moved to the man's feet. He contemplated the toes of Tice's boots, then gently grasped his left ankle and lifted his leg enough to view his boot back. After lowering Tice's leg, Holmes repeated his actions on the right.

Stepping from the body, Holmes lifted his gaze to the upper stories of the house. "I take it that the question is whether he was pushed from that open window or jumped of his own volition."

A fleeting look of chagrin crossed the inspector's face before he huffed a laugh. "Well done, Mr. Holmes. That's exactly the case."

"I have seen all I need to see here; you may remove his body now," said Holmes as he strode toward the house. "Let us examine the room from which he descended."

We mounted the stairs and reached the first landing when a door was flung open and a muscular, fair-haired young man stood on the threshold. I wondered if his untucked shirt and unkempt hair was typical for him, or if it indicated his current emotional state.

He clutched the door jamb with whitened knuckles and narrowed his red-rimmed eyes. "You must be Sherlock Holmes and Dr. Watson. I told the inspector and now I tell you: Edgar did not kill himself!"

"So you've said, Mr. Elliott," Hopkins replied with more patience than I expected. "Once we have finished upstairs we will speak with you."

Elliott's jaw assumed a pugnacious angle. "I will await you." With a brisk nod, he stepped back and pointedly left the door open.

Holmes lifted one brow, but remained silent as Hopkins led us up two additional flights.

"This was Mr. Tice's studio," Hopkins said as we walked into the surprisingly cheerful chamber. A row of tall north-facing French windows were set into the back wall and, despite the dreary weather, brightly illuminated the space. One window stood open, the frame warped and split, several panes of glass cracked or missing. A chill wind invaded the room.

Obviously arranged as an artist's studio, the majority of the room was devoted to the tools of his trade, including a large easel with a canvas upon

273

it, stacks of finished paintings, and a small platform upon which sat a ladder-back chair and lengths of fustian and silk. An ash-filled fireplace was located in the far wall, with a settee, several armchairs, and a cloth-covered work table residing between it and a small aperture that faced the street. The breeze from the open window ruffled the tablecloth and sent a small blizzard of paper chasing around the legs of the settee.

Holmes began a quick inspection of the chamber, striding around the chairs and settee, his nimble fingers sliding along the stained upholstery. Several used tumblers stood upon the table. One armchair had been drawn apart, near the open window. At its feet a tumbler lay overturned beside a decanter that matched the ones in the tantalus from the dining room. The stopper rested to one side and a scarce quarter-inch of liquid was left.

Hopkins continued. "Mr. Tice was, as you can see, a painter. He shared his quarters with Mr. Thomas Elliott, a sculptor who occupies the first floor rooms. His studio is located in the outbuilding."

"Despite Mr. Elliott's protestation, do you think it suicide?" I asked.

"Perhaps." Hopkins shrugged. "He did not leave a note, however, and as you heard, at least one other person believes it to be otherwise. I hope Mr. Holmes can uncover evidence for one possibility or the other."

Holmes grunted as he squatted on the hearth, sifting through the ashes with the poker.

Hopkins opened his mouth to speak, thought the better of it, and rubbed his chin. His gaze never left the form of my friend as Holmes moved on to the open window. Minutely studying the low sill, less than a foot above the floor, he then leaned out so far I gasped and took an involuntary step toward him. After examining the exterior wall, he knelt and turned his attention to the battered plaster and wainscoting beneath the window.

"Well, Mr. Holmes?" Inspector Hopkins followed his movements with a wary eye.

Holmes glanced at him. "You know my methods, Inspector. I will not venture an explanation until I have all the facts."

With a sigh, Hopkins turned to me. "What do you think, Doctor?"

I gestured toward the decanter and glasses. "If he was the worse for drink, it would not be an unusual tragedy."

"So you believe it to be an accident, rather than murder or suicide?" asked Hopkins.

"It is certainly a strong possibility."

Hopkins frowned. "I would rather have a more definitive answer."

"Come, Inspector," I laughed. "I have learned caution. If Sherlock Holmes will not venture an answer, neither will I."

Holmes rose and dusted off his hands, then paused, his gaze traveling around the room. With two long strides he reached the stack of finished canvases propped against the wall and bent to look through them.

Curious, I joined him, and we contemplated a series of well-executed but pedestrian landscapes, still-life studies, and allegorical scenes featuring a lovely young woman. "Do you suppose he earned much from his work?" I asked Holmes as I contemplated several studies of an autumnal field. I had seen similar paintings in our local pub.

"Unlikely, unless one desires the commonplace." Holmes moved to another pile and continued his perusal. He paused at the third canvas, then stooped to examine it more closely. "It appears Mr. Edgar Tice decided to experiment with his subject matter. This was completed recently."

I looked at the painting – what appeared at first glance to be an uninspired portrait of the same attractive young lady who appeared in the mythical paintings – and leaned down, my gaze drawn to her soulful eyes. I frowned, disturbed by . . . *something* in the portrait. "This is . . . unusual."

With a nod, Holmes rose and crossed to where the easel stood. It was positioned so that the painting propped on it could not be seen from elsewhere in the room. I approached it reluctantly, joined by the inspector.

We both gasped when we saw what stood on the wooden crosspiece. A painting, true, but the painting itself had been defaced, large portions smeared or covered with thick black paint. What could still be seen showed, in broad brush strokes, the artist's intent: Another portrait of the same young woman. Yet a sense of disquietude, of profound unease, permeated the canvas, with corruption blossoming just beneath the surface, evident even in the ruined sketch. I shuddered, and could only imagine the effect the finished, unblemished portrait would have upon its viewers. Even Hopkins's phlegmatic practicality appeared shaken as he grimaced and shook his head. Holmes, however, examined it minutely, pausing at several points to peer at it so closely that his hawk-like nose almost touched the paint.

Eventually, to my relief, Holmes turned away. "I take it his personal chambers are on the floor below?"

"Yes, they are," said Hopkins. We descended to the second floor, where Holmes spent fewer than five minutes examining Tice's spartan sitting room, furnished with one upholstered chair and a small side table, and his surprisingly opulent bedroom. The bed was of carved mahogany and took up most of the room. I wondered how Tice had managed to manoeuver it into the small chamber. Rich brocade hangings harkened to the Orient, while a heavy fur lay across the counterpane and lent a barbaric air. There was not room for the three of us, so Hopkins and I stood by the door.

When Holmes finished, he merely remarked, "Now let us hear what Mr. Elliott wishes to say."

We trooped down the stairs and joined the young man in his chambers. A small sitting room faced the street front, and from it an open door led to a bedchamber. An unmade bed with an iron bedstead was just visible through the portal. The tiny room had a threadbare look and appeared furnished with castoffs. The furniture was of good quality, but forty years out of date, the fabric on the uncomfortable-looking settee and chairs faded and thin with age.

After greeting us with a nod and grunt, Elliott threw himself into a chair which creaked alarmingly. Holmes moved directly to the window and glanced outside before standing by the hearth, his keen eyes fixed on Elliott. That left the settee for Hopkins and me, and it was indeed as uncomfortable as it looked.

"Do you know whom Mr. Tice entertained last night?" asked Holmes.

Elliott looked startled. "How did you – Ah, the glasses we used. Of course, Annie has not been up to the studio to clean." He shrugged. "It was the usual collection of friends. I was there, along with Edgar's brother, Randolph. Georgie – Lady Georgiana Beaufort – and Daphne Beaufort. Daphne modeled for him occasionally. Also Charles Plunkett, another painter. We often gathered in Edgar's studio after dinner, especially when he wished to show us a new work."

Holmes studied Elliott for a long moment. "And did he show you a new work last night?"

Elliott sat up and leaned forward, his reddened eyes glittering fever-bright. "He wasn't yet finished and was reluctant to let us see it, but eventually we persuaded him. It's remarkable – I don't doubt it will cause a stir amongst the entire artistic community."

"I don't doubt it either," said the inspector dryly. I could only silently agree.

Elliott glared at him. "Of course, the ignorant are skeptical. Every artistic advance is met with resistance."

Before Hopkins could respond, Holmes spoke. "Was Miss Daphne Beaufort the model for this artistic departure?"

"Yes."

"Did the others share your excitement?"

With a frown, Elliott slumped back in the chair. "Randolph knows nothing of art and makes no bones about his ignorance. Georgie, however, pretends to knowledge she does not possess. I thought perhaps Charles would understand Edgar's vision, but he was as discouraging as the others."

"And what was Miss Daphne Beaufort's reaction?"

276

Elliott's frown deepened. "She burst into tears and begged Edgar to destroy the painting. Poor Edgar! Initially he attempted to laugh off the criticism, but by the time Daphne began to weep he was extremely upset – understandably so!" Elliott leapt to his feet. "The very friends who should have been his strongest supporters turn on him and make *him* – the genius amongst them all! – doubt his abilities and talent. By this time whisky had loosened *certain* tongues and made emotions more volatile."

"Whose tongue in particular?" Hopkins asked.

Elliott's jaw set and his lip curled. "Georgie, for one, laid into Edgar when she should have maintained a womanly reticence. She considers herself an authority on art merely because her insipid works are popular and have gained attention from the Academy! Edgar paid far too much attention to her opinion, and as a result, his own artistic vision was undermined."

"From what you say," Hopkins said mildly, "it is possible that Mr. Tice became despondent at the response to his work, and after everyone left he decided to end his life."

"Never!" cried Elliott. He paced rapidly around the small room. "He believed me when I said it was the best thing he had done, and that once he finished the portrait and received the accolades he deserved, the naysayers would change their minds – *especially* Georgie."

Holmes leaned against the mantelpiece and regarded Elliott with half-lidded eyes. "I only know Lady Georgiana through her artistic works, but she appears to be quite formidable."

Elliott snorted and muttered something about unnatural females.

"What of Miss Daphne Beaufort?" continued Holmes. "I take it she is related to Lady Georgiana."

"Yes, yes, she is." Elliott brushed back a lock of hair that had fallen over his high forehead. "She is Georgie's cousin. Her parents died when she was young, and she came to live with Georgie. She's a lovely little thing who fancies herself a poetess, but is more decorative than useful. She is best suited as a model and poses for several of us, including Georgie and Edgar."

"Does she model for you?"

"Yes. As well as for Charles and a few other painters."

"So Miss Daphne wept when she saw the painting last night."

"Yes, indeed. Of course, she did not understand what Edgar was doing and completely misconstrued his intent. She was upsetting everyone, so Charles offered to take her home. I'm afraid he has a *tendresse* for her, and unfortunately, it affected his art."

"Did Lady Georgiana accompany them?"

He scowled. "No, she was still flaying Edgar over the portrait. I spoke up for him, but she ignored my reasoned arguments. Finally I could bear it no longer and left."

"When did you repair to your bed?"

"I don't remember. I sat in front of the fire for a while and had another drink or two. Then I fell asleep in the chair and heard nothing until Annie screamed this morning when she found Edgar."

We were interrupted by a knock. A constable stood on the threshold and nodded at Hopkins.

"Beg pardon, Inspector, but you told me to find you when Mr. Randolph Tice arrived. He's in the parlor."

"Very good, Constable. We'll join him in a few minutes."

"You mentioned Randolph Tice earlier," said Holmes. "Was he still in the studio when you left?"

Elliott hesitated, his brow furrowing. "I don't remember him leaving, so he may have been. You will have to ask him."

Hopkins rose. "Thank you for your time, Mr. Elliott."

"It wouldn't surprise me," Elliott said as we moved toward the door, "if Georgie had something to do with this business."

Holmes stopped and regarded him intently. "Of what are you accusing her? Murder?"

"I'm not accusing anyone of anything. But when you meet her, do not be fooled by her attempts to charm you: That damned woman is involved in Edgar's death in some fashion."

Randolph Tice awaited us in the small parlor. A tall, composed young man, he greeted us with an old-fashioned gravity. He sat with his hands folded beneath his chin as Hopkins related what we knew thus far, nodding solemnly, yet did not appear unduly upset at the news of his brother's death.

"I was always afraid Edgar would not live a long life," he said with a sigh when Hopkins finished. "He lived every day so fully, and sacrificed much for his art."

Holmes asked him about the previous evening, and his version of events corresponded with Elliott's, at least until he spoke of Lady Georgiana.

"She has always been protective of Daphne, ever since Daphne was orphaned and came to live with her. Elliott?" His laugh at the inspector's question was as dry as dust. "Thomas has resented Georgie since she received accolades from the Academy – accolades he felt Edgar should have received. And yet even I, unschooled as I am, recognized that Edgar's abilities and talent were . . . ." He lifted one shoulder. "Lesser. To her credit, Georgie attempted to explain why Daphne reacted so strongly to the portrait, and what Edgar could do to make it less objectionable. Edgar did not want to listen at first, but he respected Georgie's abilities and artistic sense, and by the time we left, he agreed that her suggestions had merit, and decided to rework the portrait."

"So at that point he did not appear in danger of taking his own life?" asked Hopkins.

Tice flinched – a small crack in his stony façade – and shook his head. "No indeed. If anything, he appeared excited and anxious to return to work."

"What would you say," said Holmes, "to the news that the painting has been defaced?"

"What?" Tice blinked, bewildered. "Edgar would *never* do that. Someone else must have joined him after Georgie and I left."

"Perhaps we should speak with Lady Georgiana, Miss Beaufort, and Mr. Plunkett," said Holmes. "They may be able to provide additional information."

"Yes. Yes, of course. After I received your note, Inspector, I sent my boy around to Georgie's. She will be expecting news, no doubt."

The Beauforts resided in an elegant, if compact, townhouse of Portland stone, located near the best addresses in London. Clearly the family fortunes were still robust, if not massive. Lady Georgiana greeted us, a tall, slender woman unexpectedly wearing breeches, waistcoat, and cravat. Her unusual attire garnered a stare and raised brow from the inspector, but Holmes appeared to take it in his stride. She reminded me of a highly bred racehorse: All long limbs and exposed nerves. Her cousin, by contrast, possessed a delicate flaxen beauty that Tice had never managed to capture in his portraits of her. Even Holmes seemed caught by her loveliness, for he bowed low over her hand, and when he rose, his gaze lingered on her face.

Behind Miss Daphne hovered a young man, swart and lean, with dark eyes that regarded us suspiciously. He was introduced as Charles Plunkett, artist and admirer of Daphne Beaufort.

Once we were seated in a tasteful drawing room, Lady Georgiana turned to Holmes.

"I assume Edgar is dead and that we are persons of interest. How did he die?"

"What makes you think that, Lady Georgiana?" asked Hopkins, unsuccessfully striving to hide his surprise.

She gave him a look of weary contempt and repeated her question to Holmes.

279

With a nod of acknowledgement, Holmes related the bare facts. Miss Daphne raised a quivering hand to her bosom as Holmes spoke of Tice's demise. She reached out with her other hand and Plunkett, who sat beside her on a settee, regarded her tenderly and took her hand between his.

"This is utterly dreadful. I feel responsible for Edgar's death," she said when Holmes finished. Her distress appeared genuine. "I lost my composure and was horrible to him, but truly his painting was too frightful . . . ." She took a shaky breath. "I told him I would never model for him again."

"You cannot blame yourself, my dear!" Plunkett held her hand tighter. "Edgar's decision to end his life was his own."

"Don't be ridiculous, Charles." Lady Georgiana snorted. "I don't for a moment believe that Edgar took his own life," she continued as she lit a cigarette. "The question therefore is: Was it an accident, or did someone intentionally kill him? What is your opinion, Mr. Holmes?"

"As far as I'm concerned," said Plunkett before Holmes could respond, "Edgar's painting of Daphne was monstrous, and he deserved whatever fate befell him, whether it be suicide, accident, or murder. Thank God that disgusting filth will never be shown in public."

I glanced at Holmes and Hopkins. Were either going to reveal that the painting had been destroyed? Neither spoke. Apparently they were going to hold this fact close, at least for the moment.

Miss Daphne turned to Plunkett. "Do not be so unkind, Charles. You heard me tell him I would never model for him again; that was sufficient. Still, I am glad the painting was not finished."

"It should be destroyed," said Plunkett, his nostrils flaring in anger. "Cut to ribbons and burnt. I would have done so myself last night if Daphne had not needed me to escort her home."

"Oh, Charles," said Miss Daphne, a pretty blush upon her smooth cheeks. "I am certain Randolph will not permit it to be exhibited now that Edgar . . . ." Her voice broke on his name.

Hopkins looked at Plunkett with the air of a coursing hound catching a scent. "What did you do after you brought Miss Beaufort home?"

"I sat with her for a while until she calmed, and then I returned to my own chambers."

"Can anyone confirm this?"

"No," said Plunkett. "I live alone, with only a woman who comes in during the day."

Lady Georgiana threw her cigarette into the fire. "Do you suspect Charles of being somehow involved in Edgar's death, Inspector? Simply because he wanted to destroy Edgar's painting?"

"He is certainly a suspect," replied Hopkins. "Especially because someone *did* deface Mr. Tice's painting."

Miss Daphne gasped and Lady Georgiana regarded Hopkins thoughtfully, but if Hopkins hoped that the news would shock Plunkett into confessing his involvement, he sadly underestimated the young man's nerve.

Plunkett laughed. "My dear Inspector, if I believed I could destroy that abomination while avoiding an inebriated and bellicose Edgar Tice and his sycophant, I would have made the effort."

"Sycophant?" Holmes glanced at the others. "Is that a general opinion about Mr. Elliott?" He looked at Randolph Tice, who shrugged.

"Yes, it is. Edgar discovered Thomas last year – "

"You mean Thomas flattered his way into Edgar's good graces," said Lady Georgiana, emitting an unladylike snort.

Randolph Tice inclined his head. "Granted. To be fair, Edgar admired Thomas's work and brought him to the attention of several gallery owners. When Thomas mentioned that he was going to be thrown out of his digs, Edgar offered him chambers and a space for his studio."

"Deferring his rent until he became established," added Lady Georgiana. "Well, of course Thomas would defend Edgar. He had too much to lose otherwise."

"Thomas is such an appalling man," murmured Miss Daphne. "Always so presumptuous. I never liked modeling for him."

Plunkett patted her shoulder. "You did so out of kindness, at Edgar's insistence."

Hopkins turned to Randolph. "Who is your brother's heir?"

"I am," he said, startled by the abrupt change in subject. "As he was mine, since we are both unmarried and have no children. The house he lived in was a gift from our late parents. And before you ask," he continued as Hopkins opened his mouth to speak, "I can prove that my business is successful and I do not need the property."

"That's as may be," said Hopkins, glaring at Tice. Was he now changing his mind and casting suspicion upon Randolph Tice?

Tice shifted as if uncomfortable with the inspector's regard, but Lady Georgiana bristled, hands on hips, as she rounded on Hopkins.

"Honestly, Inspector, if you believe that Randolph would have anything to do with Edgar's death, then you're even more of an idiot than you appear."

Before Hopkins could reply, Holmes stood, hiding his smile behind his raised hand. "Let us all return to Edgar Tice's studio, and I will shed some light on the subject of his death."

"What?" said Hopkins, his surprise at Holmes's assertion evident. "Tell me!"

"All in good time, Inspector," said Holmes with a dry laugh.

He headed toward the door. The others stared at each other for a moment before rising and hurrying after him.

"Mr. Holmes? Inspector? What are you doing?" asked Thomas Elliott, peering from his chamber door as we traipsed up the stairs to the top floor.

"Mr. Holmes is going to reveal all," said Lady Georgiana. "Come along, Thomas. You may as well join the party."

Elliott hesitated, and Holmes chimed in. "Yes, Mr. Elliott. Your presence would be of immeasurable help."

Taking a reluctant step forward, Elliott glanced at Holmes, a dubious expression on his face. He let out a squawk of surprise as Hopkins took his arm and urged him forward.

We foregathered in the studio, where Holmes waved the women to the settee and the men to the chairs, while he stood before the defaced painting, his hands clasped behind his back as he regarded his audience. Energy suffused his lean form and imbued even the simplest gesture with purpose, a stark contrast to the languishing man I witnessed this morning.

"Let me reconstruct the events of last night," he began. "After showing his painting and receiving a negative reaction from his friends and colleagues, Edgar Tice remained alone in his studio. The fire had burned bright, the whisky flowed freely, and therefore the room was stuffy, so he opened a window. Then he pulled up a chair and sat contemplating his work while finishing off another glass."

Elliott snorted. "Come, now. You cannot know this, Mr. Holmes."

"Indeed I can," he replied. "The evidence is before us. One must learn to observe and interpret it, however."

At Elliott's dubious look I spoke. "Holmes speaks the truth, for I have witnessed it many times. If you do not believe me, just ask any of his many clients."

"Thank you, Watson," Holmes said with a smile. "As I was saying: Tice sat dozing in a whisky-soaked stupor when a member of the party who had been in the studio earlier returned. This person crept into the room, expecting it to be empty, only to discover a slumbering Tice still there. They walked to the portrait, careful not to wake Tice, picked up a brush and began their mission of destruction.

"At this point, Tice awoke and leapt to his feet, enraged by this wanton act. Our visitor, startled by his actions, turned. Tice stumbled forward and was shoved away. He tripped over the hem of his dressing gown, crashed against the partially open window, and tumbled to the pavement below."

"Horrible," murmured Lady Georgiana. The color had drained from her face, and when she lit a cigarette, her hands shook.

"Oh, Mr. Holmes!" Miss Daphne choked out a sob and bowed her head.

"That's enough!" cried Plunkett, his fists clenched. "You are upsetting Daphne and Georgie!"

"I insist on continuing, Mr. Plunkett," said Holmes, his collected calm rebuking Plunkett's ire. "I am certain that Lady Georgiana and Miss Beaufort have sufficient strength and courage to hear the truth."

"Yes, of course," said Lady Georgiana, putting her cigarette to her pale lips and inhaling deeply.

Miss Daphne raised her head and gave Plunkett a tremulous smile. "I am anxious to hear what Mr. Holmes has to say. Please continue."

After giving a theatrical bow, Holmes regarded the group of expectant faces.

"Who was this visitor? One of the most difficult aspects of this case was the surfeit of suspects, each with a sufficient motive." He gestured toward Lady Georgiana. "Was it Her Ladyship, who exerted so much artistic influence on Tice?"

"I knew it!" cried Elliott. "I knew she was responsible!"

"Quiet, Mr. Elliott," said Hopkins.

Muttering, Elliott subsided.

Holmes waited a moment, then continued. "Perhaps it was his brother Randolph, who also admires Lady Georgiana?" He turned to Elliott. "Or Thomas Elliott, whose unbridled admiration of his patron may have led to disillusionment and hatred? Or could it have been Charles Plunkett, defending his muse and object of interest?"

He paused, ignoring the general outcry and exclamations of defense. At that moment he reminded me of a coiled serpent, waiting to lash out.

"Or . . . ." The serpent reared and struck. ". . . was it Miss Daphne Beaufort? After all, in many ways she had the most to lose, for Tice's portrait would have purportedly revealed her soul to the world and ruined her reputation."

"Nonsense!" cried Plunkett, while Elliott assumed a pugilistic stance, muttering about thrashing Holmes. Elliott subsided when Hopkins clapped a heavy hand on his shoulder. Lady Georgiana cried, "Ridiculous!", and Randolph Tice remained silent, yet watchful.

"Mr. Holmes!" Miss Daphne rose, her delicate hand pressed to her breast, the picture of wounded womanhood. "This is the merest conjecture."

With a shake of his head, Holmes stepped forward. "I am afraid the evidence against you is marked and compelling. While you defaced the painting some of the wet paint transferred to your hands, and when you shoved Edgar Tice traces of color were left on his dressing gown and shirt. Although you attempted to wash away the paint on your hands, you could not completely remove it all – there is a smudge of carmine on your ring finger, and a trace of black on the side of your thumb."

"That is easily explained. I model for several painters," she said, her lovely blue eyes blazing in indignation. "It is not unusual for me to discover smudges of paint on my hands and garments."

Holmes raised a brow and continued. "In addition, you did not notice that a lock of your hair brushed against the canvas, not only leaving behind several tell-tale strands, but also picking up a little of the wet paint." His long fingers lifted a lock of her hair, and even from a distance I could see a trace of dark color on her blond tresses.

She hurriedly stepped away from Holmes, only to meet the solid wall of Inspector Hopkins. With a flutter of her lace-edged handkerchief, she dabbed at the corners of her eyes. "How can you be so ungallant, Mr. Holmes?"

"On the contrary, I *am* being gallant, Miss Beaufort. I do not believe you intended to kill Edgar Tice when you pushed him. He startled you, and you reacted in fright. Unfortunately, the window behind him was open, and when Tice tripped over the hem of his dressing gown, he fell. It was a series of unfortunate circumstances that led to his death."

"That's for a jury to decide," said the inspector, his large hand closing around her wrist. "Come with me, miss."

Miss Daphne let out a little cry and tugged ineffectually against his grasp.

Lady Georgiana hurried to her side. "That is not necessary, Inspector. I will accompany Daphne to ensure she is properly treated."

Hopkins bristled for a moment, then sighed and reluctantly released Miss Daphne's wrist. "Very well, Your Ladyship," he said. "I suppose there's nothing I can do to convince you otherwise? No, I didn't think so." With another heartfelt sigh, he ushered the two women from the room.

"Well!" Plunkett shook his head. "I can scarce believe it, Mr. Holmes. That Daphne would do such a thing . . ."

"It's inconceivable," said Elliott. "Why, she's such a meek little thing, a womanly woman."

Holmes smiled briefly. "Desperation can stiffen the resolve of even the most mild temperament, gentlemen. And remember, she has lived with Lady Georgiana for many years – no doubt Her Ladyship's example of courage and fortitude influenced Miss Beaufort."

284

Randolph Tice looked around the studio. "I suppose I must thank you for resolving the mystery of my brother's death, Mr. Holmes, but the knowledge brings no peace. Merely sadness at the loss of one life and the ruin of another." He quickly crossed the room and followed after Hopkins and the women.

"Such a tragic loss of Edgar's talent," muttered Elliott. "All because of a weak woman. Excuse me. I must ask Mr. Tice about his intentions regarding my tenancy." He hurried out the door.

Plunkett came over to Holmes, hand outstretched. "I will thank you if no one else will, Mr. Holmes. It is better to know the truth than remain blinded by falsehood, but I cannot find it in my heart to condemn Daphne for her actions. After all, she did not mean to kill Edgar. I pray the jury absolves her of a charge of murder, and when she's a free woman, I hope she will accept my offer of marriage."

Holmes shook Plunkett's hand. "I will do my best to convince them."

Once we were alone in the studio, Holmes returned to the defaced portrait and regarded it for several moments.

"It is unfortunate," he said, "that Edgar Tice's artistic abilities were so limited and his attempts to paint a masterpiece so ill-conceived. I'm afraid his jealousy and resentment of Lady Georgiana's abilities inadvertently led to his downfall."

"Miss Beaufort can hardly be blamed for reacting so when he approached," I said. "I hope, when all this is over, she and Plunkett are happy together."

"I shall do my best to ensure that is the case, as least as regards her trial." Holmes pulled out his pocket watch and glanced at it. "Ah well, Watson. Not every resolution is a happy one, even when we have solved the case. Now I believe we have time for an early supper at Romano's before attending Ysaÿe's concert."

The Adventure of the
Sunken Parsley
by Mark Alberstat
From *Part III: 1896-1929* (2015)

The summer heat of 1898 had somewhat abated as Mr. Sherlock Holmes and I enjoyed a rare morning of inactivity in early September. We had left the city on several occasions throughout the all-too-short British summer, but each of those trips had been in response to a summons for Holmes to help untangle the rat's nest of clues and scents of some mystery laid before us. This morning, however, was a leisurely one. We sat in front of a cold fireplace, tobacco at hand, and a variety of the daily papers scattered about our intimate sitting room.

The year so far had been a busy one. My notes, however, indicate that there was only one case which I could lay before the public, and that was the affair at Wisteria Lodge. The other undertakings of my friend Sherlock Holmes were to that point either inconclusive, repetitive tropes from previous exploits, or too delicate for those involved to even consider exploring in the public press.

"Is it your eyesight or your reflexes, Watson?" asked Holmes.

"My eyesight or my reflexes? What are you getting at, Holmes?" I replied

"Is it your eyesight or your reflexes that are not quite what they used to be to allow you to be hit so hard on the knee with a cricket ball that you are not playing today?"

"Once again, I feel you are partially a warlock. How on Earth did you know I was hit yesterday? You did not see me come in after the match, and I was seated here when you came down to breakfast. And, I would like to add, it is neither my eyesight nor my reflexes. I was distracted by someone in the crowd which led to my injury," I replied.

"Yes, someone in the crowd. I am sure that was it. As to how I know you were hit is simplicity itself. There in an account in this paper of the Players versus Gentlemen match in which you were participated yesterday at Lords. That was the second day of a three-day match. Although today's activities do not start for another two hours, you are clearly not preparing to be there. That raises the question as to why. You are sitting in the chair a bit more stiffly then is your usual relaxed mode, and your left leg is crossed over your right, an atypical pose for you. I have to conclude an injury to your leg is keeping you home today, and being hit in the leg by a pitched ball seems the most likely injury event to a non-sportsman like myself."

"As is often the case, Holmes, you are correct in your observations and conclusions. Although I hate to let my side down, I just can't make it to the pitch at Lord's today, despite it being a stone's throw from our door. If I were there, the pull to put on my whites and have a go would be too strong and, I feel, detrimental to the Gentlemen who were kind enough to invite me to play with them," I said.

"Your injury could not have come at a better time. I am in need of a sounding board, and you would do well with some country air and a ramble to reinvigorate your leg,"

"Sounds capital, Holmes. Where are we off to?"

"Hertford. County town for Hertfordshire. If you would be so kind as to reach for the timetable, we can plan our trip."

My military background did me proud, as within ninety minutes Holmes and I found ourselves settling into a first-class carriage that was pulling out of London's Liverpool Station. Holmes said it was to be a day trip, so nothing more was needed other than a Bradshaw.

The countryside often put Holmes in a philosophic mood, and today was no different. Although attached to the great metropolis by a thousand filaments, he longed for the clean air and solitude of the realms beyond. He often talked about buying a cottage somewhere, and as he gazed out the window, I was sure he was thinking about it again.

"How many pounds of honey per annum, Holmes?" I asked.

"Honey? Pounds per annum? My dear Watson, you are attempting to break into my thoughts as I have often done to you on occasion. Well done, well done indeed," replied Holmes.

"However, I will disappoint you and inform you that I was not thinking of my retirement cottage, but the mystery at hand."

"We have slightly over an hour in this carriage for me to give you an outline of the errand we are on. An hour to pass through the metropolis and into the pastoral setting of Hertfordshire's farms. Sadly, Watson, we are heading into dark matters, a far cry from Austen's *Pride and Prejudice*, set in this bucolic locale," said Holmes, gazing out the window.

"And what is it that whisks us out of the city and into rural England, Holmes?"

"A summons, Watson. A summons from Inspector Neal."

"I am not aware of that name."

"Possibly not. Neal is still young and putting in his time away from the city. He does have promise and shows enough intelligence to call me in when he is out of his depth. This is one such incident," said Holmes.

"Neal has a murder on his hands, Watson. A murder with no physical trauma, and the local doctor has said that his initial tests for poison have been inconclusive. This is why you are with me. You may see something medically that the local doctor has missed, and with your ever-growing knowledge of murders, thanks to my practice and our partnership, you may be considered an expert in your own right."

These were indeed high words of praise from Holmes. However, finding fault in another professional man's work and opinion is something I did not look forward to.

"The Thorntons have been a prominent family in the town since Elizabethan times, and their estate, Hartham House, at one time was the largest in the county. You may remember, Watson, that Queen Elizabeth spent time in Hertford when the Plague was on in London. It was the Thorntons who hosted her until Hertford Castle was ready for the Queen and her retinue. Today's family, of course, does not host royalty, but they still have cache and sway in the town, if not the county."

"And the murder, Holmes? Who has been murdered?"

"Always the man of action. Sir Evan Thornton is dead, Watson. He is the latest patriarch of the family and was found deceased in his bed this morning. He and his wife, Lady Elizabeth, have separate bedrooms, and it was Sir Evan's valet who found him. From the pained expression on his face, the state of his nightclothes, and the bed itself, it was instantly believed that Sir Evan did not die peacefully," said Holmes.

"And there are no suspects? No smoking gun?"

"No, there are no smoking guns, as you put it, Watson. After the body was found, the local doctor was immediately sent for. Neal tells me in a telegram that what this local practitioner found was so far out of the ordinary that he immediately thought of us. You for your medical background, and myself to see and find things which he cannot."

With that brief *précis*, we arrived at Hertford Station. We were immediately met by Inspector Neal when we alighted the train.

"So good of you to come on such short notice, Mr. Holmes," said Neal.

"Murder rarely finds a convenient time, Inspector."

"Quite so, quite so. Hartham House is just at the other end of town," said the inspector, issuing us into a carriage which was clearly marked as property of the local constabulary.

"As you instructed, Mr. Holmes, the body has not been moved. The rest of the house has also been left as it was when I arrived earlier this morning and began the investigation," said Neal.

"Tell us about the household. Who lives there, size of staff and the property itself," commanded Holmes.

"The primary concerns in the house are Mr. and Mrs. Thornton, of course, but also Mrs. Thornton's brother, who arrived a couple of months ago. He is here studying horticulture, and splits his time between the estate and a rental property in London. The household staff includes Sir Evan's valet, Michaels, who is the only staff who lives on the estate. He is much more than a valet and butler to Sir Evan. He assists in running the estate. There are a few other domestic staff who do not live in the house, as well as a full-time gardener. Lady Thornton is expecting us."

"What can you tell us about Sir Evan and his wife?" asked Holmes.

"Well, sir, they are generally well-liked in the town. They are the benefactors for various charities and events through the year, which brings them in contact with most of the town. They received their honorary titles just last year for the work they have done with the local poor. Lady Thornton has established three charities in the town, and her husband donated land and resources for people to grow their own produce. Despite their prominence, Sir Evan has never sought public office, and seems to spend most of his time managing the various businesses the family owns, puttering in his extensive gardens which are open to the public once a year, and attending various private functions through the summer months. Sir Evan was born in this house some forty years ago. His father was a bit of a queer duck, and had the boy schooled locally and not sent away as most of their class do," reported Neal.

"And Lady Elizabeth?"

"Almost the polar opposite, Mr. Holmes. Although also well-liked in town, she is not from here, and when I say 'here,' I mean to say England. Sir Evan took a two-year world-tour after his father died, and he arrived back on these shores a married man. Lady Elizabeth is actually an Elizabetta who grew up rich and privileged in Italy. She is a charming, warm woman who has captivated the local social scene and has turned more than a few heads. But here we are, and you can meet her momentarily for yourself."

We alighted from the carriage and were standing in front of a large three-storey block of a manor house. The door we were about to enter was set into the right front façade of the home. Its curved header was mimicked in all of the long windows on this, the ground floor of the home. I glanced about as we entered the portico and saw that the house stood on a large plot of land that was probably once a much larger estate.

We were greeted at the door by Michaels, the Thornton's valet and butler, who informed us we could wait in the library for Mrs. Thornton to come down and speak to us.

"Before we do that," said Holmes, "I would like to examine the body."

"Right this way, Mr. Holmes," replied Neal, leading us up the central stairs and into a well-appointed bedroom.

Sir Evan Thornton's body was on the bed, covered by a single sheet. Neal closed the door behind us and Holmes removed the temporary shroud.

Sir Evan's face was contorted in a paroxysm of agony. His knees were drawn up to his chest and his hands were clenched.

"Note the rigidity and the facial expression. This was not a natural death. What do you make of it, Watson?" asked Holmes.

I leaned over and looked into the corpse's eyes and mouth. The eyes were that of any dead man, and the mouth and odour from it were also no different. Many poisons leave traces or tell-tale signs in both locations, but in this case there was nothing. From a small mark on the arm it was clear that the local doctor had drawn blood to have it tested.

Holmes watched me as I made my examination of the body. As I rose and stepped away, he asked for my opinion.

"I would have to agree with the local doctor. At this point I would say poison or poisons unknown is the cause," I replied.

After this morbid examination, the three of us left the death room and walked downstairs and into the library.

The library was a typical one for a country estate. The room, which featured doors leading into the garden, was lined with book cases. A long table dominated one end of the room, while a large, heavy desk commanded respect at the other. As we waited, the ever-curious Holmes wandered the room, looking at the collection of rare and not-so-rare books.

"Mark my words, Neal. You can learn a lot about a man by the books he keeps, and even more by the books he reads," said Holmes, looking over the shelves near the desk.

Shortly afterwards, Michaels opened the door and Lady Thornton, dressed in full mourning, glided into the room, aided by a man who could only be her brother.

"Gentlemen, I am Lady Elizabetta Thornton, and this is my brother, Mario Conti," said our host as we introduced ourselves.

Lady Elizabetta was a raven-haired Italian beauty.

"I will do whatever I can to help you in your investigation. My husband's murderer must be found. Stop at nothing, the cost is immaterial," she said.

"Madam, I am here to find the truth, not a pay day," replied Holmes. "Can we begin with last night?"

"Certainly, Mr. Holmes," said Lady Elizabetta, sitting on the settee, while her brother stood resolutely behind her.

"My husband returned home late from the city. He often returns on the six p.m. train, but that night it was the 8:15. He was picked up at the station by Michaels. I saw my husband briefly and then retired for the evening. I know nothing more of his movements until the next morning when Michaels found him."

"Do you know who he saw while in the city?" asked Holmes.

"No sir, I do not. My husband kept the various business aspects of the estate very close to himself. He once told me the firm of lawyers he uses, or I should say used, but I have no idea what took him to London yesterday," answered Lady Elizabetta.

"Very succinct, Lady Thornton, thank you. Mr. Conti, did you see Sir Evan yesterday evening?"

"I did, indeed. In fact, I dined with him, which, no doubt, Michaels will confirm, since he served the meal. I was also in the city that day, doing some research at your British Museum. I arrived here about 7:45 and discovered that my brother-in-law had not yet returned but was expected soon, so I waited for him. We had some matters to discuss and I saw no reason to delay. I may as well tell you now, the conversation over dinner was a heated one, as I am sure the spying staff will report."

"And what was it that you were discussing?" asked Holmes.

"None of your concern, I can assure you."

"That is for me to decide. What matters did you discuss, heatedly, with the late Sir Evan?" repeated Holmes.

Conti glanced down at his seated sister; she looked up at him and nodded slightly, giving her permission to discuss what must have been a private subject its public airing.

"We were discussing a member of staff, and also my sister's return to Italy. The marriage has been less than she dreamt of, and she was looking for a split. We are staunch Catholics and revere the word from Rome. We know there will be no divorce, but a separation of thousands of miles will help the situation. Sir Evan would have nothing to do with the scheme and threatened to cut her off financially should she ever even attempt to leave England," said Conti.

"Surely your family fortune would be enough," said Holmes.

"The fortune is not what it once was, and our father, who is a strong nationalist, was very hurt when his only daughter left Italy to be with an English knight," replied Conti.

"You corroborate this, Lady Thornton?" asked Holmes.

"Yes, it is true, and it now looks bad for us, but it is true. I loved Evan when we met, and when we travelled together around Italy and the rest of the continent. He seemed to this young girl so worldly, so knowledgeable, I was swept off my feet. When we came to this house, he became a different person. He was so involved in the estate and the local community, he forgot about me and the life we had planned to share. He was more concerned with his house, the grounds, and the gardens, than he was with his new bride," said Lady Thornton.

"I told myself this would change. He would, as you say, come around. He didn't, and after five years of this marriage, I decided to leave him. By this time, my brother was here studying and I confided in him. We went to my husband as a united front, but were rebuffed and denied as if we were merely asking to redecorate a room," continued Lady Thornton.

Holmes looked over at Inspector Neal and said, "I would like to talk to the valet now."

"You have nothing more to ask us, Mr. Holmes?" asked Lady Thornton.

"Not at the moment. Your statements are clear and concise, and I do not want to keep you any longer than necessary. I am sure you have arrangements to make, and further questions can be asked later."

Lady Thornton and her brother left the room and Michaels was invited in. He soon confirmed the tone and content of the dinner conversation which Conti had disclosed.

"How long have you been with the family?" asked Holmes.

"Man and boy, Mr. Holmes. I started here in the stables when I was just a lad and my father was the game keeper. I went to school with Sir Evan, and also went with him as his valet when he was on his Grand Tour. The estate and Sir Evan has changed a lot over the years," reminisced Michaels. "The estate has gotten smaller, with outer parts being sold off or given away to the poor. Sir Evan expanded the garden and now wants to eat as much as he can from his own property. Did you know, Mr. Holmes, we grow four different types of carrots? And that's just a start of the variety of vegetables gown right here."

"Did Sir Evan actually do the gardening, or was that left up to staff?" asked Holmes.

"Oh no, sir. Sir Evan was in the garden most days during the season, and planning and reading about gardening through the winter. Those bookcases there," said Michaels, pointing to three glass-fronted cases near the large desk, "are full of books on the subject and his own journals and plan books. Mr. Conti was the same. Although they didn't agree on all topics, as you have heard, they certainly did when it came to matters of the soil and garden. I have been of assistance to both of them, although, of course, much more assistance to Sir Evan, having served him for so many years. I take some pride in being able to say there is not a bed, a tree or a plant on the grounds that I do not know, or have not had a hand in planting, pruning or shaping. "

"Thank you, Michaels. That will be all for now," said Holmes. It was just as Michaels was leaving the room that a local constable came in and handed Neal a sealed envelope.

"This will be the coroner's report, Mr. Holmes. I asked the office to send it to me, wherever I was."

"Excellent. It may prove to be interesting reading," said Holmes.

Neal sat at the desk, with Holmes and me standing over his shoulders. The report was one page and outlined Sir Evan's general health, age and other vitals. The final paragraph was the critical part for us. However, after each of us reading, the conclusions we were no further ahead.

"Well, Mr. Holmes. Death by poison unknown. Nothing much new here, I'm afraid," said Neal.

"On the contrary. It confirms our earlier suspicions, rules out other possibilities, and sets us on our track. Let us walk in the garden and think," replied Holmes.

Our forty-minute walk through the famed gardens was a quiet one. Holmes had brought along his briar-root pipe, a favourite of his for country walks. The two detectives walked together while I trailed behind them. The beds ranged from showy flowers, which I have not the faintest idea of what they are, to a large vegetable and herb patch, which featured items I was more familiar with. Several times Holmes stopped at a bed, examined a plant or two, and continued.

"Like the library, Neal, a man's hobbies can tell much about the person. In this case, I believe we can learn as much about his death as we can his life," said Holmes.

"Mr. Holmes, I know of your queer ways and obtuse remarks, but I am completely at sea if you think I can learn about who killed Sir Evan by a stroll around the garden," replied Neal.

"Like my friend Watson here, you see but you do not observe," said Holmes.

By this time, we had reached the front of the house again. Michaels was standing near the police brougham, and Conti was on the top step, examining a large ornamental planter.

"I am here at the behest of my sister, Mr. Holmes. Is there anything further you need from any of us?"

"Not at the moment, thank you," said Holmes as we approached the four-wheeler.

"I believe I have forgotten my walking stick in the garden," added Holmes. "I will just nip round and retrieve it, I will only be a moment," Holmes said as he hurried away.

Holmes returned a few minutes later without his stick.

"Age is a cruel master, Mr. Conti. I don't believe I had my stick with me at all today. Tricks of the mind," said Holmes, stepping into the brougham.

"Please let your sister know I will be in touch in a day or two. We will get to the bottom of this, be assured."

"What now, Mr. Holmes? I don't see that we are any further ahead in this murder investigation," asked Neal.

"On the contrary. We are near the end, I believe. It is back to the police station for you, and back to London for Watson and me. Can you meet us in at Baker Street in London for dinner tomorrow evening? I think by then, the fog shall lift and I will provide you with a solution to this very pretty little murder," said Holmes.

"Yes, of course. But what shall I do until then?" asked Neal.

"Whatever policemen in the country do. Except, I would advise you not to dine at Hartham House."

With that we drove back to the station and were in our Baker Street rooms before sunset.

"Before dinner, Watson, I would like to conduct a chemical experiment. You are welcome to assist me if you care to."

"Today's exertions and the meandering garden walk has not helped by injured knee at all. Also, your experiments often put up such foul smells I may not be down for dinner at all. However, for now I will retire to my room and rest," I replied, leaving our sitting room to Holmes's machinations.

When I awoke two hours later, I was pleasantly surprised with the clearness of the air. When I made my way down to our sitting room, Holmes sat amidst a scattering of papers, a satisfied look upon his face.

"Well, Holmes, you don't have to be a detective to see that you are pleased with something. However, from the air and lack of an acrid smell, I would suggest that you did not, after all, conduct any experiments."

"Quite the opposite," said Holmes. "I did, and they were a success. One cup of butter will never be the same, but this time the experiment was self-contained and proved my theory regarding the Thornton murder."

"Clearly he was murdered with poison, Holmes. However, how you could sit here and positively discover how or with what is beyond me," I replied.

"Not the biggest stretch for us, but a pretty little case in a pretty little corner of our country," said Holmes. "I do hope that Neal has fathomed his way through it better than you, Watson."

"So, you will not tell me who killed Sir Evan?"

"Not at the moment. You know my love for the dramatic. All will be revealed at dinner tomorrow when the good inspector joins us. Until then,

Mrs. Hudson has prepared a full cold dinner for us, which we shouldn't put off much longer."

The next day was a long one for me. Not only was I anxiously awaiting Inspector Neal to arrive so we could get on with the explanation of the murder, but my knee had swollen due to the previous day's outings, and I read in the paper that The Gentlemen had lost the match, an outcome my superior batting prowess may have been able to avoid.

Time did pass, as it always does, and we soon heard a knock on our door. Inspector Neal was led into our room by our landlady. As Mrs. Hudson was about to leave, Holmes said, "We will now take that dinner you and I had discussed, Mrs. Hudson."

She closed the door, and the three of us stood around the cold fireplace.

"Well, Mr. Holmes. Here we are. I am no further ahead in the murder investigation, but I certainly hope you are."

"Murder, and especially poisonings, are nothing to discuss on an empty stomach. Once our dinner is laid out, and we are sitting enjoying Mrs. Hudson's repast, all shall be revealed," said Holmes.

While we were waiting for our landlady to set the table for the three of us and bring out a cornucopia of cold dishes for our dinner, we discussed the latest news from Scotland Yard. The trials and tribulations of the growing force was of interest to me, while Holmes seemed, of course, most keen on the C.I.D., or Criminal Investigations Division. After mulling its existence and structure, we were ready to sit down.

"Now, Inspector. Our landlady is not renowned for her cooking, but she is certainly more than adequate. Before we partake in the cold joint, I would like to bring your attention to the long serving dish with two squares of butter on it. Squares identical to these aided me in unravelling our Hertfordshire mystery."

"Really, Mr. Holmes? You have me at a complete loss," replied the inspector.

"Perhaps so. Allow me to recreate a small experiment I conducted here yesterday evening."

With that, Holmes gestured toward the long, glass-covered dish containing the two squares of butter. He then revealed two smaller glass dishes. Each of these, seemingly, had parsley in them, and I commented as much.

"You are correct, Watson. They do seem alike, and they do seem like parsley. Both of these samples I liberated from the garden at Hartham House yesterday when I returned for my mislaid walking stick."

"The sample on the right is the type of parsley found all too often on the side of plates in restaurants throughout the city and the country. The parsley on the left is something very different indeed," said Holmes.

Holmes then took a pair of pincers from his laboratory table and put a few springs of each in its corresponding square of butter.

"Now, gentlemen, I request from you nothing more than some patience," said Holmes.

With five minutes, the results of the experiment were clear. The parsley on the right pad of butter was just as Holmes had placed it. The one on the left, however, had sunk three-quarters of the way through the butter and would soon be resting on the bottom of the dish. The butter around that piece of parsley was melted and oozing into a puddle.

"Gentlemen, let me introduce to you the very rare, *petroselinum virdi mortem*, or Green-Leafed Death, as it is known in parts of northern Italy. It is particularly insidious, in that it initially tastes and acts like any other type of parsley. Once it mixes with food and other acids in the victim's stomach, however, death surely follows."

"But what is it, Holmes?" I asked.

"It is a distant relative of the common parsley plant, but one that has a long and checkered past. This is what Sir Evan died from, and this is why the coroner could not find it in any toxicology books. The plant is virtually unknown outside of a small area around Lake Como, and even there it is rare and hardly ever grown in a garden. As soon as the leaves are picked, the plant excretes a very toxic, acid-like sap. The few sprigs I brought back with me almost ate through the envelope in which I placed them," said Holmes.

"But how did you find this, Mr. Holmes?" stammered Neal.

"I found it because I was looking for it. When the coroner's report spoke of unknown poisons, and we were at an estate known for its gardens, my mind immediately linked the two. At that point, of course, I only had a suspicion, but that would soon be proven to be true."

"As we walked around the garden," continued Holmes, "I noticed that many of the beds thrived with a type of planting called 'companion gardening'. There were actually a few books on the subject in the library; the library I told you to pay attention to, Neal."

"During the walk, I noticed that a rose bed was fringed with parsley plants. The dark green of the parsley set off the delicate roses nicely, and the companion planting helps both thrive. In the vegetable beds, I found more parsley. However, there was one bed that had a slightly neglected look about it, despite it showing some signs of care. On closer inspection, I noticed that one parsley plant had a dead patch all around it. This is the plant I returned to and took a snippet of for my experiment."

"But who gave Sir Evan the poisonous parsley?" asked Neal.

"That we shall soon discover. If I am not mistaken, that is Mr. Conti I hear in our entrance way, coming to join us for dinner. Quickly now, Watson. Cover up the two butters and follow my lead."

Just then, Mr. Conti entered our sitting room. The three of us rose to greet our new guest.

"I came as requested, Mr. Holmes, although I do regret leaving my sister at such a time."

"And I thank you for your indulgence, sir. We were just about to sit down for dinner, if you would care to join us. Michaels was kind enough to send us a fresh-produce package," said Holmes, striding back to the table.

"Here we have some fresh carrots and beets from the estate's garden, which will go lovely with this parsley butter," said Holmes lifting the covers off the two squares of butter.

"Won't you join us?" asked Holmes, taking a bread roll from a heap of them on the table and slathering some of the tainted butter on it.

Conti stared at the two butters and stammered, "These items came from the Chequers Estate?"

"Indeed. In addition to the telegram I sent to you to come here this evening, I sent one to Michaels to let him know how we were progressing, and he was kind enough to send this fine selection back."

Conti rushed over to Holmes, snatched the dinner roll out of his hand and placed the covers back on the exposed dishes.

"You mustn't eat any of this," he declared.

"Come, come, I am sure it is all fine, is it not?" replied Holmes.

"No, Mr. Holmes, I assure you it is not!" replied Conti. "This is poison and was meant for you," he said, pointing to the parsley that had melted through the butter.

"Time to tell your tale, Mr. Conti. Be warned, however, Neal here will take down a complete recording of that tale, and his notes may be used in court."

"That is quite alright. It began about eighteen months ago when I received a letter from my sister. It was clear she was no longer happy with her husband, her situation, and her future. He never raised a hand to her, Mr. Holmes, but he abused and belittled her in a hundred different ways. She wanted out and away from him."

"I had been planning on a visit before, but that letter sealed my plans. I was in Hertfordshire within two weeks. I used my interest in horticulture and the chance to study at the British Museum and Sir Evan's own library as a guise for the trip and extended stay. "

"My sister and I decided we would make a united front and approach her husband about a separation. We did, one Saturday morning a month ago. He did not take it lightly. He flew into a rage and railed at us. For a man who is often reserved, he yelled and went on, loud enough and long enough for there to be no doubt among any of the staff as to what we were discussing. It was clear that my wife's husband was not going to let her leave. He said they could lead independent lives under the same roof, but that was as far as he would allow."

"We left Sir Evan in the library. As we did, Michaels went in. He seemed to always be lurking somewhere obvious in the house."

"After that initial discussion, if you can call it one, Sir Evan wouldn't speak to me except on the subject of horticulture. On that point we talked often and freely. If I were to bring the subject of my sister into the conversation, he would either put an end to the conversation, or rage at me for bringing up a closed subject."

"While I was in the garden one day, I noticed this plant," continued Conti. "Where I come from it is a known poison, but it is far from common. Anyone with an interest in plants, however, will have come across it and know its evil legacy. I knew that neither I nor Sir Evan planted it. Sir Evan had been far too busy with other aspects of the estate, and I would never grow something so deadly in an open garden. It is not an easy plant to remove, Mr. Holmes, or I would have pulled it from the ground then and there. The leaves, as you know, are very dangerous and must be handled correctly. I made a mental note to return with proper gloves and a spade to remove it from the garden and burn it."

"Later that day," continued Conti "I returned to the bed, but before I got there, I saw Michaels tending it. It was he who had planted the Green Death; I knew then that I was dealing with a very serious-minded man and refrained from approaching him. A man who grows poisons in the open is not to be lightly dealt with. I approached Sir Evan about the matter that evening, and he was dead by morning. Mr. Holmes, Michaels murdered his employer and has tried to do the same to you!"

"Calm yourself, Mr. Conti. I know. In addition to the telegram that I sent to yourself to join us, I took the liberty of sending another to Inspector Neal's office with instructions to arrest Michaels. By now, he should be making himself at home in a holding cell in the Hertford police station."

With that, Holmes removed the tainted parsley from the table and invited our guests to dine with us.

"But how did you know it was Michaels?" asked Neal.

"My first suspicions naturally fell on yourself, Mr. Conti. However, when I saw the dead patch around the suspected poison, I realized it couldn't be you. You would be aware of what plants can co-exist with the Green Death and would have been able to hide it better."

"I also surmised that when you and Sir Evan were discussing a member of such a small staff, it may have been Michaels. I also noticed that Michaels kept very close at hand when we were questioning Lady Elizabeth. It seemed more than usual staff curiosity. When Michaels entered and Lady Elizabeth left, the look in his eyes was unmistakable. He is in love with your sister, Mr. Conti. He was angered that Sir Evan would not allow her her freedom. I believe he had seeds for this plant from when he visited Italy with Sir Evan years ago. Why he kept it all this time is difficult to say. A look at the history of this plant does show that more than one staff member has murdered their employer with it. Maybe he found the history of it before and kept it in the back of his mind. It is not always an easy thing to plumb the depths of the mind of a murderer."

"Another murderer brought to heel," I said to Holmes later that evening, after our guests had departed. "Not often you bring down a villain by watching parsley sink in butter."

"Very true, Watson. This may be a fine study for your chronicles. The parsley not only brought down a murderer, but I was also able to garnish a fine fee from Lady Elizabeth," added Holmes with a chuckle.

When Spaghetti was Served
at the Diogenes Club
by John Farrell
From *Part XXXV: "However Improbable . . . ." (1897-1919)* (2022)

It was the first, and only, time that spaghetti was served in the dining room of the Diogenes Club. Spaghetti was not something that suited the peculiar sensibilities of the Diogenes Club's rather unusual membership.

Most of all, there was the noise involved in eating the Italian specialty. Silence was the principal driving force of the Diogenes, and that silence was cherished in the club's dining room as nowhere else. Waiters were given dinner orders in writing. Each diner had every sort of condiment, salt cellar, and pepper mill available individually so no one need ever ask for anything from a fellow member. Even the click of knife and fork on China and the gurgle of wine poured into crystal were carefully minimized lest a member come to the attention of the Committee to be admonished for creating a scene.

There were a few members, the more adventurous, who enjoyed their brief encounter with Italian cooking, but many of the others made it clear that such an honor would not again be welcome. Roast beef, they felt, was good enough for honest English gentleman, and the peasant foods of southern climes were not a suitable replacement. And so, even when served to a group of generally elderly and conservative gentlemen as a special honor, spaghetti was not a success.

That spaghetti appeared even once at the Diogenes was the inadvertent fault of Mr. Mycroft Holmes. It was not his intent to either challenge or educate the pallets of his fellow members. Indeed, if the truth be told, he would have rather avoided the whole matter.

Still, when the King of Italy insisted on offering his hospitality and the services of his personal chef to the club for an evening's gustatorial pleasure, it was difficult for the club to reject the proposal without offending His Majesty. It must be said that the wines provided from the Royal cellars, the liqueurs, the delicious soup, shrimp caught in the Mediterranean and brought on ice to London, and beefsteak in the Florentine style all proved extraordinary. The spaghetti, however, was a failure. The relevant facts follow.

Mr. Mycroft Holmes much preferred to conduct official business, Her Majesty's business, in the comfortable office that his Queen had provided for those matters on a quiet floor of the Foreign Office. His life was such that he preferred to keep his affairs, each in its proper place. The office was for matters of government, the Diogenes Club his personal refuge. But when the Foreign Secretary asked that he meet with the secretary to the Italian Ambassador, Count Cipriano Livorno, in a non-official manner and at a place where privacy was certain and press comment could be avoided, he realized that the request was one of great political importance, and he agreed to meet the ambassador in the Stranger's Room at his club, the only place where conversation was allowed, if only barely tolerated within its confines.

The Foreign Secretary was also a member of the Diogenes, a membership he owed to Mr. Mycroft Holmes's good offices. He knew there were several members of the Diogenes who were wont to consider current British foreign policy to be rather too liberal, especially that cautious friendship with France, which these members remembered only as the home of that upstart, Napoleon the First. With such a reactionary membership, it was felt the Count should appear *incognito*. He arrived on a Tuesday in November, a wet and gray day on which pedestrians hurried on their way, shivering under their ineffectual umbrellas.

From his comfortable seat in the Stranger's Room, Mycroft Holmes had been watching the passing scene. Presently, an elegantly dressed gentleman came into view, wearing a shiny black silk top hat and Van Dyke beard. He stepped from a hansom under the club's *porte cochere*. Mycroft Holmes, without moving from his chair, signaled to his favorite waiter to bring two double Scotches to his table.

The gentleman who entered the room was a study in understated elegance. His frock coat was of conventional cut, but of a cloth of great beauty. His boots, tiny and pointed, were as sharp as his beard and matched his slicked-back hair in their glossy blackness.

The Count, operating under the *nom-de-guerre* of Signore Cipriano, was hardly five feet tall and moved with a quick, bird-like gait that showed a crisp intelligence and a careful awareness of his surroundings. In the sometime-violent world of Italian royal politics, that awareness had more than once avoided a serious and violent moment of crisis.

Count Livorno knew Mycroft Holmes at sight. His corpulent figure, dark, intelligent eyes, and broad, bland face hid an encyclopedic knowledge of British foreign affairs and, in his ten years as secretary to the Italian Ambassador in London, the diplomat had come to trust Mycroft Holmes's judgment in political matters. He had also heard of Sherlock Holmes – as who hadn't in London? – but never before had he had the ill-fortune to be confronted with a matter that required that gentleman's knowledge of crime.

Signore Cipriano, the Count's alter ego, had been created by an over-eager member of the Italian Embassy staff, and the Count had been warned to maintain the secret of his identity with vigor, so as he stepped across the Stranger's Room, he rather more loudly than was quite necessary called out to Mycroft Holmes.

"Ah, Mr. Holmes. I am Signore Cipriano. It is so good of you to see me. The directors of the company that employs me need advice on British export law and you were recommended to us as an expert. It is kind of you to see me here in your club."

Truth be told, Mycroft Holmes was nonplussed by Count Livorno's effusive greeting, but his diplomatic training was more than enough for the crisis. Ignoring the raised eyebrows of several members, he used a flipper-like hand to guide his guest to a comfortable armchair and as the Count sat down, he leaned over him and whispered into his ear, "No need to overplay your character, my dear Count Livorno. Here in the Diogenes, no one will notice you at all. It is a part of the inherent courtesy of the club that we make a point of never noticing each other, except when unavoidably necessary."

"Ah, you will excuse me, I am sure," the Count said in a much quieter voice, and in a much less exaggerated manner, "but our recent tragedy and, perhaps, undue caution on the part of my Embassy colleagues, has made me more than a bit sensitive."

"Your feelings are understandable, of course," Mycroft Holmes replied. "I understand that you are here to consult me about the death of a young man in your office?"

From Mycroft Holmes's manner, if not his words, it was clear that he knew much more about the matter than he admitted.

"Do, first, have a sip of that Scotch. I have it on authority from a medical friend of my brother's that whisky is a nerve tonic, and this is one of the best twelve-year-old single malts anywhere, available only to the Royal Family and, by the Prince of Wales' graciousness, to our cellar."

The Count raised his glass, toasted in gesture to his host, and sipped some of the golden liquid, holding it briefly on his tongue before swallowing. He uttered a little sigh before speaking.

"In Italy we have some of the finest wines, and some of the most ancient of vineyards but, if I may say so, there is nothing we produce, not even our finest brandies or our herbal liqueurs, which are as complex and rewarding as the whiskys of the British Isles. I trust you will hold that opinion as a diplomatic secret."

"Your secret I will keep. I am afraid the reputation of the whisky is already broadcast. Come, though, and tell me of your problem. It must be

302

a serious one indeed to require the precautions you have undertaken to protect it."

"It is no less than murder that I come to ask you about," the Count said in an emotional whisper. "At the least, I believe it is murder, though I cannot explain how the murder was committed, cannot find a motive for it, and my colleagues, while they are as shocked as I am at the event, do not believe it to be anything more than an accidental death."

"Pray give me all the details, Count Livorno, even the most trivial, and I will do my best to give you an answer." Sitting back in his armchair, his large fist closed around the crystal tumbler, Mycroft Holmes looked at the ceiling and prepared to listen.

"You must first understand how our Embassy functions to realize the terrible impact this event has had on all of us there," Count Livorno said in a voice strained with anguish. "Italy has been in a political furor for years, with attacks on government officials only one of many problems afflicting our nation, which is both one of the oldest in Europe, dating from our Roman history, and one of the newest, reunited within living memory. While our government has, from time to time, recalled the current Italian ambassador and replaced him with someone more representative of the then-current faction, our staff here in London has remained largely unchanged, like a family. It is felt this is safer, since we can be certain of the long-term loyalties of those who have served for many years.

"Still," said the Italian nobleman, pausing for a healthy sip of the whisky, "we do require new staff members from time to time, and they are chosen carefully, based not only on educational success, but family ties and reputation as well. I know this seems old-fashioned, but in Italy, family is an important consideration, and even those appointed to junior positions are certain to belong to at least the cadet branches of important families that have a long history of loyalty to the royal family.

"Such a one was Giovanni Martinelli, who came to us just three months ago. Although he was young – twenty-seven years old, I believe – his good looks and bright smile made him seem several years younger, which certainly did him no harm with the older women who act as typewriters and translators on our staff. Martinelli came of a fine family. His mother's father lost his life in the revolution that put King Victore Emmanuelle on the throne, and his father had fought with the rebels as well.

"Further, his academic accomplishments were remarkable. He had studied Latin and Greek in his church-school, and at University showed an even greater facility for languages. He spoke perfect French, and six different Italian dialects. This is an important factor in success in our young and still loosely unified nation. This is not to mention how, in one

303

year at Oxford, he acquired a command of accent-less English. It was considered a notable achievement.

"He was certainly marked to go far in our service. His good looks and considerable personal charm – never a disadvantage in the diplomatic world – together with his linguistic skills, would certainly have been matched by knowledge gained by experience, and soon enough would have raised him to an important rank. In three months, he'd already attracted the favorable notice of the Ambassador, who sent a letter to Martinelli's father praising his son. He was slated for a career of great service to his country. Yet now he is dead, and no one can offer a reasonable explanation for that death."

"Allow me," Mycroft Holmes said, "to interrupt your very admirable narrative. No doubt you would benefit from another whisky, which I will order for you." He did so with a nod and Mr. Holmes made a hand-signal to the waiter across the room. "Pray continue."

"Thank you, sir," replied the Count. "It is true that this matter has been one of great emotional distress for all of us, and especially for me, because I must admit I found in young Martinelli many of the attributes I might have looked for in a son, if I had one. His mysterious death shocked me as much as anyone in the Embassy. The fact that it remains unexplained is even more deeply troubling."

"Tell me the details of his death, then, and let us see what we can conclude. There are few human mysteries that will not yield to human ratiocination, and those others must be left to the Church authorities for their consideration."

The Count crossed himself. "Indeed, Mr. Holmes, you are right, and I hope this is not one of those. We shall see. It was only last week that this happened. Today is Tuesday, and it was just a week ago, in the afternoon, that we noticed that Giovanni Martinelli was not himself."

"How so?"

"The young man in question was usually a picture of perfect physical health," Count Cipriano said. "He enjoyed rowing in the park, horseback riding, and football. He had even played your English Rugby and found it entertaining. Martinelli had a healthy appetite and especially enjoyed the bitter Italian liqueur called Campari, which he drank with relish every afternoon at our office during what we like to call our 'teatime', though we Italians have doubts about the health-giving properties of that beverage and usually prefer wine or an aperitif in the afternoon.

"Last Tuesday at luncheon, the young man ate nothing, saying that he had no appetite whatsoever and plead that his stomach was slightly upset. Nor did he drink anything more than a little water that afternoon. He complained of a headache and slight dizziness as well. I suggested he visit a physician, but he said again it was just a mild stomach upset and I thought no more of it.

"The very next day, Wednesday last, he came to the office at his usual early time, though we all could clearly see that he did not feel well. We urged him to go home or seek medical assistance, but the young often feel they are immortal, and in truth dyspepsia is not a fatal illness. Again he ate little at lunch, and seemed ill at ease throughout what would have been an otherwise convivial meal.

"He returned to his office and there complained to a colleague about a severe headache and worse – dizziness. Shortly thereafter he experienced convulsions and collapsed, barely breathing. We called in the local physician who handles Embassy cases, but there was apparently nothing he could do. He applied various stimulants, including volatile salts, but Martinelli never regained consciousness, and his heart beat and breathing weakened and then stopped entirely."

"There would be no autopsy or coroner's inquest required, I quite understand, since the death occurred in what is technically Italian soil," Mycroft Holmes said. "Nonetheless, the physician must have had some idea what caused the death?'

"He had no idea whatsoever, save for the conventional. He said there were no indications of poisoning by any of the well-known means, and the symptoms – dizziness and a weakness of the heart – might well be the explanation. But I knew this was a vigorous young man in the peak of condition, and I do not believe that he had a weak heart.

"The Ambassador would prefer to ignore the matter, and has refused to do more than send a telegram of regret to Martinelli's family and to the young noblewoman to whom he was betrothed. I am before you without official brief, but I feel this young man deserved better of his country, and I was able to ask a favor of one of your ministers, who was glad to accommodate me. Thus, I am here to consult you privately."

"You will pardon my frankness, then, Count, when I say that you have left at least one important fact out of your otherwise detailed account of the affair."

"And that is?" the Count said with a little asperity.

"While I feel that your concern for this afflicted young man is genuine, I must wonder whether there is a more political reason for your concern. Bluntly, did Giovanni Martinelli have access to any important Embassy secrets?"

"Mr. Holmes!" said the Count, rising.

"My dear Count," said Mycroft Holmes in a voice of soothing condolence, "I do not wish to know your government's secrets, if indeed there are any we do not already know. I am acting here purely in a capacity of criminal investigator, and I must inquire as to whether there is a motive for Martinelli's death. Did he know anything that that might have compromised him or your legation? Is there a motive that might indicate that his death was anything but a natural one?"

"Martinelli, despite his family contacts and his linguistic abilities, was still merely a junior clerk in our office, Mr. Holmes," the Count said. "He could not have known anything more about our government's affairs than the day-to-day calendar of activities. He would not have been privy to diplomatic communiques, had no access to diplomatic cyphers, and did not involve himself in any more serious activities in the office. It would have been some months before he was trusted with those *mattes* in any way."

"That is all perfectly clear, then," said Mycroft Holmes. "Allow me, then, one more question, and I think that I shall be able to advise you of what you will find it necessary to do."

"And that question is?" said the Count, sitting forward in his seat in eagerness.

"You looked at Giovanni Martinelli after his death?"

"Yes, I did. It was a sad sight, Mr. Holmes."

"Then no doubt you noticed that his skin, the whites of his eyes, and especially his gums were bright yellow?"

The Count sat back in his chair in amazement. "How could you have possibly known that?" he asked in incredulity. It is almost as though you were there!"

"It does not matter how I know it, but only that I do. You wish my advice?"

"Most certainly."

"It is very urgent. You must return to your Embassy at once and cancel or delay your king's upcoming visit to Queen Victoria."

"That cannot be done. As you yourself know, we have spent more than a year arranging for King Umberto's arrival. He will not admit to anyone stopping his visit at this late date."

"Nonetheless, it must be done," said Mycroft Holmes. "If your ambassador cannot manage affairs, then I personally will make sure the visit is canceled. It is that urgent. Surely King Umberto might find himself indisposed for a few days. Perhaps an unannounced visit to a European spa might be arranged. I can tell you that this matter of urgency can be taken under advisement and solved in a few days. But you must delay His Majesty's arrival."

"Mr. Holmes, I came to you for your advice and I must be willing to take it," the Count said. "I will go at once and do my best to delay His

306

Majesty, with the assurance that if I cannot, you will be able to arrange that feat."

"Like me, Count, you have a lifetime of service to your country, and you know, as I do, that in the final accounting, it is not the kings and queens, who are detached from day-to-day matters, nor the ministers serving short terms, who have the power to affect daily decisions. I am sure that you can persuade your king that a brief rest for his health is in his best interest, and while he rests, I am sure I can explain the death of your young clerk."

The Count left in haste to carry out his mission, and Mycroft Holmes signaled to the club's commissionaire for a telegram form. On it he wrote:

> *Sherlock Holmes*
> *221b Baker Street*
> *London, W1*
>
> *Brother: Clerk in Italian Embassy died last Wednesday, two weeks before arrival of Italian King on State visit. Stop. Clerk had bright yellow skin, eyes, and gums. Stop. You will know what to do. Stop.*
>
> *Mycroft*

It was just one week later, on a day of glorious sunshine and warm breezes, that the ill-disguised Signore Cipriano visited Mycroft Holmes for a second time in the Stranger's Room of The Diogenes. This time the elegant little man knew not to introduce himself so publicly, and he settled into the armchair that Mycroft Holmes indicated, accepted his whisky, and waited for his host to begin the conversation.

"First, if I may, allow me to offer a toast to the health of King Umberto," Mycroft said with a rare smile. "I understand he was feeling under the weather last week and had to postpone his visit here."

"You most of all know his health was affected," Count Cipriano said.

"And because I know that, I can safely say that I am sure he will recover his full health immediately."

"That I will gladly toast," said the Count with more enthusiasm than he had shown hitherto. "Does this mean that you know what happened to Giovanni Martinelli?"

"Oh, I knew that from the end of our last interview," Mycroft Holmes said off-handedly. "It merely took this long to find and catch those responsible."

307

"But that is fantastic, almost unbelievable, Signore Holmes," the Count said. "You know only what I know of the incident, yet you were able to discern something I did not."

"While it was true that I knew no more of the incident than you – indeed a good deal less – I possess a more specialized knowledge and was able to act immediately on it."

"Please do not keep me in suspense, sir. I must know what you have discovered."

"Well, it has been said of the Holmes family that we have a penchant for the dramatic, which I believe is more evident in my brother than myself. Nonetheless, I think the story will be better told in an orderly fashion than in pieces. Here, to begin, is the counterfoil of the wire I sent to my brother as you left last Wednesday. I think you will find it of some interest."

Count Cipriano grabbed the piece of paper eagerly from Mycroft Holmes's hand but, after reading it through twice, seemed no more illuminated than before.

"What does it mean, Mr. Holmes?" he asked with a little exasperation in his voice. "I can see nothing in it that explains anything."

"Before we go into details, perhaps you should read this telegram I received a few hours ago, immediately after which I sent for you." He handed the Count a telegram he first removed from his billfold:

Brother:

You will no doubt be interested to read that Friend Lestrade has added to his laurels by capturing anarchist bomb ring in Eastside house this morning. Stop.

Sherlock

"There are more details here in this afternoon's earliest edition of *The Daily Mail*, which you may not have seen."

Count Cipriano Livorno took the newspaper from Mycroft Holmes. It had been folded so that one small story was at the center:

Scotland Yard has just announced that an anarchist bomb-building ring has been captured in an otherwise unremarkable house in suburban London. The arrests were supervised by the well-known Scotland Yard Detective Inspector G. Lestrade, the man who on many occasions has been able to use his vast experience to solve cases beyond the ken of the city's various private detectives, including Mr. Sherlock Holmes.

Mr. Lestrade bravely led a group of twenty constables in surrounding the house in question, where they arrested six men. Of apparently Sicilian origin, they were using the house to manufacture explosives and bombs to be used in undoubtedly dastardly plans. More will be known after further investigation but, in the meanwhile, the people of London can breathe easier knowing that Scotland Yard's Inspector Lestrade is still at work.

"I must admit that I am as confused as ever," the Count shook his head. "I notice that this 'G. Lestrade' must be the man to whom your brother refers. Did you anticipate his plans, or know of them when I consulted you? You should have told me then and I might have been able to forestall His Majesty's feigned illness."

"Calm yourself, my dear Count. Until today, I knew nothing of Lestrade's activities – nor my brother's, for that matter. I am not a man of action, as you may have perceived. I prefer to sit and contemplate while others do the more strenuous work. I did not know that Lestrade would conduct this morning's raid, nor that it would lead to the capture of six men and an explosives laboratory. But I had deduced the existence of the laboratory, the bombs, and the plot against the life of King Umberto before you left here last week."

"How could you have known all that on such scanty information? Surely there was nothing of a plot in what I told you."

"On the contrary, there was in your story everything I needed to know, once I added to your narrative certain data which I happened to have in mind – indeed, information which you also know. To that knowledge, I added a few quickly-reached conclusions."

"Information I knew already?" the Count said with astonishment.

"Certainly," said Mycroft Holmes placidly. "You knew your King Umberto was planning a to Great Britain and would arrive in a few days' time. I knew it, as I had played a part in making the detailed arrangements for the visit. Most everyone in London knew of it, for that matter, from newspaper accounts. You failed to connect Giovanni Martinelli's death with the impending royal visit."

"I still don't see the connection."

"Nonetheless there is one. The suspicious death of an Italian Embassy official, no matter how junior, less than a fortnight before the visit of the king, seemed to be a coincidence that is remarkably suggestive."

"Now that you speak it, I recognize the fact. But I must admit that I was too grieved to think of that at the time. Does that mean that Martinelli was involved with the plotters?"

"It might have. At that time, I was still collecting evidence and merely stored away the fact for further consideration. It was suspicious, but I needed further information, and when you described the details of the young man's death, I was certain of the fact. Your astonishment when I described the color of the dead man's skin, eyes and gums confirmed my hypothesis, and I knew at once there was a serious threat to King Umberto's safety."

"How could you possibly know that?" asked the Count. "And I admit that hard to believe that Giovanni was part of the plot."

"It will be better if we take matters one at a time. Let me first relieve your mind about your clerk. I can conclusively state that he was a victim of the conspiracy, not a member of it. Although I held him suspect at first, as soon as you made certain the circumstances of his death, his innocence was obvious. He had clearly died of some sort of poisoning, as you also suspected.

"It is highly unlikely that a conspirator would kill himself before a plot had come to fruition. Nor would his fellow conspirators allow him to die in your office in great pain since, if he knew anything incriminating, he might blurt it out. No, it was clearly a case of murder, though I doubt we will be able to prove that these bomb-makers were his murderers, at least not in a court of law."

"But the threat to His Majesty?"

"That was inherent in the details of Martinelli's death. It was clear there was a bomb plot involved."

"But he died of poisoning, not from an explosion," the still perplexed diplomat cried out.

"Exactly. The poison was the key to the bomb plot. We are far from the days of your own Lucretia Borgia, Count Livorno, and I feel sure," Mycroft Holmes continued with a raised eyebrow, "poison is not much a part of current Italian diplomacy.

"One of many subjects to which I have given special attention is the effects and symptoms of poison, and your description of Martinelli's illness and death was suggestive. Combined with my supposition that his death had something to do with King Umberto's visit, I asked you about young Martinelli's yellow pallor and hit the mark."

"You knew, then, what killed Martinelli?"

"Yes. Signore Martinelli was killed by the ingestion, over several days, of a fatal dose of picric acid."

"Picric acid?"

"Certainly you have heard of it?"

"As you discerned, I am not a very good chemist, Signore Holmes."

"Nor, if I may add, do you interest yourself in military matters."

"No, that has never been one of my duties."

"If it had been, you would have certainly heard of picric acid, for it is the high explosive of choice for artillery shells in our murderous modern world. Your government, that of Her Imperial Majesty, the Germans, the French, and others, have devised special formulas for picric acid to use in their high explosives. I understand there have been experimental attempts to use dynamite as a military explosive, but that explosive has proven too unstable so far."

"Yet surely these men who were arrested were not military men?"

"Certainly not. The picric acid that is used for military purposes is stabilized and is specially manufactured. But picric acid itself is easily manufactured by a skilled chemist, and the yellow crystalline acid is what is called a percussive explosive. It can be set off with a fuse or, if the fuse fails, throwing the container or a bomb full of the acid onto hard ground can set it off. Anarchists find it the most practical explosive available, much more powerful than black powder, easily manufactured, and stable so long as the crystals are kept under water.

"Picric acid also has medicinal uses, especially in dilute solutions applied to serious burns. It can cause poisoning if too much is applied, and can be fatal if ingested. But its rather bitter flavor makes that a rare occurrence. Your young friend liked bitter aperitifs, so it wasn't at all difficult to slip a fatal dose of only a few grains of picric acid into several drinks. The symptoms you mentioned – inability to eat, dizziness, headache – are all typical of picric acid poisoning, which cannot be detected after death – save for the yellow skin of the victim."

"How you guessed all of this is incredible."

"No guessing was involved, I assure you," said Mycroft Holmes. "Once I suspected there was picric acid in the case, it was obvious that a plot against someone's life was in the offing. King Umberto was the obvious – indeed the *only* target associated with both anarchist plotting and the Italian Embassy.

"The telegram I sent to brother Sherlock explained everything he needed to know, and I relied on his taking action. He has all the family energy. I have none."

"But Signore Holmes," the Count asked, "I still do not see how your Inspector Lestrade was able to find the plotters with such ease."

"Ah, Lestrade. Lestrade is not a man of cleverness, but like a hound, once given a scent, he is inexorable. My brother, as he has so often in the past, gave the old hound the scent. I talked to him briefly this morning: He has a telephone, but uses it only grudgingly.

"It was, as he said, an elementary investigation. I knew from the facts which you provided had that young Martinelli had most certainly died from picric acid poisoning, and that picric acid was an anarchist tool.

"Brother Sherlock saw as much immediately from my telegram. He was able, with little difficulty, to find where Martinelli spent his evenings, and was able to trace his friends, if we may call them that, since it was they who poisoned him. They extracted the information they needed from the young man and then, since their plot was near fruition, coldly eliminated him to remove a potential witness."

"But surely Martinelli wasn't in on their plot?"

"Well, not exactly. He knew nothing of their plans and seems to have given them no secrets. The king's travel agenda was common knowledge within the Italian diplomatic corps, and Martinelli's single indiscretion served to confirm those plans. Once the plotters were sure of the final dates, they no longer needed Martinelli, who might inadvertently give them away, and so they disposed of him. It was their choice of picric acid as a poison that gave me and my brother the one clue we needed."

"But how did your brother go from poison and a plot against our King to Inspector Lestrade's raid on the conspirators this morning?"

"He night never hear me admit it, but brother Sherlock is a master of disguise. He went to the cafe where Martinelli was a regular customer and overheard a good deal, though nothing incriminating. I should liked to have seen him disguised as an Italian workingman. I knew he had enough of the language to get by, of course, but I'm sure I would be amused at his choice of clothing.

"In quick order, Sherlock was able to identify several men who were – to his mind – suspicious, and he followed one of them home. My brother finds such a matter simplicity itself. The man he followed went to a detached suburban villa which seemed, to all except a trained observer, as innocent a dwelling as you might find anywhere in London."

"What, then, gave it away?"

"I will tell you what my brother told me: 'It was the dead pigeons.'"

"Dead pigeons?"

"Yes, dead pigeons. You see, in making picric acid, deadly fumes are produced that have to be removed from the laboratory by special ventilation. The plotters apparently vented their fumes through one of the chimneys in the house, and the pigeons who spend their nights near the warm chimney pots were overcome by fumes.

"You will have noticed that you never see dead pigeons in London, despite the large flocks in our public squares. Pigeons, when ill, hide and are rarely found dead. When Brother Sherlock found four dead pigeons, all within a few feet of the house's chimney, he knew that picric acid fumes had hilled them.

"Lestrade, who is always willing to take my brother's advice when he can gain credit from it, quickly assembled a large force of constables and quietly surrounded the house. Early this morning, when all in the house were fast asleep, he sprang his trap, arresting seven men, and found considerable explosives already made into bombs, plus the equipment and chemicals for making more. Lestrade will, as always, be commended for his acumen in the newspapers, and neither my brother nor I will not be mentioned."

"And Martinelli's murderer will be punished," the Count said firmly.

"Possibly, possibly not," Mycroft Holmes replied. "Certainly, the plot to kill your king has been destroyed, and Martinelli's murderers caught. The Crown will likely turn the plotters over to your government for prosecution in conspiring to kill King Umberto. The plotters are, from my brother's account, fanatical and unlikely to incriminate one another. With little prodding, I dare say Her Majesty's government will also turn over the particulars regarding the case of the murdered young Martinelli for you to prove."

The Count nodded. "I believe that is what will occur. I regret the loss of your young friend but I am glad their plans regarding His Majesty have failed. I am sure that he will want to reward you and your brother for your singular services in this painful matter."

For Sherlock Holmes that reward proved to be a discreet but heavy gold ring with the royal crest on it, an elegant piece which the detective often wore.

For Mycroft Holmes and the Diogenes Club, it was a fine dinner prepared by the king's personal chef- a dinner enjoyed by some members and decidedly not enjoyed by others.

The experiment was not repeated.

The Adventure of the White Roses
by Tracy J. Revels
From *Part XXVII: 2021 Annual (1898-1928)* (2021)

"My fiancé tells me that I am being overwrought, perhaps even a bit hysterical, Mr. Holmes. Yet, I know what I saw and what I heard. It is too late to do my poor father, or Mr. Latham, any good – but perhaps you can save their friend, who I believe is in great danger."

These words were spoken by a small, rather plain young woman swathed in mourning. Her raised veil revealed a simple face, with wide eyes and a firm, hard mouth. She had introduced herself as Miss Sarah Gibbons, daughter of the late Professor Sterling Gibbons of Essex College. Though far from beautiful, or even memorable in her face and figure, there was such a determined quality to her words that my friend could hardly refuse to hear her story.

"Your father authored a book on the Great Rebellion in America, did he not?"

Our visitor gave a little smile of pride. "He did indeed, Mr. Holmes. His specialty was the history of the American nation. Father and his friends were in America during that war. Let me show you." She produced a small photograph in a leather frame. It showed three dashing young men lounging around an encampment, smoking cigars and playing cards, as if they were blissfully unaware of the great struggle all around them.

"They do not appear to be soldiers," I observed.

"Mr. Colin Latham was a photographer. My father was a writer, and Sir Howard Blakely was . . . I suppose 'adventurer' might be the word for it. They thought it would be thrilling to see the great conflict at close range. Father hoped to write a book, and Mr. Latham to sell his pictures. Sir Howard?" The lady shrugged. "There was some falling out among them after they returned to England. I have never met Sir Howard, but Mr. Latham lived in a secluded cottage on the ocean, just a few miles from our village.

"Father had retired from his college. Five years ago, he and my mother were in a terrible carriage accident, which she did not survive, and which left Father badly crippled. Shortly afterward, Father was diagnosed with consumption and told he must have sea air to survive. After that,

Father tutored a handful of village lads, but otherwise our life was quiet and uneventful. That is, until recently."

The lady shivered, despite the warmth of the rooms.

"I have thought of little besides the events of the last months, but I have no wish to recount them unless I am certain that you will hear my case."

"We are all attention," Holmes said.

"It was the first of March when my father received a letter that upset him. It came in the post, but I couldn't tell you anything about it, as I attached no special significance to it. Father was sitting at his desk, working his way through the mail, and I was seated in a chair not five feet away, when I heard him give a horrible gasp. I turned to find his face as pale was death.

"'Papa, what is wrong?' I asked.

"He would not reply. Before I could rise from my chair, he took the letter and the envelope and consigned them both to the fire. He staggered back to his seat and slumped forward on his desk. I was ready to shout for our housekeeper to send for the doctor, but he caught my wrist. His hand was ever so cold.

"'Sarah, no, it is nothing. Now, child, please – bring me some brandy and leave me. I must finish my letters.'

"I had no wish to depart, but he was most insistent. The brandy seemed to restore him, and I removed myself only as far as my room and listened quite intently, so that I could run to his aid if needed. By supper, he was more himself."

"And you never learned the subject of the letter?"

"Father never spoke of it again, though from that day forward he became much more cautious. When we walked to church on the Sabbath, his eyes would dart about, and he was much more nervous than I could ever recall. But I had become engaged the previous Christmas, and there were times when I assumed Papa's nerves were nothing more than distress over my coming marriage.

"Then, in mid-April, Mr. Latham arrived. We had not seen him since New Year's Day. I was just leaving for the market, with a basket over my arm, when he came stomping up the lane like some kind of human locomotive. He was a short, stout man, with great grizzled side-whiskers, and a large high hat. As he drew closer, I saw that his face was red, and he was clutching a letter in his hand."

"'Why, Mr. Latham, whatever brings you here?' I asked.

"'I must speak with your father, immediately. Is he about?'

"I directed him to the study. He rushed by me without another word – he had always been an eccentric, strange man, a confirmed bachelor and a recluse, but on that morning, he was so uncivil that I was left quite astonished. I followed him into the house. He had already gone up the stairs and was bellowing for my father.

"'For God's sake, man, lower your voice,' Father said. 'Do you want the entire village to hear you?'

"With that, the study door slammed. I shooed away our puzzled housekeeper and tiptoed up the stairs, placing my ear to the portal. My father's tone was soft and low, but I distinctively heard Mr. Latham say, 'So you have had a letter too?' After several minutes, I heard, 'And what of this? Look. I found them scattered all about my house, even on my roof. Tell me how! How can this be?' There was furious pacing and more indistinct muttering. Mr. Latham shouted, 'Damn Blakely, it was all his fault!' I had just time to jump away from the door before Mr. Latham threw it open and stormed out of our house, uttering the most terrible oaths. He never saw me in the passage and was gone before I could recover my poise."

I found myself caught up in the drama of her story. It was easy to imagine the old village house, the elderly scholar, the strange friend, and the frightened girl. "What did you do?" I asked.

"I waited a few moments, and then I entered the study. Father didn't see me come in, for he was looking out the window, no doubt watching his friend go down the road. My eyes, however, were drawn to something that hadn't been there before – a single white rose upon my father's desk.

"'I fear we must cease our relations with Latham,' Father said, as he turned. 'The man has taken to drink. I hope he was not vulgar to you.'

"'He seemed very upset.'

"Father nodded. 'He has an idea that he is being persecuted. We must not allow his delusions to intrude upon our happiness. Shouldn't you be at the market already?'

"I pointed to the flower on the desk. Father laughed – I tell you that my blood ran cold, for the sound was nothing like his usual mirth. It was hollow and false.

"'Oh, Widow Grimbly gave it to me this morning. What a silly person she is. I think she has it in her head that I will marry her when you are gone. Now run along, child.'

"I couldn't imagine why my father would tell such an atrocious falsehood, but my nerves were so rattled that I left the house and went to see Eddie, my betrothed. He laughed it away.

"'Old men have queer secrets, Dearest. Don't let it worry you.'

"I tried to follow his advice, but a week later Inspector Callahan of Scotland Yard arrived at our door with terrible news that Father's friend had been murdered. Mr. Latham's body had washed up on the shore some ten miles from his seaside cottage."

"And why was his death presumed to be foul play?" Holmes asked.

"Because it was well known, despite his residence near the beach, that Mr. Latham avoided the ocean. He did not sail or fish or swim. When his body was found, it was fully clothed, though so badly battered by the rocks that it was difficult to state what he had died of – whether he had drowned or been harmed in some other way before he was thrown into the waters. And, stranger still, his wallet was found still tucked inside his breast pocket, filled with notes. The inspector wanted to know if Father suspected anyone in the affair. Father said no, but I knew he was not telling the full truth. I walked with the inspector to the gate. Just as he was about to step into his carriage, he mentioned something that nearly caused me to faint.

"'There was one very strange thing about Mr. Latham's home. The place was littered with withered white roses – a hundred or more of them. He must have been an exceptionally fine gardener.'

"Father's behavior became more fearful afterward. It was all I could do to coax him down to take a meal. My maternal aunt, who resides in London, had arranged for me to spend a week shopping for my trousseau. I was reluctant to leave, but Father insisted that I go. After two days, I couldn't stop thinking about him, and I returned home. Our housekeeper met me at the door.

"'Miss Sarah, you must tell your young man to stop it. I know he means well, but it will kill the professor.'

"'What on earth are you talking about?'

"'The roses, Miss! When we awoke this morning, we found roses scattered all about the place – in the yard, the steps, even some down the chimneys. Lovely white roses. I know that your fellow is very romantic, but – '

"Mr. Holmes, no sprinter ever ran faster than I did. Father was in terrible distress. I shut the door and begged him to tell me what this meant. A few times, I thought he would speak, but then the words choked him into silence.

"That was a week ago. For two days, nothing occurred, and Father appeared to rally. A little fair was opening in our village, which Eddie wished to attend. I tried to get Father to come with us, but he insisted he was too old. It was a beautiful day and we had a grand time, enjoying all the treats. There was a dance afterward, so it was nearly midnight before we returned home. Much to my surprise, Father was not in his room, and the housekeeper was already abed. I was alarmed, but then I recalled how often Father had walked across the lane to our neighbor's house and fallen asleep in a chair beside that kind gentleman's fireplace. I was certain he had done so again, and it seemed better to retire than to knock up another household.

"The next morning . . . I was awakened by our housekeeper's scream."

The lady's sudden distress at the memory was evident in her face, which had gone ghostly pale. Holmes raised a hand.

"I read of the event in the newspapers – I shall summarize and you may correct me if I err. Your father's body was found beneath a large oak tree in the yard, in the rear of the house. His neck and numerous other bones were broken. The coroner ruled it was a death by misadventure, that your father had climbed the tree and fallen from its branches."

"As if Father were a schoolboy, scampering up to steal robins' eggs!" the young woman wailed. "He was weak, in poor health, and crippled. He certainly could not have climbed a tree, nor jumped to it from a window."

"And there was another discovery. A great deal of money was found in his pockets."

"Yes, nearly two-hundred pounds were stuffed into his clothing. It was almost all of his savings."

"Did you tell the police about the roses?"

Miss Gibbons nodded. "Inspector Callahan came to investigate. He dismissed the roses as a lark, something concocted by Father's pupils to honor my impending nuptials. Afterward, I looked through Father's papers, but there was nothing in them, except . . . Father had a journal from his time in America. I couldn't find it. The housekeeper told me that, while I was at my aunt's, she saw Father destroy it in the fireplace."

Holmes nodded. "As a consequence, you fear for the safety of Sir Howard."

"It is the only connection I can make. Father had so few friends, and I cannot imagine why he would burn his American diary unless there was something in it that was dangerous. Eddie tells I have no right to bother a man of Sir Howard's status, and that he will think me some kind of maniac. Yet at the same time, I would never wish upon his daughter the sorrow that has come upon me."

Holmes rose, extending his hand. "Leave it to us, Miss Gibbons. I did a service for the Blakely family in the past, enough to gain me admittance to Sir Howard's august presence. I will alert him of the danger he's in, and perhaps unravel the mystery of your father's murder in the process."

"It was murder, then."

"Yes, dear lady, I am certain that it was."

Miss Gibbons left our suite with a sorrowful heart, but expressing her great trust in Holmes to bring her father's killer to justice. As her footsteps faded away, my friend lit his pipe and turned to me.

"What do you make of it, Watson?"

"It is clearly a case of blackmail!" I said. "The money in Gibbons' pockets is proof that he hoped to meet his persecutor while his daughter was away and pay him to trouble them no more. One would have thought the villain would have taken the money."

"That the offering remained in the dead men's pockets – for remember that Latham also had substantial cash upon his body – proves blackmail was never the intention," Holmes corrected. "No, our murderer is not motivated by monetary gain. He is out for revenge. This speaks to vengeance."

"For what crime?"

"That we cannot know without more data. Tell me what you make of the roses."

"A warning, of course. A signal of intent, designed to terrorize the victims."

"Excellent. You scintillate today."

"And white roses are the symbol of the House of York!"

Holmes lifted an eyebrow. "Are you accusing Richard III of this crime as well? Isn't it enough that he must take the blame for the deaths of the princes in the Tower upon his rather crooked shoulders?"

"I only mean that this may be related to Gibbons's profession. He was a historian. Perhaps one of his students is at the bottom of this."

"And I will remind you that he was a historian of the *American* experience, not the British."

"Do you have a better interpretation of their meaning?"

"I have none, beside the obvious one – that the roses were designed to alarm the intended victims, that Inspector Callahan is an incompetent oaf, and that whatever the secret was, Professor Gibbons preferred death to its revelation. A few words to his daughter could have saved him, yet he refused to utter the truth. What could be so horrific?" Holmes rose and knocked out his pipe. "It is too late to start for the Blakely seat tonight, but I shall send a telegram and request an audience for tomorrow. Be ready to start at five, Doctor!"

As we made our way toward the little village that was closest to Blakely Manor, Holmes gave me a quick sketch of the family's history, drawn from his voluminous Index. The estate had once numbered in the thousands of acres, but was now reduced to a single manor and its rents. Sir Howard had few accomplishments, but his daughter was a remarkable

319

beauty. The young lady was currently enjoying a splendid Continental debut, accompanied by her mother. The son, only ten years old, was at Eton.

"This is good fortune for us," Holmes said, as we disembarked. "The presence of the womenfolk might complicate a frank discussion of Sir Howard's past. I doubt he will recall me, as my service – "

"Mr. Sherlock Holmes!"

The hailing cry came from a young blond man in country attire, his boots considerably muddy. He held out a hand to my friend.

"You must be a wizard indeed, sir – and flown in on a broomstick, to have arrived here so promptly. Why, I sent the telegram to you only five minutes ago! I had no hopes of a reply by now, much less your actual presence."

"I fear you have me at a disadvantage, for I possess no supernatural powers."

"I am Constable Byron Price. I've read of your work and much admire it – and I have just sent a message requesting your assistance."

"About a murder?"

"Indeed."

"Of Sir Howard Blakely?"

Price gasped. "Why – yes – though I think I spot your trick. Only the murder of such an important individual would lead to you being summoned."

Holmes raised a hand. "Recently, a letter disturbed Sir Howard and then a shower of white roses occurred on his property."

Price stepped backward so quickly he nearly toppled from the platform. "Sir! Do not dispute that you are magical if you know these things already. You must have the second sight!"

"Allow me to prove I do not. Where was the body found?"

"That is the most baffling aspect of the entire business. Come, I will take you there."

We were soon ensconced in a comfortable landau, making our way out of the little village and toward the manor. The smells of early summer were rich upon the air, and lively noises were rising a country fair being set up in a meadow. Merry birdsong all around us made a strange accompaniment to Price's dark tale.

"Between us, Sir Howard was a disgrace to his title. He neglected his duties to his cottagers and gained a rather black reputation in these parts for dissolute behavior. His gambling debts were substantial. I've heard rumors that he'd begun to sell off some of the family pictures, as well as furnishings that date back to the Tudors."

"So he was a man with enemies?" I asked.

"Many – known and unknown. He was also in regular trouble over women. No servant girl stayed employed for more than a month, he was so odious with them. You see, Mr. Holmes, I already have my work cut out for me, sorting through all the people who could have wanted him dead. Ah, we've arrived. I apologize ahead of time for your shoes. They will probably be quite ruined."

Our vehicle had halted before a newly planted field. The earth was dark and loamy, still wet from the rain of the previous evening. Our guide halted us and pointed to a quartet in the center of the field.

"That's Chapman, standing there with my men. He was passing by at about six this morning with his son, setting out for work at the next farm, when he saw the body in the field. He ran to it, realized that the man was dead, then sent his lad on a plough-horse for us. Here's the devilish part, Mr. Holmes – there are no marks in the field. The earth is perfect for taking footprints or the tracks of wheels or animals, but there is absolutely no impression anywhere around the body! Sir Howard was a bit disheveled, with a broken bone or two, but he died from having his throat cut."

"Indeed?" Holmes asked, as we carefully followed the single trail the policemen had worn into the soil, as a way to reach the body without disturbing the evidence of the immaculate field.

"It seems impossible, but the corpse is nearly drained. There is only a wound on his throat to account for it. Of course, that means he was killed elsewhere and brought here." We reached the body, which lay upon its back. Sir Howard had been a handsome, silver-haired man, with a robust physique. His clothing spoke to a privileged life. A diamond stickpin glittered amid the gory bloodstain on his ascot, and a gold watch dangled from his silken waistcoat.

Holmes knelt, subjecting the body to a quick and intricate inspection. "Robbery does not seem to be the motive. I perceive that, along with his other accessories, he has maintained at least three gold rings on his fingers."

"And this was in his pocket," Price said, holding out a black velvet bag. He emptied the contents into his own palm. I counted a half-dozen pearls, easily worth a thousand pounds or more.

"I doubt that his wife would have approved of him robbing her jewel box so flagrantly," Holmes said, rising and making an attempt to brush the muck from his trousers.

"Lady Blakely has a temper, she does – my missus used to work for her," one of the policemen volunteered. "Sir Howard better be glad he got himself murdered."

"That's enough out of you," Price warned. "Mr. Holmes . . . I confess I am out of my depth here. Most crimes in our little village involved stolen apples or pilfered pears. What should I do?"

"You must follow procedure," Holmes said. "You have already spoken with the household staff?"

"Only briefly. The butler mentioned that his master had recently been disturbed by a letter, and that white roses had fallen on his house. That is why I believed you were clairvoyant."

"Continue with your interviews," Holmes said. "If possible, keep the news of Sir Howard's death confined to yourself and your men until tomorrow."

The officer nodded eagerly. "And what will you do, sir?"

"Doctor Watson and I have not enjoyed a day in the country in a very long time. I believe we shall go to the fair."

I was baffled as to why Holmes hadn't also chosen to retire to the manor, to poke around the grounds or ask questions of the servants, but there was little I could do except conform to his will. The fair was brimming with all the simple recreations rural folks enjoyed. Children danced around a maypole while a brass band tooted and honked in enthusiastic, if rather tuneless, accompaniment. Pies, flowers, and pigs were being judged. A variety of games were set up, to test one's skill at knocking down milk bottles or popping balloons with darts. Holmes insisted that I enter a shooting match, since I had my service revolver with me, and I'm proud to write that a lovely village maiden pinned the second-place red ribbon to my jacket. There was a Punch-and-Judy show, a carousel, even an elephant and a clever little monkey on exhibit. After a few hours, I found myself caught up in the laughter of the children, the general gaiety of the crowd.

The afternoon was drawing to a close, and most of the townspeople were beginning to depart, when Holmes drew my attention to the attraction at the corner of the fair. It was a large balloon with a wicker basket. Much to my surprise, it was painted not with a Union Jack, but with a crude approximation of the American Stars and Stripes. A sign announced that an ascent of a half-hour, courtesy of Professional Aeronaut Theodore Vance, was available for six shillings per passenger. The aeronaut, a trim and handsome man with a slender black mustache, was making some adjustments to the moorings as we approached.

"Is it too late to go up?" Holmes asked. I can only imagine the look I must have given my friend as he made this request. I don't consider myself a cowardly fellow, but I have no great love of heights, and the very thought of dangling above all of creation in a tiny basket made my head spin and my stomach pitch.

"I'm sorry, but I'm done for today."

"It wouldn't take long," Holmes said, with the air of an annoyed tourist, "and I can pay handsomely for the privilege. Of course, I would need to be careful, as you do have something of a habit of throwing your passengers overboard."

The man had crouched down to secure a knot, but he rose suddenly, spinning around with a fiery expression. "My vehicle is perfectly safe, and I've had no complaints."

"Dead men tell different tales." Holmes reached into his coat and pulled out a single white rose that he must have purloined from one of the stalls. "Your calling card, Mr. Vance."

The effect was astonishing. The aeronaut drew back, his face going pale, his teeth bared at us. "What is the meaning of this?"

"Murder. And I would like to know why."

"You're a funny kind of policeman."

"I am not the official forces. My name is Sherlock Holmes, and I am a consulting detective. The daughter of one of your victims has engaged me."

"Am I under arrest?"

"You will be, very soon."

"Then perhaps I have time enough for a drink? I'd prefer not to be dragged off to prison thirsty."

Holmes made an elegant gesture, and we found ourselves walking beside the man into the local public house, which was doing a brisk business. Holmes signaled for our quarry to be seated with his back to the wall, which he did with no protest. He accepted a mug of ale with a quick salute.

"You wish to hear my story? Well, it is worth hearing." He drank deeply. "I was born in Virginia in 1847. I had a twin sister, Barbara. Our parents were poor, honest people, but they perished in a cholera epidemic when we were only four, and a judge gave us to a wretched tavern keeper in Fredericksburg. We were told we must work for him until we were both twenty-one. We were treated much like the Negro slaves, forced to labor night and day, wearing ragged clothes and never having enough to eat. When the war came, I swore that I would run away and join the Union Army and kill every man who took another man's freedom. But I was too young, and I was small and underfed, so that I appeared even younger than my years.

"In December of 1862, our small town was the focus of both armies. The Confederates took to the hills, and the Union men marched through in pursuit of them. Our master fled to the plantation of a friend, but we were left behind and told to guard the tavern. What chance did children have against armies? Both sides came through and plucked our establishment bare.

"That day, as the terrible battle raged just beyond the town, three men came into our tavern. It was obvious that they were not soldiers. Their voices betrayed them as foreigners. The one they called Blakely was clearly wealthier than the others. He wore a fine coat, had a diamond stickpin in his tie, and generally told the others what they should do. He demanded we serve them dinner and offered to pay us in gold. We scratched up what provisions we could find, and poured the single bottle of whisky that was left to us. The men talked and smoked, and we hoped they would pay us and go about their business.

"Then Blakely cast his evil eyes upon my sister. He began to speak to her in vulgar ways, and when she ran out of the room in mortified tears, I told him to leave. He merely laughed at me and called to his friends to 'Hold the lad!' The one they addressed as Latham was a stout man. He knocked me down, kicked me until I coughed up blood, and then knelt upon my back, nearly crushing me. Blakely left the room, and I heard my sister screaming. I fought and kicked, but the man atop me was too heavy to be dislodged. The third man, the one they called Gibbons, stood in the doorway. He averted his eyes from the scene. He would not come to my aid or my sister's.

"It seemed like an hour passed. Finally, Blakely came back into the room, smirking. Our tavern was called The White Rose, named for the flowers which grew on a trellis beside the door. He had plucked one, which he threw at me."

Vance took up his glass again, but only stared down into it.

"There was no doctor to come and tend Barbara's wounds. She took a fever. Before a week passed, she was dead. Over her grave, I vowed eternal vengeance."

"How did you come upon your singular career?" Holmes asked.

"After I buried my sister, I ran away to the Union lines, thinking that perhaps I could become a camp servant or cook, if not a soldier. The army had observational balloons, and I was fascinated by them. A friendly officer saw my wonder. He took me on as an assistant and taught me everything there was to know about being an aeronaut. After the war, he adopted me as a son, and I was as loved by his wife and children as I had been despised by my former master. We toured the country with his balloon, performing ascents at hundreds of fairs. It was a fine life for many years, but I remained haunted by Barbara's fate. I saved all the money I

324

could, and when at last I had enough, I said goodbye to my friends and came to England.

"For the last five years I have devoted myself to finding the evil men who killed my sister. I invested in a balloon and established myself in the circuit of rural entertainers. At last, this spring, I saw my opportunity. First, I sent each man a letter, telling the offender that the hour of reckoning had come. Then I went above and showered his dwelling with white roses. Afterward, I sent him a note saying that he might purchase forgiveness if he would meet me in a private place of my choosing." Vance looked up with a snarl. "I did not want money. I only used it as a lure, to convince them to meet me – to lull them into thinking they would survive the encounter. I did not steal so much as a penny. I killed each man and took his body aloft, to leave it in a place that would strike fear and wonder into those who might find it. But I see my little trick of dropping Blakely's corpse in the field did not fool you, sir."

"It was impossible for his body to have been placed there in any other manner," Holmes said. "It was the singularity of the thing that made the method clear."

Vance nodded. "My vanity was my undoing. I do not regret killing them, even if I hang for it. But I am not a thief, nor do I bear any ill will against their families. My job is done. My sister's soul can rest. So often I have felt her presence beside me, in the basket. Last evening, when Blakely was slain, I sensed her spirit flying up into the heavens, to reside with the angels."

At just that moment, a shout – more of a war cry – erupted from the bar. A massive, red-headed man swung his meaty fist at the equally large man beside him, who retaliated by grabbing a bottle and breaking it over the assailant's head. The entire room was thrown into chaos as men leapt up, shouting encouragement, some of them eager to join the fray, others trying futilely to halt it. Vance abruptly hurled his mug at my friend, nearly crashing it into his skull. Before I could react, the American, who was clearly much stronger than his trim frame suggested, had flipped the table over. We toppled to the floor. Vance disappeared into the crowd of writhing, struggling bodies.

"Holmes!" I called. "Holmes, hurry!" I gained my feet and darted forward, but when I looked back, Holmes was casually brushing off his coat. "He will escape!"

"That is certainly his intention," my friend said. Police whistles sounded, causing the knot of fighting men to untangle, and at last we were outside.

"Where would he go?" I said.

"His route is obvious. Let us return to the fairground."

We broke into a run, reaching our destination in a matter of minutes. Vance had already cast off all but one of his moorings. As we ran up, he sliced the final rope with a knife and the balloon began to rise. I drew my pistol from my pocket.

"Watson, no!" Holmes yelled, slapping the weapon away.

"I could have stopped him!" I protested, watching helplessly as the balloon went silently away into the night's clouds.

"What goes up must come down," Holmes replied. "If you had injured or killed him, it would trouble your conscience. Come – let us see if we can find a room at this hour."

The next morning, Holmes sat smoking at the breakfast table of the little hotel where we had retired. He had been silent all evening, making no further comment upon the investigation or the remarkable story we had heard from the murderer. At last, he pushed his plate away and tapped out his cigarette.

"Watson, you have frequently commented on my propensity to play judge and jury, or perhaps even God. But I am troubled by this case. My responsibly to the law lies in one direction, my duty to justice in another, and my obligation to my client in a third.

"Hear me out. Theodore Vance is a confessed murderer. By the laws of England, he should be tried and hanged. Yet upon hearing his story – and there is no doubt in my mind it is a true one, for what other motive could this man have possessed? I am inclined to think that justice has been served. Clearly my client is in no danger, but she is owed the truth about her father's demise. However, it is impossible to explain the murder without engaging with the motive."

"It will break the young lady's heart," I said. "She clearly adored her father."

"Indeed. And one must ask, what good will come of this? This revelation might put a strain upon her engagement, or even her marriage. Is it right to steal happiness from her?"

"She asked you for the truth."

"And she deserves no less. Ah, but here is Price – looking rather distraught, I think."

The constable's face was drawn and pale. His hair was uncombed, and he had clearly not paused to shave. He collapsed into a chair.

"Troubles come in threes, do they not? First the murder of Sir Howard, then the brawl at the pub, and now our poor balloonist, who vanished in the night!"

"What has happened?"

"I just received a telegram. His balloon was spotted in the waves off Dover. The basket was smashed upon the rocks. They are still looking for his body."

Miss Sarah Gibbons's eyes were damp with tears, but she quickly mastered her emotions. She seemed satisfied with Holmes's explanation that her father's murder was connected to an American tragedy, decades in the past.

"It is a sad story, but one that has been concluded," Holmes said. "Do not allow it to affect your happy memories of your father or cause you to fear for your future."

"You have learned evil things that you do not wish to tell me," she said.

Holmes nodded solemnly. "You are very perceptive. I would ask you to allow me to serve as a guardian for these unpleasant facts and hold them in a kind of trust for you."

The lady smiled. "I have lived a sheltered life. Father – *Papa* – was always so protective of me. He said the world was wicked, and he was far from perfect, but he would shield me from all harm, as long as he lived. You are clearly a man of wisdom and experience, Mr. Holmes. If you are satisfied that my father has received justice, I will ask no more. Perhaps in the future, when my feelings will not matter, Doctor Watson might record this story for posterity. Thank you, sir, for finding the truth."

Miss Gibbons took her leave. She went on to marry and lived a happy life, but a few weeks ago we received a note from her husband, saying that she had perished from influenza. Poor Constable Price never solved his case, and some of the more sensational newspapers had a field day speculating that Sir Howard Blakely had fallen victim to the legendary leaping demon named Spring Heeled Jack.

A month after Vance disappeared, Holmes and I were walking through Regent's Park. Two children, a boy and a girl so alike they might have been twins, skipped by, towing a single red balloon between them. Something in the image sparked a thought.

"Vance is not dead," I murmured.

"Assuredly, he is not," Holmes answered. "He was a master of the art of navigating the air. It would have been simplicity itself to bring his device to the ground and then abandon it, allowing it to soar unguided over the Channel. He is doubtless on his way back to America. One day, he will face a higher judge than any in this empire and we, perhaps, will receive credit for our measure of mercy."

The Colourful Skein of Life
by Julie McKuras
From *Part XXX: More Christmas Adventures (1897-1928)* (2021)

In looking back at the varied and interesting cases which I shared with Sherlock Holmes, I find a number which involved one of the greatest celebrations in the Christian calendar. "The Blue Carbuncle" hinged more on a goose than the day, but Christmas played a much larger role in another investigation. I hesitated for a number of years to put pen to paper about a story that combines the joys of Christmas with a criminal who preyed on the weaknesses of others. The time has come to record it, in hopes that it might alert those vulnerable souls who may cross with those who would betray them.

I arose one December morning, having slept in later than was my routine. Dressed and ready for the day, I entered the sitting room where I found Holmes standing by the cheery fire, staring at the plugs and dottles scattered on the mantelpiece. Leaving him to his thoughts, I crossed the room to the window. Silhouetted against the gray sky, the tree branches in the distant park were mostly bare, the last obstinate dead leaves hanging on until the cold winter winds came to take them.

Seating myself at the breakfast table, I examined the various dishes. "Holmes, you appear lost in thought this morning." He often neglected meals when engaged in an interesting case, but nothing had presented itself recently. The case I described as "The Adventure of the Priory School" was seven months past, and like the citizens of London I was focused on hopes for a peaceful Christmas and a happy 1902. After pouring my coffee, I dug into the ham and eggs while eying the orange marmalade.

Holmes approached the table, pipe in hand. "I received a communication from Mycroft early this morning. I thought it was a summons to his club, but he plans to visit us here. Rather soon, actually." When Holmes misses an opportunity to poke fun at my healthy appetite, it confirms that his attention is elsewhere. "He wrote that it is a matter of pressing importance requiring a private setting."

"More private than the Stranger's Room?" Mycroft generally preferred we meet at the Diogenes Club, which afforded solitude to those unsociable men who exhibited little or no interest in their fellow members. I finished my meal while unsuccessfully trying to recall any subjects which would cause Mycroft to interrupt his work day and – more remarkably – to alter his routine.

Shortly after Mrs. Hudson cleared the table and the fire was stirred, we heard heavy footsteps on the stairs. The door opened and Mycroft Holmes blew in, filling the doorway. Cheeks reddened by the cold, his coat and muffler trailing behind him, he went to the hearth without a word of greeting to warm his great hands. Accustomed to the two brothers attempting to outdo each other with their deductions, I waited for the usual exchange to start, but Mycroft immediately began to relate the reason for his visit.

He dropped into a chair and positioned himself. "As you know, bits of information and innuendo find their way to my office in Whitehall, and a most consequential situation has come to my attention. It involves the initial plans for a battleship with armaments so large and so advanced that it will revolutionize naval warfare. Robert Payne-Owen is in charge of the project and, recognizing the need for secrecy, only four men meet with him in his office. Yet despite precautions, we've had two unsolicited inquiries about supplying ammunition which could only be used with the new guns. When questioned, both companies responded that their proposals were made 'assuming' there would be a need in the future. There's never been a question of improper or illegal behaviour on either Payne-Owen's part or the others, and an after-hours search of their offices exposed nothing untoward. But if munitions manufacturers have information like this, we have to ask: What else might have left his office – or any other office in Whitehall for that matter?"

There was silence in the room as we considered the implications. Holmes spoke first. "And you need someone unconnected to Whitehall to look into this?"

"An appropriate observation, since we don't know where the leak or leaks originates. There are several other situations. For instance, one involves a cabinet member named Talman who had a change of heart about his earlier announcement that he wouldn't stand for re-election. He's only told two close allies about his decision, but within days, heinous, unfounded attacks about his moral character have been made in conversation and in the press." He held up a newspaper. "This is what appeared yesterday. *'Talman Feels Women Who Want the Vote Should be Beaten by Their Husbands.'* Last week, one issue carried a comment that Talman felt children of the poor were too ignorant to benefit from school and should seek physical labor instead. They're repeated *ad nauseum* with 'You all know about this' so it's almost impossible to refute such anonymous claims." Mycroft crumbled the newspaper and threw it into the fire where it quickly crumbled to ashes. "There's more, but no indication who started this character assassination. Suspicions point to who benefits from his downfall – in this case, a certain political adversary."

I found this appalling. "What kind of a gentleman would do that?"

"The type of gentleman who often runs for office, Watson." Holmes smirked, and began to pace, chin upon his chest.

"Payne-Owen's group and the cabinet member I mentioned are independent of each other. There are additional situations, yet the only commonality is that they've originated within the same time period. I fear there's more and consulted my sources, not all of them upstanding examples of our citizenry, but they're useful as they provide a window into your forte, the criminal world. Other matters outside of the government came to light which would never have been revealed if not for our inquiries. There are questions about a bank's instability, blackmail, substantial thefts on the docks, and a large department store. I've written down the names of those concerned for your review." He handed the list to his brother. "I have two requests for you two. One: I'd like you to consult your friends in low places to see if you can determine more about the origins of these crimes outside the sphere of Whitehall. Two: I've come up with a plan to begin to ascertain where the government leaks exist, and hope you'll agree to help."

Holmes rubbed his hands together. "What part do we play?"

Mycroft shifted uneasily in his chair, suddenly quiet as if at a loss for words. After a brief pause he answered. "We're going to begin by searching Payne-Owen's home."

"You want us to break into his house?" Holmes and I had some experience in this skill, as I've documented.

"Not exactly break in. Sir Thomas Ellington, the head of the department in question, has agreed we have to start somewhere with our investigation. Ellington asked Payne-Owen and his wife to stand in as hosts at the annual department Christmas party, claiming his wife is ill. Payne-Owen is ambitious, with hopes to assume Sir Thomas's position after he retires, and Ellington has hinted that this will indicate who will replace him. Mrs. Payne-Owen is anxious for the social opportunities such a post might provide, so they were quick to agree, knowing they will appear the gracious hosts without incurring personal expense or preparations, a perfect situation for anyone with ambition. The party for the department management and families is set at their home on December 13th."

I often thought myself intuitively slow compared to Holmes and this was one such instance.

"If we're not breaking in, will the party be a distraction for us to sneak into the house? We can't blend in as guests, or are we the hired help?"

"Not exactly. Sir Thomas is hiring entertainers and providing extra help, decorations, food, and gifts for the children. There will be about fifty guests in total, myself included. Sherlock, I know you've always had a flare for the dramatic, so you will be our thespian. Once the guests are settled, the program will begin with you performing a dramatic reading of a portion of *A Christmas Carol* and selected Christmas poems. Afterwards, using some excuse, you will retreat to the kitchen near the back stairway and, instead of returning to the party, you'll use those stairs to access and search their personal rooms. While you're doing that, a magician and then a musician will perform, followed by a break while the guests feast on cakes and puddings. Afterwards, Father Christmas will appear and greet each child and give them a gift. More carols and thanks to the hosts will conclude the festive afternoon, and hopefully your search. It should keep the hosts occupied."

"If our 'actor' is searching the premises, will I be assisting him?'

"No, Doctor. Until you're called upon for your official role, you will station yourself by the front stairways to observe if any members of the household wander in your direction. Should they use the stairs, you will cough loudly enough for Sherlock to hear you."

"What is my 'official' role besides watching for anyone going upstairs?"

"You will be Father Christmas's helper."

Holmes looked me up and down. "Watson an elf? I think he'd look rather smart with pointed ears." Needless to say, I found it less amusing, but knew if there was a question of a traitor, I would do whatever was asked. "And what will you be doing while this is happening? Dining with the guests?"

If Mycroft was a bit uneasy when he explained the plan, his reluctance to share more was plain to see. "I have a vital responsibility in this diversion. I'm sure you'll find this hilarious, but I shall be playing Father Christmas."

Holmes was rarely given to boisterous laughter, but today was an exception. He laughed until I thought he might weep. Finally catching his breath, he asked "And exactly how much experience do you have entertaining children?"

Jaw clenched, Mycroft looked at his brother for a moment before he spoke. "My work within the government has prepared me for working with children, if not in age then certainly in temperament."

Holmes's laughter tapered off as he assessed the grave expression on Mycroft's face. Walking to his brother he placed his hand on his shoulder. "If you're willing to act as Father Christmas, I'm sure I speak for both of us when I say we will do as you ask." He looked quite serious. "For King and Country."

He turned to me as I repeated it. "For King and Country."

The few days until the party passed both slowly and quickly. While decorations were hung in shops, families planned their holidays, and churches prepared for the holy season, Holmes rehearsed his story and poems and scoured the newspapers for reports of potentially related events. He spent the evenings in his old haunts with those who kept their ears to the ground for news of criminal doings. One night he returned to Baker Street just before midnight as I was preparing to retire.

"What news tonight?" I asked.

When he removed his coat I saw he was wearing workman's clothing. "It's a misspent evening when Shinwell Johnson can't put his finger on what's going on, other than talk among the lower elements of a new game in town. A plot to ruin a large banking firm with rumors about financial losses, a major department store with questions about selling stolen goods, blackmail, and unparalleled thefts on the docks have all arisen in the past few months. I don't trust coincidence, and if Moriarty and Milverton hadn't gone to their final rewards, I would have thought one or both of them might be connected to this. Tomorrow night we'll call at a spot Shinwell recommended. It's the type of place that might attract those who could cause troubles on the docks."

The next day I tried to focus on the book I was reading, but Holmes's repetitive recitation of Clement Moore's "The Night Before Christmas" distracted me. The day dragged on, but when darkness fell we prepared for our evening's work. Holmes had clothing to convince anyone we were dock workers, and added whiskers and grease smudges completed our disguise. Holmes stopped as were ready to exit. "Watson, we'll be visiting one of the most contemptable establishments in London. Violence isn't uncommon there. Perhaps it would be wise to bring your service revolver."

I patted my coat pocket. "Ready, should it be needed."

A hansom cab delivered us to a point within walking distance of the docks. The cold wind and effluence from the Thames assailed us, and within moments we came upon what I hoped might be the welcoming warmth of the tavern. I expected to see a blazing fire inside, but the accumulated dirt of years on the windows made that impossible. Once through the door, no boughs of holly or baubles greeted us, and the dim lighting barely penetrated the smoke that hung in the air. Holmes leaned over and said quietly "Welcome to the 3B's Pub. Watch your pocket and your back. The men here generally pose no danger, but it's hard to pick those who do from those who don't."

The floor was sticky and unwashed, which described everything else within the pub. With the door closed against the cold, the smell of the river still permeated the 3B's, but wasn't enough to mask the odors from so many hard-working, hollow-eyed men. Trying to forget the day as they huddled alone over glasses of cheap gin and ale, they drank, knowing the next day would be no easier. Making our way to the bar, we found two stools. I saw Holmes looking cautiously around the room, but his eyes stopped at one table with two men.

"Wouldn't be staring back there if I was you, mate." The man sitting next to Holmes spoke quietly and never looked up from his drink, which he held with cracked and reddened hands. He was a thin man with a long scar of the left cheek of his drawn face, a hat pulled low over his brow. "That's bad business going on." Holmes's brows rose slightly, surprised that he'd been noticed. Our seatmate rotated an inch in our direction and appraised us with a keen eye. "You ain't been here any time that I am, and I'm here 'most every night."

"We've no use for bad business, friend. We're just off the *Della May* and saw this spot." Holmes motioned to the barkeep that we'd like two glasses of ale. The glasses looked as unwashed as everything else in the tavern.

Our new acquaintance took a healthy drink of his gin. "Name's Rudy. So you're sailors, huh? Men with clean hands like you don't stumble on this place too often." He tilted his head imperceptibly toward the corner table. "That gent, the one with the dark hair and eyes, has soft, clean hands and nails. His clothes are clean too. Acts all friendly – finds someone and buys them a few drinks. That isn't something that happens here, at least until he started coming in this summer."

I looked past Holmes to Rudy. "So what's the problem if he wants to buy a man a drink?"

"Maybe nothing, maybe something. Whoever he's talking up gets tipsy, but he doesn't, not really. When his new chum is in his cups, that gent starts asking questions about ships and cargo coming and out, like he knows where they work but real casual like. Best to avoid him."

He finished his drink and looked us over. "Probably won't see you at the 3B's again." We left about ten minutes after his departure.

We retraced our route and found a cab willing to take us, only after seeing we had the funds to pay the fare. Holmes sat deep in thought for a moment, then roused himself. "I've always fancied myself a perceptive observer of others, but our friend Rudy turned the tables on us. He spotted us from the moment we sat down – probably from the minute we walked in. I knew that gentleman in the corner didn't belong there, but what hubris, what arrogance for me to think others don't note much from a person's appearance."

I was somewhat taken aback by this admission. "That may be, but are those incidences at the 3B's simply the common thefts which have always occurred, what with the value of the cargo shipped in and out?"

"Many a desperate man has found a day's work or ill-gotten goods on the docks. Yet Shinwell Johnson, whose own bad reputation allows him to know the workings of the criminal world, knew nothing beyond the rumor that something, or someone new was involved. The genial gentleman from the 3B's wants to know about shipping schedules and cargo which doesn't appear to have any commonalities with what Mycroft described. Questions remain if such disparate events have more than the common thread of timing and worse, if someone new has taken the vacated position at the centre of the criminal web. I can't put the pieces of this peculiar puzzle together."

Sinking into the silence that often marked his contemplative moods, he didn't speak as we exited the cab and, once upstairs, removed his coat. As he sank into a chair, I went up to my room and prepared myself for bed. Looking back as I departed the sitting room, I saw Holmes with his pipe in hand. I doubted he would rest that night and wondered if I would be able to sleep should he take up his violin.

I awoke the morning of Saturday, December 13th, huddled beneath the covers. No sunshine showed through the windows and a quick glimpse revealed a light snow was falling, perfect for the holiday revelries at the Payne-Owen household. I dressed and found Holmes settled at our dining table. He looked up. "So nice of you to join me this morning. Mrs. Hudson prepared a particularly pleasing breakfast."

I felt Mrs. Hudson always prepared a pleasing breakfast, while Holmes was rarely so complimentary. In between bites of his eggs, bacon, fish, and crumpets with the strawberry jam that Mrs. Hudson put up the past summer, he continued. "Mycroft sent a note early this morning along with our costumes for today. He's arriving at the Payne-Owen home about one o'clock, and we are to arrive no later than two, as the guests are expected at 2:30."

At the appointed time, we changed into our costumes. Mine was a simple red waistcoat, a green cravat, and a holly boutonniere. When he emerged from his bedchamber, I would have sworn I was looking at the author of *A Christmas Carol.* With his hair brushed forward in a strange style with curls at his temples, a neat goatee, and his suit and cravat, he could have been Charles Dickens himself. With a theatrical flourish, he carried a cane. Noticing my inspection of his outfit, he patted his waistcoat pocket. "It's in my pocket." I was glad his well-used burgling kit was close at hand, as it was sure to be used.

A quick carriage ride brought us to the Payne-Owens' lovely home in Eaton Square. The maid who answered the door quickly put us in our place, reminding us that the back door was used "by tradesmen and the like" before closing the door in our faces. Taking her direction, we rounded the houses and found the back door. Once admitted inside, we were shown to the first floor great room where the party was to be held. It was a hub of activity, with Mycroft directing the setting of the tables and chairs with a mere wave of his hand, making sure the chairs faced the stage and not the stairs. We approached him, weaving between those preparing the party needs.

Holmes appraised his brother, focusing on his midsection. "Mycroft, I see your padding is in place for your Jolly Old Elf costume."

"Ah yes, I see your wit and tongue are as sharp as ever. Are you both clear on what's to be done?" We agreed, and it wasn't long before we heard the guests entering.

The afternoon went off according to Mycroft's plan. The guests were led to the party room and Sir Thomas, with Payne-Owen and his wife at his side, welcomed them. After Sir Thomas gave a brief introduction, Holmes took the stage. As I noted early in my association with him, the stage lost a fine actor. When the applause subsided, he took his leave and, after accepting a few "Well done!" accolades, I saw him talk to one of the maids who gestured down a hallway. With a slight nod in my direction, he left the room.

The program continued. Mesmerized by the magician, the children could be heard whispering, "How did he do that?" with each trick. They sang along with the musicians and afterwards, there were delighted squeals as they filled their plates with the sweets and other treats laid on long tables. The families returned to their seats and, once their plates were empty, there was an announcement that a surprise was in store for them. All eyes widened when Father Christmas took the stage and I stood beside him. Mycroft cut a compelling figure, resplendent in his red robes, a convincing beard and locks, and a hearty laugh. The children were relatively patient as they waited to see the great man, anticipating how long it would be before it was their turn. Keeping an eye on the stairs, I led each child to Mycroft, who greeted them and asked their names. While I found the correctly tagged gift, he talked with them about their hopes for a Merry Christmas, and I wondered if the stage might have lost another fine actor as he put the boys and girls at ease. Their parents looked on, obviously proud of their children and their good manners. When each child had his or her moment, they took their seats. As the final carol was sung, I saw Holmes slip down the stairs and rejoin the group.

Sir Thomas took the stage and thanked the girls and boys for being so well behaved and his "dear friends", Mr. and Mrs. Payne-Owen, for their generosity and hospitality. It didn't take long after the guests bid their thanks that we were able to take our leave. Back in Baker Street, we waited until Mycroft arrived, and when we were seated Holmes began his narrative.

"There are two parts of this story regarding this afternoon. Let me start with my search of Payne-Owen's private rooms. As planned, I made my way upstairs where I searched the bedchamber and his office. It was all very tidy with nothing of consequence. No safe, no locked desk drawers, no loose incriminating papers, no cryptic messages or addresses, nothing. This doesn't exonerate Payne-Owen, of course, but I found no evidence of his involvement."

Mycroft nodded his head. "Frankly I couldn't imagine there would be, but it was a place to start."

"It was decidedly unproductive. But I can't say the same for what happened in the kitchen." Mycroft and I exchanged glances, wondering what Holmes found interesting. "After my performance, I went to the kitchen where I found the cook in her rocking chair, wrapped in a shawl with knitting in her lap. She agreed to my request for a cup of something soothing and, as she laid her knitting on the table to put the kettle on, I saw the scarf had a series of unevenly spaced knots in one row and some small holes in the next. She noticed I was looking at it, and moved her red yarn and needles under her chair just as Mrs. Payne-Owen swept into the kitchen."

Never missing the chance for a dramatic pause, Holmes walked to the window and looked at the darkened street below. "Apparently she frowns upon the help entertaining the hired entertainers in the kitchen, or so I gathered. 'Cook, the children need more fruit punch, and we need more lemons for the tea. You should have noticed, but it appears you're busy with this gentleman.' With that parting shot she left for the party room, but not before I saw the expression on the cook's face. It was pure hatred. I decided further conversation with her might prove productive."

"We're in the midst of questionable treason and other crimes, and you chose to question the help about the enmity she holds for the lady of the house?"

"Yes Mycroft, I did. In a home like the Payne-Owens', the help attend to the homeowner's every need, yet are often treated as if they're invisible unless there's a problem. With that invisibility and presumed loyalty, the conversation among family or with guests is often less than circumspect, so it's possible she heard something that shouldn't have been shared. Once Mrs. Payne-Owen was out of sight, I asked her, 'That one's got her nose up in the air. Is she always like that?'

"'No, she's usually worse. Not many a kind or thankful word from her, I can tell you.' She collected the punch and lemons and called a maid to take them up to the party room.

"'Sorry, I didn't introduce myself. I'm Edmund. And you're . . . ?'

"'It's not 'Cook'. I'm Beryl. I'm not sure Mrs. High-and-Mighty even knows my name. She only speaks to me to tell me what's wrong.'

"'Nice to meet you, Beryl. My nan used to knit quite a bit, so I feel right at home with you here in the kitchen.' I pointed to her yarn. 'Making that for someone? Thought I saw some knots and holes in it.'

"She became a bit flustered and was quick to make light of the mistakes, telling me she'd fix it later, but something was off with her. She was nervous, more interested in talking about Mrs. Payne-Owen and how she treats the servants, but is all too holy when others are around, always talking about her Christian charity. She said 'At least that means we get time off on Sunday morning to go to church services. Not her fancy church where she goes to be seen, mind you. I go to St. Anselm's and I'll be taking this scarf in tomorrow.' Apparently there's other parishioners who are in service like her, and join in donating knitted goods."

I'm not as intuitive as Holmes and failed to see where this was going. "So you know the lady of the house isn't as kind as she puts on and the cook takes her knitting to church, but what bearing does this have on the leaked information and crimes?"

"As our friend Rudy from the 3B's said: 'Maybe nothing, maybe something.' My instincts tell me an ignored older woman, destined to live out her life in someone else's kitchen, may have a story of her own. And something is nagging at me about that knitting. Tomorrow is Sunday, and a good day to observe the cook at her church."

After dining on a cold supper, Mycroft left us. Holmes pulled several books and a number of cards from his index, and then settled in for what I surmised was related to his question about knitting, although why this particular subject interested him escaped me. He was still reading when I began nodding off.

The next morning dawned with overcast skies and no sun to melt the previous day's snow. I could hear Holmes stirring in the sitting room.

"Watson! I was just about to rouse you for our Sunday services. Sabbath or not, the cook has to prepare breakfast for the Payne-Owens, so we'll attend the ten o'clock service. She didn't see you, so no need to alter your appearance, but it's a different situation for me. I'll join you shortly."

While he dressed, I had a light breakfast and looked at the newspaper. As familiar as I was with Holmes's disguises, when he entered the room I was taken aback by his ability to transform himself. He appeared much older with gray hair, poor posture which made him appear shorter, thick spectacles, a bulbous nose, and slightly bucked teeth. His waistline, normally so thin, had required a bit of extra padding in his costume of a middle-class clerk.

"How do I look? Do you think Beryl will recognize me as the distinguished actor from yesterday?"

I assured him that as I could barely discern his features, I doubted she would either, particularly as he'd worn a different disguise when they met. We were soon off to St. Anselm's. The light snow provided an appropriate holiday setting for the faithful who were entering the church to celebrate the third Sunday of Advent. The church embodied both beauty and simplicity, and while I admired the stained-glass windows, religious symbols, and statuary, Holmes scanned the assembled as we found a pew. It was a lovely service, and when it was over, the faithful filed out, thanking the priest who stood by the door to talk with the communicants. There were groups and individuals remaining inside, some in prayer and others in conversation with friends and family. In only a moment Holmes nudged me, and tilted his head toward a side aisle. "That's Beryl and it's certainly her knitted goods in that bag." The cook walked to an alcove where a small cluster of quiet churchwomen were sitting. Suddenly, Holmes sat forward and grabbed my arm.

"Take note of the new arrival. Do you see how the others are focused on her? I recognize her."

I found nothing familiar or outstanding in her appearance. Her features were rather plain, her clothing and hat what one might expect of a servant in her Sunday best. "Who is she?"

"She's *my* – or should I say *Escott the plumber's* – former fiancée, Agatha."

"Milverton's housemaid? It's been what, almost three years since you've seen her. Are you sure?" Having never seen the ill-used servant before, her entrance had no impact on me.

"Yes, it's her. I wonder if a piece of this puzzle may have fallen into place." His attention returned to the group as the women spoke quietly, placing a few items in an empty spot near Agatha, who appeared to soundlessly dominate the group.

"They're not here as a group of friends, but to see Agatha, aren't they?"

"My assumption as well. I'm fairly certain we're closer to discovering what's happening, but our time here is limited." Although

338

they'd been together for only a short period, the ladies were already picking up their other belongings as if to leave. "I think we should follow Agatha."

As she left the church, we kept out of Agatha's sight. She carried a few small bags down the steps and dropped them next to a waiting landau. The coachman jumped down in haste and held the door for her, giving her his arm as she climbed inside, then placed the bags at her feet. He resumed his seat and, taking the reins, pulled into the street. We were able to hail a hansom to follow them at a distance and as we settled in, Holmes said, "One doesn't often see a maid met by a landau and such an attentive driver. It's going to prove rather interesting to see who Agatha is working for since the demise of Mr. Milverton."

With that, he removed his facial disguise and wig. Leaving the area with the church and surrounding small shops, we entered an area with fashionable homes. The landau turned into a mews and Holmes alerted the driver to stop. He paid him and jumped out, with me fast behind him. As we rounded the corner we saw Agatha, followed by the driver, enter the back of a large but not overly ostentatious house.

"We'll ask Mycroft to see who actually owns this house, which is presumably where she works. For now, a call at the Payne-Owens' home is in order." I reminded Holmes that Beryl could reasonably be expected to be preparing the midday meal. There was a brisk breeze but it was a short walk to Eaton Square, the snow covering some of the unpleasantness normally found in the streets. In hopes of avoiding Mr. or Mrs. Payne-Owen, we went to the back door where we were invited inside by a servant when Holmes told her it was vital we speak to Beryl. She showed us into the kitchen, a warm and comfortable room with the odor of cooking hanging in the air. There was a woman standing at the counter and she looked at both of us, especially at Holmes.

"Good day, Beryl. You might not remember me from the party yesterday." She looked unsure if she did. "I'm not an actor as I told you, and my name isn't Edmund. I'm Sherlock Holmes, and this is my associate Dr. John Watson." Her face paled and she put her hand on her chest. "I take it you've heard of us." I moved toward her, feeling it might be best for her to sit down.

"What is it you want with me?" Her question was a simple yet suspicious one. Holmes sat across from her, and leaned forward, elbows on his knees. In a calm voice he said "Beryl, let's not draw this out. When I was here yesterday, I noticed evident errors in your knitting and your nervousness when I mentioned them. Your reaction bothered me, and I think they weren't mistakes at all, but intentional. A woman at church taught you how to use a code to relay information, didn't she? Things you've overheard in this house about Mr. Payne-Owen's government work – particularly about a new ship."

Beryl's head was down and I could see the tears begin to roll down her cheeks. She spoke softly. "I've known this day would come."

Holmes was known for his gentleness toward women. "I believe things will go a bit easier for you if you cooperate. Please, tell us the whole story from the beginning."

It took her a minute to gather her thoughts. "I've gone over and over what happened, trying to understand how it got this far. I've always been a cook, and after my last family moved to Italy last year, it took a while before I found this position. I have no family nearby, just a sister in Dover, and I don't get a chance to meet people, so I joined St. Anselm's and their knitting group. I feel good helping with the charity work along with five or six women." She shifted uncomfortably, keeping her eyes cast downwards. "Sometime last spring, Charlotte joined our group. She was friendly and got everyone talking and laughing, and it didn't take long before we all looked forward to our brief time together after Sunday services. She was so interested in us, and complimentary. But it didn't last."

"She said her name is Charlotte?" Beryl nodded. "When did your time with Charlotte change?"

"Maybe mid-summer? She started complaining about how the family she served treated her. That's something we all have in common, one way or another, and it didn't take long before the short time we have after church turned into talking about our problems. You know, it felt good to share that, like I wasn't alone. We gabbed about the lady of the house, how the mister approached the pretty maids, all of the little things that happen every day. But some of it wasn't all that nice, and some of it should never have been repeated."

"Like what you overheard about the plans Mr. Payne-Owen is working on?" There was an edge in Holmes's voice.

"Mr. Holmes, much as I don't like the mistress, the mister isn't a bad sort. I heard him talking about a big new ship with the missus, but I didn't know it was such a secret. I guess I felt a bit special working for someone like him who's in charge of something so important."

Holmes was on his feet, hands on the back of his chair. "Go on with your story."

"One Sunday as we were leaving, I saw Charlotte pull one of our group, Margaret, aside and talk to her. The next week I asked her what it was about since she'd looked so unhappy, but she wouldn't say a word. Two weeks later it was the same thing, only with Ruth, and before long it was my turn. It turns out Charlotte listened to our gossip – not as a friend, but so she could use it against us."

"What did she threaten she was going to do with your gossip?"

"That's the bad part, Mr. Holmes. She'd already done it. Told me she'd sold that bit about the big guns to a company or two. Said she'd tell Payne-Owen that I was gossiping about him and his department secrets and if I wanted to keep my position, I'd tell her more of what I hear. I'm certain that's what's happened with Margaret, Ruth, Grace, Rose, and Winifred too. I'm so ashamed that I don't even want to attend church anymore, but Charlotte let me know if I stop, she'll tell Mr. Payne-Owen her story, and then what will happen to me?"

It was grim, and one could see the air of unhappiness and shame that hung over her. She resumed her tale. "I should have quit as soon as it happened. I went through what little money I'd saved before I found this situation, and if I left then for Dover and my sister's tea shop, I'd have gone with little to offer other than my baking. Staying here, I thought I could save some money to help with the shop – especially since Charlotte started giving us envelopes with a pound or two now and then. She acted like it was to help us, but that's not why she did it. We all took that dirty money and with the knitting, it tied us to her like a boat anchor. That fear of being found out has tortured me every day."

I'd been listening quietly, but there was a point that bothered me. "Beryl, you're together with these women on Sundays. Why don't you simply tell Charlotte your secrets instead of using some involved knitting code? That has to take a lot of time."

"It was just idle gossip when we talked in church, but by the time we were all tangled up with her, she wanted to make sure no one overheard whatever secrets we had to tell her. She didn't want notes because if one was lost or read over a shoulder she'd have a problem, and we don't have enough time away from work to go meet her. She showed us how to knit coded messages with names, numbers, and the like. The scarf you saw Mr. Holmes? Mine indicated exactly how many guns were on the ship. And you're right, Dr. Watson. I spend many evening hours knitting after a long day in the kitchen, but it isn't as if I have something to pass on every week."

Holmes was silent for a moment. "Beryl, before we leave you, one thing we do need to know for whom your fellow knitters work – and please note if you know what could be used against them. I hope you understand that I can't speak for what happens next, but I'm not going to say anything to Mr. Payne-Owen until we learn a bit more."

Beryl nodded and then spent some time writing down the names of her group with the information Holmes requested. "I know who they work for and what they said, but not where they live. And Mr. Holmes? I'm not going to try to run away, no matter how much I wish I could."

We left the unhappy cook of Eaton Square and went home to Baker Street. Holmes turned his attention to his index, comparing the names of the employers to his entries. It wasn't long before he looked me "Ah! Beryl's friend Ruth works for a leading officer of the bank that's been accused of financial problems. Margaret works for an actor who bribed a member of the press to write a terrible review of another actor's performance, thus limiting his competition for stage roles. Rose is a maid at a vicarage, one that a certain Lord visited to privately confess his problem of stealing small items from friends and shops. There's a few more notes here, but I think we can see how the information Agatha gathers is used by her employer."

Taking the list, I read the entries. "It also include Grace's employer, who doesn't seem to be engaged in anything criminal, but has responsibility for awarding a number of government contracts. That might be of interest to business concerns. But the other is something else. Winifred recently discovered that her employer embezzled money from elderly widows. But I see no mention of the other crimes Mycroft mentioned."

"You're right. He indicated there were two authors, a large department store, and a cabinet member who were experiencing difficulties, so one might presume Agatha and others in the same employ are insinuating themselves across the city in order to gain information. This may be more widespread than we know." He replaced his index file and took a chair. "There's nothing we can do this evening, Watson. Tomorrow, when Mycroft determines who owns the house where Agatha works, a visit to see who else lives there will be in order." Holmes leaned back into the chair cushion, Persian slipper in one hand and pipe in the other. "I think it will be advantageous for Mycroft and Inspector Morton to accompany us."

At first light, I awakened to the sound of Holmes's voice and found him at his desk having just completed a telephone conversation. "Mycroft has arranged for Inspector Morton to meet us at nine o'clock at the home where we saw Agatha. Hopefully her employer, Mr. Milton Charles according to Mycroft, will be there and we can find who else is working for him." Glancing at his watch, he suggested we leave within the hour. His nervous energy was evident as he paced around the room, and as I'd learned over the years, it was best not to interrupt him.

A few minutes before nine we met Mycroft on the corner we'd visited only the day before. Looking down the street, on the opposite corner we saw Inspector Morton and two members of the force. They walked toward us and we met not far from the house.

Mycroft looked at them. "It's just the three of you?"

The inspector shook his head. "No, I sent four others to the mews in case the rats decide to leave the sinking ship out the back way. Are we ready?" Nodding in agreement, we went up the front steps where Morton rang the bell. A lovely young maid answered the door and before she could say a word, we entered the house. Mycroft handed her his coat, much to her surprise.

Holmes smiled at her. "I believe you have a woman named Agatha working here? We need to talk to her."

She looked confused. "There's no one works here named Agatha. Do you mean Miss Agatha?"

That stopped Holmes in his tracks but he recovered quickly. "Yes. Please tell the lady of the house that an old friend has come to see her." She left us standing in the foyer as she went to announce us. He looked at me with an expression I seldom saw and said softly "I think it's possible that I underestimated my former fiancée."

Morton instructed the two police officers to remain near the front door as she returned. We were shown to an elegantly appointed morning room where Agatha and a man were seated comfortably in cushioned chairs. Well dressed, obviously at ease as they enjoyed their morning coffee, they turned slightly to look at their four visitors. A moment passed as Holmes and Agatha viewed each other. Having spent a great deal of time in the company of women, the quality and cost of her dress and jewelry was easy to identify, and out of place for the dowdy woman we'd seen at the church.

Agatha stood and was the first to speak. "You! I hoped I'd never see you again."

"Having followed you home from church yesterday, we decided to call to wish you the Compliments of the Season. Seeing you two so cozy, must I accept that it's too late to rekindle our romance?"

We'd been so intent on Agatha that it took a moment before I recognized her dark-haired, dark-eyed companion. "Different clothes and place, but you're the friendly gent from the 3B's who likes to get men drunk and find out what's coming into and out of the docks." He had no visible reaction other than the tightening of his hands on the arms of his chair.

Holmes turned his attention to the man. "So he is. Mycroft, Inspector Morton, may I introduce the gentleman behind the scene, Mr. Milton Charles. I'm sure we can depend on his good will to help us unravel and identify his web of criminals, Agatha included, who are engaged in theft, espionage, and blackmail. And please, don't insult us by denying it."

There was a brief pause and to everyone's surprise, Agatha began to laugh, quietly at first but then she laughed until she was bent over. "You prat, he's not Milton Charles. There is no Milton Charles."

It wasn't often that Holmes was caught flat-footed, but flat-footed he was. Every one of us stood in silence, waiting to see what would happen next. Collecting himself, a tight grin spread across his face. "Agatha, or Charlotte as you're known at St Anselm's, we came here thinking you were in this gentleman's employ. Then I wondered if you were partners with him. But he works for you, doesn't he?"

"The great Sherlock Holmes, or Escott if you prefer, thinks he's figured it out. Seems neither of us is always who we say we are, does it?" She paused, hands on her hips. "What is it you think you know?"

"I have five women from St. Anselm's who can provide proof of your blackmail, and I'm sure a thorough search of this house will provide even more evidence of the unfortunates you and your hirelings have preyed upon. Inspector Morton, please have your men look for notes about her accomplices and any knitted items as well." Morton left the room to instruct several of his officers currently in the mews to examine the house while others remained on guard. "By the way Agatha, now that your future is looking a bit bleak, perhaps you'll tell us how you came to be the spider in the centre of this extensive web"

I hastened to add, "And I think we'd like to know about this knitting code Holmes referred to."

Despite her current illegal vocation, she was a proud woman, torn between refuting the accusations and touting her ownership. "I can tell by the looks on your faces that you never considered a mere housemaid could do what I have." She pointed at Holmes. "You took advantage of me when I worked for Milverton. Both of you thought all I could do was keep his house tidy, but I watched him and knew what he was doing to make a pretty penny. I saw those letters that he locked up when people came to see him or when he left the house, but while he was home he sometimes left them out on his desk. Then he met his untimely end, which was timely for me. Most of what he had was destroyed, but I had a few odds and ends tucked away and thought if he could make a living blackmailing people, so could I. It's an easy thing to find people who work on the wrong side of the law, like Alvin here, to help, but it's taken two years to get where I am."

Holmes rarely expressed his anger. "And you did it by making those poor women think you were a household servant like them."

"That's all they expected of someone like me, so it wasn't difficult. That's what you thought when you saw me at church, so why wouldn't they? I know what their lives are like and how to talk to them. It was simple, actually."

I asked again. "But what about the knitting?"

"Milverton might have been a miserable old git, but he had a good library, and I used to sneak a book or two to read. Amazing what you can learn from Charles Dickens."

Holmes turned to us. "She's referring to the *tricoteuse* in *A Tale of Two Cities*. She knit the names of the guillotine's victims into her work."

"Very good, Holmes. Madame Defarge did teach me a thing or two. I made a fairly simple pattern for the alphabet and numbers and made sure those women learned it."

It was at that moment that one of Morton's men called to him. "Inspector, you should come look at this." Leaving the two officers to watch Agatha and her male companion, we followed Morton into the nearby study. The officer held up a sheaf of papers. "Sir, there's lists of names and some accounting that may be what you want." Mycroft took the bundle and examined several papers, and then said "This is exactly what we're looking for."

Our day was a long one which ended in the removal of Agatha, Alvin, and a number of the household staff to jail. Mycroft summoned a carriage and a few men from Whitehall to box up the papers, as well as several piles of knitted goods, all carefully labeled with the names of those who'd knitted them. Suffice it to say, this evidence was only the beginning of her downfall.

It was some days before we heard from Mycroft. He joined us in Baker Street on Christmas Eve, and after Mrs. Hudson's fine dinner we relaxed by the fire, each with a whisky-and-soda. Holmes spoke first. "Mycroft, I've been quite patient and promised myself I would wait to inquire about what official progress has been made regarding Agatha and her entourage."

"It isn't patience when it's only been a bit more than a week since arrests were made and her records seized. It's fair to say that Agatha's successful venture will collapse under the weight of her own tidy files. We know whom she hired to find those with information to pass on. The unfortunates they coerced are maids, cooks, secretaries, footmen, stableboys, and clerks. Most did Agatha's bidding because they knew if they failed to provide the information she wanted, their employers would be informed about their indiscretions and they'd be arrested – or in the very least, sacked without a reference, all because a loose piece of information or gossip fell on the wrong ears. Others did it because they were unhappy with their situations and saw a way out. Her dogsbody Alvin plied those on the docks with drink which loosened their tongues. It hasn't been decided what will happen to each of them."

"Why did Agatha go to St. Anselm's herself when she could have used one of her agents? If it wasn't for Holmes spotting her, do you think the case would have been settled so quickly?"

"Excellent question, Doctor." Taking a sip of his whisky, Mycroft continued. "She attended the church as a child and still had great fondness for it. Sadly it wasn't enough to redeem her. But I have a question for you, Sherlock. You told us that what focused your attention on Beryl and your question about knitting. I don't recall such domestic skills interested you, although it certainly led in the correct direction."

"It was the details which interested me. When I first met her, she had a lacy shawl over her shoulders, which would have required some skill to make. The simple scarf she was knitting had obvious flaws, and when I pointed them out, she tried to distract me with her comments about Mrs. Payne-Owen. She said she'd fix the holes and knots before she took it church the next day, but I couldn't see how she could do that in such a short time. Anyone who could knit such a shawl as hers wouldn't make those mistakes – and then it occurred to me it must be purposeful. Perhaps it was my appearance as Dickens that prompted a vague memory of a knitting code which I confirmed when I looked at my copy of *A Tale of Two Cities*."

We were all silent for a moment as we considered the toll that would be paid by so many because of one woman's greed. "A more charitable attitude from their employers would have made those in service far less susceptible to Agatha's plots," I said.

"You're right," agreed Mycroft. "If more respect was shown to them, it would have been a different story, and I hope when more of this is revealed there will be lessons learned. But that's the subject for another day. And speaking of charity, tonight it's fitting that we raise a glass to the spirit of the Holy Day we're celebrating. As Mr. Dickens wrote, this should be a reminder that we should honor Christmas in our hearts, and try to keep it all the year." We rose, and holding a glass, we toasted the spirit of Christmas.

Holmes raised his glass again, and added "And to the colourful skein of life."

About the Contributors

Mark Alberstat, BSI, ("Halifax") has been an active Sherlockian since his teens when he started his local society, The Spence Munros. He co-edits, with his wife JoAnn, the quarterly Sherlockian journal, *Canadian Holmes*, and has contributed many talks and articles on Conan Doyle and sport. Recently he spoke at the annual history of baseball symposium in Cooperstown, New York, about Conan Doyle's love of baseball. He can be reached at *markalberstat@gmail.com*

Marino C. Alvarez, Ed.D., BSI ("Hilton Soames") is professor emeritus at Tennessee State University and was a senior research scientist at the Center of Excellence in Information Systems. He is co-author of *The Art of Educating with V Diagrams*, Cambridge University Press, and *The Little Book: Conceptual Elements of Research*, Rowman & Littlefield. Alvarez is the author of *A Professor Reflects on Sherlock Holmes*, MX Publishing, London and co-editor of *Education Never Ends: Educators, Education and the Sherlockian Canon*, BSI Press. His Sherlockian articles appear in *The Baker Street Journal, The Canadian Holmes Journal, The Saturday Review of* Literature, and in chapters in BSI Publications, *The Quiet Man* and *The Staunton Tragedy*. Sherlockian scion investitures include Circulo Holmes (Barcelona Spain), Nashville Scholars of the Three Pipe Problem, The Occupants of the Full House, and is Founding and Charter Member of the 1885 Shillings. He is the recipient of the Association of Literacy and Researchers Laureate Award and the A.B. Herr Award, and the only recipient of both the Teacher-of-the-Year and Distinguished Researcher-of-the-Year Awards at Tennessee State University. Alvarez was inducted into the Bruce High School Hall of Fame and the West Virginia University College of Education and Human Resources Hall of Fame and the recipient of the WVU Distinguished Alumnus Aware 2019.

Brian Belanger, PSI, is a publisher, illustrator, graphic designer, editor, and author. In 2015, he co-founded Belanger Books publishing company along with his brother, author Derrick Belanger. His illustrations have appeared in *The Essential Sherlock Holmes* and *Sherlock Holmes: A Three-Pipe Christmas*, and in children's books such as *The MacDougall Twins with Sherlock Holmes* series, *Dragonella*, and *Scones and Bones on Baker Street*. Brian has published a number of Sherlock Holmes anthologies and novels through Belanger Books, as well as new editions of August Derleth's classic Solar Pons mysteries. Brian continues to design all of the covers for Belanger Books, and since 2016 he has designed the majority of book covers for MX Publishing. In 2019, Brian received his investiture in the PSI as "Sir Ronald Duveen." More recently, he illustrated a comic book featuring the band The Moonlight Initiative, created the logo for the Arthur Conan Doyle Society and designed *The Great Game of Sherlock Holmes* card game. Find him online at:
www.belangerbooks.com and
www.redbubble.com/people/zhahadun and
zhahadun.wixsite.com/221b.

Peter Calamai, BSI, ("The *Leeds* Mercury") was a resident of Ottawa. He was a reporter, editor, and foreign correspondent with major Canadian newspapers since 1966. For half those years, he worked five minutes' walk from the Rideau Canal and the Commissariat Building. When editor of the Ottawa Citizen's editorial pages, Calamai had the good fortune to spend an afternoon interviewing canal historian Robert Legget. He was an active Sherlockian since the mid-1990's, concentrating on Holmes and the Victorian press.

Honours included designation as a Master Bootmaker by Canada's leading Sherlockian society and investiture in the *Baker Street Irregulars* as "The Leeds Mercury", a name taken from *The Hound of the Baskervilles*.

Catherine Cooke, BSI, ("The Book of Life") is the Chairman of The Sherlock Holmes Society of London and an invested member of the BSI and ASH. She received the Society's Tony Howlett Award for 2014 and Tony and Freda Howlett Literary Award for 2017. She won the BSI Morley-Montgomery Award for 2005. She is a Fellow of the Chartered Institute of Library and Information Professionals and won the BIC/cilip RFID Innovation in Libraries Award for 2009. She was awarded the British Empire Medal for services to libraries in the January 2020 New Year's Honours List. Having spent many years managing and developing the IT systems of Westminster Libraries and their Sherlock Holmes Collection, she is now retired and volunteering on the latter.

Carla Coupe, BSI, ("London Bridge") fell into writing short stories almost without noticing. Two of her short stories – "Rear View Murder" in *Chesapeake Crimes II* and "Dangerous Crossing" in *Chesapeake Crimes 3* – were nominated for Agatha Awards. She has written a number of Sherlock Holmes pastiches, which have appeared in *Sherlock Holmes Mystery Magazine*, *Sherlock's Home: The Empty House*, *Irene's Cabinet*, and other anthologies. Her story "The Book of Tobit" was included in *The Best American Mystery Stories of 2012*.

David Stuart Davies, BSI, ("Sir Ralph Musgrave") is a long time Sherlockian. He is a member of *Sherlock Holmes Society of London* and an invested *Baker Street Irregular*. He is a writer and editor and author of six Sherlock Holmes novels – the latest being *Sherlock Holmes: The Devil's Promise* (Titan), and two books on the films of the Great Detective. He has also penned two plays about Holmes and *Bending the Willow*, a volume about Jeremy Brett playing Sherlock. David is a member of the national committee of the *Crime Writer's Association* and edits their monthly magazine, *Red Herrings*. He has edited various collections of mystery & supernatural fiction and is the author of two crime series: one set in the Second World War featuring the detective Johnny One Eye, and another based in Yorkshire in the 1980's with DI Paul Snow. The latest novel in this series is *Innocent Blood* (Mystery Press).

Sir Arthur Conan Doyle (1859-1930) *Holmes Chronicler Emeritus*. If not for him, this anthology would not exist. Author, physician, patriot, sportsman, spiritualist, husband and father, and advocate for the oppressed. He is remembered and honored for the purposes of this collection by being the man who introduced Sherlock Holmes to the world. Through fifty-six Holmes short stories, four novels, and additional Apocryphal entries, Doyle revolutionized mystery stories and also greatly influenced and improved police forensic methods and techniques for the betterment of all. *Steel True Blade Straight*.

Steve Emecz's main field is technology, in which he has been working for about twenty-five years. Steve is a regular speaker at trade shows and his tech career has taken him to more than fifty countries – so he's no stranger to planes and airports. In 2008, MX published its first Sherlock Holmes book, and MX has gone on to become the largest specialist Holmes publisher in the world with over 500 books. MX is a social enterprise and supports three main causes. The first is Happy Life, a children's rescue project in Nairobi, Kenya, where he and his wife, Sharon, spend every Christmas at the rescue centre in Kasarani. They have written two editions of a short book about the project, *The Happy Life Story*. The second is Undershaw, Sir Arthur Conan Doyle's former home, which is a school for children with learning disabilities for which Steve is a patron. Steve has been a mentor for the World Food Programme for several years, and was part of the Nobel Peace Prize winning team in 2020.

John F. Farrell Jr., BSI, ("The Tiger of San Pedro") was born and raised in San Pedro, California. He became interested in Sherlock Holmes in the late 1960's. He joined *The Non-Canonical Calabashes* (A Sherlock Holmes scion Society) where he met and became friends with another Sherlockian, Sean Wright. He collaborated with Mr. Wright on *The Sherlock Holmes Cookbook*. Later he was a member of *The Goose Club of the Alpha Inn*. He submitted articles to *The Baker Street Journal*. *The Baker Street Irregulars* awarded him the title The Tiger of San Pedro in 1981. He was proud to include "*BSI*" after his name. John made his living as a classical music and play reviewer for multiple newspapers in the Los Angeles area. He passed away in 2015 while he was writing a review. He left behind his family and many friends. He has been accurately described by those that knew him as larger than life.

Lyndsay Faye, BSI, ("Kitty Winter") grew up in the Pacific Northwest, graduating from Notre Dame de Namur University. She worked as a professional actress throughout the Bay Area for several years before moving to New York. Her first novel was the critically acclaimed pastiche *Dust and Shadow: An Account of the Ripper Killings by Dr. John H Watson*. Faye's love of her adopted city led her to research the origins of the New York City Police Department, as related in the *Edgar*-nominated Timothy Wilde trilogy. She is a frequent writer for the *Strand Magazine* and the Eisner-nominated comic *Watson and Holmes*. She is a very proud member of the *Baker Street Babes, Actor's Equity Association, Mystery Writers of America, The Adventuresses of Sherlock Holmes*, and *The Baker Street Irregulars*. Her works have currently been translated into fourteen languages.

In The Baker Street Irregulars, **Sonia Fetherston**, BSI, is known by her titular investiture, "The Solitary Cyclist." A longtime advertising and public relations professional in her native Pacific Northwest, she now devotes herself to dabbling in Sherlockiana. Sonia's byline often appears in *The Baker Street Journal* and other Sherlockian publications the world over. A multiple award-winner for her essays on the Great Setective, she is also the author of the books *Prince of the Realm: The Most Irregular James Bliss Austin* (2014), *Commissionaire: Julian Wolff and his Baker Street Irregulars* (2020), and *"Wiggins": Tom Stix and the Baker Street Irregulars"* (coming in 2024), all biographies of illustrious Sherlockians. Her literary criticism has appeared in numerous anthologies and textbooks. She's a member of several Sherlockian societies including Seattle's *Sound of the Baskervilles*, and *The Speckled Band of Boston*.

Mark A. Gagen BSI, ("Sir James Damery") is co-founder of Wessex Press, sponsor of the popular *From Gillette to Brett* conferences, and publisher of *The Sherlock Holmes Reference Library* and many other fine Sherlockian titles. A life-long Holmes enthusiast, he is a member of *The Baker Street Irregulars* and *The Illustrious Clients of Indianapolis*. A graphic artist by profession, his work is often seen on the covers of *The Baker Street Journal* and various BSI books.

Jayantika Ganguly BSI, ("The Great Agra Treasure") is the General Secretary and Editor of the *Sherlock Holmes Society of India*, a member of the *Sherlock Holmes Society of London*, and the *Czech Sherlock Holmes Society*. She is the author of *The Holmes Sutra* (MX 2014). She is a corporate lawyer working with one of the Big Six law firms.

John Atkinson Grimshaw (1836-1893) was born in Leeds, England. His amazing paintings, usually featuring twilight or night scenes illuminated by gas-lamps or moonlight, are easily recognizable, and are often used on the covers of books about The Great Detective to set the mood, as shadowy figures move in the distance through misty mysterious settings and over rain-slicked streets.

Jeffrey Hatcher, BSI, ("The Five Orange Pips") is a playwright and screenwriter. His plays have been produced on Broadway, Off-Broadway, and in theaters throughout the U.S. and around the world. They include *Three Viewings, Scotland Road, The Turn of the Screw, Compleat Female Stage Beauty, Mrs. Mannerly, Murderers, Smash, Korczak's Children, The Government Inspector, A Picasso, The Alchemist, Key Largo, Dr. Jekyll and Mr. Hyde,* and his Sherlock Holmes plays *Sherlock Holmes and the Adventure of the Suicide Club, Sherlock Holmes and the Ice Palace Murders,* and *Holmes and Watson.* His film work includes the screenplays for *Stage Beauty, Casanova, The Duchess, Mr. Holmes,* and *The Good Liar.* For television, he has written episodes of *Columbo* and *The Mentalist* and the TV movie *Murder at the Cannes Film Festival.* He has received grants and awards from the NEA, TCG, Lila Wallace Fund, Rosenthal New Play Prize, Frankel Award, Charles MacArthur Fellowship Award, McKnight Foundation, Jerome Foundation, and a Barrymore Award for Best New Play. He has been twice nominated for an Edgar Award. He is a member and/or alumnus of The Playwrights Center, the Dramatists Guild, the Writers Guild, and New Dramatists.

Nancy Holder, BSI, ("Beryl Garcia") is a *New York Times* bestselling author who lives in Washington state. She has received 6 Bram Stoker Awards from the Horror Writers Association and the 2019 Grand Master "Faust" Award from the International Association of Media Tie-in Writers. She has written numerous Sherlockian pastiches and articles and is a member of several Sherlockian societies including *The Sound of the Baskervilles* and *The Sherlock Holmes Society of London.* She also writes and edits comic books and pulp fiction. Forthcoming works include two new comic book and graphic novel series with her writing partner, Alan Philipson.

Roger Johnson, BSI, (*"Pall Mall Gazette"*), ASH, PSI, etc, is a member of more Holmesian societies than he can remember, thanks to his (so far) 16 years as editor of The Sherlock Holmes Journal, and 32 years as editor of *The District Messenger.* The latter, the newsletter of *The Sherlock Holmes Society of London,* is now in the safe hands of Jean Upton, with whom he collaborated on the well-received book, The Sherlock Holmes Miscellany. Roger is resigned to the fact that he will never match the Duke of Holdernesse, whose name was followed by "half the alphabet".

Leslie S. Klinger, BSI, ("The Abbey Grange") is the editor of *The New Annotated Sherlock Holmes* and many other books on Holmes, Watson, and the Victorian age.

Arlene Mantin Levy, RN, retired to Colorado in 2015. She practiced as a Critical Care/Trauma Specialist for thirty-eight years in Miami, Florida. During the last four years in Florida, she was a member of the scion *Tropical Deerstalker.* After moving to Evergreen, she and her late husband Mark Levy were members of the scion *Dr. Watson's Neglected Patients.*

Mark Levy, BSI, ("Don Juan Murillo") was an intellectual property attorney and a member of the *Baker Street Irregulars.* He held a B.S. degree in Physics from NYU Polytechnic University, a J.D. degree from New York Law School, and an M.A. degree in creative

352

writing from Wilkes University. His passion was writing. He contributed articles or letters to *The Baker Street Journal*, *The New York Times*, *The Mensa Bulletin*, *The Skeptical Inquirer*, *The Bulletin of the Atomic Scientists*, *Videomaker* Magazine, and *The Journal of Irreproducible Results*. His short, humorous essays were broadcast on the public radio show, *Weekend Radio*, and he wrote a collection of those polymathic essays, *Trophy Envy*. He passed away in 2021.

Ann Margaret Lewis, BSI, ("The Polyphonic Motets of Lassus") attended Michigan State University, where she received her Bachelor's Degree in English Literature. She began her writing career writing tie-in children's books and short stories for DC Comics. She then published two editions of the *book Star Wars: The New Essential Guide to Alien Species* for Random House. She is the author of the award-winning *Murder in the Vatican: The Church Mysteries of Sherlock Holmes* (Wessex Press), as well as *The Watson Chronicles: A Sherlock Holmes Novel* in Stories (Wessex Press). She is also a classical singer.

Bonnie MacBird, BSI, ("Art in the Blood"), ASH has loved Sherlock Holmes since breathlessly devouring The Canon at ten. She has degrees in music and film from Stanford, is the original writer of the movie *TRON*, won three Emmys for documentary film, studied Shakespearean acting at Oxford, and divides her time between her home in Los Angeles and a lodgings in London. She runs *The Sherlock Breakfast Club* and a play-reading series in Los Angeles, where she also teaches writing at UCLA Extension. Her Sherlockian first novel, *Art in the Blood* (HarperCollins 2015) dealt with kidnapping, murder, and an art theft, and challenged Holmes's artistic nature and his friendship with Watson to the limits. Her subsequenet Holmes novels are *Unquiet Spirits*, *The Devil's Due*, *The Three Locks*, *What Child is This?*

David Marcum plays *The Game* with deadly seriousness. He first discovered Sherlock Holmes in 1975 at the age of ten, and since that time, he has collected, read, and chronologicized literally thousands of traditional Holmes pastiches in the form of novels, short stories, radio and television episodes, movies and scripts, comics, fan-fiction, and unpublished manuscripts. He is the author of over one-hundred Sherlockian pastiches, some published in anthologies and magazines such as *The Strand*, and others collected in his own books, *The Papers of Sherlock Holmes*, *Sherlock Holmes and A Quantity of Debt*, *Sherlock Holmes – Tangled Skeins*, *Sherlock Holmes and The Eye of Heka*, and *The Complete Papers of Sherlock Holmes.* He has edited over sixty books, including several dozen traditional Sherlockian anthologies, such as the ongoing series *The MX Book of New Sherlock Holmes Stories*, which he created in 2015. This collection is now thirty-six volumes, with more in preparation. He was responsible for bringing back August Derleth's Solar Pons for a new generation, first with his collection of authorized Pons stories, *The Papers of Solar Pons*, and then by editing the reissued authorized versions of the original Pons books, and then several volumes of new Pons adventures, including his *The Further Papers of Solar Pons*. He has done the same for the adventures of Dr. Thorndyke, and has plans for similar projects in the future. He has contributed numerous essays to various publications, and is a member of a number of Sherlockian groups and Scions. His irregular Sherlockian blog, *A Seventeen Step Program*, addresses various topics related to his favorite book friends (as his son used to call them when he was small), and can be found at *http://17stepprogram.blogspot.com/* He is a member of the Mystery Writers of America, and is a licensed Civil Engineer, living in Tennessee with his wife and son. Since the age of nineteen, he has worn a deerstalker as his regular-and-only hat. In 2013, he and his deerstalker were finally able make his first trip-of-a-lifetime Holmes Pilgrimage to

England, with return Pilgrimages in 2015 and 2016, where you may have spotted him. If you ever run into him and his deerstalker out and about, feel free to say hello!

Steve Mason, BSI, ("The Fortescue Scholarship") has considered himself a Sherlockian since the first time he found his Father's copy of *The Hound of the Baskervilles* at seven years old. He is currently the head of *The Crew of the Barque Lone Star*, a Dallas-Fort Worth scion society, as well as the Chair of the Communications Committee for *The Beacon Society*. He administers The Fortescue Scholarship Exam, and is the primary editor of the Sherlock Spotlight, on behalf of *The Beacon Society*, and is one of the co-creators of *Baker Street Elementary*, a weekly comic strip that reveals the first adventures of Holmes and Watson. He also was one of the co-creators of *The Legion of Zoom* virtual society, supporting efforts of societies who have kept the memory green on the internet. He has received his investitures in the *BSI* and *ASH*.

Julie McKuras BSI, ("The Duchess of Devonshire"), ASH, discovered Sherlock Holmes at the age of eleven through the late night magic of the Basil Rathbone and Nigel Bruce films. It was a bonus to learn there were actually books written by Sir Arthur Conan Doyle. She served as the President of *The Norwegian Explorers of Minnesota* for nine years, and has been on the board of *The Friends of the Sherlock Holmes Collections* since 1997, editing their quarterly newsletter since 1999. Julie was the first editor of *The BSI Trust* newsletter as well. She is a frequent contributor to the *Friends* newsletter, and has had articles published in the *Baker Street Journal*, London's *Sherlock Holmes Journal*, *Through the Magic Door*, and *The Serpentine Muse*. Her essays have been included in *The Norwegian Explorers Christmas Annuals*, *Sir Arthur Conan Doyle and Sherlock Holmes: Essays and Art on The Doctor and The Detective*, "A Note on the Sherlock Holmes Collections" published in *The Horror of the Heights*, *Violets and Vitriol*, and *Sherlock Holmes in the Heartland: The Illustrious Clients Fifth Casebook*. She is a co-editor of *The Missing Misadventures of Sherlock Holmes*, and with Susan Vizoskie, she co-edited *Sherlockian Heresies*. Julie has been a speaker at a number of conferences and events, such as *The Sherlock Holmes Society of London*'s Statue Festival, Holmes Under the Arch, the Newberry Library, From Gillette to Brett, and the 2014 Reichenbach Irregulars Conference in Davos. She lives in Apple Valley, Minnesota with her husband, Mike, and with her children, their spouses, and her three grandchildren nearby.

Jacquelynn Morris, BSI, ("The Lion's Mane") ASH, JHWS, is a member of several Sherlock Holmes societies in the Mid-Atlantic area of the U.S.A., but her home group is Watson's Tin Box in Maryland. She is the founder of *A Scintillation of Scions*, an annual Sherlock Holmes symposium. She has been published in the BSI Manuscript Series, *The Wrong Passage*, as well as in *About Sixty* and *About Being a Sherlockian* (Wildside Press). Jacquelynn was the U.S. liaison for the Undershaw Preservation Trust for several years, until Undershaw was purchased to become part of Stepping Stones School.

Sidney Paget (1860-1908), a few of whose illustrations are used within this anthology, was born in London, and like his two older brothers, became a famed illustrator and painter. He completed over three-hundred-and-fifty drawings for the Sherlock Holmes stories that were first published in *The Strand* magazine, defining Holmes's image forever after in the public mind.

Otto Penzler, BSI, ("The King of Bohemia") proprietor of The Mysterious Bookshop in New York City, founded The Mysterious Press in 1975, and publishes e-books through *MysteriousPress.com*. Penzler has won two Edgar Awards, *The Mystery Writers of*

354

America's Ellery Queen Award, and The Raven. He has been given Lifetime Achievement awards by Noircon and *The Strand Magazine*. He founded two new publishing companies in 2018, Penzler Publishers, reissuing American Mystery Classics in hardcover and trade paperback, and Scarlet, which publishes original psychological suspense novels. He has edited more than sixty anthologies.

Chris Redmond, BSI, ("Billy") is the author of *A Sherlock Holmes Handbook*, *In Bed with Sherlock Holmes*, and other books, as well as many Sherlockian articles. He is a member of the *Baker Street Irregulars*, *The Bootmakers of Toronto*, *The Adventuresses of Sherlock Holmes*, and other societies. He lives in Waterloo, Ontario, Canada.

Tracy J. Revels, BSI, ("A Black Sequin-Covered Dinner-Dress") a Sherlockian from the age of eleven, is a professor of history and the Laura and Winston Hoy Professor of Humanities at Wofford College in Spartanburg, South Carolina. She is a member of *The Survivors of the Gloria Scott* and *The Studious Scarlets Society*, and is a past recipient of the Beacon Society Award. Almost every semester, she teaches a class that covers The Canon, either to college students or to senior citizens. She is also the author of three supernatural Sherlockian pastiches with MX (*Shadowfall*, *Shadowblood*, and *Shadowwraith*), and a regular contributor to her scion's newsletter. She also has some notoriety as an author of very silly skits: For proof, see "The Adventure of the Adversarial Adventuress" and "Occupy Baker Street" on YouTube. When not studying Sherlock, she can be found researching the history of her native state, and has written books on Florida in the Civil War and on the development of Florida's tourism industry.

Steven Rothman BSI, ("The Valley of Fear") has been the editor of *The Baker Street Journal* since 2000. He edited *The Standard Doyle Company: Christopher Morley on Sherlock Holmes* (1990) and *"A Remarkable Mixture": Award-Winning Articles from* The Baker Street Journal (2008). Other publications include *To Keep the Memory Green: Reflections on the Life of Richard Lancelyn Green 1953–2004* (2007, co-edited with Nicholas Utechin), and *Out of the Abyss: A Facsimile of the Original Manuscript of "The Empty House" by Sir Arthur Conan Doyle* (2014, co-edited with Robert Katz and Andrew Solberg). He is invested in the *Baker Street Irregulars* as *"The Valley of Fear."*

Nicholas Utechin, BSI ("The Ancient British Barrow") joined *The Sherlock Holmes Society of London* in 1966, aged fourteen. Ten years later he became Editor of *The Sherlock Holmes Journal* – a position he held for thirty years. The year 1976 also saw the publication of two Holmes pastiches he co-wrote: *The Earthquake Machine* and *Hellbirds.*. He was a *Baker Street Irregular*, an honorary senior member of the *Sons of the the Copper Beeches* Scion society, a founding member of the *John H. Watson Society*, and contributed extensively to Sherlockian scholarship over the decades. The fact that he was related to Basil Rathbone could have something to do with this madness. In another life, he was a senior producer and occasional presenter for BBC Radio in the field of current affairs. After retiring, he lived in Oxford, U.K., with his wife, Annie, following the careers of their two sons with interest, and the lives of their two grandchildren with love. He believed that he knew quite a lot about fine wine and silent films (meeting and interviewing Lillian Gish was something special,) and was lucky enough to own a Sidney Paget original (sadly not one for a Sherlock Holmes story.) He passed away in 2022.

DeForeest Wright III has a day job as a baker for Ralphs grocery stores. It helps support his love for books. A long-time lover of literature, especially of the Sherlock Holmes tales, he spends his time away from the oven hunched over novels, poetry, anthologies, or any tome on philosophy, mathematics, science, or martial arts he can find, sipping an espresso if one is to hand. He writes prose and poetry in his off hours and currently hosts "The Sunless Sea Open-Mic: Spoken Word and Poetry Show" at the Unurban Coffee House in Santa Monica. He was glad to team up writing with his father.

Sean Wright, BSI, ("The Manor House Case") makes his home in Santa Clarita, a charming city at the entrance of the high desert in Southern California. For sixteen years, features and articles under his byline appeared in *The Tidings* – now *The Angelus News*, publications of the Roman Catholic Archdiocese of Los Angeles. Continuing his education in 2007, Mr. Wright graduated from Grand Canyon University, attaining a Bachelor of Arts degree in Christian Studies with a *summa cum laude*. He then attained a Master of Arts degree, also in Christian Studies. Once active in the entertainment industry, and in an abortive attempt to revive dramatic radio in 1976 with his beloved mentor, the late Daws Butler, directing, Mr. Wright co-produced and wrote the syndicated *New Radio Adventures of Sherlock Holmes*, starring the late Edward Mulhare as the Great Detective. Mr. Wright has written for several television quiz shows and remains proud of his work for *The Quiz Kid's Challenge* and the popular TV quiz show *Jeopardy!* for which the Academy of Television Arts and Sciences honored him in 1985 with an Emmy nomination in the field of writing. Honored with membership in The Baker Street Irregulars as "The Manor House Case" after founding The Non-Canonical Calabashes, the Sherlock Holmes Society of Los Angeles in 1970, Mr. Wright has written for *The Baker Street Journal* and *Mystery Magazine*. Since 1971, he has conducted lectures on Sherlock Holmes's influence on literature and cinema for libraries, colleges, and private organizations, including MENSA. Mr. Wright's whimsical *Sherlock Holmes Cookbook* (Drake), created with John Farrell, BSI, was published in 1976, and a mystery novel, *Enter the Lion: a Posthumous Memoir of Mycroft Holmes* (Hawthorne), "edited" with Michael Hodel, BSI, followed in 1979. As director general of The Plot Thickens Mystery Company, Mr .Wright originated hosting "mystery parties" in homes, restaurants, and offices, as well as producing and directing the very first "Mystery Train" tours on Amtrak beginning in 1982.

The MX Book of New Sherlock Holmes Stories
Edited by David Marcum
(MX Publishing, 2015-   )

"This is the finest volume of Sherlockian fiction I have ever read, and I have read, literally, thousands." – Philip K. Jones

"Beyond Impressive . . . This is a splendid venture for a great cause!
– Roger Johnson, Editor, *The Sherlock Holmes Journal,*
The Sherlock Holmes Society of London

In Preparation
Part XXXVI (and XXXVIII and XXXIX???) – 2023 Annual
. . . and more to come!

The MX Book of New Sherlock Holmes Stories
Edited by David Marcum
(MX Publishing, 2015-   )

<u>*Publishers Weekly*</u> says:

Part VI: *The traditional pastiche is alive and well . . . .*

Part VII: *Sherlockians eager for faithful-to-the-canon
plots and characters will be delighted.*

Part VIII: *The imagination of the contributors in coming up with variations on the
volume's theme is matched by their ingenious resolutions.*

Part IX: *The 18 stories . . . will satisfy fans of Conan Doyle's originals. Sherlockians will
rejoice that more volumes are on the way.*

Part X: *. . . new Sherlock Holmes adventures of consistently high quality.*

Part XI: *. . . an essential volume for Sherlock Holmes fans.*

Part XII: *. . . continues to amaze with the number of high-quality pastiches.*

Part XIII: *. . . Amazingly, Marcum has found 22 superb pastiches . . . This is more catnip
for fans of stories faithful to Conan Doyle's original*

Part XIV: *. . . this standout anthology of 21 short stories written
in the spirit of Conan Doyle's originals.*

Part XV: *Stories pitting Sherlock Holmes against seemingly supernatural phenomena
highlight Marcum's 15th anthology of superior short pastiches.*

Part XVI: *Marcum has once again done fans of Conan Doyle's originals a service.*

Part XVII: *This is yet another impressive array of new but traditional Holmes stories.*

Part XVIII: *Sherlockians will again be grateful to Marcum and
MX for high-quality new Holmes tales.*

Part XIX: *Inventive plots and intriguing explorations of aspects of Dr. Watson's life and
beliefs lift the 24 pastiches in Marcum's impressive 19th Sherlock Holmes anthology*

Part XX: *Marcum's reserve of high-quality new Holmes exploits seems endless.*

Part XXI: *This is another must-have for Sherlockians.*

Part XXII: *Marcum's superlative 22nd Sherlock Holmes pastiche anthology features 21
short stories that successfully emulate the spirit of Conan Doyle's originals while
expanding on the canon's tantalizing references to mysteries Dr. Watson
never got around to chronicling.*

Part XXIII: *Marcum's well of talented authors able to mimic the
feel of The Canon seems bottomless.*

Part XXIV: *Marcum's expertise at selecting high-quality
pastiches remains impressive.*

Part XXVIII: *All entries adhere to the spirit, language, and characterizations of
Conan Doyle's originals, evincing the deep pool of talent Marcum has access to.
Against the odds, this series remains strong, hundreds of stories in.*

Part XXXI: *. . . yet another stellar anthology of 21 short pastiches that
effectively mimic the originals . . . Marcum's diligent searches for high-quality
stories has again paid off for Sherlockians.*

The MX Book of New Sherlock Holmes Stories
Edited by David Marcum
(MX Publishing, 2015-   )

MX Publishing

MX Publishing is the world's largest specialist Sherlock Holmes publisher, with over five-hundred titles and over two-hundred authors creating the latest in Sherlock Holmes fiction and non-fiction

The catalogue includes several award winning books, and over two-hundred-and-fifty have been converted into audio.

MX Publishing also has one of the largest communities of Holmes fans on Facebook, with regular contributions from dozens of authors.

www.mxpublishing.com

@mxpublishing on Facebook, Twitter, and Instagram